Unwilling Helper

Phil Whitney

Completely Novel Edition

© 2018 Phil Whitney

Distributed by Completely Novel

ISBN 9781787232297

Author's Note

Although this novel deals with very real issues and as much as possible of the background information is correct, it is a work of fiction. With the exception of current and former politicians to whom reference is made: David Cameron, Roberto Maroni and Lina Merlin, all characters in this book are the products solely of my imagination and any resemblance they may bear to persons living or dead are completely coincidental.

Sadly, there is a lot of misinformation about refugees, both in Britain and in Italy, particularly about the financial support available to them. Often, when outraged comments appear on social media about the amount of money given to refugees each day, they do not appreciate that hardly any of this money goes directly to the refugees. I hope that, in some small way, my novel will help people gain a better understanding and become more compassionate.

This novel is the third in a loose trilogy set almost entirely in Italy and covering the period from 1934 to 2018. Each of the three can be read as a stand-alone novel, however, as the second and third novels sometimes refer to earlier outcomes, I would suggest that, if you think you may read more than one of the novels, you start with 'Relative Values' and then move on to 'Affairs of State' before reading 'Unwilling Helper'. If you have already read the first two novels then I'm sure you will enjoy this one – and thank you for your continued support.

Acknowledgements

As usual, I would like to thank Lucia for her support while I have been writing this novel. I would also like to thank the many friends, both in England and in Italy who have either knowingly or unknowingly provided me with background information and ideas for this story. I would also like to thank those who provided constructive feedback after reading 'Relative Values' and 'Affairs of State'.

Part One – Sicily

Chapter One

At five thirty in the morning there was still a faint chill in the air and he considered pulling the light cover over him and going back to sleep, but then thought better of it. If he didn't send a message to Giulia to confirm that he'd look after the pool and empty the bins, then her husband would do it before leaving for work. Although Totò wouldn't mind, he knew that the informal arrangement he had was very convenient so, after a couple of minutes lying listening to the faint sounds of seabirds, he swung his legs off the rough home-made bed and reached for his phone. *Menu – Messaggi – Crea messaggio – Contatti recenti –* Giulia, top of the list of course: it must be nearly three weeks since he'd used the phone to call anyone else, and other than the mechanic who'd got the old *motorino* going for him, no-one had rung or messaged him. 'Amazing,' he thought, 'if I were back in England, there would be plenty of messages offering to reclaim bank charges, get me a discount on a new boiler, or obtain several thousand pounds of compensation for my "accident", as if!' *'Arrivo'* he typed in, and pressed the "OK" button below where the screen said *"invia"* to send the message.

As he walked up the road to the holiday complex ten minutes later, he thought again about the text messages that arrived regularly in England fishing for business. He wondered what they would say if he responded to one of those telling him he was due compensation for his accident, 'Hello, I'd like you to get me compensation for the "accident" that ended my career and cost me my marriage. - What happened? - I made a mistake; did what I thought was right, trusted the wrong people and got stuffed – Not an accident? - Self-inflicted wounds – OK then better take me off your database. He laughed to himself; did the fact he was still thinking about it mean he was still bitter? Yes, of course he was bitter – bitter with the person or persons who'd let him down, and bitter about his ex-wife. But, on the other hand, would he swap his life now for his previous life if he were offered the opportunity? No chance.

The holiday complex, which consisted of a dozen small bungalows, each with their own South or South-East facing terrace for outdoor eating, was situated on the crest of the hill on the opposite side of the road to his own old shepherd's hut. The pleasant modern villa in which Giulia lived with her husband Totò, their young son and Totò's mother Armida, was to the left of the steep driveway leading into the complex, at the highest point, while the twelve bungalows were arranged around the curve of the hillside just beyond the villa.

He passed the villa and the first two bungalows before taking the path to the natural terrace below, where a kidney shaped infinity pool had been built with a rock feature in the middle, and surrounded by an area of decking where a number of sun-loungers were folded and had been placed face down on the ground. Set about thirty metres back from one end of the pool was the shower-block and behind that, hidden from view of all but the most curious of guests was the pool-house where the filtration plant was housed and tools for the pool were stored.

The robotic pool cleaner was attached to the trickle charger in the pool-house and, after disconnecting it, he carefully lifted it outside and turned it over for a cursory check of the condition of the brushes before carrying it over to the far end of the pool where a gentle ramp for wheelchair access had been constructed. Once he had activated the robot and watched it slide down the ramp to the bottom of the pool, he did his round of the bins which, at this early stage of the season, contained very little, and collected all the contents into a single large bag that he took up to the top of the driveway to collect and take down to the communal bins when he had finished.

By the time he got back to the pool, the edge of the sun was just creeping over the shoulder of the distant Stromboli and the first rays were just beginning to caress the far side of the infinity pool giving, just for a minute or two, an unearthly purple-orange border separating earth and sky. He watched for a moment then, glancing around to make sure that there were no unusually early risers amongst the few guests, quickly stripped off his shorts and t-shirt and dived into the pool. Chilled by the night air and without the heat retention in the surrounding ground that it would have in a month or so, the water made him gasp and it was not until he had completed almost three complete circuits of the pool that he began to feel comfortable.

After ten minutes, as the automatic pool cleaner continued to crawl around the base of the pool, he hauled himself quickly out, picked up his clothes and ran over to the showers. Once the sun moved completely above Stromboli, the whole complex was suffused in a crisp morning light with only a few wispy clouds interrupting the azure sky. Back at the pool, he walked down the ramp and waited in the thigh deep shallow end until the pool cleaner came close enough for him to redirect it up the ramp. He turned it off and, after tipping it on its side for a moment to allow any excess water to drain away, carried it back to the pool-house where he reconnected the trickle charger.

The communal *cassonetti* for the rubbish were sited about a hundred and fifty metres further down the road than the start of the rough track to his shepherd's hut but, as the view over the southern coast of Lipari Island and the view of the picturesque town of Lipari itself was so stunning, he always enjoyed the walk to the bins and back.

Having dropped the rubbish bag into the bin, he walked slightly further down the road, lowered himself onto the low wall on the other side and just sat quietly for five minutes looking over the picturesque old part of town and along the coastline towards Stromboli trying to ignore both the past and the future and focus only on the beauty of the here and now. Finally. A gruff *'Buongiorno'* from the owner of the olive grove that nestled on the hillside below him, brought him out of his reverie.

'Another good one,' he said, looking at the clear sky.

The local, who was wearing a heavy fleece, despite the brush-cutter he held making it clear that he was about to engage on a morning's hard physical work amongst the olives, gave a non-committal grunt, clearly not impressed by the shorts and t-shirt before allowing a grudging, 'Spring should be here soon,' to acknowledge the fine weather.

Luke grinned and raised himself to his feet and began to make his way back to his hut, throwing a cheery, *'Buon lavoro,'* over his shoulder as he did so.

He was back at the hut just after seven and decided that it was still too early to walk down the steep back road into the town to stock up on provisions so he may as well make the most of the good weather. Slipping a light fleece over his t-shirt, he disconnected his e-reader from one of the wires that dangled from his ceiling, picked up one of his two plastic chairs and moved everything outside into the early morning sunshine. Downloading novels was one of the few luxuries he allowed himself, or needed – and even then, many of those he downloaded were available for free on special promotions. Some of the free books were very good, occasionally he found one that was disappointing, but this time he had allowed himself the luxury of splashing out on a full priced book which, as the author was really JK Rowling writing under a pseudonym, he had no doubt would be excellent.

The latest adventures of Cormoran Strike and his assistant Robin Ellacott were just as gripping as he'd expected and it was with some reluctance that he closed the book down at the end of Chapter Twelve just after nine o' clock. He knew that even this early in the year it was a good idea to have made the long walk up from the town with his shopping before the sun reached its zenith, and in any case, it wouldn't do any harm to use one of his mini solar panels to recharge his device.

The road down began in a dip a little further up the hill and was, for the most part, enclosed by high walls for much of the way. Occasionally, however, there were glimpses of sumptuous villas near the top and then, increasingly, business premises in various states of repair lower down. One of these, which always brought a smile to his face, was an apparently thriving boatyard to and from which boats could only be transported either by large tractors, which it was difficult to imagine manoeuvring between the high walls of the narrow lane or by military helicopter. He had no doubt that the former was the case and looked forward with interest to the day when he would be able to watch one of the larger boats being moved.

At the bottom of the hill, the narrow lane passed under the main road which took a wider sweep around the headland removing some of the severity of the gradient, and beyond that, climbed again slightly before entering the modern part of the town by the hospital. Beyond the hospital he greeted the man setting out his trays of fruit and vegetables outside the general store, telling him that he'd be calling in on his way back, and continued down into the heart of the old town.

Ignoring the shops and restaurants on the main pedestrianised street through the centre of the town, he cut through to the more picturesque Via Umberto that led down to the smaller of the two harbours. As it was still before ten in the morning and only the end of March, the normally busy street was almost deserted with the majority of the businesses there yet to open up. An exception to this, however, was the *Enoteca* on his left just before the curve where he knew that the sea would come in to view. The owner, who Luke knew lived above the premises, was cleaning the tops of the tables when he entered through the door which was propped open with a mop bucket, although he could see from the light on the front of the coffee maker that it was turned on.

'*Buongiorno*, Gilberto. Any chance of a coffee and a *brioche*.'

'*Buongiorno,* Luke. I can do you a coffee in a minute – only two more tables to do, then I can wash my hands… Alright. That's done… Gilda's just popped over to the baker's to pick up today's stock of bread of pastries; do you want to wait a couple of minutes till she gets back, or do you want the coffee now?'

'I'll have one now and another one with a *brioche* in a few minutes, if that's OK.'

Gilberto who, for some reason, always made Luke think of a pirate, smiled. 'The customer's always right - you know that.'

'And if the customer wanted to use your computer to send an e-mail?' asked Luke, pulling a memory stick out of his pocket.

'Go on then, seeing as there are no other customers in at the moment, but make sure you don't tell anyone that I let you –

especially not Gilda. She's always reminding me that if I let customers use it, we'll end up with viruses.'

'Don't worry. Gilda knows that, as I don't have an internet connection up on the hill, the only virus I'm likely to pick up is a cold... and even that's unlikely. This memory stick has only been on my internet free computer and on yours.' He made his way through the faded bead curtain that separated the bar area from Gilberto's little office and pushed the memory stick into one of the USB ports. 'Anything exciting been happening in the town?' he asked, as he clicked on 'File Explorer' and then scrolled down to the H Drive.

'I can see you've only been here for a few months. Nothing ever happens between November and Easter – it's only when the tourists are here that we get competitive and it's every man for himself. Old habits take a long time to die out and it's not so long ago that if we didn't all pull together and help each other, lots of people wouldn't have survived the winters.'

Luke entered the recipient's address, wrote 'Darius' in the subject box, attached file number 19 from the memory stick and pressed 'Send', before continuing the light hearted conversation as he closed down his e-mail account and withdrew the memory stick. 'What? No gossip at all? Surely not everyone goes into hibernation over the winter!'

It was Gilberto's turn to smile, 'You asked if anything exciting had been happening; you didn't ask if there was any gossip.'

Luke raised an eyebrow, 'Well?'

'You know how it works. People chat when they have too much free time; someone wonders where someone else got the money from to buy a new car, or someone mentions having seen a common acquaintance talking to a stranger - a bit of idle speculation – just for fun; another person hears it and embroiders the story a bit before they tell someone else and, before you know it, half the town is gossiping about it.'

'And that doesn't lead to any problems?'

Gilberto shrugged, 'occasionally there's a fight; once every few years someone even gets killed, but it's only because people have nothing else to do. Everyone knows that if you hear a rumour in winter, it's very unlikely to be true. I don't think that there's anything out of the ordinary at the moment; I could tell you about a couple of rumoured affairs, but you don't know the people involved so it wouldn't mean anything to you.'

'OK Never mind - Hi Gilda. How's things?' he added as a stocky woman with a warm friendly face, about ten years her husband's junior entered the wine bar.

'Hello,' she replied in English, and then, reverting to Italian, 'I imagine that you're waiting for one of these,' and she put the plastic crate she was carrying on the nearest table.

'Actually, I was just waiting to see your smile… but I may as well have a *brioche* while I'm here.'

'Don't forget what I was just telling you,' said Gilberto with mock severity as he made Luke's second coffee.

As Luke made his way back up the hill, a plastic bag full of provisions in each hand, he looked at the boatyard again and an idea for number twenty began to develop in his mind.

By the time he had found appropriate storage places in his hut and in the nearby habitable cave, the idea was almost fully formed; the main lines of dialogue were being played out inside his head and the plot just needed fine-tuning. All that was really missing was the visual aspect and he knew, from experience, that the best way to arrange the various images was to shut himself off from the beautiful sights around that tended to distract him.

He would usually not have bothered starting the next episode immediately after sending off the previous one, but the idea that he had had as he passed the boatyard, and the dialogue in his head was so clear, that he decided to leave 'Robert Galbraith' until later and concentrate on his own work.

Twenty minutes later, he was lying calmly on his bed looking up at the ceiling and using the bumps, wires, shadows and flaking paintwork to create the sequence of images he could work from. As he lay, an intermittent buzzing, which increased then died away, then increased and almost died away again, but gradually growing louder each time it reappeared, filtered into his consciousness. Realising that it must be one of the reconditioned scooters that were available for hire to tourists down at the larger port, he wondered where they were going, assuming that they must have taken a wrong turn as the road became no more than a bridlepath less than two kilometres further on.

The sound of the engine died as the scooter came to a halt at the side of the road facing the front of his hut, leaving only the very faint distant sound of the brush-cutter down the road to disturb the peace that he treasured.

He sighed, wondering which language the tourist would use to ask him the way; would it be the type of tourist who always made the effort to learn at least a few words of the local language wherever they went, or would it be one of those who expected everyone, all over the world, to be able to speak their own language particularly, in the case of his fellow Englishmen, if they spoke it loudly enough. It was unlikely to be an Italian – most Italians would view a holiday by the sea in March as a sign of insanity; if they were French, Spanish or Portuguese he would do the best he could to send them on their way in their own language, if they were German or Scandinavian he would have to use English and, if they were English or American he would sprinkle just enough English words in his Italian to make sure they got the meaning but the last thing he wanted was to get into conversation with them and have to explain why was there. He raised himself from the bed and moved over to sit on the rough wooden chair just inside the open doorway.

The woman who picked her way carefully across the broken ground between the road and his old shepherd's hut as she fumbled with the chinstrap of her helmet was wearing ankle length, low-heeled brown leather boots below deliberately distressed denim jeans and a tightly buttoned denim jacket. When she reached a spot about five metres from the door, she finally managed to undo the clasp, lift the helmet off and toss her head to allow a mane of medium length auburn hair to free itself, glinting in the still low sunlight as it did so.

She turned her head slightly so that she was looking directly at him and gave a broad smile that failed to fully mask the uncertainty in her eyes. Luke drew his head back slightly into the shadow of the hut, hoping that the contrast between the dark opening to the hut and the clear blue sky and sunlight behind it would make it difficult for her to recognise him. She stopped.

'Hello, Luke.' He remained silent. 'Finding you took quite a bit of effort. Are you coming out? Or are you going to ask me in?'

He looked up, 'I've got nothing to say; I'm sorry you've had a wasted journey but if you go back down to the town now, you should be able to catch the eleven o'clock ferry back to Milazzo.'

She sighed and, with the edge of one of her boots, pushed to one side a few small stones that lay on the ground in front of her and then lowered herself down and sat cross-legged in the space she had cleared. He watched her undo the buttons of her jacket and lean back, hands resting on the ground to either side behind her. She closed her eyes and turned her face towards the sun's rays giving him the opportunity to remind himself of the contours of her figure and the chiselled precision of her profile. He looked, even though he knew that that was what he was intended to do and why she intended him to look. 'A cup of tea would be nice - or, if you can't manage that, then I suppose a glass of water would do,' she said without opening her eyes.

'You've got a nerve – I don't know how you dare show your face here after what you did – You can have a cup of tea, then go – I've got nothing to say to you and I don't want you to ever show your face here again.' He got up and moved the small gas stove outside the front of the hut.

'It wasn't my fault, you know,' she said, looking down into the mug of tea cupped between her hands. 'I was out of the country. They sent me over to Tunisia then on to Egypt to cover the uprisings; by the time I was back in the country your trial was over and they'd locked you away – You hadn't appealed and there was nothing I could do about it.'

'Phbbt! How about not writing the article in the first place! You said that most of what I told you would only be published after the hearing, and even then, only if it went badly so I could tell my side of the story…. Instead...' his voice tailed off and he shook his head.

'Instead, the editor took my file off the computer, took out all the bits that explained why you did what you did, that would have been seen as mitigating circumstances, and just published the parts that explained what you did – You didn't stand a chance after that.' There was an uneasy silence for a minute, then she continued, 'I tried to come and see you in prison, to explain and say how sorry I was – but you weren't prepared to see me.'

He glared at her, 'I trusted you. You said you understood. "If they throw you out of the force, I'll make sure everyone knows why you did it, that everyone hears your side of the story" - instead it was my interview with you that convicted me, ended my career and got me six years inside, reduced to three for good behaviour.'

'I'm sorry,' she said again, 'I really am!' and she looked down into her now empty mug again, letting her hair hang forward so that he wouldn't see the tears forming in her eyes.

'Do you think it's easy for a cop who gets sent to prison? Even if you haven't been a real cop, just a backroom boy working with computers – once someone 'accidentally' lets it slip, you're a marked man.' He suddenly pulled his t-shirt over the top of his head and twisted his right shoulder forwards towards her, 'Look at that,' he said angrily. Indicating a series of burn marks on the rear of the shoulder and the top part of his back. 'Cigarette burns! That's what happens to cops who end up inside – and I was relatively lucky! And you just have to take it. React once and that's your remission for good behaviour gone.'

The stool he had given her fell over as she stood up suddenly, no longer bothering to hide the tears in her eyes. She took a step towards him and raised a hand; he braced himself for the slap that he knew was coming but, when her hand came down it rested on his left shoulder as her head came down and her lips brushed the topmost burn scars on his right shoulder. He was too surprised to speak as she turned, grabbed her helmet and made her way back to the road. 'I'll be back,' she shouted without turning. 'We need to talk.'

He felt a wave of relief sweep over him as he listened to the sound of her engine fade into the distance as she took the first of the big bends that descended around the edge of the hill, although it was a relief tinged with sadness. If she'd meant what she'd said about coming back then he'd need to think about moving on and finding somewhere else where he could live in anonymity for as long as he chose. He could just imagine the way the British tabloids would present the story of the disgraced former police officer, luxuriating in the sunshine on an idyllic Mediterranean island while out on licence, while the hard-working British Public who had footed the bill for his stay in prison, suffered the consequences of the government's austerity package. She might have been telling the truth about how the previous article had come to be published, but he was pretty sure that she was here now to do a follow-up story; and once she'd done one and told people where he was, there was nothing to stop others from following.

Finishing the story that he'd been thinking about earlier seemed the most sensible thing to do, then, if he had to move, he wouldn't need to worry about missing the next fortnightly deadline that was the good thing about creativity coming in bursts.

Once he'd settled down, however, with the slim line graphics tablet attached to his note-book, he didn't find it as easy as he'd expected to get the images he'd been thinking of down onto the tablets. When he tried to give characters hair - even characters that he'd drawn many times before - what came to mind was the sunlight glistening in her auburn hair as she shook it out, and when he tried to draw figures, the contours that came to mind were those that had been in evidence as she had leaned back and rested on her hands. Finally, he threw down the stylus and disconnected the note-book from the wires connecting it to one of the solar panels on the roof.

He had no intention of walking back into the town again but he knew that if he climbed up to the back of the nearest of Giulia's bungalows, he should be able to get a good enough signal to be able to use Google and other search engines to find out more about her. It probably wouldn't make any difference, but at least it would make him feel that, if she did come back, he'd be meeting her on slightly more equal terms. He would also be able to get an idea about what some of the other people from his former life were up to.

Once he was connected to the internet, the first thing he did was to look at the website of the unpleasant tabloid that she had worked for. 'Idiot' he thought. 'How could I have ever believed that someone decent, whose word I could trust could work for paper like that?', then he put her name in the site's 'Advanced search Filters' section and came up with twenty-seven stories with her by-line attached to them. None of the stories were dated any more recently than March 2011 and all the stories from that year, with the notable exception of the article exposing him, had been about the Arab Spring, initially in Tunisia and then in Egypt.

Slightly surprised, he exited the newspaper's site and put her name into a more general search engine. He was somewhat surprised to see that there was no sign of her on any of the major social media sites, although he realised that she could well be using a nom de plume on Facebook. There was a link back to the tabloid site, which he ignored, and instead used a site called *journalisted.com* that referenced all known articles by all current and recent journalists. From here he deduced that she must have been working as a freelance since leaving the tabloid and the majority of articles since then appeared to be either for the Huffington Post or for the online news-feed of Al Jazeera. Recent articles seemed to be more infrequent and the majority dealt with the situation of the refugees trickling into Europe out of the war-torn countries of the Middle East and Africa. Out of curiosity, he compared the most recent article credited to her with one on the same subject published on the same day by the tabloid she had previously worked for. There was an abyss between the two stories; the tabloid focused on the potential effects of more refugees being added to the 'hordes of scroungers' already making unsustainable demands on public services in Britain, urging people to vote to leave the European Union in the forthcoming referendum so that Britain's borders could be hermetically sealed; the article on the Al Jazeera site however, focused on the human tragedy of the refugees, illustrated the hardships facing them and carried a number of quotes from refugees, all of whom were effectively saying that while they were in desperate need of shelter, they also wished to return to their original homes as soon as was possible. Having read and compared the articles, he felt somewhat less antagonistic towards her than he had before.

As the visit had stirred up memories of the past and reminded him of his grievances, he used his ex-mother-in-law's account name and password to log into Facebook from where he was able to access his ex-wife's home page. He still wasn't quite sure whether he blamed her or blamed himself for her having left him while he was in prison, but felt the need to check and make sure she was alright. It didn't take long for him to reassure himself on that score: her profile stated that she was 'in a relationship' and, while every photograph in which they had appeared together seemed to have been deleted, there were some recent photographs taken during a break in Mauritius, presumably by whoever she was now 'in a relationship' with. He wondered if it was anyone he knew and felt a surge of jealousy although, strangely, the beach photographs of her left him unmoved. Perhaps one day he would be able to resist the urge to find out what she was doing and stop blaming himself for having ruined their marriage. In prison, he'd been used to hearing other inmates whose wives or partners had left them after they'd been put away, swearing vengeance and heaping abuse on their former partners. While he sympathized with their position, he didn't feel he could share it: 'to love and to cherish till death do us part,' he thought. But it wasn't death who had parted them; he had, by being sent to prison. He hadn't thought he would be caught out, but he'd known what the consequences would be if he were and that meant that he was the one responsible for the separation.

For almost the first time since he'd moved into the shepherd's hut, he didn't sleep well. He wasn't sure whether he wanted her to come back again so he could ask her why she'd left the tabloid, or whether he just wanted her to disappear and let him go back to the simple life again, insulated from his past for as long as he wanted it to remain that way or, to put it another way, for as long as it took for his past to forget about him.

As it was still early in the year, the warmth in the ground was only superficial so the water in the pool did not retain its heat overnight and his early morning dips required him to swim quite vigorously to keep warm. The exercise did him good and he felt much better as he made his way back to his hut deciding to go for a long walk later and see what wild herbs he could recognise and collect.

When he got back to the hut, however, he found she was already there, sitting on the bench he had made outside the door; he wasn't sure how to react.

'Buongiorno,' she said, holding out a brown paper-bag, 'I need to practice my Italian… and I brought some *brioches* for *la prima colazione* – as a peace offering. I read a series of novels where the tradition was that when you had eaten together in someone's house there was a cessation of hostilities… at least for the duration of that visit.'

He smiled, despite his determination not to trust her again, 'I wouldn't have expected a tabloid journalist to be so well read; however, if you've read the whole series, you'll remember "the red wedding", so forgive me if I'm sceptical. I always find it best to assume that everyone successful has read Machiavelli…. *Caffè?'*

She nodded, and seemed to Luke to be more relaxed as she sat on the bench. He got the stove out and prepared the *macchinetta* for the espresso. *'Tazzine* for the espresso are just inside on the left; I think there are a couple of sachets of sugar as well, if you need them. Make yourself useful, since I don't seem to be able to get rid of you.' She rose and went inside for the cups.

'Shall I bring a couple of plates as well?'

'No. A few crumbs outside won't do any harm and the less washing-up the better.'

Apart from a mumbled, 'thanks', when he handed her the coffee, neither of them spoke until the last *brioche* had been finished. Luke was the first to finish and studied her carefully as she took her last two bites of the food, watching the delicate movements of her throat as she swallowed and then followed the path of her fingers as she carefully brushed the last traces of sugar from the corner of her lips.

'Well?' he said brusquely as she gave her fingers a little wipe on the outside of her thighs.

'Well what?' she replied, startled by the sudden change in atmosphere.

'You said yesterday that we need to talk, and now here we are, so let's get on with it. I assume that whatever I say, you'll dig around until you got enough information or gossip to do a nice article about how the corrupt ex-cop gets to lie about in the sunshine. So ask me what you need to ask then you can leave. At least this way we might end up with a little bit of truth in the article.' He leaned forward so that he was intimidatingly close to her, and looked her directly in the eye.

She stood up, brushing his forehead with her hip as she did so, took a few steps away from him and stood looking silently down the valley for a while. He watched her, warily.

'I understand why you don't like me,' she gave a little laugh, 'No… I understand why you hate me… and I fully understand why you don't trust me… I get it… I really do! All I ask is that you listen to me. Then I'll answer any questions you want to ask me. And then… If you want me to, I'll go away and you'll probably never see me again.' She turned to face him and he saw with surprise that there were tears in her eyes. He asked himself how genuine the tears were but decided that, for now, he'd give her the benefit of the doubt.

'I was going to go for a long walk, but…' he trailed off as his eyes fell to her boots and the tight jeans.

Interpreting his look correctly, she said, 'It's OK. I've got a pair of shorts and some trainers with me, just in case you'd left after I found you yesterday. They're in the helmet box on the scooter; I'll get them, if you don't mind…' she looked towards the hut.

'Be my guest,' he said.

When they set off, ten minutes later, she had exchanged the jeans for a pair of loose fitting bermuda shorts into the pockets of which she had transferred as much as she could out of her bag and the pockets of her jacket which she had dispensed with. He had suggested that she kept her jacket with her as it could be quite windy up on the top of the peninsula at the Observatory, but she had shrugged and said that she wasn't worried about a few goose-pimples; most of the time they were walking it would be pleasantly warm and a few minutes feeling cold was far preferable to having to carry her jacket for ages or wear it as they walked when she really didn't need it.

They walked along the road in the opposite direction to Lipari town and for the first few minutes there was no sea-view as a ridge separated the road from the slopes that dropped away steeply towards the sea. When they emerged there were good, if not spectacular views across the strait towards the neighbouring island of Vulcano and he could sense her disappointment when, after a few hundred metres he took a right fork, apparently away from the sea along a road that rose quite steeply with a high stone wall on one side and rising scrubland, from which they were separated by a wire mesh fence, on the other. 'Explain again about the article,' he said, speaking for the first time since they had left the hut.

'A couple of days after I'd done the interview, I was called in by the Deputy Editor and told that as one of the senior foreign reporters had got appendicitis, I was being sent out to Tunisia that afternoon to cover the disturbances there. He said it was an assignment that would probably last a few days – a couple of weeks at most – and that as soon as everything blew over, I'd be on the way back. You probably remember that, at the time, no-one had any idea of how big what was happening in Tunisia would get and what the knock on effect would be on other countries in the region. I'm still not sure whether it was just bad luck that it was me who got sent out, or if it was just a convenient way to get me out of the way.'

'And why would they want to do that?'

'I don't know. That certainly wasn't how I saw it at the time and I'm fairly sure that the Deputy Editor was genuine when he told me to go out there – it's just that, because of what happened later, I did wonder who had suggested to him that I was the one who should be sent. There were other, more experienced journalists who could have been sent, who probably should have been sent, but I suppose that at the time, it never crossed my mind to ask, or even think, why me? It was only because of what happened later that I started to wonder.'

He looked at her quizzically, 'Go on.'

'When we get sent away on assignment, any work-in-progress that we've been working on before we go away, has to be saved on a 'safe area' of the paper's hard-drive so that, if anything happens to us or to our laptops, while we're away, our work isn't lost. It also stops us from breaking our contracts and selling scoops to the highest bidder – but that's not relevant in this case. Anyway, I downloaded everything I had onto my secure area of the server – it didn't amount to much other than the recording of the interview with you and, in theory, only senior editorial staff and some of the IT support team would be able to access it. Now, after I'd been in Tunisia for a while, when I was expecting to come home, I got a message telling me that I had to get to Cairo because things were starting to happen there and, as I'd seen what was happening in Tunisia it was essential that I was in Egypt too.'

'And the article?'

'To be honest, while I was in the Middle East, I hardly thought about it, if at all. If you remember, the agreement was that I wouldn't publish anything until after the hearing so it didn't seem important at the time – I was too busy rushing round Cairo and other places, thinking I was the next Kate Adie. Most of the time, I was absolutely worn out whenever I wasn't working and most days didn't even have time to look on the paper's website to see what comments people were leaving about my articles. It was an old university friend who sent me a text commenting on what a stir my article had caused and that I ought to look at some of the comments. Even then, I assumed that he was talking about one of the Egypt articles and I left it a few days before I found out that that wasn't what he meant.'

'I thought you said that everything was saved in a safe area that no-one could access?'

She shook her head, 'Not quite. I said that only senior editorial staff and some of the techies would be able to access it – but there was no reason why they should. In fact, I can't see how they would have time to check through what's stored in everyone's safe areas. It might be paranoia but I think that I was singled out for some reason.'

'Maybe,' said Luke, 'or it could be that someone has written and installed a programme that flags up the presence of specific keywords or strings of keywords in stored information. If they have then the contents of your draft articles could have been flashed up for attention as soon as you uploaded them.'

Her expression indicated that she found this explanation hard to believe, 'But the words in the draft, and in other things that were in there that didn't get published, were mainly pretty ordinary words. Almost every article by everyone would get flagged up if they were using a programme like the one you described.'

He shook his head, 'Believe me; these programmes can be fairly subtle. Most of the Social Media sites claim to have set up filters to flag up words to do with pornography and terrorism. The reason they're not as effective as they should be is because the parameters they use are too vague, but they can be very, very specific. You're right when you say that most of the words in the interview were fairly commonplace, but I mentioned names as well. One of those names probably wouldn't ring any alarm bells, but finding several of them in the same article would be very unusual.' She was silent for a while as she digested the explanation he had given her, so he prompted her to continue. 'So what did you do when you saw the article that had been published under your name? Just ignore it and think about your career?' he asked, unable to veil a touch of bitterness.

'You've got every right to be angry but that's not fair… I told you, I didn't know anything about the article until several days after it had appeared. I managed to get hold of the Deputy Editor who'd sent me out and he claimed to know nothing about it either – "concentrating on foreign affairs", he said. He suggested that I should take it up with the Editor herself, if I wasn't happy, and I told him that I would, and that I wouldn't be filing any more stories from the Middle-East until I'd had at least an explanation and preferably both an explanation and an apology, then I hung up on him. I spent an hour and a half that night and another four hours the following morning trying to get through to the editor, but couldn't even get her PA. Then, the following evening, Oliver Peacock, the journalist I'd originally stood-in for in Tunisia, turned up at my hotel, told me I'd been dismissed for gross misconduct and handed me a plane ticket back to Gatwick.'

'And that's when you started writing for Huffington Post and Al Jazeera.'

'Not immediately. Even though there was no way I could have worked for that paper again, I couldn't have that "dismissal for gross misconduct' on my record, so I went to see a lawyer. They looked into it and advised me not to take it to court on the basis that I'd threatened not to write any more articles and then hung up on them. Apparently, what I'd said, could be construed as putting me in breach of contract and, as they were willing to make an ex-gratia payment, the best I could hope to achieve if I insisted on taking them to court was peppercorn damages and I wouldn't be awarded costs. That didn't really leave me with much of a choice. The Huff accepted the first article from me three or four weeks later.'

They walked on in silence for a few minutes then, as they crested a rise, a view over the sea, back towards mainland Sicily opened up to their left. She stopped and gasped but Luke took her arm just above the elbow and pulled gently. 'Come on. Another five minutes. The view's really worth stopping for up there,' and he indicated a point at the top of the next rise where both the road and the island seemed to come to an end, forming a triangle against the sky – a triangle crowned with a pinkish-brown building surrounded by radio masts and with a large satellite-dish on the side resembling, from that distance, a rose attached to the side of an old lady's hat.

When they reached the Observatory, the building itself, which was surrounded by high mesh fencing, looked a little shabby, but the view over the sea was spectacular. 'That's Vulcano,' he said, pointing to the island in front of them, 'and that small one in front of it, is Vulcanello. From here they look like two separate islands, but they're actually joined by a flat strip of land. And in the distance, obviously, you can see Sicily.'

'Is it dormant?' she asked, and he laughed.

'Look carefully. You can't see any smoke coming out of the crater as it disperses before it reaches the rim but, there are various points on the sides of the island where you can see wisps of smoke coming out. I don't know much about volcanoes but I'd assume that they're acting a bit like the valve on a pressure cooker.'

'And people live there? Even though it's still active?'

He shrugged, 'People have lived there on and off for hundreds of years and there hasn't been a significant eruption since 1890. Vines growing on volcanic rock produce a very good wine and plenty of tourists come to try the hot mud baths.'

'I think I'll give them a miss. I never really saw the appeal of getting dirty.'

'Come on,' he said suddenly, lightly touching her elbow again.'

'Where to now? I thought we could sit and admire the view for a bit.'

'Just follow me,' he said, and led her down the steps from the *piazzale* where the road came to an end. At the foot of the steps was a stony path that wound its way towards the point of a slightly lower headland in front of them through aromatic mediterranean scrub.

When they got there, the view of Vulcano and Vulcanello was even clearer but Luke indicated that she should look along the Lipari coastline to their right. This time, she didn't gasp, she just stood with her mouth half open looking at the landscape. 'Those rocks,' she said, 'they look just like the ones on Capri – you know – the ones that are on all the postcards. Its… it's beautiful.'

'*I faraglioni*,' said Luke. 'The name just means the rock stacks. There are a few in Italy, but because, in England, we only know the ones on Capri, we assume that the name is unique to them while really it just describes the geological formation. There are some more spectacular ones near the Gargano National Park on Italy's east coast, and then these on Lipari. In summer you can get boat trips that will take you right up to them.'

'Can we get down there?' she asked, pointing to the shoreline below them and to their left, where there appeared to be a deserted beach.

'We can… but it's a bit of a scramble, especially on the way back up. If we go back towards the hut, there's a point where there's a proper path down to the sea. The beach is much smaller than that one, but they're all stony anyway, so they're uncomfortable to move around on.'

'Alright, you're the one who knows the way around.'

They walked back to within half a kilometre of the hut, mainly in silence, before Luke indicated that they should take a driveway to their right that appeared to lead to a large, modern house with multiple boundaries. After a few yards of driveway, however, he turned through a gap in the fence and onto a narrow path that snaked its way through the scrub, down towards the sea.

'When I saw you this morning, I was determined I wasn't going to believe a word you said.'

'And now?'

'And now, I'm undecided. You tell a good story... but then you would, wouldn't you? You're a journalist. Let's just say that, for the moment, I'm prepared to keep an open mind – but now you need to tell me why you're here.'

She didn't reply for a moment, as she negotiated her way around a straggly bush with obvious thorns. 'I needed to apologise to you - to explain.'

He snorted, 'Yes, of course you did. If what you said before was true, and my instinct is to believe you, then you don't have anything to apologise for – and the amount of effort you must have put into tracking me down – you must be mad if it was just so you could explain. What difference does it make to you if I understand - or to me for that matter - understanding doesn't give me my career back, or my wife... does it?'

He held out a hand to help her over a rough bit of path where one edge had crumbled down the hillside. She ignored his hand, 'To apologise and explain and... and to ask for your help.'

He stopped suddenly, causing her to bump into him, 'What? You must be crazy! Why on earth would I want to help you? Even if it wasn't entirely your fault, it was still your article that changed my life.'

'Can we talk about this when we get to the bottom...please?' she asked imploringly.

He shrugged a shoulder, turned and carried on down, not bothering anymore to offer a hand on the rougher parts of the path.

Finally, without another word being spoken between them, they reached a small stony beach that was lapped by crystal-clear water that gradually merged into turquoise and amethyst as it stretched out towards Vulcanello. She sat down on a flat stone that was somewhat larger than the others and put her arms around her knees that she pulled up to her chest. He stood and waited for her to begin.

'As you know I've been writing for the Huffington Post and Al Jazeera amongst others, you've probably also seen that most of what I've written recently is about the refugees. Most of what's been published has been about the Syrians and Sudanese coming across to Lesbos from Turkey, or travelling overland up through the Balkans and Central Europe. What you won't have seen recently are any articles about the refugees arriving in Italy from Tunisia or Libya. It's not that I haven't been writing them, it's just that they're not top of the news agenda at the moment – partly because the flow always slows down during the winter, but also because that was last year's news agenda. Public attention, particularly in England, has moved on, although it will turn back again when we get to summer.'

'So what?' he said, puzzled… 'I don't mean "So what – who cares about the refugees", I mean, so what – what's that got to do with me? I don't have a television, I rarely listen to the radio, and I only have infrequent internet access – certainly not enough to get a real grip of the refugee crisis.'

She ignored his question. 'People don't talk about it – mainly because most people don't care but of the refugees who have arrived in Italy over the past three years -that's of the refugees who we know have arrived, there could be many more! - well over three thousand unaccompanied minors are now unaccounted for – no-one has any idea where they are or what's happened to them – and most people don't want to know. I want to find out what's happening and, if possible, put a stop to it.'

He turned and looked out to sea, 'I still don't see what that's got to do with me.'

'It's got nothing to do with you. No more than it's got to do with anyone else in Sicily. The only difference is, that I know you, and I know that you're not happy when you see injustices and you're also prepared to stick your neck out to help others.'

He remained facing the sea for a couple of minutes, without saying anything. When he finally turned, his face was serious with an air of sadness. 'I suppose I should be flattered that you asked me to do this but, I'm sorry... I can't.' He saw her head drop and felt guilty, knowing that she was trying to hide her disappointment. 'When you're let out before the end of your tariff, you're let out on licence for the rest of the time you were sentenced for. There are very strict conditions and, if you breach them, you can be picked up and locked up for the rest of your sentence. I really can't go back inside... those burns I showed you yesterday are just a foretaste of what could happen to me if I get sent back.'

He watched her for a few moments, wondering how she would react and hoping she wasn't going to cry but, when she raised her head she had managed to squeeze out a smile. 'I'm sorry. I shouldn't have asked... are we going for a swim?'

'What?' he asked, surprised. 'It's the end of March – it will be freezing.' She was already undoing her laces.

'Come on - don't they call people like you "nesh" where you come from? You'll enjoy it once you're in.' She undid the buckle of her belt and slid the zip down as she stood up, allowing the shorts to slide down around her ankles. She then gripped the bottom edge of her t-shirt and in one flowing movement pulled it up over her head and allowed it to fall on the stones by her side. She then reached round behind her to undo the clasp on her bra and dropped that on top of the t-shirt before tiptoeing carefully over the stones towards the water.'

'Come on,' she repeated as she entered. Luke thought about it for a moment and then sat down on the stones. He watched her ease her way in and then gasp as a little wave took the water further up her thighs than she had expected, then she dove forward and, for three or four seconds, was just a mermaid-like blur under the surface. When she came up for air, she struck out in a strong front crawl for about twenty strokes and then turned and returned towards the shore using breaststroke.

When she had come as near as she could while still remaining under water, she called, 'What's the matter? This would be a hot summer day in England – it's fine after the first few seconds.'

'It's not that. It's the stones. I don't know why but I've always found it difficult to walk barefoot on little stones. I usually bring a pair of plastic sandals with me when I come down to the beach. I've already been in the pool before you came up this morning, and believe me, the water in an unheated pool feels much colder than the sea.'

She gave a few more energetic strokes away from the shore and then came closer again. 'I'll give you the benefit of the doubt, but tomorrow I expect you to prove it.'

He cursed inwardly; he was sure that life would be far less complicated if she went away sooner rather than later. He was determined not to like her and he knew that that would be more difficult now that she had overcome his active dislike of her.

'It's lovely once you get over the initial shock', she called, and then struck out again.

He shook his head decisively, 'Another time - for now I'm quite happy sitting here.' Actually, he would have really liked to be in the water with her. He enjoyed his swims in the pool every morning but it wasn't the same as being with someone else, especially – the thought came unbidden, giving him no time to repress it – when that someone else was as attractive as she was. If he tried to go in without anything on his feet though, he knew how awkwardly self-conscious he would feel as he gingerly made his way over the unevenly sized small pebbles – evidently much more self-conscious than she was, he thought, as he watched her turn onto her back in the water, laughing as she did so.

When she emerged from the water, she came carefully over the stones, arms raised to help her balance and looking down to make sure she kept her footing. As she did so, he was able to observe her more attentively without fear of being noticed, knowing that, although in many ways he would be glad when she was out of his life again, the image of her in his mind would take much longer to fade away. He pulled his t-shirt off over his head when she was within two metres of the edge of the water and held it out towards her.

'Here. Dry yourself with this.'

'Thanks, but it's alright. I can just slip my things on; it's not cold so I'll dry out on the way back.'

'Take it. People round here don't know you, but I'm not walking back along the road with someone who looks like a contestant from the Miss-Lipari-wet-t-shirt-competition; my reputation would never recover.'

She laughed and accepted his shirt. 'I thought that women around the Med were more liberated now. I didn't expect you to be so prudish.'

He smiled, 'You shouldn't believe what you read in the tabloids… there are strict, if unwritten, codes of behaviour and woe betide anyone who breaks them. You'll be giving tourists a bad name.'

There were a couple of small boats, probably local fishermen, in the channel separating Lipari from Vulcano and he watched them, half turned away from her, as she quickly dried herself and slipped on her own clothes. He remembered the first time he had been on holiday abroad with Judi and how reticent she had been at first to go topless, until she had realised that, on the beach at Agay, she had been the one who stood out and attracted attention as one of the very few younger women to be chastely attired. That had been when they were both still students inter-railing round Europe, imposing on friends and relatives or camping out if there was no-one they could persuade to give them a bed and feed them. They had thought they were a perfect match then, and it was only later when the nature of his job had meant that he often had to work late, and she began to move in more exalted circles that there had been the first signs of tension. Even then, he knew she was proud of his rapid promotions and was looking forward to the time when he would have more control over his working patterns. Everything would have been fine, if it hadn't been for the journalists.

He hadn't disliked the journalist from the News of the World who occasionally bought him a drink and gently prodded him for newsworthy information. He'd known what the journalist wanted and had occasionally teased him by appearing to be on the verge of giving him something then stopping just short. The journalist had known that he wasn't going to get anything from Luke but had been happy to play along and most of the time they'd argued about football – the journalist was quite happy to pay for the drinks and claim it back on expenses. Unfortunately, not everyone who'd been groomed by the journalist had been as discreet as Luke and one or two had accepted expense payments from the newspaper in exchange for information. When the officers who had given information, and the journalist himself, were caught up in Operation Elveden, every officer who had had any contact with the journalist was scrutinised as part of the process. That scrutiny had revealed that Luke had spent a considerable amount of time finding out the location, and tracking the movements of an elderly Italian lawyer now living incognito in Switzerland. Luke was suspected of having passed that information on, and the lawyer had later been murdered.

Although the evidence that he had been researching the lawyer was incontrovertible, the evidence that he had passed it on was much weaker and he had hoped that the result of his disciplinary proceedings would be a demotion and an official warning. Knowing, however, that the lawyer had been a very influential man and had almost certainly had equally powerful friends in the English establishment, he had decided to give the keen young journalist from the country's leading mid-range tabloid, an exclusive interview, on the understanding that he would have the final say over which parts were used and when it should be published. The girl had given him assurances; he'd believed her – and it had ruined him.

Those thirty seconds thinking about the past helped to harden his heart against her again and when he turned round and she returned his t-shirt with a smile, he didn't return it. 'Come on,' he said brusquely, and turned back towards the path leading away from the sea, 'we need to be getting back.' She followed him without a word but let out a little sigh as she did so.

He had to slow down before they reached the top of the path as she was falling behind and he felt a guilty pang as he saw the sea-water seeping through her shorts and realised how they must be chafing. He held out a hand to help her as she got closer. 'Sorry, my past caught up with me and I lost it for a bit.' He glanced down at her shorts and she blushed slightly and then smiled.

'You've got every right... I'll be fine in a minute when we're back on the road and I can take smaller steps.' He kept hold of her hand as he slowly led her up the last few metres to the road.

Ten minutes later they were back at the hut. 'Wait here a minute,' and he disappeared through the door. When he came out he had everything he needed to make tea which he placed down next to the stove. 'I'll make some tea while you get those damp things off. It'll have to be Earl Grey as I've no milk left for normal tea.' He smiled as he registered her surprised expression, realising what she must be thinking.

'There's a pair of tracksuit bottoms and one of my t-shirts on the chair; you can slip those on while the others dry. Bring your clothes out and I'll hang them in the sun behind the hut. They'll dry in no time, even if I rinse the underwear in fresh water first.'

'That's nice of you, but there's no need – not to mention that getting water up here must be difficult – you don't want to waste it on my... things.' He laughed as he saw the effort she made to find a bland word without connotations, thinking that it actually had the opposite effect in allowing him to use his imagination.

'Don't tell anyone, but there's a little natural spring in one of the caves over there,' he used his head to indicate a small outcrop thirty metres to his left, where a tumbledown building, even more dilapidated than his hut, seemed to lean drunkenly against the rock. 'It's part of my land, so I suppose the spring belongs to me. Everything round here is volcanic, so I get warm water throughout the year. It's only a trickle but I've linked it to three connected water tanks, so I've always got water available.'

She was impressed. 'Is it drinking water?'

He shrugged, 'I assume that it's pretty much the same water as at the old Saint Calogero spa, just up the coast. I know that bathing in the waters was meant to be good for a range of different illnesses but

I haven't heard of them being drunk. The water I'm using for the tea comes out of a bottle. Go on; go and get changed.'

She looked disarmingly vulnerable sitting cross-legged, sipping tea, dressed in the dark-blue tracksuit bottoms that were far too big for her and a white t-shirt with Karl Marx informing people that he'd warned them 'that this would happen' emblazoned across the front, hanging loosely and exposing one delicate shoulder and collar bone. 'You haven't told me how you managed to track me down,' he said, in a tone that implied it was a question rather than a statement. She smiled, 'I'm not completely useless as an investigative journalist. Even I have friends who can get me bits of information and then all I had to do was to piece them together.'

'And you found enough bits of information to lead you here,' he said, looking round him with some incredulity.

'Not exactly - I found enough to suggest that you were in the Aeolian Islands and I gave myself ten days to find you. I'm booked in down in the town for one more night then I'm booked in at a little place in Acquacalda, at the other end of the island, for the next couple of days. If I didn't find you near Lipari, I was going to try round there for a couple of days and then move across to Salina and have a look there.'

'So how did you find me here?' he asked, making a vague circular gesture with his hand to take in the hut and the area around it.

'Most of the bars are fairly quiet at the moment and their owners like to chat with the few customers they have. The dishy young barman down at the bar near the harbour was obviously keen to impress and we got talking about the films that have been made on the island. I said I supposed that they must send people over to check things out before they decided to film here and he said that there were always people here sent down to check out locations. I asked him how he knew and he said he could always tell when different people came to the island. When I laughed and said he was making it up, he claimed that there were at least three people on the island now who he was sure worked for film companies.'

Luke groaned, 'Don't tell me that I'm one of them.' He shook his head in frustration and she laughed.

'If it's any consolation, you were the third one on his list. The first one is a property developer looking for land and it's just possible that he was right about the second one.'

'And how did you know that this place was mine?'

'That was simple. I moved on to another bar and the friendly barman told me that you lived somewhere up on the hill, and the man in the general stores at the bottom of the hill told me what your place looked like.'

'That was good of him,' said Luke sarcastically.

'Don't be too hard on him. I told him that I was your cousin and wanted to pay you a surprise visit.'

He bowed his head in disgust.

They sat in silence for a while. He asked himself whether he would ever be free to make a new life for himself and she watched him carefully.

'So, wherever I go, there are always going to be people who can track me down if they want to.'

A little smile played around the corners of her mouth. 'I'd like to think that I could, but then it's a bit easier for me than it is for "people". Isn't it?'

He lifted his face and fixed her eyes with his. 'And how do you work that out? What makes you so special?'

She held his gaze. 'I think I understand you better than most other people. Not only did you tell me all those things in the interview, but I researched you fairly thoroughly before I did the interview and then again after I came back from the Middle East.'

'Surely, any other competent journalist could do the research you did before the interview and your former employers have still got the original tape, haven't they?'

She nodded.

'And they could also do the research that you've done since then, couldn't they?'

'They could,' she agreed, 'but they'd have to have some idea where to start, and they weren't there when I did the interview, so they wouldn't have the clues from your body language.'

'What do you mean? What clues?'

'Oh, just little things: when you smiled and when you didn't; the points at which you crossed or uncrossed your legs; and particularly the way you leaned slightly forward to impress me with your sincerity when you weren't telling the whole truth.'

He shook his head and smiled. 'You're fishing. Everything in the interview that was brought up in court, I admitted to – under oath.'

'I know you did. I've read the transcript - several times. I was surprised that you didn't offer a better defence at first, then after I realised that you were protecting someone, maybe even more than one person.' She paused to allow him to object, but he sat impassively so she continued. 'I know that several of your superiors testified to say how gifted you were but I don't think you could have found out all you did without help from Italy – help from someone you really wanted to protect.'

'An interesting theory. But if there had been someone I was protecting, wouldn't the best way to protect them have been to defend myself and be declared innocent?' He smiled.

'It would, if you could have been certain of defending yourself successfully, but you couldn't be sure of that because there were flaws in your story that would have been revealed under cross-examination. You would probably have been convicted anyway and they would have refused parole until you had given them the name of your accomplice or accomplices.'

'As I said, it's an interesting theory, but it sounds a bit far-fetched. Why did nobody think of that at the time?'

'Because they were too keen to see you behind bars, so that whoever had been asked to make an example of you, would please the right people. Tell me that I'm wrong?'

'I wouldn't dream of it. I'm flattered that you think I'm so Machiavellian – he was always my favourite political theorist.'

'So what do you plan to do now that you've found me, and I've explained that I can't help you? Do you still intend to move on to Acquacalda or are you leaving tomorrow to get on with your investigation?'

She thought for a moment and then, without looking up said hesitantly, 'I ought to move on… but, Acquacalda's not too far away, is it?... If I stayed, would you be willing to show me around the rest of the island? - I- I'd really like that- and you did say that you'd come in the sea tomorrow.' She raised her head and looked anxiously into his eyes.

It was his chance to free himself of her – probably for ever – and he knew he should show no weakness and tell her to leave the island as soon as possible. He should ignore what he felt when he looked at her, or listened to her voice, or saw her laugh, or watched her lithe, almost naked body glide through the sea – the effect of those sights and sounds was only to be expected when you'd been living on your own for several months, and he was sure he'd get over them.

He had to do it and he hardened his heart and opened his mouth to tell her to leave the island, but the words that came out of his mouth as his eyes rested on the delicately sculpted hollow above her collar bone were not the words that he'd intended.

Chapter Two

'On my way. Probably away a few days from tomorrow – will call when back' Send. He hoped he wasn't making a silly mistake, but it was too late now. He had told her over a pizza down in the town the previous evening that he was prepared to accept that she probably wasn't the duplicitous, scheming bitch that his mind had created over the past five years, and that she hadn't intended to do the damage that she had, although he'd never be able to forget the consequences of her article. He'd thought initially that she was offended by the way he'd put it, but then she'd laughed heartily and said that if ever she came to write her memoirs, she'd put in 'not a duplicitous, scheming bitch' as one of the compliments she most treasured.

They had eaten in a characteristic little restaurant on the same street as Gilberto's *Enoteca* and, after they had eaten, Luke declined coffee at the restaurant and led the way down the road to Gilberto's.

When Gilda came over to take their order, he had given her his most winning smile, 'You're looking lovely tonight, Gilda.'

She had rolled her eyes theatrically, 'What do you want?'

'Due caffè, una grappa, un limoncello, per favore.'

'And?' she had said resignedly.

That had earned another smile from Luke, 'Well. Now that you've reminded me... I don't suppose I could use your computer for a minute to send another file, could I?'

Gilda had glanced round the other customers, 'Next time one of us needs to go in the office, we'll put the computer on. You can slip in after that- but don't make it obvious!'

'Thankyou, Gilda. I don't know what I'd do without you.' She had shaken her head and moved away.

'You could have used my I-pad. I know you haven't got internet but I'm sure you could have transferred whatever you need to send using Bluetooth.'

'What? Leave my innermost secrets on a journalist's computer. I've heard that that's not always a good idea.' She coloured and lowered her head and he took pity on her. 'I'm sorry; that was unfair. I've been earning enough money to get by on by writing some teenage adventure stories for a magazine back in the UK. I'm ahead of schedule at the moment but I decided that, as I'm not sure when I'll next get the chance, I'd send the next one over now. I finished it off after you'd gone this afternoon. I think it's probably better if all the stories are sent from the same computer, or at least from computers that have no connection at all to Luke Garvey.'

'Isn't that a bit paranoid?' she had asked with a smile.

'Possibly, but I'm afraid that's what comes of having worked as a computer analyst for the police.'

Before calling at her *pensione*, he passed by one of the two car hire companies based down in the port. He knew that there was one price for tourists and one for locals and, as he knew the manager, Sebastiano, quite well from evenings spent watching football on the big screen in one of the bars, he felt it was better if he conducted the negotiations.

Ten minutes later, he had agreed a very good deal for the three-day hire of an old but recently serviced Citroen Mehari, and had agreed that a second driver would be allowed at no extra cost so long as they didn't take it off the island.

'You really need to exchange your English licence for an Italian one, if you're going to stay here. In theory you can get fined if you don't get it changed within six months of becoming resident.

'Theories are wonderful, Seb. Just write down my English address on your form and officially, I'm a tourist just like all the others.'

Sebastiano shrugged, 'OK I'll just need to take a copy of this. I just thought I'd let you know.'

'And your thoughtfulness is much appreciated. We'll bring the other licence in when we pick the car up in twenty minutes or so.'

'I'm here to collect Signorina Simons' he said clearly into the intercom next to the bell of the pensione. There was an indistinct reply and, at the same time, the door, which was set into a larger door, clicked open. Inside, a passageway led through to a courtyard where an old Fiat 500 and two well-used scooters had been left. A stairway on the right led up to a landing above the passageway and a notice fastened to the wall at the foot of the stairs bore the legend *'Pensione Girasole 2 Piano'*. He ascended the staircase and arrived at an open doorway, inside which he could see Layla handing over some money to pay her bill.

'Buongiorno,' he called.

'Good morning,' she responded and the man who was counting the money gave a glance his way and a small acknowledging nod before finishing counting the notes.

'Bene. Tutto a posto,' said the man, satisfied that the money was correct. 'Enjoy the rest of your stay in Italy and please tell your friends to come here in future.'

'I will,' she said, *'Arrivederci.'*

Luke stepped forward and took her rucksack, swinging it over his shoulder, said *'Buongiorno'* to the hotelier and led the way back onto the street.

'I suppose we'd better go straight to Acquacalda,' she said, 'I don't really fancy walking round with these bags all day.'

He explained that he had arranged for a car and suggested that, as the road to Acquacalda passed close to the islands best beaches, they should buy themselves some rolls, some prosciutto and a couple of bottles of water in the supermarket across the road, so that they could have a picnic lunch. Although the beach was still covered in small pebbles, there was a rudimentary shower so they wouldn't need to spend the rest of the day encased in salt.

She agreed that it was an excellent suggestion and said that she would also buy something to cook that evening, as the place she'd arranged to stay was meant to have a small kitchen. 'I'll also buy myself a swimming costume so you won't be shocked or embarrassed again if we're seen by anyone you know.'

'Haven't you got one in here?' he asked, patting the strap of the rucksack to indicate what he meant by "here".

'I wasn't coming for a holiday when I came here, and I certainly couldn't afford to stay anywhere with a pool.'

'How about this one?' he asked innocently, holding out probably the dullest one-piece black swimsuit it was possible to imagine. 'It's probably suitably tasteful.' He saw her face fall.

'Do you really think so?' she asked without any enthusiasm and then laughed as he couldn't keep his face straight any longer. 'I was worried you were serious for a minute.'

'I'm not sure that the supermarket's the best place for costumes,' he said. 'There's a place just up the road with a much more eye-catching selection in the window and, as there'll be hardly anyone else on the beach and I'll have no-one else to look at, I'm quite happy to encourage you to pay to buy a better one.'

She shook her head, 'Your altruism amazes me, but I don't think that designer swimwear is really necessary. I don't think I'll be getting the black one but there are some quite adequate bikinis here and, as you've said, there won't be any competition so adequate will do just fine.'

Finally, they made their way down to the port where the white Mehari was waiting outside for them. Layla looked at it dubiously. 'What is it? Are you sure it will go? It doesn't look like any car I've ever driven!'

He laughed, 'You'll love it after a few minutes – it's the next best thing to a Mini-Moke. 'She looked at him blankly. 'Come on. They need to take a photocopy of your licence so that you're covered by the insurance too.'

Her look changed to one of horror, 'You're expecting me to drive! Have you seen where that gear-lever is?'

'Only in an emergency. Come on.'

Half an hour later, Luke pulled the Mehari into a lay-by on the right hand side of the road opposite what appeared to be an old abandoned factory. The steep hillside behind the factory was almost pure white with occasional dark shadows where recesses had been carved out of the rock. The remnants of an old bridge stretched across the road from the factory and jutted out towards the sea.

'Chalk?' asked Layla, looking at the factory with curiosity.

Luke shook his head, 'Pumice – you know, the stuff that you pay a fortune for to rub the hard bits of skin off your feet – it's one of the results of volcanic eruptions when the lava flows cool down and solidify. You either get pure white pumice or, depending on chemical reactions that are way too complicated for me to understand, jet black obsidian. If you look in any of the souvenir shops, you'll see plenty of jewellery and little ornaments carved out of obsidian. It's shiny and black, and even though it's not as easy to carve as pumice, it looks much more impressive. People used to believe that dragons lived in volcanoes breathing fire, so some people call obsidian, dragon glass. – See, I'm a fount of useless information; you'll be glad to get away from me in a few days.'

'And that's why you've stopped here, is it? So you can put your master-plan into operation.'

'Actually, no. The thought didn't strike me until after I'd stopped... There aren't really any natural beaches on Lipari, but on this side of the island, where the pumice mines are, the little bays and coves beneath the factories were developed so that boats could get close in and take the pumice over to the mainland. The last of the factories closed down in the seventies, I think, and the bays have been adapted to provide bathing establishments. They can get quite busy in summer, although most people arrive there on boats from Lipari or Cannareto, rather than by scrambling down the paths from the road, like we're going to do.'

By tacit agreement, they managed to get through the rest of the day and evening without mentioning the difficult issues from the past and without her renewing her request for his help, even though neither of them doubted that a time would come when the issues would bubble to the surface again.

The beach was virtually deserted: a few people came down the path, stayed for between half an hour and an hour and then made their way back up to the road, while one, clearly northern European couple with three small children were dropped off by boat and stayed a couple of hours before Luke saw the father make a call as a prelude to the family making their way to the small jetty at the southern end of the beach. Ten minutes later, the water-taxi that had brought them, flying the Jolly Roger above a second flag made up of a red and a yellow triangle with a three legged emblem in the middle, pulled carefully up against the jetty and a rugged man with long hair and a shaggy beard, held out a hand to assist first the mother, then the three children and finally the father to board the boat.

'Is that the flag of Lipari? The emblem looks a bit like that of the Isle of Man.'

He grinned, 'Are you ready for your second lesson of the day?' She smiled, nodded her head and lay back carefully on the stones closing her eyes and turning her face so that it faced the sun.

'Right. The emblem of the three legs radiating from a central point like the spokes on a wheel is called a *trinacria*, which back in the Roman period was the word for a three-pointed star. If you sort of half close your eyes and squint a bit at a map of Sicily, it looks pretty much like a star with three points, and the same applies to the Isle of Man. When the allies invaded in forty-three they wanted to separate Sicily from Fascist Italy and set it up as an independent republic. That's when they came up with the red and yellow flag with the three legs that seem to be running round a little gorgon's head in the middle – although the *trinacria* had been used on Sicilian coins well over two thousand years ago. The flag was…'

'Enough! I can't take it anymore,' she said pressing her hands over her ears, 'put those plastic sandals on and let's go for a swim.'

He laughed and began to slip the beach-sandals on, 'I don't know. I must be destined to spend my whole life looking for a cultured woman – surely there must be one somewhere!' She threw a piece of pumice at him and stood up.

'Come on. Race you into the water.'

The race was no contest; although she got a head start as he pulled the second sandal on, they gave him such an advantage that he easily outstripped her, and his early morning dips in the pool, and familiarity with the point at which the water suddenly deepened, meant that he had no hesitation in diving forwards after just four strides in the water. When he lifted his head out of the water and rolled over to look back, she was still easing herself gingerly into the water. He swam back towards her and then stopped a few metres from her and reached down to remove his sandals before throwing them past her onto the beach.

'I thought you needed those,' she said, pausing as she turned to watch them land.

'Either I can get out very slowly and inelegantly, or somebody kind could get out first and throw them in to me, but I much prefer to swim in bare feet.' He watched as she made her mind up and dived forward into the water. She passed within fifty centimetres of him, just below the surface of the water, arms close to her sides and legs kicking purposefully; he raised one of his own hands feeling a sudden urge to let it trail along her body as she slipped past, but thought better of it, and kept the hand raised until she was clear of him.

The water was cold, but by the time they had swum out far enough to see round the headland into the next bay, neither of them felt it anymore.

'See what I mean', he said, pointing to the abandoned industrial works above the bay, 'Everywhere that's now a beach, used to be a busy industrial port. It's only really been in the last thirty or forty years that tourism has replaced the island's traditional sources of income, and many people here only just manage to survive throughout the year.'

'So why did you decide to make it your home?'

'Because I could,' he said and, rolling onto his back, struck out towards their beach. She watched for a few seconds and then, after casting a last look at the other little beach, followed him.

When they reached the shore, she went first and then paddled carefully back in to give him his sandals so he could get out. As he was now the more stable one on the stones, he offered her his hand to help her up the beach – an offer that was declined with a smile.

After a quick cold shower at the far end of the beach, they returned to the spot where they had left their things. 'What do you mean, because you could?' she asked him as he lowered himself down onto the pumice pebbles near her.

'It's complicated and would probably bore you,' he said dismissively.

'Try me. I'm sure it will be more interesting than the story of the Sicilian flag.'

'Alright, but don't complain this time.'

'I promise I'll try not to. If it does get boring, I can always go to sleep and pretend to be concentrating on your story. Go on.'

'Your research will have told you that my aunt in Italy had a younger sister called Francesca. Now Francesca's been in a vegetative state for the last twelve years after the incident where my aunt and uncle were killed, and ever since the accident all her assets have been dealt with by her father under power of attorney... You're following so far? ... OK - Well, ten years or so before the accident, Francesca and her then boyfriend were touring Sicily and the smaller islands on a BMW motorbike....'

'Being a BMW makes a difference, does it?'

He ignored her, and continued. 'When they were here, Francesca saw the hut and its surrounding land and absolutely loved it. The boyfriend, who apparently was besotted by her, made a few enquiries and found out that it could be bought for next to nothing and bought it for her.'

'No!'

He smiled, 'It's true; although when I say next to nothing, I really do mean next to nothing. I've seen the sale documents and he got it for three hundred and fifty thousand lire, which must have been about a hundred and ten pounds at the time.'

'That's still pretty impressive! I can't remember any boyfriend spending that much on me.'

'Anyway... I never met him as they split up a few months later, although I can vaguely remember my uncle saying that the boyfriend had been a bit of a jerk. Actually he used an Italian term, *"figlio di papa"*, which means a young man who's given everything he wants by his parents without having to work hard for anything. I suppose the literal translation would be "Daddy's boy", but the term "spoilt brat" would probably be more accurate, despite not conveying the family relationship... where was I, I've lost my thread.'

'Boyfriend, gift, power of attorney,' she offered helpfully.

'Oh yes, that's right. Her father's getting on a bit now and two years ago the power of attorney was transferred to one of my cousins. She's never been here, and has no interest in the land and so she suggested that I could give it a go down here until I decided what to do next. That's all there is to it, really – told you it was pretty dull.'

'And have you?'

'Have I what?' he asked, puzzled.

'Decided what to do next?'

'Aah. I see... At the moment there isn't a next. I'm on licence for another nineteen months and I'm quite happy living a simple life here at the moment, amongst friendly, genuine people who live life at their own pace.'

'Great,' she said, in a voice that implied she thought the opposite. 'Have you thought about writing pastorals? There will we sit upon the rocks – and see the shepherds feed their flocks - by shallow rivers, to whose falls – melodious birds sing madrigals.'

'Ha, ha. Very funny!' he said, and lay back on his towel.

They lay still and silent for a while, each pursuing their own thoughts. She was the first to break the silence, 'I suppose it was the least she could do for you, wasn't it?'

'Sorry?' he said, taken by surprise again.

'Your cousin. She owed you a big favour, didn't she?'

'I don't know what you mean.'

'Have it your way, but I think that you deliberately kept her name out of it and took all the blame on yourself at the trial.' There was silence again, and this time, it lasted until they were ready to leave.

They found the mini-apartment that Layla had agreed to rent near the far end of the village of Acquacalda, which was, for the most part, a single row of buildings on the landward side of the main road that dipped down into the bay and then ran along for three hundred metres before climbing up again. It was only after the road began to climb again, that a second, minor one split off and continued to run along the shore for another hundred metres or so. The apartment was on the upper floor of a house and had clearly been created out of roof space to try and create income from the summer flows of tourists. A flight of rickety steps had been built up the side of the house, so that guests had their own independent entrance, which they were grateful for. The woman who owned it made it obvious that she was not happy that there were two of them as Layla had not mentioned that when she booked, and said that it would make a difference to the amount of tourist tax that was payable. Although Luke was sure that none of the money that Layla was paying would ever be declared to anyone, whether that be the local tourist office or the national tax authorities, he understood how hard it was for the islanders to make ends meet and passed over a twenty euro note that 'should cover the extra taxes payable.'

The inside of the apartment was what an estate-agent would have described as "compact"; there was a small bathroom in one corner with toilet, sink and shower, a kitchenette to one side with a sink, a two ring hob, a small fridge and a microwave, which seemed clean and relatively modern, while in the main part of the room it was clear that the table and chairs would need to be pushed to one side when the sofa-bed was opened. The best feature of the apartment, however was the large roof-terrace in front of the French-windows, which offered spectacular views of the island of Salina in front of them and the distant outline of Alicudi.

'I didn't realise it would be so small,' she said, as soon as the *signora* had left them to their own devices,' looking towards the sofa-bed with a concerned look on her face. 'When the description said that there was a sofa-bed, I thought it meant as well as a proper bed – I didn't think.'

He smiled, 'Don't worry. I think it's wider than most of the sofa-beds you'd get back in England – and if it's not wide enough, I can always sleep on the floor. It won't be very different from my bed back at the hut.'

'We'll try it, but if anyone has to sleep on the floor, it should be me; I was the one who asked you to come with me.'

'I'll tell you what,' he said, 'we'll give it a try and if it doesn't work out, I can always get the car, go back to the hut, and come back first thing in the morning with some fresh bread.'

She smiled and nodded, then opened the cupboard under the sink to check the cooking utensils, before straightening up again. 'Right. Now I want you to go out for a walk, for at least an hour and a half while I cook.'

'An hour and a half! Can't I just sit on the terrace and read a book?'

'No. I want you well away while I'm cooking, otherwise, you'll be curious and keep coming in and looking, and sticking your finger in to taste things, and offering advice – and we'll end up arguing - Go!'

Trying to adopt a pained expression, he gave in and left, taking his tablet with him so he could sit on the sea-front and read.

When he came back, he could smell something wonderful before he was halfway up the steps leading up to the apartment and realised for the first time that they had hardly eaten all day and that the sea air had given him an appetite.

'Am I allowed back in now?' he asked, as he reached the top of the stairs. 'I've brought some wine.'

'Hi. You can set the table. It will be ready in about ten minutes if you're hungry – otherwise I can turn it off and heat it up again later.'

'Ten minutes will be fine. What do we need on the table?'

'Fork, glass, a couple of sheets of kitchen paper each – and maybe a knife if you're a finicky eater who doesn't like getting his fingers dirty.'

A pan was on one of the gas-rings and he could see that she had constructed a home-made steamer on top using a colander and a pan lid. He moved closer to the cooker and leaned towards it but then withdrew swiftly as he was threatened with a wooden spoon. 'Alright. I give in. I'll wait until it's ready,' he said, stepping away from the spoon. 'Shall I put the table out on the terrace, it's still quite pleasant out?' She shrugged and he took it as assent.

Setting the table took less than a minute and his offer of more assistance was declined so he had nothing else to do but sit down at the table and look out towards Salina where he could just see the first lights being turned on, despite there still being plenty of time before they were really needed.

When she finally emerged she placed a large plate full of couscous covered with a rich and highly fragrant sauce, in which he could see that there were chickpeas, chunks of sweet potato, squash and large pieces of octopus.

'It smells wonderful,' he said as she re-emerged with her own, somewhat smaller plate, 'I haven't had couscous for ages.'

'Hopefully, this will be a bit different to the couscous you can buy in supermarkets and just add a bit of boiling water to and then mix in a glug of olive-oil. This was cooked by steaming it over the sauce, the North-African way.'

'I'm impressed.'

'You'd better taste it first before you're too liberal with your compliments – you might not like it.' He did as she suggested.

'I'm even more impressed now.'

She gave a little smile and began eating.

The meal was one of the best he'd had in a long time. All the different flavours of the spices she had used, and the variety of textures, particularly the locally caught octopus, made every mouthful an experience to savour. The litre of rough local red wine that had been the only choice on offer at that time of year in the little village shop also went well with the octopus and, by the time they had finished, the bottle was almost empty. They had bought a bottle of Malvasia dessert wine in the supermarket that morning and decided that it would be a shame not to at least try it, to round off the meal, although Layla insisted on only having a very small amount as she said she already felt a little light-headed.

Luke insisted on tidying up and doing the washing up when they had finished while she remained at the table sipping her Malvasia. Out of the corner of his eye, he could see her studying him as he worked, and was careful not to turn his head towards her until he had finished, by which time she had lowered her eyes.

He smiled, 'Where did you learn to cook like that? It reminds me of some of the tagines I ate when we went on holiday to Morocco – but this was much better.'

'It should be much better. I assume that when you went to Morocco, you only ate in tourist restaurants, or at least only in restaurants in areas where there are a lot of tourists – what do you expect?'

'I'm not disagreeing – but that doesn't tell me where you learnt to cook like that.'

She shrugged dismissively, 'When I was in Tunisia and Egypt, it wasn't just watching revolutions and people being shot, I had to eat as well, and sometimes that meant being fed by the local people who individually, whatever side they took in the revolution, were always charming and incredibly hospitable... And, apart from that, my mother was quite widely travelled, so I learnt some things from her.'

'Well, if you learnt to cook like that from her, feel free to pass on my compliments next time you see her.' He laughed and turned away, the two thirds of a litre of wine he had drunk making him miss the sad look on her face as she lowered it. 'It's still fairly early. Let's go for a walk to work off some of the calories and help clear our heads.'

They walked back along the road by the sea until they reached the main road again and then Luke turned to walk up the hill away from the sea.

'Can't we carry on along the bay by the sea? I like to hear the sound of the water against the pebbles, especially that gentle shuerre sound as the water drains back into the sea,' she said, putting an arm through his.

'Say that again he said with a laugh – I liked that.'

'Shhhuerrrre,' she said, turning her face towards his and pushing her lower jaw and bottom lip forwards as she imitated the sound of the sea with her eyes semi-closed. He felt an almost irresistible desire to kiss her and began to slowly move his face down towards hers.

Almost irresistible, but not quite. He knew that they had both drunk a fair amount and that the urge he felt was just the effect of the wine; he also remembered who she was and what she was responsible for. He pulled his head back and, pressing his arm to his side so that hers remained a prisoner, said brusquely, 'Come on... you'll be able to hear the waves from the apartment later – we're near enough to the sea.' He began to walk her up the hill and continued to do so for almost twenty minutes despite feeling the drag on his arm of her mute protest.

Eventually he stopped at a point where the road turned sharply to the left away from the sea. 'This way,' and he stepped over the guard-rail on the right hand side of the road; as he still had her arm, she had no choice but to follow him. He pushed aside a bush and led her onto a narrow flat area before the hillside fell steeply away towards the sea. 'Look,' he said, and pointed out to sea.

From where they stood, not only was the island of Salina clearly visible ahead of them, with the lights of its several small settlements glittering in the dark, but to the left were two apparently smaller islands which he explained were Alicudi and Filicudi, while to their right were two other islands, the shoulder of one of which was silhouetted against a red glow that appeared to shimmer as she tried to focus on it. 'San Pietro and Stromboli. There's another little island in between but it's hidden by San Pietro. A couple of times a week, you can get night-time boat trips from Lipari that take people round the back of Stromboli so you get a better view of the sparks it sends out... but most of the time – so long as the weather's fine – I like to see it from here. I think it helps put things into perspective.'

She didn't respond for a while, just stood there looking, before finally and with a smaller voice than usual murmuring 'Thankyou.' He was careful not to make the mistake of looking her in the face again.

When they had clambered back over the guard-rail, she placed her arm through his again, but he could feel that she was was far more relaxed and although they returned to the village enveloped in the same silence with which they had departed, there was much less tension in the air.

As they reached the junction, she suggested that they could walk across the pebbly beach to the sea's edge and he was happy to follow her although warning that they needed to be careful in the dark as the surface was very uneven.

Having lived on the island for over a year without television, radio or any other form of evening entertainment, he had got used to going to bed early and rising early to make the most of the light so, even though it was only just ten o'clock, they decided to go to bed soon after arriving back at the apartment. He opened the bed-settee while she was in the bathroom and made the bed with the sheets and quilt that had been provided. The somewhat cramped space that was left between the bed and the wall did not look appealing and he decided that it would be best to try each taking one side of the bed and hope for the best. When she came out of the bathroom wearing a simple pair of cotton pyjamas that he was pleased to see were not particularly flattering, she raised no objection to this suggestion and climbed into the far side of the bed. He took his own turn in the bathroom, put on a pair of running shorts that he had packed for the purpose and, emerging from the bathroom, turned off the light and climbed into bed trying to stay as close to the edge as he could.

As the room was small, they had left one of the french-windows wide open behind the long curtains to let some air in while they slept. When he woke up, sometime between two and three in the morning, the curtain was flapping and he could hear that not only had a wind got up during the night but that it had brought rain with it. He slipped quietly out of the side of the bed so as not to disturb her and made his way over to the window to see if there was any way of blocking it partially open. Just as he reached it, a distant flash of lightening revealed Layla sitting on one of the loungers on the terrace with her knees pulled up to her chest. The now almost empty bottle of Malvasia lay on the floor beside her alongside a glass now half full of rainwater, showing that she had been there for some time.

He stepped quickly outside and crouched in the rain beside her. When he cupped his fingers under her chin and gently lifted and turned her face towards him, he saw that there were tears running down her cheeks. Allowing her chin to slip down again, he placed his left arm behind her back and his right behind her knees and bracing his own back, lifted her gently up and carried her back into the room. He tried to lower her onto her feet but realised immediately that she was incapable of standing up on her own so repositioned her and let her down onto one of the dining chairs that he had pushed against the wall when he had opened the sofa-bed.

When he was reasonably sure that she would not slip off the chair, he left her for a moment and mixed a teaspoon of salt into half a glass of water and then placed the glass in the bathroom. Returning to Layla, he placed her arms behind his neck and then, managing to slip his own arms behind her back lifted her to her feet. She muttered incoherently as she rested her head on his shoulder until, with difficulty, he managed to turn her around and walk her into the bathroom where he first forced her to drink some of the salt water and then, bending her over the toilet-bowl, poked his finger into her throat until she gagged and deposited much of the Malvasia into the toilet.

After making her drink a couple of glasses of water, he stripped off her sodden clothes and placed her under the shower before towelling her down, slipping one of his t-shirts on her and putting her to bed although by this time she was crying again and seemed to think she was talking to someone called Aida.

He woke up more than two hours before her in the morning and, although he knew he ought to walk along to the shop to get something in for breakfast, he decided it was better not to leave her alone and went out onto the terrace with a glass of water and his book. Eventually, after he had read several chapters, he heard her stirring and then, a couple of minutes later, she emerged onto the terrace still wearing his t-shirt and looking somewhat haggard. He couldn't help smiling as he took in the immaculate legs, the oversized yellow t-shirt with its 'Keep the asylum seekers and deport the Daily Express' slogan and the drawn face with the black-rimmed eyes surrounded by a mass of wild hair. She did not return his smile.

'What happened?' she mumbled, and looking down at the t-shirt blushed and said 'Did you…?'

He shook his head. 'You've got nothing to worry about… Look. Why don't you have a shower while I go and get something for breakfast?'

She gave a little nod and then grimaced as the nod made her head throb.

'You'll feel a lot better when you've got something inside you and you start to feel like a human being again,' he reassured her.

He had to more or less force-feed her the bread and Nutella, that were all he'd been able to get hold of, but when she had finished and had been convinced that it wasn't going to come straight back up again, she admitted that she felt a lot better. He sent her out to the terrace while he made two more mugs of tea and then joined her.

'How bad was it?' she asked quietly, looking down into her tea.

'It was pretty bad... I have seen worse, but only on those documentaries meant to shock us about what young people get up to on holiday when they think no-one's looking. Is it something you do regularly?' He raised an eyebrow as he asked.

'Oh, my God. I'm so ashamed... You probably won't believe me, but nothing like that's ever happened to me before. I can't remember ever being more than slightly tipsy, and that was only when I was a teenager – I'll never touch another drop of alcohol again!'

'Don't worry. I believe you. A regular heavy drinker would have been able to take far more than you did and still be standing up. You'll be fine going back to being just a normal drinker in a couple of days. The lesson will have done you good.'

She was silent for a time then looked up, blushing. 'I think I need to know exactly what happened. It feels awkward thanking you for what you did... and didn't do... without having the embarrassment of knowing exactly what it was... the last thing I remember was looking out over the other islands from the top of the hill... I know it's going to be embarrassing but I think I have to hear it – as part of my penance.' So he told her, while trying to gloss over his showering her, drying her and slipping his t-shirt on her as quickly as possible.

When he had finished, she stood up slowly, leaned over to squeeze his hand and said 'Thankyou,' then she added, 'and really, nothing else happened?' He looked at her and she blushed deeply, 'I mean, people always tell us never to get drunk because men are just waiting for us to let our defences down.'

He looked at her thoughtfully. 'I'm not sure what I can say that won't make me sound like a character out of a nineteenth century novel… the phrases that come to mind are ones like "your honour is intact, madam" and "I am a gentleman", but they sound far too pompous don't they? How about if I just say that comatose women have no appeal for me and leave it at that?' She smiled.

'Who's Aida?' he asked casually, and her face froze.

'What do you know about Aida?' she responded, her voice catching as she spoke and her eyes open wide.

'Very little. At one stage last night you were doing a lot of fairly incoherent muttering, and Aida was one of names that stuck in my mind because of the opera – I love Verdi.'

She sighed, 'I suppose, after last night, you deserve to know all the truth, but can we leave it until later on when I'm feeling a bit less shaky. It's quite a complicated story and I promise not to hide anything from you but, this morning, I'd really like you to take me somewhere nice and peaceful – hopefully where I can have a swim as well.'

'Deal,' he said, 'Ready in ten minutes?'

He took her over the top of the island, driving very carefully so as not to upset her stomach, stopping at the bar in Pianoconte to get some sandwiches made up and to buy a large bottle of water and some oranges. From there it only took a few minutes down a side-road before they arrived at the old Thermal Baths of San Calogero where they parked behind two other cars and a scooter. At the Spa, for a contribution of two euros each, an enthusiastic volunteer showed them around the old complex giving them the historical background and then left them alone to look at the exhibition of local art on the ground floor.

The paintings in the exhibition were mainly abstract and, with the exception of a handful that seemed to have captured some exciting colour harmonies suggestive of a range of emotions, there was not much that caused them to linger and they were soon out in the sunshine again. Below the spa buildings, and only accessible from the spa was an old cart track that led down to within a hundred metres of the sea, and from there a narrow path snaked its way down to a small strip of pebble.

By the time they had spent fifteen minutes in the sea, swimming vigorously to keep warm, it was clear that Layla was feeling much better, although she was still shivering after she had dried herself off and dressed.

'We'll call in at the hut... it's much nearer than Acquacalda, and there should be enough tepid water stored in the cave to wash the salt off us. I'll be able to lend you a big thick jumper as well, if you still need it after a cup of tea and our sandwiches.'

She washed first and then dressed and made each of them a large cup of tea while he disappeared into the cave to wash. Anyone passing would have been struck by the contrast in their attire, as he took the mug she held out towards him and sat on the camping chair next to her. She was wearing a large green fleece that was much too big for her over a pair of bermuda-shorts while he now sported a sleeveless black t-shirt over a pair of tatty faded denim jeans.

'Aida was my sister... She died last year... and yesterday would have been her birthday... the first birthday since she died.' He stretched out a hand towards her, but she ignored it.

'I'm sorry,' he said, at a loss to think of anything more appropriate or sensitive to say. It was as if he hadn't spoken.

'I've never really talked about her to anyone before – but I think I need to – if you don't mind.'

This time he managed to reach her hand with his, 'Of course I don't mind, but... can I make a suggestion?... let's buy some food in for tonight and then go back to the apartment... that way you can talk as much or as little as you need and we don't have anything else to think about – OK?'

She nodded. 'OK. But can we keep off the wine tonight, please?'

He laughed, 'As it's obviously my turn to cook tonight, I can't promise that there won't be any wine in what I cook, but the alcohol content should evaporate away. I may have a glass myself, but that doesn't mean you have to.'

By the time they were back at the apartment, the spring sun had disappeared around the corner of the island and each put on the warmest clothing they had available before sitting out on the sun-loungers on the terrace.

When they were settled, he looked at her and said, 'It's entirely up to you whether you tell me or not. You don't have to... but if you think that talking would help you, then... then I'm here.' He was rewarded with a weak smile as she drew her breath in.

'Like I said, Aida was my sister and, as far as I'm concerned she was the cleverest, most argumentative, headstrong, annoying, beautiful and wonderful person who ever lived – as you can imagine, we had quite an up and down relationship but I always knew that if ever I really needed her that she would be there for me, no matter what I'd done.'

'Wow!'

She smiled at him through tears that he couldn't be sure were tears of joy from happy memories or tears of sadness for her loss – probably, he thought, she didn't know herself.

'The trouble is, I can't really explain Aida to you, and what it was that made her so special without telling you about our background, and it's not really straightforward – you can't imagine how complicated families can be.' Luke smiled to himself, remembering what his uncle Paul had told him about how some of the Italian side of the family had been closely linked to Mussolini's regime – but he said nothing. 'I need to go back nearly a hundred years to when my great-grandfather was an important academic at the University of Tripoli, fairly well off with a wife from a leading Berber family, and well regarded by officials in the Italian regime – Libya was an Italian colony of course from 1911 onwards. My grandmother, Lina, was their first child – the first of five and, according to my mother, very beautiful when she was young, but also fairly rebellious – I'm afraid it runs in the family.' She glanced at him and smiled. 'Well, when she was only twenty, she fell in love. Nothing wrong with that you might think, but she was already destined for marriage with the eldest son of a leading family in Benghazi and the man she fell in love with was a dashing young Italian Captain on the staff of the Italian Governor. Normally, her parents would have been able to insist that she went ahead with the arranged marriage and that would have been that, but at that time, you didn't upset the colonial administration and it appears that Capitano Carlo Maria de Simone was a great favourite with Ettore Bastico the Governor-General.' She paused to take a drink of the orange juice they had bought.

'So you're part Libyan and part Italian,' said Luke, surprised, 'You always seemed to have something a little bit exotic about you, but I couldn't quite put my finger on it – maybe because I've always been used to seeing Italians.'

'Not quite. I'm part Libyan, but not part Italian. My grandmother and her captain were married in forty-two and Carlo Maria was killed in the fighting in forty-three, or escaped with those Italians who didn't surrender, which amounts to pretty much the same thing. The big problem was that my grandmother had pretty much burnt her boats with her family when she'd shamed them by reneging on the arranged marriage, so she couldn't expect any help from them; the only one who seems to have had any contact with her was her youngest brother, Mohammed, but he was only seventeen at the time... Somehow she survived, I have my suspicions how but I'd rather not think about it – she was only twenty-four and a very attractive woman. Anyway, by the middle of 1944 she was living with a Major Phillips, a pen-pusher rather than a fighter, who was part of the new British administration in Tripolitania as the British sector of Libya was called. He was my grandfather.'

'Almost as British as me then. I have to go a generation further back to find my Italian ancestor – although there are a few Irish bits thrown into the mix here and there.'

She gave a wry smile in acknowledgement of his interruption and then continued, 'The one thing that we're very bad at in my family seems to be in choosing our men, although it was Lina, my grandmother, who probably had the least luck of all. Steady, reliable, comfortably boring Major Phillips was promoted in 1947 and became a Colonel attached to the staff of General Sir Rob McGregor MacDonald Lockhart when he was appointed Acting Governor of the North West Frontier in India that June. When he left Libya, he gave my grandmother two hundred pounds so that she could look after herself and her eleven month old baby, and that was that. My grandmother had assumed that she'd be spending the rest of her life with Major Phillips and had named my mother Dagny, which means "a new day begins" in Arabic – some new day!'

'And I assume the gallant Major was never seen again?'

She shook her head and surprised him by laughing, 'Not in Libya, but apparently he died of a fever in what is now part of Pakistan after a child bit his hand – poetic justice, wouldn't you say?' The question was clearly rhetorical and required no more than a complicit smile as a response.

'My grandmother was an intelligent woman, even if she was a bad judge of men, and she soon realised that what seemed like a fair sized sum would soon disappear and, as she had no family to turn to – even her younger brother, Mohammed, had distanced himself from her after she'd taken up with my grandfather – she decided that she would use her money in getting to Europe. I don't know much about the next couple of years; I know they travelled up through Italy, but not much more than that, until, after a few months in West Germany, they ended up in Belgium where they found a room in a house of Arab exiles in the suburb of Brussels that became notorious after the terrorist attacks in Paris last year.'

'Meeringen – or something like that?' he asked quizzically.

'Molenbeek,' she corrected. 'She wasn't the sort of woman who ever gave up and she somehow changed her name from De Simone to the more Belgian sounding Simons and got a job in a shop where she eventually became manager and succeeded in buying her own flat. Somewhere along the way she managed to acquire Belgian citizenship and make sure that her daughter, my mother, worked hard through school and eventually qualified as a teacher although she never managed to get a permanent contract.' She paused. 'If they'd stayed in Belgium who knows what would have happened but, in 1971 Britain joined the Common Market and she got the idea that if she moved over to Britain, she might be able to find her Major again.'

'Didn't he die in Pakistan?'

'He did, but she didn't know that at the time. Anyway, even when she found out, as she was never one for looking backwards, she decided to stay in England where she gave some private French lessons and did a little bit of translation work. Unfortunately, she developed ovarian cancer and died in 1978 without ever finding happiness and before she had chance to see her first grandchild.

'My mother, Dagny, was someone who everyone seems to have liked; although she never had the physical beauty that her mother had had she seems to have had plenty of boyfriends when she was young, but never anyone she wanted to settle down with until she moved to a different school in North London as Head of Art. I told you earlier that, in my family we're very bad at choosing our men, and Mum was no exception. She didn't have a car and one evening, after a parents' evening, the Deputy Head offered her a lift home as it was on his way. After that... I'm sure you could tell the story yourself - he wasn't happy in his marriage – his wife didn't love him – he was only staying for the sake of the children – he wished his wife were more like her – as soon as his eldest had done his 'O' levels he was going to leave her, although of course he would never hurt his children. After that, he was always polite and friendly in school, without appearing pushy and, the next time he offered her a lift home, she asked if he had time to pop in for a coffee - and that was that. Aida was born in March 1979 and he was very distant for a while then, after a few months – I suppose it would be bitchy to say when she'd got her figure back, he started paying her attention again, although he insisted that there could be no more pregnancies.'

'Aaah!' said Luke.

She smiled, 'Your life might have been different if he'd got his way!.. As it happened, Aida's had been a difficult pregnancy and the Doctors had told mum that she was unlikely to be able to have any more children. She felt that that allowed her to tell my father that she definitely couldn't have any more. They continued to see each other irregularly for the next few years; occasionally he'd tell her that he was on the verge of leaving his wife, but she never really believed him. Then, as his Christmas present for 1986, she had to tell him that she was pregnant again, although it was likely that she'd lose the baby. He said that he hoped she did – that it would be better for everyone. She never spoke to him again and somehow, I was born the following June, several weeks premature.'

'And your father?'

'He was a few years older than Mum, so fortunately he retired from teaching a couple of years later and she never had to have any more to do with him. She could – maybe should – have pursued him through the Child Support Agency to make him contribute towards the upbringing of his children but she didn't. She told me later that if she had, the people who would have ended up suffering most would have been his other children and it wasn't their fault that their father was a scumbag... I've seen him - in the distance - I wanted to know what he looked like - and I've even spoken to my half-siblings, without them having any idea who I was, of course.'

'You wouldn't want to get to know them?'

She threw her head back and laughed, a hearty laugh that for some reason made him feel warm inside. He watched her until she'd finished and looked at him again. 'I'm sorry,' she said, 'One of them is a Chartered Accountant and the other is an Actuary, and if you have a stereotype of a chartered accountant in your head, then you will know exactly what my half siblings are like. I wish them no ill, but I can't imagine anyone with whom I have less in common.' She stopped and seemed to be wondering how to continue, or whether to continue at all.

Luke waited a minute patiently, then offered, 'Shall I make a cup of tea.' She smiled and nodded, and he went inside, giving her time to gather her thoughts.

'We forgot to get milk, so it's black I'm afraid. We finished the other milk this morning.'

'So long as it's hot and wet, it will do. Thankyou,' she said with a smile. 'And thankyou for giving me a few minutes to pull myself together – the next bit is the difficult bit.'

He turned his hands up in front of him and shrugged his shoulders, 'You don't have to tell me any more, if you don't want to; it's none of my business, really.'

She smiled, 'I know. But I told you, I've never spoken to anyone about this before and, if you don't mind me telling you – I think that, in a way, it's probably therapeutic.'

'Alright, but remember you can stop whenever you want to.'

She nodded.. 'My mother, Dagny, died of breast cancer in 2002 when I was just fifteen and Aida was twenty-three. Aida was a medical student at the time, trying to juggle dealing with mum's illness, looking after a sulky teenage sister who was convinced that the whole world was against her, getting through the final year of her degree and carrying on a pretty passionate relationship with an anarcho-communist who believed in direct action. What she'd kept from both me, and from mum before she died, was that they'd both been involved in the Bradford riots in 2001, and were facing charges. They were both up in court less than a week after Mum's funeral; Jack compounded what he'd already done by telling the judge that he didn't recognise the authority of the fascist state so they gave him five years. Fortunately, Aida, mindful of having to look after me, pleaded guilty and expressed remorse; the solicitor that the court had appointed to represent her gave an excellent speech in mitigation and she got off with a six month suspended sentence, but it cost her her university place. She never complained, never said I held her back; she just got a job in a dodgy private care home that somehow managed to get round the requirement for staff to be CRB cleared and put up with me for the next fifteen months until I was officially able to leave school.'

'And then?' he asked, unable to restrain his curiosity after she stopped and looked out to sea.

'And then, she made me do the bursary applications and sixth-form entry exams for five different boarding schools. I hated her at the time and told her I wished that the judge had sent her to prison as well, but she knew what was best for me and never stopped pushing me, even though private schools represented everything that she hated most about Britain. Somehow I got a place at a school in Staffordshire. The only good thing about it was that, if you managed to sneak out, it wasn't too far to Alton Towers. It wasn't until I was half way through university that I really realised how much she'd sacrificed for me and what an ungrateful little brat I was.'

'What happened to the boyfriend? I can't imagine he would have approved of Aida sending you to a private school, even if he understood her pleading guilty in court.'

She shook her head, 'Ah, Jack. Poor Jack. I told you that we don't have a very good track record in choosing our men. Jack got religion when he was in prison. You would have expected him to end up on drugs or something like that, but not Jack. Jack got religion; he's now a Jehovah's Witness or a Seventh Day Adventist or something like that... Shame really, I liked Jack.'

She stood up and walked to the edge of the little terrace and looked out over the sea. 'Aida had always intended to work for Medecins Sans Frontiers, but that wasn't possible once she'd been thrown out of medical school, so she went to work for Amnesty. Back in 2011, just after I'd been sent out to Tunis, she managed to get sent to Libya, somewhere she'd always wanted to go. She's slightly darker than me and once she put a head-scarf on could easily pass without being noticed in a country like Libya where there were lots of people of mixed heritage. While she was there, as well as trying to get to grips with the humanitarian issues, she also tried to see if she could track down any members of our grandmother's family, and I think that that's why, when Amnesty pulled most of their workers out, because it was just too dangerous, she insisted on staying behind. It might also have been, of course, that by then she knew there was something wrong with her and, with her medical training, probably suspected that it was terminal.'

Luke wanted to get up and go and put his arms around her, but something told him that it would be the wrong thing to do at that moment and instead, he waited patiently.

Layla leaned forward against the balustrade, her head bowed and her voice thick with emotion, so he had to strain to hear her words. 'She didn't have much access to the internet as all the infrastructure in the main Libyan cities was in ruins or jealously guarded and reserved by the various alternative governments who claimed to rule the country but, just before Christmas in 2014, she managed to send me quite a long e-mail, telling me she was really proud of some articles that she'd read by me and how she would have really liked to see me again so that we could have got to know each other as adults, but that she had really important things to do over in Libya and wouldn't be able to get home. Even though conditions were really terrible out there, she managed to put a positive spin on it so that I wouldn't worry too much about her but, at the end, she said that I should go and see my Doctor and ask to have a BRCA test… I'd never heard of a BRCA test, and I hardly ever go to the doctor so I just dismissed it as her giving me some big-sister, substitute mother advice, and I forgot all about it.

'I didn't hear from her again until April and then I got a hand written letter that had taken nearly five weeks to get to me. I know that letter off by heart, I've read it so many times, and often, when I try to sleep, I can hear her saying the words as clear as if she were standing next to me – "Dear Layla, If you've been along to have the test that I told you to do in my last e-mail, you'll have put two and two together and realised that I have terminal breast cancer, just as our mother did. Don't get angry and throw this letter down yet (I understand you better than you think, little sister)" – and she'd drawn in a smiley face! – "If you haven't had the test done, I'm sure this will be a bit of a shock but, the way genetics works means that you've only got a fifty percent chance of having the defective gene that's caused both mine and Mum's breast cancers and, almost certainly, grandma's ovarian cancer. Even if you have, it is very rare for it to develop before you are thirty and the doctors will tell you that there is a way of taking away the risk. If you are in that situation, I want you to promise me that you'll do what the doctors say." She was right when she said she understood me; I did throw the letter to one side at that point, because I couldn't imagine how anything else could be of any importance. I didn't read the rest until the end of May, when I'd had confirmation that she was dead from a French aid worker who'd also stayed out there. But I did work up the courage to go and ask for the test a few days after I got her letter. Luckily, I was in the clear – my one positive legacy from my disappointing father seems to be a fully functioning BRCA gene.' She paused again, but something told him that she hadn't yet finished.

'The middle part of the letter was mainly spent trying to make me feel better – telling me that it wasn't very painful, that she had friends to look after her and that she'd enjoyed her life – I'm sure that most of it was nonsense, but I was grateful to her for still trying to protect me. After that, though, what she had to tell me came as a bit of a bombshell. She'd managed to track down the orphaned daughter of a cousin of my mother – the younger son of my grandmother Lina's youngest brother, Mohammed...'

'Wait a minute, let me make sure I've got this straight,' he mentally drew a family tree, 'so Mohammed was Lina's youngest brother – the one who stuck by her at first. His son would have been your mother's cousin, but she never met him.'

'That's right. And this son, Omar, was apparently working for Gheddafi, so when the revolution and civil war came, he, his wife, and their seven year old son – another Mohammed were killed in one of the airstrikes. Somehow, their daughter Zahra, who was eight at the time, wasn't at home and survived. Aida was fairly sure that the family who were looking after Zahra had taken any assets that Omar had had left and were now fairly keen to get Zahra off their hands. They claimed to be more or less penniless but said that if Aida could pay, they could arrange for Zahra to be on one of the boats that was leaving for Italy. There seemed to be no other chance of saving her, even Aida would have struggled to get out of the country at that point, and there was no chance in the condition she was in. The family clearly wanted to be rid of Zahra, and the thought of what would happen to her if she were turned out onto the streets didn't bear thinking about. Reluctantly, Aida agreed and somehow scraped the money together to buy Zahra a place on a boat that was leaving two weeks later for Lampedusa. That would have been three weeks before I got the letter and almost eight weeks before I read it. The only positive thing is that the French aid worker said he was sure that the girl had got the boat – Aida died the following day, but Georges said that she was smiling when she died and that her last coherent sentence was that her sister would look after Zahra.'

This time, he knew that she was finished and that the only thing he could do was to get up and put a tenuous arm around her shoulders; there was nothing to say, *'Che sará, quel che* sará' he thought.

Although she was only three years younger than him, she seemed suddenly vulnerable and very young as he held her against him with her tears soaking into the shoulder of his fleece and he knew that he could no longer let her just sail into the distance after these few days on the island. The story she had told him was an incomplete one and he knew that he had to know how it ended, whether the ending were good or bad. Not to help her find the answers she was looking for – and hopefully the girl Zahra at the same time – would be like reading a thrilling book and then finding that the last chapter was missing. Even if it meant having to buy a second copy – it just had to be done. Then, he'd be able to go back to his uncomplicated life on the island.

'Ciao bellissima! How are things at the centre of the earth?'

'Luke! How are you? Where are you? You haven't rung me for ages – *stronzo!'*

He laughed, 'You know me, Mati; I only ring when I need something.'

'That's because you know the answers always going to be yes for my favourite cousin.'

'I'm your only cousin, Mati. You don't have the luxury of choice like I do. You should be honoured that I've rung you and not Alessio.'

'I am. I am. Now answer my questions before you tell me what I can do for you.'

'I'm fine – probably better than I've felt at any time in the last five years. Fit and ready for anything. As for where I am – at the moment I'm looking across the sea at Salina where I can see lights twinkling in all the little houses as if there were a gathering of fairies.'

'How poetic – you must be in good spirits – I'm pleased, you've been hiding yourself away and sulking for far too long.'

He adopted a hurt tone, 'I have not been sulking; I've been reflecting and meditating and now I feel spiritually enriched.'

'Whatever! You've either been out in the sun for too long without a hat or you're in love and, as it's the end of March, I know where I'm putting my money.'

'Well you'd lose it,' he said, feeling momentarily, although inexplicable, irritated, 'but, seeing as you want to throw your money around I do really need you to do me a very big favour.'

'Good news,' he said as he went back into the apartment, 'my cousin has just agreed to find a suitable second-hand car on the internet and buy and insure it for me. Hopefully, she'll be able to sort things out over the next couple of days and let me know where to pick it up.'

She caught her breath, 'So you really meant it when you said you'd come with me and help me. I thought you'd change your mind when I stopped crying. I didn't mean... I never thought...'

'I know you didn't. I'm coming because I want to know the end of the story – no other reason. And don't think you can get whatever you want just by crying. In general, I try and keep away from people who cry. Let's not have any misunderstanding – I'll help you to follow this through, then you go off and win your Pulitzer prize, or whatever it is that journalists yearn for, and maybe be an adoptive mother as well, while I can just fade back into peaceful obscurity and we'll all live happily ever after.'

'Thankyou... for everything... and thank your cousin as well – That's Matilde, isn't it? The one who works at C.E.R.N.'

'That's the one. The really brainy one in the family. One of the few Italians under forty to have a regular job, and they pay her far more than she has the time to spend, so I'm doing her a favour in letting her lend me some money.'

'But don't you need to see a second hand car before you buy one? How will she know what's suitable?'

'Don't worry about Mati. She's a real petrol-head; that's what took her into engineering and from there she was fast-tracked into C.E.R.N. Apart from it being her money that she'll be spending, she knows more about cars than I do... Anyway, put your shoes on, we're going for a walk before I amaze you with the quality of my mushroom risotto.'

She looked at him with a teasing smile – the first smile he'd seen on her face since they'd returned to the apartment, 'Yes master. Your wish is my command.' He smiled.

His risotto was declared a success and she did allow herself a single glass of the white wine he'd bought to cook with to go with it. As they had the previous night, they were in bed before ten although this time both of them were feeling emotionally drained and were asleep after a few minutes.

He dreamed of Judi, dreamed that they were on their honeymoon, running through the Corsican surf, chasing each other across the sand and laughing contentedly. It was the first time in a long time that he'd dreamed of his ex-wife and even longer since his dreams of her had been pleasant. When he woke up, it seemed at first as if the dream had turned into reality; he had rolled over as he slept and his right leg was pressed against a smooth warm piece of flesh that was almost certainly a thigh, while wisps of dark hair lay across his shoulder and collar bone. He savoured the sensations for a minute, wondering if he were still dreaming, soothed by the gentle sound of the sea in the background.

When he opened his eyes again, he was looking into a pair of deep brown eyes less than thirty centimetres from his own that seemed to have a warm amber-like glow in the rays of early morning sunshine that had sneaked in through a gap in the curtains.

'*Buongiorno*. You looked so peaceful while you were sleeping,' she said with a smile.

He suddenly remembered where he was and who he was with and pulled away in embarrassment. 'I'm sorry. I didn't know... I mean...'

'Shhh...It's alright I don't mind. It felt somehow reassuring – sort of innocent.' She smiled again. He did not move back towards her.

'I'm sorry. I was dreaming about my wife. You should have kicked me or used an elbow to get rid of me.' She sighed and rolled over so she was facing the other way.

'What?' he said, surprised, but all he got in response was the sight of the back of her head shaking.

She was uncharacteristically moody and irritable throughout breakfast and for the first part of the morning. He had suggested that they should use the day to explore the neighbouring island of Salina, which they could see clearly from their terrace. To get there, however, they had to drive back across the island and down into the larger of Lipari's two ports to catch one of the regular ferry services; fortunately, as Salina was the next island in the chain, most of the ferries that left for the other islands called at Salina on the way to their final destination.

Luke arranged to leave the Mehari outside the office of the car hire company, so they had no need to pay for parking, and then went to the ticket office to check the schedules and buy the tickets. Luckily, it was possible to journey outwards on a ferry that called into Santa Marina and catch one of the day's last ferries back from Rinella on the southern side of the island. They had nearly twenty minutes to wait on the jetty before the first Salina bound ferry called into the island, and Layla spent most of it leaning on the rail and looking almost vacantly out to sea; he decided to ignore her until such time as she was herself again – or at least what he had become used to considering as herself – and sat on one of the bollards, intending to skim through the day's *Quotidiano di Sicilia*, pausing to give more attention to articles about refugees. To his horror, the first twelve pages of the paper were all about two bombings that had taken place in Brussels the day before. The majority of articles were speculative but the main facts were known: two presumed ISIS terrorists had exploded bombs inside Brussels airport, and a third had blown up an underground train several minutes later, catching some of those who had been trying to get away from the area of the first explosions. There were human interest stories telling how some people had escaped because they had changed their plans at the last minute or had moved away from the check in desks for a moment to take a phone call. There were stories of members of the public helping the injured and of Members and officials of the European Parliament trying to do whatever they could to help.

Then, of course, there were comments by so-called 'experts' either passing judgements on the Belgian security protocols or, inevitably, linking the attacks to the flow of refugees into Europe and calling for draconian methods to be taken and for the Schengen agreement, guaranteeing free movement between European states, to be suspended and strict border controls introduced.

It was clear that the bulk of the paper had been put together before the articles about the attacks had been written and was surprised to see that when they talked about the 'Refugee Crisis' the paper seemed to be concentrating on the flood of refugees making the short sea crossing from Turkey to the Greek Island of Lesbos, and the difficulties of the journey many were then attempting up through the Balkans in an attempt to claim asylum in Germany.

There had recently been a crisis summit of European leaders, to which the Prime Minister of Turkey had also been invited. He had been aware of, and applauded, the policy followed by the German government the previous year of welcoming refugees and trying to integrate them, but was fairly sure that they could not have anticipated the incomprehensible policies being championed by the United States, the United Kingdom and, to a lesser extent other western countries which only seemed to serve to increase the number of people flooding out of Syria. Russia were following their own interests and didn't really seem to care what anyone else thought, whilst France's kneejerk reaction after the December 2015 terrorist attacks in Paris was understandable, if likely to be ultimately counter-productive. He shook his head in disgust, as he read a quote from David Cameron, which was obviously aimed more at pleasing the Daily Mail readers back in England, than at his fellow European leaders.

The previous year, the papers had been full of terrible stories of refugees either just managing to make it as far as Lampedusa, off Sicily's southern coast, or being picked out of the sea – dead or alive – after their boats had capsized. It was only towards the back of the paper, where the news tended to be more parochial, that he read that by the end of February almost one hundred and thirty six thousand refugees had made sea crossings to Europe since the start of the year and that almost ten percent of those had arrived in the Sicilian islands of Lampedusa and Pantelleria.

As their boat came around the corner of the bay, he stood up and walked over to her. 'I think you'd better have a look at this… There were more terrorist attacks in Brussels yesterday with over thirty people killed.' He handed her the paper.

She began to flick through the paper, taking in the headlines and the images, as they boarded the boat then, as they sat down, she passed it back to him, a worried look on her face. 'Can you summarise the main articles for me – I'm afraid they're a bit much for my Italian.'

He agreed, and the exercise took up most of the sea journey to Santa Marina. She gazed moodily out of the window while he translated while at the same time keeping an eye on the rolling twenty-four-hour news-service on the big-screen he could just see at the other end of the almost empty saloon. In what he estimated were seats for over two hundred people, there were probably no more than a dozen, and the stairs up to the upper seating area were cordoned off. He wondered whether there would have been the political will back in Britain to keep an obviously loss making service running for its social benefits. The boats probably ran at something close to full capacity in the intense summer season, but it was certainly nothing like that now.

Suddenly, as the note of the ship's engines changed, and the spray against the window that had been their near constant companion since leaving Lipari, fell away as the boat slowed, she gripped his arm tightly, 'Look. Look at them,' she said excitedly, 'Dolphins!'

He leaned forward and across her to see out. 'Maybe,' he said, as a forked black tail disappeared under the surface. 'There are various types of dolphins around the islands – particularly this one because of the vegetation – but you also sometimes see whales and sharks.'

'Sharks! You didn't tell me that yesterday when we were in the sea – or the day before when you let me go in on my own.'

He laughed, pleased to see that she seemed to have forgotten whatever it was that had put her in a bad mood. 'I've never seen anyone being eaten by a shark before – but on the other hand, neither has anyone else I've ever spoken to on the islands. I assume that someone would have said something if there were any danger at all.'

'Nevertheless, I'll keep my eyes open next time you think of an excuse to send me into the sea on my own.'

'I've got my plastic sandals in the bag, so you should be safe today – unless you fall into a volcano, of course.'

'I thought it was Vulcano and Stromboli where the volcanoes are.'

'Stromboli's the most active currently, and Vulcano is one of the most recent to have had a significant eruption – back in the 1890s I think – but all the islands in the group are volcanic, going down a long way under the sea. That's one of the reasons why the area is so popular with dolphins, whales, sharks and turtle. The water gets very deep quickly and the minerals produced by the volcanoes and the run off from the vegetation mean that the water here is an ideal breeding ground for plankton…'

'So little fish come and eat the plankton and big fish come and eat the little fish.'

'Pretty much, although most of the cetaceans – that's the collective name for the dolphins and the others - are also quite happy to feed directly on plankton. Did you know that?'

'Enough!' she said, feigning horror. 'If you can't resist the urge to educate me, could you please drip feed me with your wisdom, otherwise it's too much.'

'Alright, alright – I don't actually know much more about marine biology but, one thing I must tell you before we get off the boat because I wouldn't be doing my job as your personal tour guide if I didn't, is that the picturesque walkway we'll be going along when we get off the boat is the one that was used in the film *"Il Postino"* when Philippe Noiret, who played the part of Pablo Neruda, arrives on the island. At the far end of the walkway there's an original poster from the movie, and set into the poster with half sticking out on one side and half on the other, is the actual bike that Massimo Troisi, the postman, rode in the film.'

'I remember seeing *"Il Postino"* at a university film club showing while I was a student. But I thought it was filmed on one of the islands near Naples.'

'Part of it was, but a lot of it was filmed here. This was the landing stage, and more of the film was shot in Rinella, which is where we'll be getting the boat from when we go back later.'

Having tacitly agreed to put the events in Brussels onto one side, the day on Salina was a great success, the magnificent and varied scenery providing enough distractions to stop either of them brooding over problems that they couldn't even begin to solve until they were back on Sicily itself.

When they disembarked in Lipari he suggested that they go for a pizza rather than cooking back at the apartment for their last evening on the island and they made their way through the centre of the town to a pizzeria he knew could always be relied on to serve quality food at reasonable, rather than tourist, prices. He put off for as long as he could telling her what he had decided on the boat as they had returned from Salina, to limit the amount of time available in which he could be persuaded to change his mind.

He insisted on splitting the bill with her when she tried to pay and then allowed her to slip her arm through his as they began to wander back through the town in the general direction of the port.

'There are a few things I need to sort out the hut before we leave the island.'

'That's fine. We can either call in there now or before we get the ferry in the morning: whichever you think is best.'

He avoided looking at her, not wanting his face to give away what he was really thinking, 'Actually, I was thinking that if you're OK about driving the car, it would be best if I went up there and you drove over to Acquacalda and then picked me up in the morning – otherwise, I can drive you over and then go back and pick you up in the morning.'

There was a slight pause, and then she said, in a tone that suggested she was trying just a little too hard to appear nonchalant, 'I'll be fine driving; it's not as though there are many cars to bump into once I'm out of Lipari itself. I should have realised that just because I've got all my things with me, it doesn't mean you won't need a bit of time to sort your things out. I'll run you up the hill before I go.'

'No,' he said, a little too brusquely. For some reason, he couldn't imagine watching her drive away from the hut, and yet he knew that there was no acceptable alternative. 'I find that the walk up the hill really helps me think, as well as helping me to sleep,' he added in a more conciliatory tone.

'That's fine,' she said as she turned and began to walk back towards the port where the Mehari was. 'What time's the ferry tomorrow?'

'There are a few ferries quite early and then a gap until eleven-thirty, so I think we should aim to catch the eight-fifty, which is the last of the early ones. It's probably easiest if I meet you down at the port outside the car-hire shop about half past eight.'

'I can come and pick you up, if you like,'

He shook his head, 'There's no point; it will probably take you as long to make your way through the town, pick me up and then come back through the town to the port again, as it would for me to walk down the more direct path. If you're there before me, you can always drop the car off.'

He needed to keep himself busy and, as soon as he was back, set to sorting everything he would need into a medium size rucksack and then stored everything else into an old tea chest that he then transported into the cave and padlocked the door he'd made covering the entrance to the cave behind the lean-to shack. After that, as the light was beginning to fade, he made his way up behind Giulia's bungalow, which he assumed was still vacant, and connected to the internet. After he had read the latest comments and articles about Brussels, he began to search for information about refugees in Sicily. It took him nearly fifty minutes to trawl though the online site of the *'Giornale di Sicilia'* and he was amazed to see that there had only been a handful of short articles about refugees during the last couple of months, and that most of those were really about alleged corruption in the way the main contract had been awarded for the construction of the refugee holding centre at Mineo near Caltagirone.

There did not appear to have been any sort of report or article about the refugees themselves since early in the month when a decomposed body had washed up on one of the beaches that it was believed had been in the sea for at least a fortnight. The last report of a boat having been helped into port was from the end of February and he was shocked to see that the authorities had no idea how many people had been on-board when it had left North Africa. It had arrived with twenty three people on-board and a further two were known to have been lost within sight of the Italian coast, but it was estimated that there could have originally been as many as forty as far as he could tell, no-one appeared to be making any great efforts to establish the truth.

Readers' comments, posted after the article were, as usual, by people at either end of the possible spectrum of opinion. This did not surprise him, as he was convinced that only people with very strong, and usually inflexible, points of view ever felt compelled to share their opinions in cyberspace. It was depressing, although not wholly unexpected, that the majority of comments were by jingoistic racists, the sort who often prefaced opinions with phrases like 'I'm not racist but...' One of these, which appeared to have been received with a number of favourable comments was particularly shocking in advocating that gunboats should be employed to fire on the mainly flimsy boats as soon as they left African territorial waters, to send a resounding message to those planning to attempt the journey themselves. The person making the comment argued that, while it was regrettable if anyone was killed during the operation, the number of lives saved in the long-run would far exceed any initial casualties. Occasionally there were pious comments arguing that Sicilians had always believed in looking after those weaker than themselves and that they should continue to extend the hand of friendship to those who made the perilous journey across the sea. He ignored the most recent comments which all seemed to be extremists blaming the previous day's terrorist attacks on refugees.

Despite ignoring these comments, there did seem to be a significant body of opinion arguing that the majority of those coming were economic migrants looking for a better life rather than genuine refugees. A few people had responded to this by pointing out that it was ridiculous to believe that someone would abandon their family, travel through war zones, live in squalid squatter camps while they waited for someone kind enough to take all their valuable goods from them in exchange for a dangerous sea-crossing in an often unseaworthy boat, crewed by even poorer refugees who had been unable to pay the full price for their passage. Before he moved off the site, one final comment caught his eye which claimed that small boats were making it to the shores of Lampedusa and Linosa every day, and he wondered why these arrivals were not being reported by the newspapers and how closely they were monitored.

Before closing the computer down, he clicked onto the Evening Standard's website to get an overview of what was happening back in England. The leading articles on the more serious pages of the website seemed to be either articles about the Brussels attacks or comments on the positions that various right-wing politicians had declared that they intended to take during the forthcoming, potentially disastrous EU referendum. There was an article in which David Cameron appeared to be claiming to have single-handedly saved Europe from the Refugee Crisis by reaching an agreement with Turkey, and another pointing out that the draft agreement reached by the EU, and to which it appeared that Cameron had contributed very little, was not only illegal under international law but would also almost certainly turn out to be unworkable in practice. Andy Burnham, the Shadow Foreign Secretary had given a scathing criticism of the government's approach but he had to click on a link to find out what the other parties were saying.

The first thing he noticed on the page to which the link took him was a photograph of the Liberal Democrat's Foreign Affairs spokesman surrounded by members of his team. Two things surprised him; the first was that Cam McCreggan, who he had known since their university days, and who he had always got on well with, despite profound differences in their political opinions, had been elevated to the House of Lords after losing his seat in the Commons the preceding May and secondly, and more importantly, that closest to him of the advisors who stood behind him was Judi. This was surprising as, when they'd been together, she'd always claimed not to be interested in politics, and although she'd seemed to like Cam when he'd introduced her to the newly elected and upwardly mobile MP after his by-election victory back in 2007, she had always after that claimed that she found politicians boring. Maybe, she'd had an epiphany, he thought – shame it had led her to the Liberal Democrats!

He used an on-line search facility to search for "Cameron McCreggan MP" and "Lord Cameron McCreggan" wondering if Judi was now working in one of his offices, but could find no list of staff on any of the sites suggested by the computer.

Despite not sleeping well, he was up very early in the morning to clean the pool and empty the bins from the holiday complex and, before he returned home to collect his things, he pushed a note through Giulia's door letting her know he was going to be away and had no idea how long it would be for. Then he walked down to the port.

Layla was already outside the car-hire shop talking to Sebastiano when he arrived and, as she gave him a little smile he guessed that he wasn't the only one who had not slept well that night. He shook hands with Sebastiano who said he hoped he enjoyed his holiday and then gave him a meaningful wink as Layla turned towards the ferry. Luke gave a little shake of the head, said 'I'll see you soon,' and then followed Layla.

The ferry was far busier than the previous day's boat to Salina had been, but was still little more than a third full and they had no trouble in finding seats where both those in front of them and those behind were unoccupied. Once the engines had started and they could talk without their voices carrying to other people, he said, almost accusingly, 'You didn't tell me that Judi was working for the Liberal Democrats – I assume you knew.'

She looked out of the window and sighed, 'I knew... but I didn't see that your knowing would have been of any benefit to you... how did you find out? Surely she didn't contact you to let you know.'

He gave a little snort that was almost a laugh, 'She hasn't contacted me since I pleaded guilty except through her lawyers. She's hardly likely to track me down to let me know that she's gone to work for a political party that I find difficult to take seriously... No, I was checking on an English news site last night to find out what's going on over there. I read about what the Tories and Labour are saying and then followed a link to see what the Lib-Dems have to say about the "Refugee Crisis". It looks from the photo at the top of the article that she's working very closely with Cam McCreggan who I've known since we were in the same cross country team at university. He was much more into real ale and heavy metal than politics at the time.'

Layla remained with her head turned towards the window but, after a few seconds asked, 'And what did the Lib-Dems have to say about the "Refugee Crisis"?'

Now it was his turn to pause, and then he laughed, 'Do you know – I was so distracted by the photograph that I forgot to read the article.'

Chapter Three

There were less than twenty passengers who alighted from the regional train when it stopped at Isernia Station in the early evening. The light had been fading ever since they had changed trains in Naples and Luke was disappointed that they had seen little of the scenery in the two hours since then. He knew that the Molise region was meant to be one of the most rural and unspoilt in Italy although he had never had the opportunity to visit before. He had read through the paper they had bought in Messina, during the four and a half hour journey to Naples after they had crossed over on the ferry to Villa San Giovanni; Layla had watched the stunning Calabrian scenery whenever they had emerged from the sometimes long tunnels, until the line had moved away from the coast, at which point she had fallen asleep.

Neither of them was feeling particularly bright as they considered who to ask where to find a hotel or *pensione* for the night, the long journey, coming after a mainly sleepless night, having taken its toll.

'There's a policeman over there, by the exit,' said Layla, nodding her head in the direction of a young *carabiniere* who stood looking bored, watching the lights of the train disappear into the distance.

'Mi scusi... Signor Garvey?' asked a woman of about their own age, as she stepped out of the shadows to their left.'

'Si. Ma lei, chi é?' asked Luke, stepping forward puzzled.

'I'm sorry; you weren't expecting me... My name is Michela Rosucci but my married name is Vichi. My father-in-law thought that you would be arriving on this train and asked me to come and meet you,' she extended her hand towards Luke.

'Vichi the *commissario*?' asked Luke, amazed, 'But how...?'

'Your cousin,' said the woman with a smile, 'Apparently you asked her to work miracles and the only way she could think of getting it done immediately, was to enlist Giacomo's help. Oh, and by the way, when you meet him in the morning, don't call him *Commissario* – he's a *Questore* now.'

After he'd introduced Layla to her as a friend, she led them to her car and opened the boot for them to throw their bags into. As Luke lifted up the front seat of the Fiat Brava for Layla to slide past and into the back seat, she mouthed a 'Who?' to him that he knew implied many other unspoken questions that he knew he would have to answer; for the moment he just gave her an enigmatic smile, partly because there were questions he needed answering himself before he could work out what to tell her.

During the five minutes it took them to arrive at a small hotel, Michela apologised for not being able to invite them for dinner, but her mother-in-law was seriously ill and needed to rest. She herself had taken a few days off work in Milan to come down and offer her in-laws as much help as she could. Luke wasn't sure what, if anything, Vichi would have told her about him so he was careful to keep the conversation on a general level during the journey.

She came into the hotel reception with them and suggested they sit on the sofa while she sorted things out with the receptionist. After a few seconds she turned and came over to them. 'I'm afraid that Giacomo didn't know you would have anyone with you, so he only booked the one room – although it is a double. The manager says that, if you prefer, he could swap you with another couple who haven't arrived yet, and who have booked a twin rather than a double.

'We'll swap it for the twin, thanks.' Michela raised an eyebrow and shot Luke a curious glance but then regained her composure and returned to the counter to complete the formalities.

'I thought that all Italian hotels were meant to take a photocopy of guests' identity documents when they arrive. He didn't even ask to see ours.'

'That must be one of the benefits of having a room sorted out by the *Questore* – normal rules obviously don't apply.'

'OK. Now you'd better start explaining to me what's going on. Why have we travelled for several hours in the opposite direction to where I need to go, and why is the *Questore* of this place that I've never heard of, doing favours for a convicted foreign criminal whose crimes led to the murder of an Italian citizen? If I remember correctly from watching Montalbano on television, a *Questore* is an important official in charge of both Police and *Carabinieri* – correct me if I'm wrong.'

He rubbed the palms of his hands over his face and then looked at her. 'When I asked my cousin if she could sort a car out for us quickly, I assumed it would be something that she could sort out over the internet - although I realised there might be some complications. When she told me that she'd managed to sort one but that I'd have to come to Isernia to get it, I imagined that it was just because with this being a fairly sparsely populated province, they might be a bit more flexible in the way they dealt with bureaucracy. Presumably, at least in this case, the reason why they can be more flexible is the same reason why they haven't asked for our passports here in the hotel. Obviously the real reason was that Mati knew the *Questore* here – which is lucky for us.'

She smiled, 'Good thinking, and very plausible... but you're not telling me everything, are you? ... When Michela said that her married name was Vichi, you said, 'and she did her best to mimic his voice and surprised tone, "Vichi the *commissario*," so it's not just your cousin who knows him, is it?' Luke looked down but didn't respond. 'If there's a good reason why you can't tell me, then so be it, but please don't lie to me or treat me like a fool.'

He flushed, 'I'm sorry. I don't think I've lied to you and it certainly wasn't my intention to treat you as a fool - it's just that there are some things - some secrets if you like - that aren't really my secrets.' He stretched out a hand as if to take her elbow but she drew back, pensive.

'Alright... but promise me that whatever secrets there are between you and this policeman aren't going to interfere with looking for Zahra.'

'They won't. And one thing I can tell you is that Vichi's a good man – if anything, having met him again can only be of benefit to us.'

'Luke. It is very good to see you again. I am glad that the circumstances are happier than the last time. *Signorina*,' he said, turning to Layla and giving a little bow, 'welcome to Isernia and please excuse my English; it is a long time that I have not spoken.'

Layla gave a wide smile and held out her hand which Vichi lifted and kissed lightly. 'Your English is much better than my Italian. I'm afraid that we English, have a well-deserved bad reputation as language learners. Unfortunately, we haven't seen much of Isernia yet, as it was dark when we arrived last night, but what we've seen so far looks charming.'

After the initial pleasantries, the three of them sat on comfortable chairs around a glass-topped coffee table to one side of Vichi's office. Vichi's secretary brought in a tray with a large coffee-pot, three *tazzine* and a bowl of sugar, then left, closing the door behind him.

'You've done well,' said Luke, taking in the office around them.

Vichi gave an unconvincing smile, 'You think so?' and when Luke didn't reply, he added, 'On a good day, I'm quite happy to be here: I can go for long walks in the hills, do a bit of skiing in the winter; there's very rarely any serious crime to worry about; we hardly ever get any visits from politicians – what could be more idyllic? And yet, most of the time, I see it as a prison – a very pleasant gilded prison – but a prison all the same.'

'Why?' said Layla, confused.

Vichi shook his head and turning to Luke, asked in Italian, 'How much does the *signorina* know about what happened?'

'Layla knows what I did, and why I served time in prison. She also believes that I was quite lucky not to have earned myself a longer sentence for conspiracy to murder.'

'You must be a very brave young woman to travel around with a renegade like this,' said Vichi, forgetting to revert back to English as he looked at Layla.

'I think I understood that,' she said. 'and while I don't usually find it easy to excuse people's faults, and Luke has never really explained, I know that there is more to it than meets the eye.'

'Layla understands reasonably well and her spoken Italian is coming along. I'm sure she won't mind if we talk in Italian; she can always stop us, if necessary, and ask me to explain.'

'Thankyou, *signorina*,' said Vichi, giving Layla a smile and then, turning back to Luke, 'I know it's none of my business, but sometimes I yearn for the days when I was a proper policeman and was allowed to ask questions. Why do you need a car in such a hurry and why didn't you just drive down from England, or hire one? I hope you're not getting me involved in anything illegal.'

'I hope so too. I'm out of prison on licence at the moment – as I'm sure you know - so I'm quite keen myself to keep out of trouble. I've been living on one of your quieter islands for the last fifteen months, so driving down from England wasn't really an option and, as I'm not sure how long we'll need a car for, hiring one would probably have ended up costing us a lot more.'

'Yes. You're probably right. Are you planning on going anywhere special or just travelling around?'

'Luke looked at the world-weary old officer with the penetrating gaze for a moment and then glanced at Layla before responding hesitantly. 'Actually, this isn't something we've discussed, as I had no idea that I'd be seeing you, but you might just be able to help us.'

Vichi tilted his head slightly and leaned back in his chair. 'Layla is part English, part Italian and also partly of Libyan descent – although she's never been to Libya. Last year a distant relative of hers – a twelve year old girl – was put on a boat in Libya and transported across to Lampedusa. Layla was unaware of this at the time, and by the time she found out, the girl had disappeared. What I'm going to try and do is to help find this girl and make sure that she's safe.'

Vichi sighed. 'You've set yourselves a very difficult task – in all probability an impossible one. I can tell you the process that's meant to be followed for all the refugees – a process that, when it works effectively, is a very good, a very humane process. Unfortunately, the project is poorly financed, a situation which, as usual, is made worse because there are always people looking for a way to cream off a percentage of any money available. There aren't enough staff, or volunteers, available to speed up the registration processes and it's quite common for refugees to just walk out of the reception centres and make their way north to try neighbouring countries. Mainly these are adults, ready to confront another long journey with very few resources but – and this is where it gets more problematic – younger detainees can often be persuaded to leave the centres by promises of help that are really very unlikely to be maintained.'

'And do you have any idea what happens to these children?'

Vichi glanced at Layla, and then, speeding up his speech so that even Luke could only just keep up, said, 'If they're lucky they end up as domestic servants, kept out of sight in some rich businessman's house. Effectively prisoners, but at least they are fed and have a roof over their head. Many of them are not ill-treated, just deprived of their freedom and made to work very hard. Some get shipped off to provide child labour in sweatshops across the middle-east, so that we can all enjoy cheap clothing and toys for our children while turning a blind-eye to how they're produced. And some, of course, end up as sex-workers. Many of them are weaned onto drugs and then, once they're dependent, they have to go out and work for their pimps or their supply will be cut off.'

Layla reached out and put a hand on Luke's forearm, 'I didn't get that?'

'He said that there are several different outcomes possible – none of them particularly desirable.'

She nodded gravely, fully aware that Luke had watered down whatever Vichi had said. 'Is there any way in which you might be able to help us,' she asked, in English but enunciating every word clearly.

Vichi shook his head sadly, 'I will try to give you advice when you need it but it is very difficult for me to do more. Ten years ago, *signorina*, I was sent here, to this beautiful, but isolated Province to get me out of the way, to wither on the vine.'

She looked at him, baffled, 'But you're a *Questore* – an important person!'

'Aaah importance. Twelve years ago, *signorina*, I was a *commissario* in Florence. It wasn't an easy job, I had difficult, complicated cases to work on, some very unpleasant criminals to contend with, but I felt I was contributing something to society, my wife was happy in the job she did, and we were paid enough to live quite comfortably. Then, I got involved in a case that I wasn't meant to be involved in, ending up knowing things that important people would have preferred me not to know. Other people who knew too much, and who felt that what they knew should be more widely known, met with unfortunate accidents; I allowed myself to be convinced that it was in my country's best interests for me to keep quiet, and to make sure that I was well out of the way of temptation, while apparently being rewarded for services rendered, I was sent here where people think I'm important.... Tell me, was I more important when I was catching criminals, or now when I'm compiling reports about boundary disputes and stolen chickens?'

There was an awkward pause, then Luke said, 'Speaking of your wife, how is she? Your daughter-in-law told us that she wasn't very well.'

Vichi smiled, the moment of bitterness having passed, 'She had a fairly big operation about three weeks ago, but she'll be fine, given time. Thank you for asking.' Then after a pause, 'Although there's not much that I can do to help you, there is one person who I trust, who I think you should go and see.'

They parked their little Mercedes A Class in the first empty space they found, which was nearly fifteen minutes' walk from the address that Vichi had given them in what Luke assumed was one of the less wealthy areas of Catania. When they were fairly sure they had located the address, they were confronted by a plain metal door inset with a moveable grill, set into the otherwise featureless side of a building. Feeling less than convinced that the address was correct, he rapped sharply on the door, stepped back and waited.

Just as he was about to make a second attempt, the metal plate behind the grill was slid to one side and a pair of hard female eyes stared out at them. 'Who are you and what do you want?' demanded a harsh voice.

Slightly taken aback by the reception, Luke paused before replying wondering if Vichi had made a mistake but then deciding to trust him. 'My name is Luke Garvey – I'm English – A friend of mine, Giacomo Vichi, told me that I'd be able to make contact with Luana Capezzi at this address.'

The eyes looked at him suspiciously. 'I'll find out if she's here. If she is, and if she wants to see you, she'll be outside in thirty minutes; come back then. If she's not waiting for you then, either she's not here or she doesn't want to see you.' The metal plate slid back into place and they were left standing outside.

Layla looked at him, 'What is this place? They don't seem very friendly.'

Luke shrugged, trying not to show the sense of disquiet that he too felt. 'Let's go and get a coffee. There's no point hanging about here and speculation isn't likely to get us anywhere. Half an hour's not too long to wait, I suppose.' There being little alternative, he put his hand lightly on her elbow and began to move towards the end of the street where there appeared to be a little more life.

Just under half an hour later, as they re-entered the street, a figure detached itself from the shadows near the door and began to make its way towards them. The woman, who Luke guessed was a few years older than he, had short dark hair framing a not unattractive face in which a pair of striking grey eyes dominated. She was wearing a zipped up black leather jacket and a pair of battered, tight-fitting black jeans over a pair of well-worn unbranded trainers. She moved towards them lithely and he noticed the well-defined muscles around her neck. He was pleased to see a warm, friendly smile appear on her face as she got closer to them and held out her hand. 'Signor Garvey, I hadn't expected to see you again – although I'm sure you don't remember having seen me before.'

He responded with a more cautious smile, 'You're right, I'm afraid I'm at a disadvantage. I have no recollection at all of our having met.'

'I didn't think you would. It was at the funeral of your aunt and uncle eleven years ago, and while you were one of the chief mourners, I was just a young police officer, in full dress uniform trying to keep in the background. I would have been surprised if you had noticed me.' She turned towards Layla and spoke to her in reasonably correct English, 'Hello, *Signorina*. My name is Luana Capezzi. I work with *Commissario* Vichi in Florence many years since. He tell me that Signor Garvey has a friend with him. Welcome to Catania. I hope I can be helping you.'

Layla stepped closer to her and smiled, holding out a hand, 'Thankyou. It's very kind of you to help. My name is Layla Simons, but please just call me Layla.' The Italian returned her smile and then turned back to Luke and changed back into Italian.

'Unless you've already eaten, I know somewhere fairly close that's nice and discreet where we can eat while you explain what I can do to help you. Vichi was very vague when he rang me as it's never wise to discuss too much sensitive business over the phone. I'm afraid you will need to translate what I say into English for Layla as my level of English is a bit basic to discuss anything complicated.'

'We haven't eaten yet and, Layla's Italian's coming on by leaps and bounds, so hopefully I won't have to translate too much.' Layla nodded to show that she had understood and to confirm what he had said.

The *trattoria* was a small one, down another side street where no tourist would ever dream of going; the decoration was simple but welcoming, there was no printed menu, and the only other diners were two groups of workmen clearly on their lunchbreak. The men at both tables were talking animatedly as they ate which Luke realised immediately would cover whatever they said to each other at the table they were given at the other end of the room. He noticed a slight dip in the level of conversation as they entered and the men appraised the two women, particularly Layla, but it returned to its previous level almost immediately and they were forgotten about.

'*Buongiorno,*' said the waiter, who Luke guessed was the owner. 'What can I bring you?'

'Water and white wine then whatever the dish of the day is today,' responded Luana.

'Still or fizzy?' asked the waiter. Luana looked at Luke and Layla and raised an eyebrow in interrogation.

'*Naturale,*' said Layla, and the waiter nodded and moved away.

'The dishes of the day are always fish based, that's why I ordered the white wine – I hope you don't mind.'

'You're the expert,' said Luke.

Luana gave a small smile and then said, 'Now. Tell me what the problem is. Why does Vichi think I might be able to help you?'

As succinctly as possible, occasionally checking his facts with Layla, Luke explained who Zahra was; why Layla wanted to find her; and everything they knew about the events prior to Zahra's disappearance. Luana listened carefully, only interrupting to ask for clarifications a couple of times when Luke's Italian failed to express something precisely enough at the first time of asking. As she listened, her expression became more and more serious and she didn't speak for a while after Luke finished his explanation.

Finally she said, 'And you say that she was twelve years old when she set off from Libya.'

Layla nodded, 'She'll be thirteen now, getting on for fourteen – if she's still alive.' She said this calmly but Luke could see her fingertips dig into the brown paper tablecloth as she spoke. He felt an urge to place his hand over hers to comfort her, but resisted in-case his compassion should be misinterpreted.

'Giacomo Vichi told us, in broad terms, what the possible outcomes are for young female refugees who go missing, so I'm under no illusions but – if there's any chance that she's somewhere where she can be rescued, I want to take it.' Luana stretched out her hand to offer the comfort that Luke had wanted to give – for a moment he felt a strange pang which almost resembled jealousy.

'I don't suppose you have a photograph of Zahra, do you?'

Layla shook her head, 'If my sister ever sent me one, it was in one of the letters that never reached me. She did say that she was attractive, lively and seemed quite old for her age – I'm not sure if that's a good thing or a bad thing.'

'I think that you need to prepared for anything but…' she glanced across at Luke before continuing, 'the one thing I wouldn't expect is good news.'

Layla looked Luana directly in the eye, 'I make my living as a freelance journalist, and over the past few years I've spent time in Tunisia, Egypt and Lebanon, so I have a pretty good idea of what the likely outcomes are for a young unaccompanied female refugee, and I realise that the chances of discovering anything are slim – but I'd never be able to live with myself if I didn't try. Giacomo Vichi thought you might be able to help me. Was he right?'

Luana sighed and shook her head, although Luke wasn't sure whether the shake indicated a refusal to help or if it implied a rueful resignation to destiny. 'For some reason, Vichi has always had an inflated view of my capabilities; if he hadn't I'd probably still be in the Police force in Florence, probably with an office of my own by now and being handed all the low level cases considered by the hierarchy to be suitable for a female to deal with. Instead, because he selected me to work with him ten years ago, he's now exiled to the back of beyond and I'm out of the force without any clear career path.'

'Your arm was in a sling!' exclaimed Luke, and Layla looked at him uncomprehendingly, 'At Paul and Rosa's funeral, your arm was in a sling because you'd been shot during the operation that arrested the ringleaders of the conspiracy against Prodi.'

Luana coloured slightly and shrugged dismissively, 'A lot of water's passed under the bridge since then – for you as well as for me.'

'You know about what happened to me then?'

She nodded, 'Because the man killed was someone with plenty of powerful friends, it made quite a stir when he was murdered on the sun-terrace of a luxurious Swiss hotel by a deranged elderly aunt, and then when a British Police officer was accused of having provided her with information to help her plan the murder, the press couldn't get enough of it.' She smiled, 'You were quite a sensation at the time.'

Now it was Luke's turn to colour, 'You shouldn't believe everything you read in the papers - what they don't know, they make up – as I'm sure you're aware,' he flicked a small sideways glance to Layla here, who looked away. 'They certainly got it wrong about my great-aunt. Maddie was anything but deranged; she knew exactly what she was doing and why she was doing it. Anyway; enough about the past. Are you going to be able to help us?'

She sighed again. 'I don't know. I can talk to people, make enquiries, try and help you work out where you need to go and what you can do, but I can't think of anything I can really do to help you; all of that will probably come to nothing.'

Layla leaned forwards, 'I didn't get all of that, but it seems to me as if the things you say you can do will be very useful. Without you, we could spend weeks asking the wrong questions to the wrong people

– and every day that goes by makes it even less likely that we'll manage to find out what happened to her.' Luke opened his mouth to translate but stopped as Luana put out a hand towards Layla's in an expression of solidarity.

After they had eaten they made their way to a quiet square in a somewhat more upmarket area of the city and ordered three beers to drink at one of the outside tables which, despite the pleasant spring sunshine were still being shunned by the Catanesi who were yet to don their summer clothes. 'We're going to drive down to Porto Empedocle tomorrow and get a ferry over to Lampedusa for two or three days. I assume that that's where the boat will have landed so it seems like the obvious place to try and pick up the trail.' said Layla when their beers had been delivered to the table. Luana pulled a face.

'I suppose it's something you can't afford to miss out, but I'd be amazed if you find out anything useful. It seems to be a waste of time you both going down there; I think the ferries to Lampedusa run overnight, so one of you could get the ferry tonight and be there by tomorrow morning. I can't see there being enough there to keep you for more than a day, so you'd only have to get one night's accommodation and then get the ferry back the next day. Have a think about it while I just go to wash my hands.' She gave a small smile and left them alone together.

'Well,' said Luke, when she'd gone, 'What do you think?'

'It seems logical, I suppose. I'd have quite liked to have seen where she landed, but it would need to be you going down there because of all the driving – I suppose I can always go and have a look at the island after all this is over – one way or the other. I suppose the only thing is, what would I be able to do here – my Italian isn't really good enough to be asking probing questions?'

'It's getting better all the time, but I'm sure that if Luana's suggested this, she must have some idea about what you could do here. I'm sure she wasn't expecting it to be you going down to Lampedusa alone.'

'What about you? It' a lot of travelling to do on your own for just a day on the island.'

He shrugged dismissively, 'Oh, you never know. I might find some interesting company on the boat,' he said, with a sudden desire to assert his independence.

She opened her mouth to reply but closed it again without speaking as Luana reappeared from inside the bar.

'Alright,' said Luke, as Luana approached. 'I'll go to Lampedusa and see if there's anything to be found out there. I assume that you can point Layla in the right direction to find out a few things here while I'm gone.' She nodded. 'Is it best to take the car over on the ferry, or should I park it up in Porto Empedocle.'

'Neither,' said Luana, and then, in English to Layla, 'You drive?'

'I can – although I haven't driven this one yet – but that shouldn't be a problem.'

'Then I think it is best that Luke take the train and leave the car with you.' Reverting to Italian, she added, 'There is a train that leaves Catania just before five that will get you to Agrigento about nine, and from there you will find regular buses for Porto Empedocle. It's expensive to take the car on the ferry and the cost of fuel and parking at the port would be far more than the train fare.'

'That's fine with me. I suppose if I need to get around the island, I can always rent a scooter for a few hours for not very much.'

The train journey was uneventful and, as the day was overcast, it was rapidly going dark even before he had to change trains in Caltanisetta, but at least he was able to read the Italian newspaper more or less from cover to cover – not that he found very much inside to interest him. Once he got to Agrigento, he quickly discovered that buses left the station for Porto Empedocle every twenty minutes which would get him to the port in good time to catch the overnight ferry. He was slightly disappointed that he would have no time to look at Porto Empedocle itself, for not only was it dark now but it would also be evening when the return ferry brought him back. To see the home town of Andrea Camilleri, one of his favourite writers, in daylight would have been interesting, but it was not to be.

When he had checked the ferry company's online site, it had told him that foot passengers must be at the port an hour before the scheduled departure time, and he was, but there was no sign of any activity on-board until a few minutes before it was due to leave. Finally the fifteen or so foot passengers were directed up a gangway before they even began to load the three lines of mainly light commercial vehicles that were waiting to board. Once on-board, he found the only open café and bought himself a hot chocolate and a grappa to help him sleep, before making his way to the lounge where he settled down in one of the reclining seats, wondering how long the ferry company would keep the large televisions on, and whether or not they would turn the lights off – or at least down – at some point.

He never found out about the lights or the televisions as, much to his surprise, he fell asleep within half an hour and wasn't even wakened by the sound of the engines as the ferry finally slipped out of the port. He slept until just after six and wasn't sure whether he'd woken naturally, or if he'd been woken by the lights and television coming back on. There were only a handful of other people scattered around the lounge and, after yawning and stretching, he made his way to the bathrooms to freshen himself up.

In the cafeteria, the pastries on display did not seem particularly appetising, and he was fairly sure that they had been left uncovered, going stale, since the previous evening. Deciding that the wisest course of action would be to put off breakfast until he was once more on dry land, he drank an *espresso* followed by a *latte macchiato* before making his way out on to the sun-deck. Disappointingly, he found that the ship was sailing through fog, or possibly early morning mist, and as a result, there were no views to be had in any direction. After ten minutes leaning on the rail, looking into the fog, he gave up and went back to the lounge where he sat down and closed his eyes, hoping to doze for at least part of the last two hours before they arrived.

By the time they arrived in the harbour at Lampedusa, the mist, or fog, was beginning to clear but not yet enough for him to be able to see more than the immediate surroundings of the docks. Throwing his rucksack over one shoulder, he made his way along the quay until he reached the Bar del Molo where he sat down on one of the metal framed chairs at an outside table under the canopy overlooking the port.

'*Desidera?*' asked a teenage waiter who appeared almost immediately at his side.

'A *cappuccino* and a *prosciutto* and *mozzarella* sandwich, please.'

While he waited, he looked out across the almost deserted esplanade towards the small boats bobbing gently near the shore, and the few somewhat larger yachts moored further out. The harbour area looked as calm and peaceful as the harbour in Lipari did on quiet Sunday mornings outside the tourist season – not at all what he'd expected.

When the waiter returned with his order, he decided it was a good subject with which to begin a conversation and, as the waiter was turning to go, he stopped him by observing that the reality of Lampedusa seemed to be very different to that projected by the news reports, and gesturing to the picturesque harbour in front of them.

The boy stopped, 'They don't bring the boats in here; they take them round to the other side,' he waved an arm vaguely to his left. The police try and keep them in the reception centre, but they don't manage with all of them – there are so many – there'll be a few round here later, when there are more customers – hoping they'll give them their loose change.'

'Beppe!' came a raspy female voice from the door to the bar. The boy turned round and Luke turned his head just in time to see a middle-aged woman, who was clearly the proprietor, jerk her thumb back over her shoulder, ordering the boy back inside.

Luke smiled, '*Buongiorno, Signora*. I'm afraid it was my fault for delaying him; I asked him a question.' She made a non-committed sound and was about to withdraw but he wasn't going to let her get away that easily. 'It must be good for business having all these extra people around. Didn't I read somewhere that they get thirty-seven euros a week each as spending money, as well as all their clothes?' He knew that this was incorrect but felt that it was likely to get the woman to open up and show him what the islanders' opinion of the refugees really was.

'They think they're in Paradise when they first get here: a roof over their heads; a mattress to sleep on; a new set of clothes and money to spend for doing nothing. It's much better than they're used to; paved with gold they think this place is - they don't realise that we have to work hard for that little bit we've got – those who're lucky enough to have a job anyway. When they first come, they don't believe it; they think we all get fed and somewhere to live without having to do anything for it. They never come and spend any money in here and we get far less tourists than we used to, because everyone thinks that we're full of refugees.'

'It must be very difficult, *Signora*,' said Luke, although without specifying for whom it must be very difficult. 'So you don't really see very much of them at all, here in the harbour?'

She looked at him suspiciously before replying as she withdrew inside, 'Too much for my liking.'

OK, he thought. At least he now had a flavour of what the locals thought about the refugees; it might be more difficult than he'd thought to pick up any useful information.

After his breakfast, he made his way up into the town behind the port, determined that finding somewhere to stay should be his first priority. He ignored the bigger hotels with sea-views and wandered round until he spotted a fading sign saying 'Pensione Delfino' down a side street. He had to ring the bell twice and wait for a couple of minutes before a woman wearing a housecoat and a headscarf appeared at the door, brush in hand.

'Hello, I'm looking for a single room for one or two nights – I'm not sure yet… Do you have any available?'

'Let me think,' said the woman, clearly pretending to consult her mental register. 'I think we can probably squeeze you in. It will be fifty euros a night – without breakfast.' He shook his head, smiled and made as if to turn away. 'Wait,' she said, hurriedly, 'I just remembered, we had a cancellation yesterday. A lovely room; I can give you a discount on it as it's last minute; how about seventy five euros for the two nights?'

'Sixty euros for the two nights – with breakfast,' he said, taking the money out of his wallet and letting her see it.

She made an effort to look as if she were considering his offer for a few seconds before stretching her hand out towards the money. He moved his hand back and removed half the money with his other hand. 'Here's the thirty for the first night; I'll let you know this evening whether I'll be needing to stay for longer.'

Taking the money, she turned back inside and he followed her to the room and was given two keys: one for the outside door, and another to the flimsy formica door to the room. Thirty was probably generous, he thought, although he did not say it out loud as he needed to stay on as good terms as possible with his landlady.

As soon as he had deposited most of his things in the room, he left again and began to wander in the direction earlier waved towards by the young waiter. After a fairly long walk, well outside the limits of the town he reached the top of a slight rise and saw, in the unexpected dip in front of him, three long white two-storey buildings with a handful of smaller buildings, all set within a perimeter fence of strong wire-mesh.

Inside the fence, he could see hundreds of people milling around and many more loitering by the entrances to the buildings. He was still too far away to distinguish individual faces but he was struck by the mixture of clothing: many were wearing fairly plain western garments but a significant minority were dressed in vibrantly coloured fabrics that they had evidently retained after their journeys, providing a strange contrast with the drab uniformity of the others. The surrounding landscape was fairly dull and strewn with grey boulders of varying sizes while the higher ground in each direction cut off all views of the sea or any of the islands other features he began to understand why the port itself had seemed surprisingly free of migrants.

At one point, outside what appeared to be the main entrance to the compound, two large white vans and a number of police and military vehicles were parked and there appeared to be some form of control point. Other men in uniform were, he noticed, to be seen in pairs or small groups at other points around the perimeter. He directed his footsteps towards the entrance.

Heads turned to watch him approach, some faces showing curiosity, some obviously pleased to see anything that might break the routine, and a few, he noticed, clearly expressing distrust and hostility.

'*Buongiorno,*' he said cheerfully, as one of the *carabinieri* stepped forwards to meet him.

'Can you identify yourself, please. This is a controlled facility and only those on official business are allowed in.'

Luke handed the man his passport but ignored the second part of the sentence. 'I'm making enquiries about a Libyan girl who I believe passed through this centre sometime last year. I wonder, is it possible to speak to the officials in charge of keeping the records? It shouldn't take very long.'

A second officer, with larger badges on each of the lapels of his short-sleeved pale blue shirt now stepped forward and took the passport from the hand of the first officer and scrutinised it before giving Luke a penetrating gaze.

'Are you a journalist?'

'No. Nine years in the British Police Force. Although I'm here on a private matter, not an official one.' He mentally crossed his fingers that the officer wouldn't bother to check his statement which, although true, was designed to be misleading – 'ex-convict' didn't have quite the same ring to it.

'*Mi dica,*' said the officer, and Luke breathed a sigh of relief.

'A thirteen year old, unaccompanied Libyan girl, travelled by boat from near Tripoli to Lampedusa in the spring of last year. The girl has distant relatives in England who are anxious to trace her, but so far there has been no news. Unfortunately, they didn't know that the girl was travelling until some time afterwards. The girl's name was - is - Zahra al-Ajd'b. I'm afraid I don't have a photograph.'

'Would you mind writing that down,' said the officer with a small smile at last, reaching into his pocket and pulling out what appeared to be a crumpled receipt from a bar. Luke took the receipt, straightened it out and took a pen out of the small shoulder-bag he carried.

'I'm sure there are some accents on some of the letters, but I've no idea where.'

The officer took the slip of paper, indicated to Luke that he should wait on one side and then disappeared into the compound.

Luke moved to the side and decided to wait close to the fence to the compound where a small crowd immediately began to form on the other side. People began to call out to him in a variety of languages: some asking for money, some for cigarettes, some asking if could give them a job and others offering a range of services. Almost immediately another officer moved over and ushered him further away from the fence, 'for your own safety.' After that he waited patiently about twenty metres away from the fence, in the shadow of one of the *carabinieri* vehicles, still the subject of some curious glances from the officers but generally ignored.

After about fifteen minutes, the officers had got used to his silent presence and were not watching him anymore. At that point, one of the officers set off walking on a trajectory that would lead him to pass very close to Luke and, as he passed him, he said in a low voice, 'Go to the Bar Muamar at ten o'clock this evening,' he then continued on his way as if he had never spoken.

When the first officer eventually returned, Luke could tell from his face as he approached that there was no good news. The officer held his hands out, palms upright as he began to speak, shrugging his shoulders at the same time. *'Mi dispiace.* When the immigrants arrive here they are no longer registered as our staff would be overwhelmed with the numbers. Originally people were registered here but since the numbers increased dramatically two years ago, we can only give them initial assistance before they are sent on to other, more permanent, welcome centres, where they can be dealt with efficiently and their applications processed. We only have records of the names of those who have required urgent medical attention, and even then, I very much doubt if all of them give us their real names.'

Luke frowned. 'How do you decide which 'welcome centre' they should be sent on to? Is it just determined by numbers or is there some other criteria.'

The officer shrugged again, 'Almost everyone here is sent on to the CARA at Mineo. What happens there, I'm afraid I can't tell you.' It was clear from the officer's tone that he considered the interview at an end so Luke thanked him for his assistance and began to retrace his steps towards the town.

Before he reached the edge of the town he heard a sound behind him and turned to find a boy with ebony black skin and sporting a big grin sliding down the bank by the side of the road. He stopped and the boy came to a halt about five feet in front of him.

'Hey, mister. You English?'

'I am. You speak English.'

'I speak: English, French, Jula, Kulango and now I learn Italian. I very useful. You take me with you, please.'

'And why would you want to come with me?' said Luke, more amused than anything else.

'Because I hear you at camp. You look for child. She dead; no use to you now. I very clever too clever to die.'

Luke smiled, 'You're a smart kid, but neither the law in Italy, nor that in England would allow me to just take you with me – even if I wanted to. And I'm not looking for the other girl for me; I'm looking for her for her family and she might still be alive.' The boy looked down at his feet like a dog hanging his head after having been beaten and Luke softened his tone. 'If there's anything I can do to help you, I'll do my best – but I can't take you away with me.' the boy looked up. 'Now, let me take you to get some food and you can tell me what it's like in the camp.'

To Luke's surprise, the boy refused to enter into any of the small restaurants in the town, explaining that many of the restaurateurs would be reluctant to serve them. Instead, he bought a selection of food at a grocery store and they shared it sitting on the deserted shore a few hundred metres to the east of the port. As they ate, it required little effort on Luke's part to draw the boy's story out of him although he was sure that parts of it were embellished. The boy's father had been a magistrate in the northern part of Côte d'Ivoire who had been removed from his position after the civil war. Although the boy, whose name was Henri, could not remember the time before his family had been reduced to near poverty, he could remember that his father had always been looked up to and consulted by other people in the village, even though he hadn't understood why at the time.

His father had died four years ago after making Henri promise that he would study for as long as he could and spend whatever he could on books so he could learn more. For three years after that he and his younger sister had been brought up by their mother – he was very vague about how she had managed to do this – until both his mother and sister had caught 'the sickness'. His sister had died after a while and his mother, who by then was very weak, had insisted that he should leave, heading north towards Europe. She had given him the limited amount of money that she had hidden away and insisted that it had been his father's wish that, as soon as he was old enough, he should go to Europe, become a doctor or a lawyer and then come back and help his country.

He gave very little detail of his journey north through Africa and Luke wasn't sure whether to question him further or whether it was best just to let him bury what were clearly terrible memories. Judi would have known what was best, he thought, she'd got a first in Psychology and was starting to make a name for herself as a psychotherapist. But Judi wasn't there. He was the one sitting here wondering what to say to a twelve year old boy who'd lived through horrors that were unimaginable for the wealthy clients who he imagined lying back in Judi's consulting room, paying a lot of money to be told that they shouldn't worry too much about the next rise in school fees. It surprised him to realise how cynical his thoughts had become about the value of what she did, and he tried to picture her smiling face but his mind could no longer get it into focus. 'Sorry. What was that?' he said, realising that Henri had stopped talking and was looking at him.

'Four. Four men with guns. They say everyone give all papers and money. Old man say not do that. Need money to eat and take boat for Italy. They laugh then they shoot old man and other six men and old woman. I say "why you not shoot me?" and man say, "You come with us. You learn to be soldier and we give you gun. So I am quiet and they tell me and two women from Niger to get in their lorry. Then they set fire to old lorry with bodies.' Luke was shocked; he was fairly sure that what the boy was telling him had really happened.

'How long did they keep you with them?' he asked, hoping that he wouldn't hear about the boy becoming a child soldier.

The boy grinned, which Luke found almost as chilling as the story he'd just heard. 'I not stay with them for long. They drive north then find house. They kick door down but nobody there. Then they take women in and tell me to wait in lorry. I wait till I hear screams then I run away and hide. They not find me again and I take some of their food from lorry.'

When Henri had finally reached the Libyan coast, he was told that there was no point looking for the smugglers as he didn't have enough money to buy his passage, but then he had heard that some smugglers would allow people to go free if they knew how to pilot a boat. Although he had never seen the sea before, he had found the smugglers and insisted that his father had been a fisherman and that he could sail any boat. They had, of course, laughed at him telling him that the wind would blow him overboard, but he'd tried again and again until finally he'd found a group who didn't trust the young man who they'd coerced into captaining their boat for them, and they had agreed he could go along to assist. Until this point, Luke was sure that the account was reasonably accurate, but he was fairly sure that the boy's account of his heroics during the crossing were the products of wishful thinking. Fortunately, the 'ship', which Luke assumed to have been a large rubber dingy with an underpowered outboard motor, had been seen by an Italian Coastguard vessel part way across and the occupants rescued and taken to Lampedusa.

Fascinating as the story about the boy's background and how he had arrived had been, what Luke really needed to know was about conditions inside the camp and he gradually got this out of Henri in a way that allowed him to get a reasonable overview that was not just Henri-centric. It seemed that at least ninety per-cent of the people in the camp were male, and almost all of those under thirty-five. They generally formed into groups depending on their ethnicity although some of the groupings were religious. Henri told him that some of the inmates were more important than others, although he wasn't able to explain why – they just were. The women tended to group together and not mix with the men except in the occasional case where both husband and wife were in the camp. Some of the women had small children or babies with them, but not very many. One of the women had given birth while they were on the boat, but the baby had been born dead and the others on the boat had insisted that it be thrown overboard. Henri didn't have much to do with the women because, although he was not yet viewed as a man, the women seemed to prefer him to stay away from them. Generally the refugees were treated with respect although there were a few policemen – or guards as Henri called them – who insisted on giving the Muslims *prosciutto* and *mortadella* telling them that if they didn't want to eat like Christians they should have stayed in Africa to eat grass and camel dung.

Henri had been in the camp for nearly two weeks, having hidden when the rest of the people he'd arrived with had been moved on to a different camp. When Luke asked why he'd done that, he explained that he would only leave the camp when he could attach himself to someone who was educated and who could help him become a doctor or a lawyer. He tried to convince the boy that he would be in a far better position once he had been moved on to one of the purpose built centres where his asylum application could be processed and where a range of organisations should be available to determine what was best for everyone. He gave Henri fifty euros in small denomination notes and warned him not to let any of the other inmates know that he had them – just in case. There was nothing more that he could do for the boy, other than give him his phone number for use in emergencies. He searched in his pocket for a scrap of paper to write it on, but Henri told him that he had a good head for numbers and had always been able to remember strings of numbers far more easily than anything else. It did not feel right to leave a twelve year old boy on his own but he knew that there was no alternative and reluctantly sent the boy on his way back to the camp carrying what was left over of the food he had bought. With a heavy heart, he set off back to his *pensione* to pick up his swimming things to refresh himself after his walk over the island.

After his swim, he again made his way back to his hotel, to try and get a couple of hours' sleep before eating again and then meeting the policeman in the Bar Muamar. He also remembered to let the owner of the *pensione* know that he would be staying for two nights as he wasn't sure what would come out of his meeting with the policeman.

The policeman, who introduced himself as Salvo, did not make a good impression on Luke; there was a forced friendliness in his manner that Luke found irritating as well as insincere. It was tragedy, he said, how many people died during the crossing from Libya; there had already been deaths this year, even though the numbers crossing had dropped during the winter, and the previous year – here he had thrown his hands in the air in a gesture of helplessness – well over four hundred had died. He explained that the majority of those whose bodies were pulled out of the sea, and a significant number of those who were found dead in the boats, were never identified and had to be buried in unmarked graves. Some of the boats didn't even make it out of Libyan waters and he had heard that there were masses of graves without names on the Libyan coast.

Although Luke knew that to certain extent, what Salvo was telling him was true, he was fairly sure that the main reason he was telling him was to convince him to give up the search sooner rather than later. The sympathy that Salvo expressed for those who died also struck him as being false. Suppressing his irritation, he thanked Salvo for his helpful advice but told him that, even if there was very little chance of success, he would not be at peace with himself unless he felt he had explored every avenue. The Italian appeared to accept this and they talked for a further half an hour about what it was like to be assigned to the island, and it was very clear that Salvo could not wait for his posting there to come to an end. Finally, Salvo said he had to go now but that, as Luke was staying, he insisted on buying him another drink before he left. Luke tried to decline but the Italian wouldn't hear of it and moved over to the bar where he engaged the olive complexioned bartender in conversation, before returning a couple of minutes later with a tall glass topped with a cocktail umbrella. 'There you are,' he said smiling and, waving away Luke's thanks, made his way towards the door, leaving Luke feeling slightly guilty and sure that he must have misjudged Salvo.

The cocktail was very good although Luke found it impossible to work out what all the ingredients were: there were definite hints of coconut and the blue tinge suggested that curacao must be one of the ingredients, but beyond that he found it difficult to guess. When he had almost finished, the bartender came over and stopped in front of him with a smile on his face. 'You like it?'

'I do. Very much. What's in it?'

The bartender's smile widened, 'House special, made from a secret recipe that's been passed down through the generations. You want another one?'

'It's probably not a good idea. It seems pretty strong.'

The barman shrugged, 'Not too strong. The taste is deceptive. Two is fine.'

Luke glanced down at his watch – quarter to ten. He had nothing else to do that evening, so why not.' He returned the barman's smile, 'Go on then. You've convinced me. Bring me another one.'

The second cocktail felt even stronger than the first and he decided he'd better take it very steadily. When he was half way down the glass, the barman again came over to him and leaned in close. 'The man you were with said you were looking for a Libyan girl.' Luke nodded, feeling his head spin slightly as he did so. 'You see the woman sitting over near the door?' He indicated a small table just inside the door where a woman wearing a long flowing pale-blue robe and a loose fitting white *niqab* or *hijab* – for the moment he couldn't remember which was which – was sitting alone with a glass of water in front of her. 'Well, she's an Arab. She comes in occasionally and sometimes I've seen her talking in the street with refugee women. I'll take you over to her.' He took Luke by the arm and guided him over towards the woman who rose and, pushing an arm through Luke's other arm, guided him out of the door.

When he awoke, he felt stiff with the early morning chill, and uncomfortable because of the small stones that were digging into him. He was in an alleyway with his back against a wall and his legs stretched out in front of him. His neck was sore as his head had tilted towards one shoulder which was resting against a staunction that had obviously stopped him falling over. His sandals had disappeared, his clothes were dishevelled and his wallet lay on the floor beside him. It took nearly a minute for his brain to slowly process where he was and begin to make some attempt at working out why he was there, before he gingerly eased his back away from the wall and slowly rolled his neck. He glanced down at his watch and discovered that it had gone, then looked around to try and gage the time by the position of the sun but it wasn't easy in the alleyway. It must be early, as the sun couldn't be very high in the sky or he'd be able to see it. The loss of the watch didn't particularly concern him: it had cost less than ten pounds soon after he'd been released from prison and he reckoned that he'd got his money's worth from it – what did irritate him was not being able to tell the time until he could replace it – probably from one of the itinerant sellers who were to be found around every seaside town in Italy.

His head felt slightly fuzzy and he could see pinpricks of light around the periphery of his vision, but he didn't have a headache and his training told him that the most likely explanation for his predicament was that he'd been drugged. As a young recruit, at the start of his training, one of the things they'd been lectured about was rohypnol, commonly known as the date-rape drug, and he was fairly sure that he'd been given that or something similar. The questions he would like to have had answered were, why? and by whom? But he recognised that the chances of finding definitive answers to either question were so slim as to be infinitesimal. He picked up his wallet and was not surprised to find that the thirty euros or so that he'd had in cash had disappeared, as had the debit card he'd had on him; it was lucky that he'd left most of his money and his other cards in the hotel – except his driving licence.

He pulled his licence out just to check that it hadn't been damaged and then frowned as he was about to slip it back inside. Whenever, he put his licence away, he automatically always put it in the same slot, facing the same way, so he always knew where it was even at times when he had lots of other cards in his wallet. The licence he held in his hand was upside down, so that when he pulled it out he would have to turn it round. He was sure that he'd never done that; whenever he pulled his licence out it was facing the way he needed. It was not something he'd ever been conscious of, but it just felt wrong and that made him think. Someone had removed his cash and card and taken his watch to make it look as if he had been taken advantage of by an opportunist thief, but they had been careful to replace his licence. Why do that? Why not just drop it or throw it to one side if they weren't going to take it?

'Because,' he thought, 'if I misplace my driving licence, that's going to cause me all sorts of problems, and could well force me to stay on Lampedusa longer.' Pleased that he had at least learned something, even if he wasn't sure what use the information would be to him, he moved slowly to the end of the alleyway and then to the end of the next street, to get his bearings so that he could make his way back to his *pensione*. There was no-one moving about in the town and once he was out of the narrow alleyway, he could tell that it couldn't have been long since dawn had broken. In a pile of rubbish waiting to be cleared, he found some cardboard and tore two pieces to place under his feet and then bound them there with some strips of old plastic bags – this allowed him to make his way slowly back to the door of the *pensione* where he keyed the code into the keybox by the door and retrieved the key to his room. His phone was where he had left it, next to the bed, and a quick look showed him that it was now a quarter to six. He had a quick shower and then crawled into bed to try and get two or three hours sleep before deciding what to do next. Fortunately, despite whatever sleep he'd had in the alleyway, he was fast asleep within five minutes of his head sinking into the pillow.

Chapter Four

'I assume that you haven't sorted out anywhere to stay yet,' said Luana, putting a hand on Layla's arm as she continued to gaze at the spot where Luke's train had rounded a gentle bend and disappeared from view.

'No, not yet. We were going to have a wander round later and see what we could find. Maybe you know of somewhere that's not too expensive.'

The light pressure on Layla's arm increased slightly as Luana gave it a little squeeze before releasing it, 'If you don't mind sharing a bathroom, and aren't expecting too much in the way of luxuries, I'd be delighted if you came to stay with me. I have a small spare room which is full of rubbish at the moment, but I'm fairly sure that there's a bed under there somewhere.' She smiled and Layla nodded, not knowing what to say but touched by the generosity of the other woman.

Luana gave her no time to feel awkward but turned purposefully towards the exit, still holding Layla's arm. 'Come on. We'd better retrieve your car from wherever you left it and see if we can find somewhere to park nearer to my flat.'

An hour later, having found a free space to park the small Mercedes not too far away, Layla followed her host into her flat and was surprised to see that it was very sparsely furnished with little on show to reveal the character of its owner. It was, however, very neat and tidy and the description of the spare room as 'full of rubbish' turned out to be very much an exaggeration: there were three cardboard boxes and two winter-coats on the bed, but other than that, she'd seen many hotel rooms that were far less ordered. Luana took the coats into her own room immediately and was about to move the boxes out when Layla stopped her, insisting that they wouldn't be in the way at all if they were just piled in the corner of the room. 'The bathroom's through there, if you need a shower or anything. Just make yourself at home… Would you like an *infusione*?'

'*Infusione*?' repeated Layla, 'I'm sorry but what's an *infusione*?'

Luana thought, 'I don't know the word in English. It is when you make a hot drink by pouring water over leaves - like tea - tea is a kind of *infusione*, but I do not have tea; I have *camomilla*, verbena and, I think I have *gelsomino* – jasmine, I think in English.'

'I think I'd like to try a *gelsomino* if you do have it – otherwise camomile will be fine.'

The small sitting room where they sat with their drinks had one wall completely covered by a large, well-stocked bookcase while the furnishings were comprised of a fairly well-worn, but comfortable looking maroon sofa, an old-fashioned television with a deep back which contrasted with the modern seventeen inch flat computer monitor that sat alongside it on a wide computer desk. Two rows of lever-arch files were neatly lined up below the desk, just far enough back as not to get in the way of the knees of anyone who used the office type swivel chair to sit and work there. While she waited for Luana to appear with the drinks, Layla looked at the books to try and get a better understanding of her host but found it difficult to understand some of the titles. Three rows were clearly full of novels, the names of many of the authors easy to recognise, even though titles had often been changed in translation; there were quite a lot of books that seemed to be legal texts while there were also a surprising amount that appeared to be in the area of what she guessed would be classed as 'Women's Studies' back in the UK, alongside about twenty-five books that she thought were about history – some clearly Italian history, and others more general.

The only ornaments in the room were three framed photographs, hung on the wall behind the computer and television; she was looking at those when Luana came back into the room. 'Are they your parents?', she said, pointing at the largest of the photographs where a couple with distinctly eighties hair styles were sitting on an upturned boat on a beach with a girl who she guessed to be about eight or nine years old, sitting below them clearly trying to adopt a glamorous pose for the camera.

'Yes. That was taken on the beach at Lido di Noto ... that's about twenty miles south of Siracusa,' she added, realising that Layla was probably not familiar enough with Sicilian geography for the name to mean much to her. 'It was the last photograph that we had as a family before my father was killed,' and then, pre-empting the obvious question from Layla, 'He was a *Maresciallo* in the *Carabinieri*, assigned as an escort to one of the anti-mafia judges – there was a car bomb and...' she shrugged her shoulders.

'That's terrible. How old were you when it happened? From the picture you can't have been much more than eight.'

'I was just eight when he died, seven when that photograph was taken. People used real film then – it wasn't like it is now where people take as many photographs as they want, whenever they want. I suppose that, in a way, it makes what we do have left, more precious because of the rarity value.'

'Is that why you joined the police when you grew up?'

Luana laughed, 'When I think about it now, it seems obvious that that's why I did it- or at least a big part of the reason. But, at the time I decided to join the police, I convinced myself that by not becoming a *carabiniere* like he was, that I was taking a completely different path – I suppose that doesn't make much sense to you as you only have one police force in England.'

'I've read about the rivalry between police and *Carabinieri* in Italy, so I think I sort of get it... That's him, as well, isn't it?' she said pointing to one of the two smaller pictures where a man sat proudly in what she guessed must be full-dress *Carabinieri* uniform.

'It is. He was always very proud of that photograph but my mother couldn't bear to look at it after he died.'

'And the last photograph; is that a brother, or a boyfriend?'

Luana turned and looked silently out of the window for a minute without speaking, until finally she sighed, 'Beniamino Venuti was a colleague of mine when we were both young police officers; he had a good sense of humour and was fun to be with. He would have liked to take the relationship on from being just friends but I was very serious and career oriented. It wasn't easy being a woman in a predominantly male force and I didn't want anyone to be able to say that I was letting my emotions get in the way of being a good police officer – then, one day, someone decided to shoot me. Ben saw what was happening just in time and knocked me out of the way, but it meant that he took the bullet for me... If you ever see a chance of happiness in life, take it – because if you don't, you'll regret it, and you might never get the chance again – carpe diem!' She turned back to face Layla, smiling, although Layla could see tears in her eyes. 'Anyway. Enough about me. Tell me everything you know about Zahra and her family in Libya.'

Over the next two hours, Layla told Luana every detail she could remember from Aida's letters and e-mails that she had already told Luke about, but also told her much more about Aida, half remembered events and looks from childhood that she intuitively felt that the other woman would be able to empathise with while Luke would have probably seen them as over-sentimental. By the time she had finished, she was sure that Luana understood why she needed to make the effort to find Zahra, or at least find out what had happened to her, and that the limited chances of success made little or no difference to this. Finally, they sat back in their chairs, each following her own train of thought for a while.

'Are you and Luke...' began Luana, and then trailed off.

Layla shook her head, 'Unfortunately, I'm the last person Luke's likely to get together with and, even though he doesn't admit it, he's still in love with his ex-wife. I'm sure that part of the reason he agreed to help me try and find Zahra was because he wants to redeem himself in her eyes, and somehow win her back.'

Luana looked at her quizzically, 'Why?'

'Why what?' said Layla, somewhat more aggressively than she'd intended – although Luana was not put off by her response.

'Firstly, I suppose; why are you the last person he'd be likely to get together with? I know I've only just met you, but you seem to get along OK.'

'We do, most of the time, but he blames me for the years he spent in prison, and because of that, for his wife leaving him.'

'But that makes no sense. He went to prison because he helped his great-aunt, or whatever relation she was, track down another relation so that she could kill him. I thought he pleaded guilty.' Layla nodded. 'So how can he blame you? Even if you were the judge, or the prosecuting magistrate – and I doubt that you were – he has to take responsibility for his own actions. It's ridiculous!'

Layla gave a sad smile and shook her head, 'It sounds fine when you put it like that, but I let him down, and if it hadn't been for me, he might have got away with what he did; his wife would still have left him – or he'd have left her – but he doesn't know that, and I can't tell him the truth because he wouldn't believe me.' She explained how she'd badgered to get an interview with Luke because the case was so unusual, and how he'd eventually agreed on condition that it wouldn't be published until he said it could be and that he retained the right to decide which parts should be left out of the published version. When she explained the circumstances in which the interview had actually been published, Luana was outraged on her behalf, partly because of the way she'd been treated by the editor and partly because Luke had refused to accept that she was blameless.

Layla gave a sad little smile but shook her head. 'If I'd been able to explain to him at the time, I think he might have understood, but with having to wait for more than four years, three of which he spent in prison, I can hardly blame him for not just saying, "Oh OK. That's all right then." can I? Especially when he thinks that that's why his wife went.'

'Why do you say, "he thinks,"?'

'When I did my research before I wrote the article, I tried to find out as much as I could about his life and his family, partly so that I'd know what questions to ask, and partly so that I'd be able to judge if he was stringing me along.'

'I'm sorry. I don't know "stringing me along".'

'Sorry. Stringing me along means convincing me that an untrue story is true. OK?' Luana nodded. 'Well while I was researching, I found that his wife was seeing an old university friend of his, who just happened to have been elected as a Liberal MP. He was seen as a rising star at the time, especially with the Liberals having gone into government as part of a coalition. Anyway, soon after Luke was sent to prison, she told him that the marriage was over because of what he'd done – wished him well for the future, but said she didn't intend to have anything more to do with him. What she didn't tell him was that she'd already moved in with his old friend. As far as I'm aware, he still doesn't know; he saw a photograph of McCreggan on the internet last week with Judi in the background, but he's convinced himself that she's just working for him.'

Luana looked dubious. 'Hmm. It sounds a bit odd to me… almost as if he's protecting himself from the risk of getting hurt again by clinging onto what he must realise is the forlorn hope of his ex-wife changing her mind. I'd say that it's time he put the past behind him and got on with the rest of his life.'

'Well,' said Layla with a wry smile, 'It's up to him... I'm going to go and turn in now, if you don't mind.'

'Turn in?'

'Sorry; turn in means go to bed. I must remember not to use idiomatic phrases.'

'No. Don't do that; it's good for my English, especially hearing them in context. Good night.'

'Buongiorno,' said Layla, stifling a yawn as she slipped into the small kitchen just after seven, surprised to see that Luana was already not only dressed but seemed to be ready to go out.

'Buongiorno,' I was going to leave you a note. I have to go into the council offices this morning to finish typing up a report and sort out a few loose ends, then from two o'clock onwards I can free myself up for a couple of days. There's nothing urgent that won't wait until next week, and I normally work hard enough to not feel guilty about disappearing. I was going to leave you a note if you weren't up when I went out. There's coffee, bread and jam in the cupboard over there, and there's a spare key to the flat on the corner of the table. Take it easy this morning; have a wander round and chat to some of the immigrant workers if you can – just to help you get a general idea of what conditions are like. You never know, you might just come across something useful – and if not,' she shrugged and smiled, 'it will be a useful introduction to the city anyway.'

When her host had gone, Layla did as she'd suggested and made herself a coffee and cut herself two pieces of bread on which she spooned what were obviously homemade peach and fig jams. After that, remembering that there was only herbal tea in the apartment, she went down into the street to find a bar where she ordered a *te' caldo*, a decision she instantly regretted as soon as the barman placed a glass of fairly hot water in front of her with a teabag, which proudly proclaimed itself as having a *'sapore classico'*, sitting in the saucer beside it. Her first taste of the so called hot tea confirmed her fears that it was, in fact, anything but a classical flavour, and she resolved to stick to *caffé* and hot chocolate for the remainder of her time in Italy.

She didn't learn much of value during the morning although, as Luana had predicted, it was interesting. She knew that while back in Britain, when people talked about 'immigrants' it was really shorthand for Eastern Europeans and Asylum Seekers who for some strange reason seemed to get lumped together, here in Southern Europe, the term was a shorthand for Africans, whether refugees or not. As in many Italian cities and resorts, most of the 'immigrants' she saw during the morning were either employed in menial jobs, as cleaners or in some of the apparently less salubrious food outlets, or working as street peddlers, each with a rucksack or sports-bag slung over one shoulder, ready to quickly pack up their wares and move on as soon as any of the municipal police appeared.

By purchasing: a mauve and emerald 'cashmere' head scarf, a watch that she was assured would go for at least two years, and a CD of African music, for a combined total of less than twenty euros, she managed to get into conversation with three of the vendors and learnt about their African homelands and about how difficult it was to get to Europe, but none of them had come over on the refugee boats or, at least, didn't admit to having done so. What they did tell her was that conditions were very hard for all immigrants, with crowded, poorly equipped living conditions and no employment protection. Most of them received their pay in cash after having at least seventy percent of it deducted for their living expenses and to repay the cost of bringing them over and finding them work. What all three wanted most of all was to earn enough money to allow them to go back to their countries of origin and make lives for themselves and their families there. As all three of those she spoke to spoke better English than Italian, and remembering the fears that right-wingers were stoking up in Britain that most migrants wanted to come to England, she asked each of the three if they had ever thought of going further north to Britain but was assured that it had never crossed their mind - England was far too cold and wet, and much too far from their families.

She met Luana again in one of the bars near the town-hall and they each had a panino before moving on. Layla asked whether the street vendors were covered by any employment legislation and Luana nearly choked on her sandwich. 'That'll be the day,' she said when she had recovered, 'unfortunately, the authorities make virtually no attempts to clamp down on the gang-masters who are the ones sourcing the counterfeit goods they sell, bringing the immigrants in more or less as slave labour and taking almost all the money they bring in. The people who are really behind it are far too influential or have protection from those who are. We've got high levels of unemployment but they'd rather bring in immigrant labour from outside because they can get away with paying amounts that no Italian would tolerate – apart from being illegal.'

'I don't get it. Why don't the unemployed object if they're being undercut by outside labour?'

'I'd like to say it's because the Sicilians have always welcomed incomers and worked hard so that all different ethnic groups get along, with each group doing what they're good at to contribute to a better overall society but, while the history books will tell you that that's the case, they're really talking about the Norman period when our rulers were able to harness the best parts of Italian, Byzantine and Arab cultures to be one of the most successful countries in Europe but, although that would have an element of truth to it, things are really very different to how they were nine hundred years ago. In part it's economics: some of these jobs just wouldn't exist if the immigrants weren't doing them, and partly it's to do with fear – there's some serious muscle working for the people who're running the show. Anyway, one problem at a time! There's someone who might be able to help, but she'll want to vet you herself first.'

'I'm intrigued.'

'Remember the place where we met yesterday?' Layla nodded. 'Well that is a theoretically church-run refuge for battered women. As part of my job with the council, I liaise with them, and I try to do whatever I can to help them, so they probably owe me a few favours.' Layla looked interested. I should only really get to see women who've been referred there by the council, but because they know I'll try to help, I often get to see other residents as well and last week, I'm fairly sure that I saw a woman who was dressed in North African clothing pass briefly by the end of a corridor. If she's still there, and if the Mother Superior will allow us to talk to her, I think there's a reasonable chance that she might have information that will point us in the right direction... Are you a Catholic?' Layla pursed her lips and shook her head. 'Never mind. It might have made things slightly easier, but only slightly.'

'My mother was nominally Muslim but the Primary School my sister and I went to was Church of England, but none of it ever meant very much to me. Only blond girls ever got to play the part of Mary in the school nativity play, so I gave up religion before I was ten.' She smiled. 'I studied the history of the Irish Troubles when I was at secondary school, which only served to teach me that Protestants and Catholics tend to be as bigoted as each other... and then, when I went to cover the Arab Spring and saw what different denominations of Muslims were capable of doing to each other, that was the last straw.'

'Just don't say that to the Mother Superior. We want her to help us, not call the exorcist.'

'I'll do my best.'

The Mother Superior's office was as unlike any other office that Layla had ever seen as she could imagine. It had clearly originally been a standard nun's cell and was no more than ten feet by seven in size with rough whitewashed stone walls and a low, uneven ceiling. The only natural light source was provided by a small, grated window, high in the middle of one of the longer walls, although this was augmented by a small reading-lamp at one end of the seemingly home-made desk behind which a severe looking woman sat very still and very upright.

The woman, who must have been in her early fifties, wore a simple white top under an unbuttoned, black, sleeveless cardigan and was bare-headed; the only article of her dress that was as expected was the large silver coloured crucifix that hung around her neck.

Layla's surprise must have shown on her face as the older woman's face relaxed into a smile as she politely gestured to her to take one of the chairs that was facing the desk. Luana crossed herself and slipped into the other chair.

'Benvenute,' she said, the smile still on her face, 'You look surprised, *signorina.'*

'I - I'm sorry - your appearance - it's not quite what I expected - I didn't mean to be rude.'

'It's alright, *signorina.* Most people get their idea of nuns from films they see and don't realise that, while we may not keep up with fashion, even our clothes have changed a little since the nineteen thirties - although, of course, we're always pleased to accept novices with good singing voices.' Layla felt herself blushing as she realised that she had indeed been thinking about The Sound of Music as she had entered the room. We still dress very traditionally on the rare occasions when our duty calls us to leave the convent, but it is not very conducive to the successful completion of our daily prayers and duties. Now, *signorina;* Luana here has given me an idea of why you are here, but I would like to hear it in your own words.'

Hesitantly at first, but then with increasing confidence, Layla recounted the story of Zahra in as much detail as she could, while the nun listened attentively. On a couple of occasions she interrupted to ask Luana if she could help her understand phrases that she wasn't sure she'd understood, but most of the time she kept her eyes fixed on Layla and gave infrequent little nods to show that she understood and to encourage her to continue.

When she had finished, the nun looked at her with troubled eyes and asked, 'And why have you come to us? We are a Catholic organisation, with only limited contact with the outside world; I assume that your relative is Muslim?'

Layla glanced across at Luana, not sure how to respond to this.

'Reverend Mother, last week, when I was here, I caught a glimpse of someone pass the far end of a corridor, who I'm sure was dressed in Muslim clothes. I thought it might be useful if Layla were to speak to her, to help her understand the background to the journeys the refugees undertake and the dangers and temptations that they face while they're travelling.'

The nun looked at Luana steadily for a while, her face inscrutable, until Luana dropped her eyes. A small sigh escaped the nun before she spoke, 'We did have an unfortunate young woman who has been brought up as a Muslim with us for a short while last week, but only until a more suitable place for her to stay could be found. Not everyone has the good fortune to be born into a Christian country and we are always happy to reach out to those who can benefit from our Christian Charity, whatever their own faith may be. Some of the young women we help demonstrate a wish to learn, and join, our faith, although that is not, of course, a precondition of the help we provide them. Our priority, of course is to give refuge to those who show an interest in learning and accepting our values.' Layla saw that Luana was about to interrupt and stretched out a hand and gently placed it on the other woman's forearm to still her. 'Unfortunately, there are occasionally cases where it appears that our best efforts are not only unlikely to succeed but that they may even have a negative effect on other, very fragile women who are in our care. Nine days ago, this young woman was delivered to our doorstep in a state of distress. We took her in and provided her with food and shelter, as we would with all of God's children, but she would not tell us her name or what problems she had, and would not attend any of our services, or even talk to the Father Confessor when he visited and refused to eat with the other women in our community. We kept her here for two nights but as it was already clear that she was openly hostile in the face of all attempts to help her, and her presence was clearly having an unsettling effect, she was transferred elsewhere before she could be a bad influence on any of our other guests. As you know,' she said, addressing herself to Luana, we have some troubled young people here.'

'May I ask where she was transferred to?' asked Layla, who despite the anger she felt inside, was determined not to make an enemy of the nun.'

Before the nun could reply it was Luana who interrupted with an air of certainty, 'Poggio Ventoso,' she said, and the nun inclined her head in confirmation. Layla looked at both in turn hoping for more explanation but soon realised that neither of the other two had any intention of expanding on the name. There was suddenly an air of tension between the two Italians and, realising that there was nothing more to be gained from their visit, Layla stood up and extended her hand towards the nun with what appeared to be a friendly smile.

'Thankyou for giving up your time to see me, Reverend Mother. You've been very helpful. The nun stood up and gave Layla's hand a brief shake that was little more than a touch.

'Deus venire, vobiscum. God go with you,' she said. 'I hope you find your relative.'

'Thankyou,' said Layla, and Luana, who was by now also on her feet and back in full control of her feelings, politely said her goodbyes and crossed herself before turning to leave the room.

The two women did not speak as they made their way out of the building except to briefly thank the doorkeeper as she opened the heavy door to let them out.

'You might have warned me that the two of you are not best of friends. I take it that this Poggio al Vento is somewhere you don't approve of?'

'It's a bit more complicated than that. Most of the time I get on very well with Sister Mara, but that's partly because the girls I take there tend to have Catholic upbringings and, even if they've drifted away, are quite happy to be guided back onto what Sister Mara would see as the only path to God. She is a kind person and does a tremendous amount of hard work to help the girls in her care - unfortunately, she can be somewhat blinkered when it comes to people who don't share her views and who she is unable to 'save'. I suspect that the Muslim

woman who was there must have fallen firmly into this category –
especially if she had her transferred to Poggio al Vento.' Layla raised
a quizzical eyebrow.

'You might have warned me that the two of you are not best of
friends. I take it that this Poggio al Vento is somewhere you don't
approve of?'

'Don't get me wrong. Unlike Sister Mara, I think that Poggio al
Vento is a wonderful place, and those who run it have done an
incredible job at rehabilitating some women with big problems, but
I'm not sure it's the right place for a vulnerable young woman, who's
obviously been through a lot and who probably speaks very little
Italian. The women at Poggio al Vento have mostly done time in
prison, for a whole range of offences; many of them have spent
considerable parts of their lives on drugs, and violence is not unheard
of."

'Tell me more,' said Layla, pointing as she spoke, to a couple of
tables outside a small unimposing bar on the far side of the
nondescript piazza they had just entered. 'I could do with a caffé.'

'Have you read *"Il Gattopardo" – "The Leopard"*?' asked Luana,
as they sat down at one of the tables, each with a small cup of
espresso and a glass of water.

'No. I think I saw the film years ago, but all I can really remember
is the music by Ravel.'

'Alright. Well, the book is really about the decline of the Sicilian
aristocracy and their changing way of life. Poggio al Vento was once
a large country estate owned by what I suppose you could describe
as decadent nobles for hundreds of years who, during the period after
the Risorgimento gradually sold off more and more of their lands to
pay the interest on their ever increasing debts in order to maintain the
appearance of grandeur. The last Count to live there actually did
rather better than his family had for several generations, as he
managed to commercialise liqueurs based on the orange and lemon
groves that had not already been sold off. He had hoped that by the
time he was ready to pass everything on to his only son, the family
fortunes would be stable again. Unfortunately, instead of putting his

son to work learning the business, and maybe even expanding it, he indulged him, gave him a decent allowance and let him do as he liked. The son, of course, squandered all the money he was given – and more! Unlike the prodigal son who returned home to have the fatted calf sacrificed in his honour, this one thought he could restore his fortune by dealing in drugs.' She paused and shook her head sadly.

'Overdose?' asked Layla.

'Yes, and no. He thought he was cleverer than the local mafia don, undercutting the mafia suppliers by sourcing and selling on inferior quality cocaine. They made him eat a considerable quantity of his own product... His father was so devastated that he left Poggio al Vento to the Region of Sicily with the provision that it had to be used for the benefit of recovering drug addicts with the guidance of the church.'

'The guidance of the church!' echoed Layla, 'How does that work?'

'It's not too surprising. There are a lot of good people in the Church who do a lot for people with drug problems throughout Italy. Some of them rely on a very rigid moralistic approach, which, in my opinion, rarely works well, but many are more open minded and practical. Fortunately the two nuns who work with the community are of the latter type and I've always got on well with them. One, at least, spent some time in prison herself, before taking the veil.'

'Just two nuns to look after the community?' asked Layla surprised.

'Only two nuns, but several paid helpers, most of whom are technically social workers. There are also usually a few volunteers, but they are very carefully selected and screened before being allowed anywhere near the place.'

'But, if the purpose of the place is to help and support recovering drug addicts, I don't see why this Muslim girl has been sent there,' said Layla, her eyes drawn together slightly in a frown.

'Exactly! That's the point - and it's not the first time that the Mother Superior has had girls moved up there who she has perceived as not fitting in. Although she does a lot of good work, a big part of the programme she puts the girls through relies on getting them to reconnect with the teachings they were given as children – before the Devil got his claws into them. That works fine with the majority of girls as almost all of us here in Italy have been through the church system as children: catechism, first-communion, confirmation and so on. But for the few, who for one reason or another, have not had a standard Italian upbringing…' she shrugged her shoulders and shook her head with a rueful expression on her face.

Although the journalist's instincts in Layla were urging her to find out more, she knew that this was not the right time. Why the girl had been transferred, and the internal politics of the Catholic Church, were not her concern. Her concern was in trying to find Zahra or, if the worst came to the worst, at least finding out what had happened to her. She felt almost as annoyed as Luana about the girl having been moved, but she realised that her irritation had a different cause; it was highly unlikely that the girl would be able to give them any useful information, even when they did get to her, and her being in a different location just meant that getting to talk to her would take up even more of her time. 'How far away is this Poggio al Vento? Can we go there today?'

'We can. But it's going to take us at least an hour to get there. If you're up for it, we'll take your car, but it's probably better if I drive: some of the roads are fairly small.'

Layla smiled, relieved. 'That's fine by me. Whenever you're ready.'

Chapter Five

It was after eleven when Luke left his hotel again, running over what he remembered of the previous evening and trying, but failing, to make sense of it all. He was grateful not to have a headache to contend with, and that did, at least indicate that his predicament had not resulted from having drunk too much, rather that, at some point, someone had slipped something into his drink. But who, and why? Could he have been the victim of a simple mugging? He remembered the training videos he'd had to watch as a young recruit – alone in a foreign country, out drinking late at night, being picked up by a woman he'd never seen before: he vaguely remembered a woman. He knew he'd been the ideal target for a mugger, but somehow it didn't feel right.

He knew he ought to call Layla and let her know how he was getting on, but he didn't because he knew how ridiculous it would sound and he just didn't want to have that conversation. The first thing he needed was a coffee, and then a swim. After that, he was sure that the way ahead would look clearer: it certainly couldn't be any more obscure.

The small bar that he chose, just behind the seafront, was almost deserted. A bored looking barmaid was playing with her phone behind the bar; two older men with the air of fishermen were playing a desultory hand of cards for a small pile of coins on the table in front of them – the whole pile probably amounted to not much more than ten euros; a third man sat at a table by the door, looking through the *Gazzetta dello Sport*. None of them paid him any attention except the barmaid who put her phone down and watched him make his way to the bar. *'Buongiorno,'* he said with a smile.

'Giorno,' said the barmaid, the corners of her mouth twitching slightly as she almost gave a welcoming smile but then obviously decided it was too much trouble.

Undeterred by the somewhat unenthusiastic welcome, Luke slipped onto one of the three stools that were close to the counter. *'Un caffè, a canolo* with *ricotta*, and a glass of water, *per favore.'* She turned to the coffee machine, emptied and replaced one of the dispensers and, having placed a small cup underneath, pressed the 'on' button, and reached under the counter for a *canolo*.

'Plain *ricotta*, *ricotta* with *pistacchio*, or *ricotta* with candied peel?'

'Plain,' he said, with another smile and, after removing his coffee cup from under the machine and placing it on a saucer in front of him, she took a plastic container out of a cool cabinet and prised the lid off.

He watched as she expertly inserted a large syringe like object into the container, extracted a white creamy substance and injected it into the shell of a *canolo*. Once she had filled the *canolo*, she picked it up using a small paper serviette from the dispenser on the counter and placed it onto a small plate in front of him, returning to her phone immediately as he began to eat.

'You must get pretty busy in here in Summer,' he remarked casually after sucking the last stray trace of ricotta from his fingers.'

With some reluctance, she put her phone down again and observed him properly for the first time. After she had scrutinised him and apparently decided that it was just a casual enquiry, she raised her bare right shoulder in a slight shrug and said, 'I suppose... I haven't worked here for that long, so I don't really know.'

'But you're from the island, aren't you? Or have you just come over for seasonal work?' he asked, keeping his tone to a casual, just passing-the-time-of-day manner.

'There are enough of us from the island to cope with the seasonal work, without needing anyone from the mainland to help out... more than enough.'

'Is that because the migrants help out?'

She snorted. 'The migrants are just passing through. They're only here because it's the nearest bit of Italy to Africa. We hardly ever see them in the town, but because of them, a lot of the other visitors have stopped coming too.'

He raised an eyebrow, 'Odd.'

'Why "odd"?' she asked, looking surprised.

He spread his hands in a what-do-I-know gesture, but then, when she thought the conversation had come to an end, added, 'I came because prices have dropped at the moment; I would have thought others would have done the same.'

She shook her head, 'Not at this time of the year, and probably not in the summer either – it's just as easy, and probably cheaper to get from the mainland to one of the Greek islands. There are a few tourists around, but it's mainly police, navy, journalists and the occasional do-gooder from the United Nations or Amnesty International.'

'United Nations! I wouldn't have thought so. It's probably just a few conmen who've found a way to make a quick buck. You shouldn't believe everything people tell you.' he responded dismissively and, putting a five euro note on the counter in front of him, stood up as if to go.

'They are!' said the girl, responding to the provocation in the way he'd hoped she would. If you don't believe me, you can see them in the bar at the Hotel Sirio, that's where they always stay.'

'OK,' he said, dismissively. *'Arrivederci,'* and he left.

The Hotel Sirio turned out to be only a few minutes' walk from the white sand beach of Cala Guitgia, on the opposite side of town to his own hotel and, after having a brief look from the outside, he decided that he would need his best clothes on if he were to eat in the restaurant there that evening. First, however, he decided that there was no point resisting the pull of the splendid beach of the so called Turquoise Bay, the pure white sand of which made a pleasant change to the small pebbly beaches he was used to on Lipari.

There was no wind and, with a clear cobalt sky, the more southerly situation of the island meant that the temperature was already up to the high teens and the soft sand was welcomingly warm. The sea was smoother than he preferred but a few minutes vigorous front crawl, followed by a more leisurely, but still purposeful, return using backstroke, left him with a healthy glow, after he'd shaken off most of the droplets of water and lain down on his towel.

Why am I here? He asked himself as he looked up into the blue, watching a creamy vapour trail form behind an aircraft that was little more than a glint in the sun, many thousands of feet above. I could spend almost as much time as I wanted, lying around on Lipari without getting involved with other people's problems. He'd ended up in the situation he was in because he'd involved himself in other people's problems before; but that was different, that was family, that was personal and he had no doubt that it had been morally right. But this? Why was he doing it? It wasn't his fight. The girl he was helping to look for was probably dead and even if she wasn't, the chances of finding her amongst all the human misery that surrounded the refugee crisis, were probably far less than finding a needle in a haystack. If he'd wanted to get involved why hadn't he just volunteered to work for Oxfam or Amnesty International or any one of the other charities that must be involved? Well, he'd do what he could on Lipari, but then that was that.

He was momentarily in shadow as two young women walked along the beach nearby. He allowed his head to tilt to one side and followed them with his eyes until they became too small to focus on. One of them had short dark hair and an hourglass figure and reminded him of Judi, the other was slightly taller with long ebony hair and a lithe but less voluptuous figure than her companion. Luke tried to focus on both, enjoying their rhythmic gait as they walked but found his eyes drawn more strongly to the taller one. As he watched her, an image of Layla came to mind, diving into the sea wearing only a pair of flimsy white knickers, as they had made their way back from the observatory what seemed like ages ago. He jerked his head round so that he was no longer focused on the lower part of the lithe girl's indigo bikini and looked towards the town. He was doing this for Layla: but why? What was he trying to prove, and what was the point anyway? She'd messed his life up and he wanted to make her sorry for that, he told himself. She'd apologised because she'd needed his help, not because she really meant it. He knew what she was up to and he knew he hadn't been taken in – so that still left the question of why he'd agreed to do it. Lying down doing nothing wasn't good for him he thought and, picking himself up, he made his way back down to the sea again.

Keeping busy made him feel better and, after a long swim, he dried himself off and then filled up a couple of hours by wandering along some of the near deserted interior roads, until he decided to buy a newspaper to occupy the rest of the time before he needed to go back and get changed. There was little of interest in the paper, but he forced himself to read it from cover to cover to avoid falling back into the confusing train of thoughts that had afflicted him on the beach.

The Hotel Sirio was a pleasant looking two-storey building with gleaming white stone decorative elements set off by what seemed to be a recently re-stuccoed yellow facade. He made his way between the large terracotta pots containing semi-tropical plants and up the three tiled steps to the terrace in front of the main entrance. Before he went in, he turned to admire the view of the bay which could be seen between other buildings and watched lights twinkling as he marvelled how much quicker night fell, the further south one went.

As he entered, a short stocky man, who he judged to be in his mid-forties looked up from behind a slightly curved, marble fronted reception desk and gave a business-like smile: *'Buonasera.'*

'Buonasera,' responded Luke. 'I was wondering if your restaurant is open to non-residents. I've been told that your seafood dishes may well be the best on the island.'

The man smiled, 'I hope we can live up to expectation. How many people is it for, sir?'

'Just me, I'm afraid.'

'In that case, sir. It's no problem at all. The hotel is not full so early in the year, so we have no problem fitting you in… If you'd like to come this way, sir, I'll take you through to the restaurant and one of the young ladies will sort you out with a table.

The best tables, closest to the window, were clearly reserved for residents and those who had booked early, and Luke was shown to a table set for two near the back of the restaurant. He waited for a few seconds before sitting down while a smiling waitress removed one of the place settings and shifted the other slightly so that it was facing the front of the restaurant.

'Da bere, Signore?' the waitress asked with a professional half smile, welcoming but not full of the over-the-top bonhomie often found amongst the staff in sea-front establishments.

'I'll have a jug of water – tap water is fine – and I'll have a half litre carafe of white please.'

'*Subito,*' she nodded and moved away towards a door that obviously led to the kitchen.

He had come to eat fairly early and was prepared to take his time over his meal, not knowing at what time the UNHCR representatives were likely to eat. Much, of course, would depend on their nationalities; if he were lucky they would be Northern Europeans which would make an early mealtime more likely and mean he wouldn't have to stay as long. He hoped that they weren't Spaniards, as they were more likely to eat much later, and he wasn't sure how long he could stretch out his meal for, and he knew he couldn't really afford to eat there again the following evening or to prolong his stay in his hotel, relatively cheap though it was, beyond that night.

When he arrived, there were only two families with small children seated in the restaurant but others, who he guessed were staying at the hotel, began to drift in as he perused the menu. As a rule, and particularly if he was eating alone, he only went to restaurants at lunchtimes when the good value daily specials were on offer and he immediately looked for the lowest cost options on the menu. His eyes, however, kept being drawn to the house specialities and, after delaying as long as he could before ordering, he convinced himself that, just for once, it was worth splashing out.

'I'll start with the *spaghetti al ragu di triglie*… and then… I think I'll have the *sarde al beccafico*.'

The waitress smiled – a more genuine smile this time – clearly approving of his choice. 'Would you like any *contorno* with that?'

He considered adding a side-dish of *capponata* but decided to resist the temptation. 'I don't think so. I'm tempted, but I think I'd better leave some room for a dessert.'

Although he was doing his best to keep an eye on the other diners in the restaurant, the mullet based sauce was so well balanced that his attention was soon fully focussed on the plate in front of him and it was only after he had finished polishing his plate with a hunk of bread so that it gleamed as if it had just come out of the dishwasher, that he noticed the two young men sitting three tables away from him.

They were in the process of ordering and one, who clearly spoke better Italian than the other was doing the bulk of the talking. When the waitress had left them, they dropped into English to talk between themselves and, although Luke could not make out much of what they were saying because of the lively talking of the families populating other tables, he was fairly sure that they were the people he was hoping to meet. One, who had close-cropped blond hair, seemed to be Scandinavian, or possibly German, but the other, who had the louder voice was either Australian or a kiwi; he'd never been able to tell the two accents apart. Most of their conversation seemed to be casual and light-hearted but every so often the tone seemed to change and, although Luke couldn't follow their conversation, he could pick out enough words to be sure that they were the people he was looking for.

As his main course arrived before the others received their starter, he was able to ignore them while he ate and give the stuffed and rolled sardines the attention and appreciation they deserved. He was delighted that the sardines had been oven-baked in the *Palermitano* style rather than fried as was more common around Catania; the distinctive taste of each of the ingredients were a delight to savour as he took and lingered over each small mouthful. When he had finished the sardines, the two men he had his eye on were only just starting their main course and so, after checking with the waitress that their *canoli* were filled at the very last minute before serving, he indulged himself with one filled with pistachio cream before finishing off with a coffee over which he lingered before paying his bill.

The two UNHCR workers asked for a beer each to take out to the terrace after they had finished eating and, after allowing a few minutes to pass, Luke ordered a glass of *passito* and followed them outside where he stood as if admiring the bay that stretched out in front of him. The two men gave him a glance when he first came out but then ignored him and carried on chatting animatedly.

After a couple of minutes, he turned towards them. 'Excuse me. I couldn't help overhearing you speaking in English. It's pretty unusual down here, at this time of year anyway. Are you on holiday?' he smiled disarmingly and took a step towards them. The Northern

European glanced at his colleague who gave a slight shrug of his shoulder and then gestured accommodatingly towards the spare chair at the table they had sat at.

'Come and join us. You on your own?'

'I am. I'm just here for a few days to do a bit of research. My name's Luke, by the way, English originally.' He held out a hand.

'Dean; all the way from Tasmania, and this is Stefan, from Sweden. What sort of research are you doing?.. Marine Biology?' his voice was friendly and it was clear he was someone who was genuinely interested in people rather than someone just making polite conversation.

Luke shook his head. He wanted to stick as close as possible to the truth but, after what had happened the previous night, he felt he ought to be a little more circumspect. 'Nothing so glamorous. I write stories for children, and I felt that with all the misinformation that they hear, it would be a good idea to write a couple of stories that help them to understand what life is really like for refugee children. I don't like all the negative propaganda they're exposed to in England, lumping refugees and economic migrants together and demonising both. I think they need to have a more realistic, and a more positive view of refugees.'

'And how is your research going? Have you had much success?'

Luke smiled ruefully, 'Not as much as I'd hoped. I did get to talk to one boy from the holding centre yesterday, and I learnt a lot from him that will be useful, but otherwise,' he shrugged, 'otherwise it's surprisingly difficult to get to talk to anyone. I expected to see a lot more migrants around the town and I thought that the authorities might be a bit more helpful than they have been,'

'You've been up to the camp up the coast?' asked the Tasmanian.

'I have, but the police and military outside seem to be very keen not to let anyone in to talk to the refugees, and they appear to be discouraging the refugees from coming out as well; I've no idea why.'

Dean snorted, and the Swede gave a wry smile and shook his head. 'You've done pretty well to get to talk to one young refugee – the chances of getting access to those in the camp are almost non-existent and, as those refugees who venture out of the camp have learned to be very wary of the reaction of some of the locals, they tend to avoid coming into the town.'

'What sort of reaction?' asked Luke, who hadn't expected to hear this and was genuinely curious.

Stefan sighed, 'Look. You have to understand that the people of Lampedusa are good people. When the first boats came... when the fishermen first started to find bodies in the sea, everyone did everything they could. When there were just a few – even when there were a few dozen – people took refugees into their own homes, they gave them food and helped clothe them – even when the official advice was that they shouldn't, that any refugees they found should be immediately handed over to the authorities for processing...'

Dean took over, 'But you've got to remember that behind the polished facade that's put on for the tourists, Lampedusa is a poor place. Most people here have work for between six and eight months a year, if they're lucky. The money they earn is partly spent on ensuring that the tourist facilities are up to scratch for the next year, and partly on making sure that they have enough to live on through the winter. Once some of them got it into their heads that the immigrants meant competition for jobs, some of them became less welcoming and gradually the atmosphere changed. Like everywhere else, there are people whose interest it is to identify scapegoats to blame for other problems, and immigrants make very convenient scapegoats. Now there are very few of them who come into town; they know that they're only here for a short time and it's better for them to wait until they're somewhere bigger.'

'You must have been here for quite a while if you've got to know all this,' said Luke, impressed.

Stefan shook his head. 'Not too long. We are here with the UNHCR, so we were well informed before we came.'

'Unfortunately,' said Dean, 'We are the UNHCR, as opposed to being with them. We're meant to keep an eye on what is happening, intervene if we see any problems, and send regular reports back to Geneva.'

'And what do your reports say?'

Dean and Stefan both eyed him for a few seconds before Dean spoke again, 'They say that as far as we are able to ascertain, the refugees are healthy and treated well while they are here... but that we find it very difficult to gain direct access to them.'

'But aren't the Italian authorities obliged to work with you? I would have thought that they'd be glad of your input.' Luke noticed a slight shake of the head from Stefan while a sardonic smile played around Dean's mouth.

'Two Italian phrases that we've learnt while we've been here are *"bella figura"* and *"brutta figura"*. The Italian authorities feel very exposed here; they want the world to see how much they do for the refugees and for the rest of the world to see them as making a *bella figura*, but it's such a massive problem that they know they can never do enough, or spend enough to resolve it. Some of their early responses were too limited to contain the situation and, at the time, they quite rightly came in for some criticism. Because of that, they're now very sensitive about keeping outsiders out – even us! We spend half our time filling forms in and getting permits stamped in various offices, and even then we're not allowed into the camp unaccompanied in case we see anything that we might interpret as *brutta figura*.'

'So the Italians aren't doing enough?'

'No,' said Dean, hesitantly. 'I wouldn't say that. I think that most of them are doing as much, if not more than could be expected. It's just that they're concerned that it might be interpreted otherwise.'

'Most of them?'

Dean paused before answering. 'The vast majority do a fantastic job but, wherever you go, you are always going to find some people who are not up to the task or, probably even worse, are looking to see how they can benefit from difficult situations.'

'In what way?' asked Luke.

Dean was about to respond when Stefan put a restraining hand on his arm. 'What did you say you did, Luke?'

Luke smiled, prepared for the question. 'I write stories for teenagers. If you've got a signal on your phone, google "Darius stories," - once you get past the references to Greek mythology, you should find references to my stories. The last one to be published was number eighteen.'

'I will look later,' said Stefan, obviously reassured. 'Are they good?'

Luke held his upturned hands out wide using an Italian gesture he'd picked up, 'I get paid for them and they keep asking for more, so someone clearly thinks they're OK.'

Dean laughed, 'So, in future, this Darius is going to be a refugee.'

'Probably not,' said Luke with a smile, 'but he may be able to befriend and help one or more refugees. I haven't really decided yet.'

'You're probably not in the right place to find out anything useful,' said Dean.

'How so?'

It was Stefan who replied, 'They are just passing through Lampedusa. Nothing can really happen to them here. They have big problems before they get here, and they can have other problems after they leave here, but in general they're safe here.'

'Dean, you said before that there are a few people who let the refugees down, even here. In what way?'

'We have no proof,' said Stefan, looking at his partner who paused before replying.

'I'm sure you'll have read, or at least heard rumours, that a lot of the minors who arrive in Italy each year cannot be accounted for.' Luke nodded. 'We're pretty sure that it doesn't happen here. We effectively count them in, and we count them out. It's later on that they get lost in the system and the figures don't add up,' he stopped.

'It feels as if there ought to be a "but" after that statement,' said Luke, looking Dean in the eye.

'We suspect – although we have no proof – that some unaccompanied kids are identified here and are then siphoned off in some way before they are officially entered into the system at their next destination.'

'I don't get it - how would that work?'

Stefan looked at him unsmiling, 'Do you know what the likely fate is of the kids who go missing?'

'I would imagine that we're talking mainly about domestic slavery and sexual exploitation,' said Luke sombrely.

'For some of them, it's almost certainly that. There are some who just manage to evade the system and who will reappear in some other European country at some point in the future, denying that they ever passed through Italy. We are concerned about them, although obviously less so, as they do have some control over their own destinies - but, yes, the ones who we really worry about are the ones who are either taken out of the system against their will, or tricked into leaving the system.'

Luke glanced at their glasses, 'Let me get you another beer. It sounds as if this isn't going to be a brief explanation.

'Good on you, mate,' said Dean appreciatively.

When they were settled with fresh drinks in front of them, Stefan raised his glass and said *'Skol'* and the others responded in kind.

'OK,' said Luke, 'So what should happen to the refugees if everything runs smoothly?'

'What should happen,' said Dean, 'is that any cases requiring emergency medical treatment are identified here on Lampedusa and moved to a suitable facility as soon as possible. Everyone gets a very basic medical check and, in theory, there's a security screening to make sure that none of the refugees are armed.'

'Why "in theory"?' asked Luke, puzzled.

Dean gave him a sad smile. 'You obviously haven't seen any of the boats that manage to make it this far, let alone those that capsize beforehand. They're so low down in the water, that it's a miracle they're still floating. Any possessions the refugees managed to get on the boats with them, will have been jettisoned over the side a long time before they get here, along with everything else that isn't absolutely essential for survival.'

'Sentiment doesn't last very long when you are as close to death as these people,' added Stefan. Anyone who dies is dumped over the side; it doesn't matter who they are: husbands, wives, friends, children, new-born babies – so possessions have no chance.'

Luke closed his eyes tightly for a moment and tried to conjure up an image of something pleasant to chase out the idea of dead newborn babies being thrown into the sea. When he opened them he said, 'OK, I get the idea – it was a stupid question.'

'Not really,' said Dean with a shrug, 'there are plenty of people who are convinced that the boats are full of well-armed jihadi terrorists, just waiting to step ashore and blow us all up.'

'I'm afraid you're right. We have plenty of newspapers back in England that are full of stories like that.'

'The famous Daily Mail,' said Stefan sourly.

'Amongst others,' muttered Luke. 'Go on.'

'As soon as possible, the refugees are moved out and ferried across to the Sicilian mainland where most of them are housed in a purpose built centre at Mineo – that's about twenty five kilometres east of Caltagirone – Once they're there, they are meant to register and then to make their formal applications for asylum. Those who make a deliberate choice to avoid the system often disappear at this stage, although the majority of those who just wander off on their own, soon get returned to the facility. In an ideal world, the centre at Mineo would be well staffed with well trained professionals and everything would be dealt with smoothly and efficiently. Unfortunately, the Italian state has massive financial problems and that means that the ideal world scenario is not one we're likely to see anytime soon - and then you've got to remember how powerful organised crime groups are here.' He lowered his voice and glanced around to make sure that they were not overheard. 'After a while, you start to notice little things, even as a tourist - mainly pretty innocuous things – the way some places are able to source things that other places can't, the way that people know someone who can help. Most of the time you just accept them because they're helpful, but if you step back a minute and think, "how are they doing this?", then you start to see that the authorities aren't really in control.'

'And you think that the Mafia is controlling the refugee programme?'

'Controlling would be stretching it a bit but I'd say that they're certainly involved. I know that there have been accusations of corruption up in Mineo connected to the contracts for building and staffing the reception centre there. I don't know the details but there's all sorts of stuff online.'

'OK. I can see how the Mafia would exploit the situation to make money, but what effect does that have on the refugees, other than meaning that there's less money available to help them?'

Stefan sighed. 'Take a step back a minute. You were asking about the unaccompanied minors who drop out of the system. Forget, for the moment, those who make a deliberate choice to abscond and find a quicker way to get to Germany or one of the Scandinavian countries where they think they'll be welcome. You mentioned the sex trade and domestic slavery.' Luke nodded. 'Well, put yourself in the position of someone who wants a sex worker or a domestic slave - how do you go about it? You can't just wander along, have a good look at all the refugees and then make your choice.'

'You need an intermediary,' muttered Luke, catching on.

Dean nodded, 'And, as we're in Sicily, any intermediary in an illegal operation has to be either from the Mafia or paying off the Mafia so that they don't object.'

'And here on Lampedusa?'

'Here on Lampedusa, the locals have limited contact with the refugees, so what you're looking for is someone who either works at the reception centre or more likely one, or more, of the security staff.'

'So what do you do about it?'

'Not enough,' replied Dean, 'We try to keep a record of how many refugees arrive at the camp; we insist that they let us know when groups are being transferred out and we make sure that we count the numbers who get on the bus at the reception centre and then off the bus and onto the boat at the port. We then let our colleagues in Porto Empedocle know and they try and meet the boat and check the numbers at the other end.'

'Try?'

'They do their best, but sometimes they have other urgent matters to see to at the camp. We only have a limited number of people and they can't be in more than one place at once but... where we have managed to check at both ends, we've never had a discrepancy of more than one, and usually the tallies match, of course, when the numbers increase, as they will when the weather improves, it will become even more difficult.'

'But surely,' exclaimed Luke, surprised, 'a discrepancy of one means that someone has gone missing. Surely, even one is a matter of concern.' Dean shook his head.

'You're right that every individual matters, but you need to remember that the movements often take place at night and it's not as easy as it should be to count at either end. An occasional discrepancy of one could very easily be due to a counting error. It is possible that someone might give the police who're accompanying them the slip while they're on the boat, but I think it's very unlikely that anyone involved in trafficking would take the risk of being caught just to get one refugee out – it would be lunacy.'

'I suppose you're right; I hadn't thought of it that way... So... when do you think that the refugees are at risk of disappearing?'

'Some of them disappear after they've left Mineo when they've already been processed and are distributed to one of the many centres that have been set up for the refugees around the country. But we suspect that many are spirited away from Mineo itself. They are meant to be registered when they first arrive there and a record is kept of when they move on, but it's almost impossible to know who is actually in the centre.' Luke looked puzzled. 'Remember, they're refugees, not prisoners and, while they're there, they're free to come and go more or less as they please. Many stay in the centre, hoping to get through to the next stage as quickly as possible but it takes time and some get frustrated. Even though they can't officially work until they've been fully processed and received papers, there are plenty of people on the look out for cheap sources of labour on a day to day basis.'

'But surely, that's easy to crack down on.'

'You'd think so, but ask yourself in whose interest it would be to crack down - think about it - the only people who suffer because of it are the workers who are displaced by the immigrants - and most of those receive some form of state benefit because they're not working - benefits that are controlled by the same people who own the businesses that employ – or exploit – the refugees. The bosses gain because they only need pay very low wages; the refugees gain because the very low wages are probably as much as many of them would have received before they became refugees and they feel they have earned some self-respect; the local mafia bosses receive a payoff from the business owners and the officials running the camp are happy that they are not trying to keep the lid on a camp that's bursting at the seams with bored refugees – on the surface there are no losers, except the general Italian taxpayer of course.'

'But?'

'But, once refugees are outside the centre - and to a large extent I'm guessing now - they can be vulnerable to less scrupulous people than the business owners and the local mafia.'

There was a moment's silence while the full import of what Dean had said, sank in, then Luke, remembering his part said, 'Well. There's certainly a lot of material here for my stories.'

'We wish you luck,' said Stefan, raising his glass.

Dean had never been to Mineo and Stefan had only spent two days there, so there was little more that they were able to tell him, but he spent another hour chatting and laughing with them before taking his leave and wishing them luck. On his way back to his hotel, he realised that he still hadn't communicated with Layla and felt suddenly guilty about it. He took out his mobile, scrolled down to her name and was about to tap the telephone icon before suddenly, and inexplicably, feeling embarrassed and pressing the message button instead. 'Getting morning ferry. CU 2morro eve.' He paused, wishing he could talk with her face to face, but then stabbed his finger down on the Send button decisively, and dropped the phone back into his pocket.

He felt the phone vibrate less than a minute later, but resisted the temptation to look at the incoming message until he was back in his hotel. 'Good. Lot to tell you.' – he smiled. As he slipped his clothes off and stepped under the fairly weak shower in his room, he couldn't help think of her diving into the sea near Lipari and then of her turning her face up towards his on the beach at Aquacalda.

Chapter Six

After he had eaten and got a couple of hours rest, Layla insisted that he tell her all about Lampedusa before she brought him up to date with what she'd found out.

'So really, Lampedusa itself was a bit of a dead end. If Zahra got that far, then we can be fairly sure that she will have been moved on to this place, Mineo. That's where we need to be trying to pick up the trail… I suppose it's even possible that she's still there: the two guys I was talking to were saying that it's not unknown for people to be there for over a year.' He felt torn between wanting to give her hope and not wanting to raise up false hopes. She had listened attentively but he could tell that she had seized on the slightly unrealistic scenario he had ended with, rather than registering the warning he had hoped to confer when he had said "if Zahra got that far." Dean and Stefan had described boats that had been recovered with dead bodies lying in the bottom as well as bloated corpses recovered from the sea, either from boats that had capsized or simply the bodies of those who had died during the journey and been unceremoniously dumped over the side. Many of these bodies had been the corpses of women and children and he knew that there was a good chance that this had been Zahra's fate.

'I agree,' responded Layla. 'From what I found out here, everything points to Mineo being the most likely place for things to have gone wrong.

'Go on,' said Luke, settling back and taking a sip from the glass of *grappa* cupped in his hand, 'tell me everything you managed to find out while I was away.'

After giving a somewhat abbreviated account of her interview with the Mother Superior in Catania, she became more animated when she described the more positive reception she had received at Poggio al Vento. 'The two nuns who are practically, if not officially, in charge of the centre were a breath of fresh air after what I'd come across earlier; both were relatively young – probably not much older than me – but they seemed to have lots of common sense and a much better grasp of the real world than I'd expected. One of them, Sister Claire, is originally Irish, although she's been over here for about fifteen years, so she was the one who showed me around and explained about the problems some of the girls there have had to face.' Layla paused as she thought about some of the horror stories she'd heard. 'She was really pleased when she heard that I could speak a bit of Arabic, and said I was welcome to spend as much time as I needed to with the refugee woman – I tried to message you, so that you'd know where I was if you came back early, but I couldn't get a signal up there.' Luke gave a small, dismissive shrug, while feeling a little uncomfortable about his own failure to communicate while he'd been away.

'Anyway, when Claire took me to her, she was sitting quietly under a tree with her arms wrapped round her legs and her chin resting on her knees. Apparently she'd told them her name and was very good at saying "please" and "thankyou", but other than that hadn't spoken. Anyway, Claire told her my name and said I was a friend, in both English and Italian and then left me with her. We sat there for a few minutes without either of us saying anything and without her even looking at me, before I decided I might just as well start talking so, using as much Arabic as I could remember, and with the odd English word thrown in when I couldn't remember the Arabic, I just chatted away for about an hour, telling her my life story. Eventually, just when I was thinking of giving up and stopped for a minute, she looked at me and said "Go on". After that, I talked for about another fifteen minutes and then asked her to tell me her story.' She paused for a while here and reached for the bottle of grappa to pour some into her own glass. She pulled a face after taking too large a sip and her eyes watered before she was able to continue.

'It wasn't easy. Once she started talking it came out in a torrent, far too fast for me to do more than just get the gist. Her accent is not one I'm familiar with and I'm only really comfortable with Arabic in short bursts, but I wanted to let her get into her flow before I interrupted her. Anyway, I managed to stop her after a bit and after that it was easier. I made sure that I asked regular questions just to make sure that I had some sort of control over what she was talking about.' Luke looked concerned, his mind going back to his police training and the warnings about not putting words into people's mouths.

'But isn't that…'

'No,' she interrupted, obviously anticipating his objection. 'Sorry, I probably didn't explain properly. I didn't mean "what she was talking about", what I should have said was the pace at which she moved from one subject to the next – you know, like she'd mention her father, and I'd ask a question about her father, so that I had chance to process what she was saying before she moved on to something else. 'She smiled, 'I'm not completely useless as an interviewer.'

'Hmmm,' he grunted, 'Go on.'

'Well… it turns out that she's from Mauritania. She and her father and two…'

'Where?'

She rolled her eyes theatrically. 'Mauritania,' she sighed at his blank look, 'I take it that Geography was not one of your best subjects at school! Mauritania is in North West Africa, just below Morocco and Algeria and above Senegal. It was one of the poorest countries around with lots of desert and not much else but then, a few years ago, they found oil which meant that people started to take a bit more notice. There are regular coups or revolutions and a fairly well ingrained caste system with generally, the fairer skinned northerners looking down on the southerners and often keeping them as slaves. In fact, in terms of number of slaves per head, it's supposed to be the worst country in the world, even though the government claims that slavery was abolished some years ago and everyone is equal.'

Luke opened his eyes wide, 'She told you all this? I thought you said that it wasn't easy to understand what she said.'

Layla laughed, 'Google and Wikipedia filled in a lot of the background details. I have to admit that I knew virtually nothing about the country before… Anyway, I was saying, for some reason, I didn't quite understand why, she, her father and her two sisters had to get out of the country and started to make their way North. One sister, the oldest, died on the way and the other two sisters had to dig a grave for her in the desert. I didn't understand all the details about the journey through Africa and, from what I did get, I'm pretty glad about that. Somehow, the father managed to arrange for the three of them to be put on one of the boats that sneak away from the Libyan coast almost every night. Probably luckily for them, they were picked up by an Italian naval vessel not long after they'd cleared Libyan territorial waters, so their time on the death trap that they'd set sail in was limited. They were taken to Lampedusa and then, after about three weeks, were transferred to Mineo, and that's where her life really began to get unpleasant.' She stopped and took another drink from her glass, although this time a much more cautious one.

'I don't know how much you were told about the Centre at Mineo, but I've done a fair bit or research since I talked to Coulibaly – the girl at Poggio al Vento, and I've found out plenty.' She paused and flicked a stray strand of hair away from an eye. 'Most of the centre was originally built to house American servicemen stationed at a nearby base, but it was left empty after the Americans closed the base down and moved away. I saw one description of it as being like a piece of anonymous American suburbia that had been lifted by aliens and dropped on the edge of a quiet old town in Sicily. Apparently it's mainly made up of detached houses neatly set out along roads with very American names like Independence Avenue and Acacia Drive but now, instead of each house holding an American serviceman's family, every room in every house now houses at least seven or eight refugees while the gardens have been converted into communal areas. It's meant to be a transit camp where refugees are processed quickly and efficiently, filed and issued with temporary papers and then resettled elsewhere, but in reality, most refugees are there for getting on for a year – some of them even longer – so it's developed into a separate town with its own laws, structures and hierarchies and its own economy.'

'You make it sound quite orderly.'

Layla grimaced. 'It's a jungle, full of wild animals… Remember there are refugees and economic migrants there from all over the Middle East and Sub-Saharan Africa; there are people from both sides of every civil war you can think of, and people from countries that have been fighting each other for so long that no-one can remember why it all started. The vast majority of those who are there are good people who just want to survive and have some sort of a chance of a life, but there's always a minority who take the view that might is right and that it's all about the survival of the fittest.' Her tone was becoming increasingly bitter as she described the centre and Luke stretched out a tentative hand to place over hers, but she moved it away a fraction before his hand arrived and carried on, clearly needing to express the anger she felt.

'The Italian officials don't help much. There aren't enough of them there to bring any sort of order to the camp and their bureaucracy takes for ever. They very rarely enter inside the ghetto and, because they don't want anyone else to know just how bad conditions are inside, they won't let any journalists, or even charity workers in, except on very tightly controlled guided tours. Most of the Mineo town council has been arrested on corruption charges and some of the left wing journalists claim that the only people with any sort of control over what goes on are the Mafia.'

She paused, and Luke took the opportunity to ask gently, 'And what did Coulibri tell you about conditions inside the centre?'

'Coulibaly,' she corrected, and sighed before continuing in a calmer voice. 'Each nationality or ethnic group has developed its own area of the camp and, in almost all cases, some of the men have taken on the role of community leaders – I suppose Kapos would be more accurate. Despite the overcrowding in the centre, there were very few Mauritanians – certainly not enough to fill one of the houses – so Coulibaly, her father and her remaining sister were placed with the Algerian Berbers. Somehow, I didn't really understand how, her father soon became one of the Kapos and, as a result, life was bearable at first – certainly a lot better than it had been during the journey... then it changed.' She stopped abruptly, stood up, and moved over to the window, where she leaned forward and pressed her head against the glass. Luke waited for what seemed like a very long time before she turned back towards him.

The light from the window was behind her, making it difficult to see her face clearly, but Luke saw her brush a traitor tear from the corner of her eye with an angry swipe of a finger. 'Coulibaly was given jobs to do around the building, but she didn't mind that as she found that she could get them all done by early afternoon and have the rest of the day pretty much free to do what she liked and what she liked was generally meeting people, so she wandered around and made friends with other young people, mainly girls, but sometimes, when she was meeting girls from some of the more enlightened ethnic groups, there would be boys there as well.'

'How old is she?' asked Luke cautiously.

'She's fifteen now – although she could easily pass for two or three years older... It was difficult to follow, not only because of the different accent but also because she used a lot of euphemisms when she told me what had happened... She hadn't been allowed to mix with boys since she was a child... I mean a young child,' she clarified bitterly. 'In the circumstances, it was probably inevitable that she thought she'd fallen in love, and the one she fell for told her he was in love as well.' She brushed her eye again.

'But he wasn't,' murmured Luke.

Layla looked at him and shrugged. 'She says that he was, and that someone found out about them and then her father got to hear about it. I suspect that "someone" found out because he was bragging about his conquest, as teenage boys like to do.' Luke decided there was nothing to be gained by objecting to the generalisation, and let it go without comment. 'Coulibaly got home one evening and was dragged inside by her father by her hair and locked in a cupboard until the next day, when she was given some water and some plain rice and then locked in again. When they eventually brought her out – she thinks it was two days later she was taken to another building and put up before some sort of Sharia court. Her father said that she had brought disgrace on the whole community and that, as far as he was concerned, she was no longer his daughter and that the court should deal with her as it saw fit. She gathered that the boy involved had met with an unfortunate accident and fainted. The next thing she remembers is one of the other Kapos - she thinks he was Ghanaian – arranging to buy her from the court...'

'Buy!' echoed Luke, 'What... like a slave?'

'Like a slave! Obviously, it was termed as paying her fine, but in reality she was handed over to him to do whatever he wanted. She was raped by him almost as soon as he got her home and then alternately either beaten or raped several more times over the next few days. He told her that she disgusted him and that he wouldn't have bought her if he'd known she hadn't undergone FGM and that he was going to sell her on outside the camp because there were Italians who would pay good money for immoral black women. Later, after one of the beatings, one of the older women told her that several of the kapos made quite a bit of money by selling young women outside the camp but couldn't say what happened to them after that.'

'So that's what happened,' said Luke excitedly, 'if she was sold and then escaped, she'll be able to help us work out what might have happened to your cousin after Mineo.'

For the first time in ages, Layla gave a small – if sad – smile as she shook her head. 'No, fortunately for Coulibaly, she's not the type to just accept her fate. After the last rape she suffered in the centre, her owner, locked the door as he left the room afterwards but hadn't noticed that there was a faulty catch on the window. She had picked up just enough Italian to make the soldier on duty at the main gate think that she was going out to find her father and, once she was out she just walked northwards until she came to a main road. She managed to get a lorry driver to stop and made him understand that she wanted a lift.'

'A good Samaritan at last.'

'Not quite,' she said, drily, 'I only ever read a children's version of "The Good Samaritan", but I don't seem to remember the Samaritan requiring payment.'

'Shit! … Sorry… he didn't rape her as well.'

Layla raised one shoulder briefly then let it fall, 'Technically, no. He wasn't unpleasant but he made it fairly clear what he wanted. If she'd said "No" then probably the worst that would have happened would have been that she would have been made to walk but, after what she'd been through already, she imagined that far worse things would happen to her if she resisted…. At least he drove her to Catania afterwards and dropped her off outside a church before disappearing.'

'Poor kid,' said Luke, and then, 'What will happen to her now?'

'She's staying at Poggio al Vento for now. Sister Claire's arranging for her to be seen by a doctor and, if she needs to, she'll be having an abortion. Luana's trying to sort out somewhere safe for her to move on to, to try and rebuild her life.'

'An abortion? I thought you said that Poggio al Vento was run by the Church,' said Luke puzzled.

He was rewarded by a genuine smile from Layla, 'It is, but I think I also mentioned that Sister Claire is not your typical nun – neither is the other one, Sister Matilde, but I didn't have as much to do with her.'

'I agree,' said Luana, two hours later, 'if you're going to pick up the trail anywhere, it's going to be at Mineo, but it's going to be very difficult… and possibly dangerous. As it's very likely that Zahra is dead, are you really sure that you want to do this?' She looked at Layla, 'Nobody could blame you if you decided you couldn't take it any further.'

Layla smiled and shook her head, 'Thank you for offering me a way out but I feel I can't stop now,' she held up a hand to forestall an objection from Luana, 'I think that you're almost certainly right about Zahra; if she didn't drown or die of thirst or disease on the journey, she was probably sold on out of the camp and died, or has been killed since then. I'm under no illusions as to the life expectancy of either domestic slaves or under-age sex-workers but… not only am I still not convinced I've tried absolutely everything, I also now feel that I owe it to Coulibaly to try and get evidence against anyone involved.'

'Evidence!' said Luana. 'And do you really think that evidence will lead to justice? I doubt very much that you'll be able to prove anything against any of those involved in the camp and those on the outside almost certainly have some very influential people behind them. Other people have tried, and failed, to bring them to justice – what makes you think you can succeed where others, with far more resources behind them have failed?'

'They didn't all fail,' said Luke quietly.

'No,' said Luana, speaking more gently now, 'Not all of them – but even those who had the most success didn't manage to completely eradicate the problem. You can remove one cancerous growth in Italy and other malignant cells that have been lying dormant will spring up to take its place.'

'I think you're right that we should continue,' said Luke looking at Layla and although he flinched he didn't withdraw his hand when she reached out to squeeze it.

Later, when Layla had gone for a shower, Luke quickly informed Luana of his encounter with the supposed Libyan girl in the bar in Lampedusa, and told her what he had worked out from the repositioning of his driving licence. He had shied away from including the episode in the otherwise comprehensive account of his time on the island that he had given them earlier.

Luana pursed her lips and shook her head, 'I suppose it's possible but...' she paused, 'I think it's pretty unlikely... As far as anyone on the island is concerned you were just a tourist taking an interest in what was happening there, whether that be as a concerned potential do-gooder or just out of ghoulish curiosity doesn't really matter. You were the only one there who knew you had a specific reason for your interest and they must be getting used to curious tourists – let's face it, a couple of years ago, most people outside Italy had probably never heard of Lampedusa, except maybe as the name of the person who wrote *"Il Gattopardo"* – now most people in Europe have heard of it, so anyone who visits the island must be curious in one way or another. In my opinion, you've over-thought this and ignored the obvious explanation.' She looked at him, a half smile on her face.

'Which is?' he sighed, although he was already realising what the answer would be.

'You were mugged... Single tourist; too much to drink; known to be keen to meet a girl, particularly an Arab girl... in lots of ways, you were a classic target and,' she paused again to judge his mood, 'being an ex-policeman, although it's an obvious one, it's probably the hardest explanation for you to accept.'

He sighed and grimaced, letting his shoulders sag slightly and gave a rueful half-smile.

Seeing that he was prepared to accept her reasoning, Luana smiled and headed for the door to the kitchen. Just before she reached it, she half turned and said, 'Maybe, what you ought to be asking yourself is why you were so vulnerable to the charms of a girl of Arab heritage?', and with a smile she continued into the kitchen.

Chapter Seven

Unlike Lampedusa, where the previously thriving tourist trade had, for the most part, managed to survive the influx of refugees and the island's new-found notoriety, any pretensions to being a tourist destination that Mineo may once have had, were now distant memories. Luana's internet search for accommodation in the town turned out to be fruitless. Not only did the main tourist accommodation sites show no results to searches for hotels, *pensioni* or rooms to rent, even the town's own website, which was clearly making a forlorn attempt to attract the innocent tourist by making no reference to the refugee camp whose name was associated with the town and whose population now outnumbered the fixed population, gave no indication that there was any accommodation to be had amongst the noteworthy churches and historic *piazze*.

'There are always people willing to take in lodgers, if you ask locally,' suggested Layla, but both Luke and Luana vetoed this idea.

'The last thing we want to do is draw attention to ourselves, unless we can't avoid it. There's no reason why two English tourists should just turn up at an out of the way village and make a massive effort to find somewhere to stay there – particularly two English tourists driving an obviously second-hand Italian car.'

Eventually, Luana found them a small *Agriturismo* about four miles from Mineo and seven miles from the camp, just outside Grammichele, which described itself as an ideal base for visiting the impressive nearby ceramics town of Caltagirone, as well as being well situated for those wishing to walk in the surrounding countryside. 'It places you near enough to the refugee centre to make access fairly easy but, at the same time, it's far enough away not to make it obvious why you're there. It's self-catering accommodation and, as the season hasn't started yet, the owner has agreed to let you have it for ten days for two hundred euros.'

What was obviously a converted agricultural building about four hundred metres from the closest house at the edge of the village seemed particularly underwhelming as they drove towards it on a rutted track but, when Elena, the owner, opened the door for them, they were pleased to see that it was clean with modern lines inside. Although not large, it was sparsely but tastefully furnished which meant that it didn't feel claustrophobic. The furniture was simple, almost minimalist and Luke suspected that there must be an IKEA somewhere on the island. Elena showed them the main living and dining area where most of the house's features were to be found, the shower-room and the main bedroom where there was just enough room to move between the wardrobe, a double bed and a simple white chest of drawers. 'You might want to keep your luggage in there,' she said, waving her hand vaguely towards a closed door next to the bedroom door, 'it will keep your bags out of your way.'

When Elena had left them, 'in there' turned out to be a second, much smaller bedroom housing a single bed and a one-drawer bedside-table. Luke immediately threw his things on the single bed and claimed the room as his own, pre-empting any discussion.

As soon as they had sorted their things out, they returned to the car and set off for a leisurely drive around the area to get their bearings and a better feel for the distances involved. Grammichele itself had a small supermarket which they determined to visit later but, after driving through the small town they began to follow signposts towards Mineo, which sat on a hilltop around two miles away as the crow flew, but more than twice as far when it was necessary to stick to the roads.

Although they knew that the centre was some distance away from the town itself, Luke pointed out that his experience on Lampedusa had demonstrated the futility of just driving up to the entrance to the camp and hoping to find out everything immediately. It was far better to get the locals talking by showing a degree of interest, and then cross-checking the information they got from various sources to work out how much they could rely on. Consequently, after finding a car park on the edge of the village next to a football pitch, they walked into the centre and found a quiet bar with a crumbling facade just off the main square.

'*Buongiorno,*' said Luke cheerily as they stepped into the almost empty bar. A heavy-set, white-shirted man looked up from his *Gazzetta dello Sport* at the table nearest the counter, grunted a somewhat indistinct reply and, after studying the intruders for a few seconds, left the paper open on the table, heaved his way upwards and moved ponderously behind the counter, from where he eyed them balefully.

'Do you have anything to eat?'

The man glanced down at an almost empty tray inside the glass-fronted counter where three slightly sad looking doughnuts were obviously left over from the morning, then catching sight of the look on Layla's face, thought better of it, '*Salame, furmaggiu o… si puttiti aspettar 'na vintina ri minuti gli arancini fatti da me mugghieri.*'

Layla looked at Luke, completely baffled by the dialect, but Luke smiled and replied to the barman, '*Penso ca fussi meglio aspettar' gli arancini.* In the meantime, we'll have a couple of beers.' The man nodded and disappeared through a door in the wall behind him. 'He said that he can either do us cheese or salami sandwiches or we can wait twenty minutes for his wife to prepare some *arancini*. I told him that we'd wait for the *arancini*.'

'Little oranges?' said Layla, puzzled.

Luke rolled his eyes, 'Did you never read Camilleri or see the series on television? One of the earliest is called *"Montalbano's arancini"*. *Arancini* are a Sicilian speciality: large stuffed and baked rice balls – I think they're called little oranges because the oil from the stuffing seeps through the rice when they're cooking and colours the breadcrumbs that they're rolled in. Trust me; a good *arancino* is a thing of beauty.' Layla didn't look entirely convinced but appeared resigned to eat whatever arrived.

As well as a genuine desire to try the *arancini*, Luke's other motive for choosing them had been to give them time to engage the bar-owner in conversation while they waited with their beers. At first Layla tried to follow what was being said but soon found that she could understand hardly anything the barman said and devoted herself to browsing the local paper instead, knowing that Luke would tell her everything she needed to know afterwards. By the time they left, having consumed a second beer to wash down the *arancini*, which she had to admit were far better than Luke's description of them, Luke and the barman appeared to be firm friends.

'Well?' she said, as they stepped out into the bright sunshine, 'What did he say? You can't imagine how irritating it is when you can only understand one side of a conversation.'

'He said that the refugees don't really affect him or his business at all. Despite efforts by the council in the past to attract tourists, there have never really been any so his customers tend to be just the locals, as they always have been. Quite a lot of refugees walk, or get lifts over to the town to do shopping, but they hardly ever come further than the edge of the town where a couple of shops have done pretty well out of selling basics to them, but he said that the sort of things they sell aren't really the sort of things that locals are interested in so he couldn't tell me much about the shops... He said that really it doesn't make much difference having the refugee camp nearby – even before, when apparently all the houses were rented by NATO to house the families of the American Air Force personnel stationed at a base just this side of Catania, they had pretty much all they needed available in the residence itself or, if they wanted more, they'd shop in Catania or in some big retail mall that's been developed between Catania and Enna over the last few years; he was a bit vague about exactly where... That was about it really. It would have seemed odd to show more than just tourist curiosity and he'd probably have clammed up if I'd pressed him, so mainly we talked about oranges and football.' He smiled and she rolled her eyes.

'I suppose that the only other thing we can do here then, is to go and have a look at these two shops; get an idea of what sort of thing they sell, and how many people use them. Then we need to work out how to move forward.'

'OK,' he said with a shrug and, taking her arm without thinking, moved off in the general direction that the bar owner had indicated.

The shops turned out to have been set up on the ground floor of some fairly ugly five storey modern buildings on the north-eastern edge of the town in an area that Luke thought must date from the late seventies or early eighties. Each apartment on the four residential floors above the shop units had a large balcony looking out over the extensive plain and towards the foothills of Mount Etna. The views were stunning, thought Luke, despite the stark modernity of the buildings which contrasted with the older part of the town.

They initially strolled past the shops, heading down the road towards the open countryside until they reached what appeared to be the final tumbledown building that could reasonably be described as forming part of Mineo. As they went down the road they passed a group of five young men going in the opposite direction. They were all jet black, wearing slightly faded t-shirts that must have once been in a range of bright colours and trousers in various states of disrepair: two wearing jeans and the other three trousers of indeterminate material; only one of the young men wore shoes which, Luke guessed, that, had been rescued from a rubbish bin somewhere. Luke and Layla smiled as they passed the men but received no answering smile.

'We could try asking one of them,' said Luke, leaning against the wall and looking in the general direction of the camp, before they turned back towards the town.

'No,' said Layla, 'there's no point. Remember that inside the camp they're pretty much split up by nationality and ethnic group. They definitely weren't from any of the Arabic nations so they wouldn't really be able to tell us much of any use. We really need to make contact with some of the Arabs, preferably Libyans, and even then, I doubt that we'll get much information when they're in a group. When I was covering the Arab Spring, people were willing to talk, off the record, when they were on their own, but otherwise they were terrified that they might be reported and punished for anything they said.'

They walked in silence for a while, their eyes taken more by the distant, postcard-like view of the still snow-capped Etna to their right where reflected sunlight was dazzling against a backdrop of dark clouds. The brilliant white with the faintest of pink tinges seemed unreal, intensifying the darkness of the sky reminding Luke of paintings of Vesuvius by Joseph Wright that he'd seen on a school trip to Derby Museum many years before. Etna wasn't Vesuvius he thought, but they had more points in common than differences, just like people. 'I'm not sure you're right,' he said suddenly as his unconscious linked his two trains of thought together.

'What?' said Layla, startled out of her own thoughts.

'I was thinking about volcanoes. About how each one is different to the next, but how really they're just different examples of the same phenomena – and it's just like people, isn't it?' He could tell from the slight furrow on her brow that he needed to do a better job of explaining. 'You said that there was no point our talking to the young men we saw because they weren't Arabs, but that's not the point is it?'

'But I…'

He interrupted, silencing her with an apologetic hand gesture, 'I'm not saying you were wrong about not trying to talk to those particular men; I'm sure you're right about people who're part of a group being unwilling to talk for a whole load of reasons, but I think you're wrong to ignore them because they're not Arabs.' He had her full attention now but could see he still needed to convince her. 'Look; what we're fairly sure is happening, both because it's logical and because people like Vichi have more or less told us, is that a significant proportion of the unaccompanied minors who go missing, as well as some of the more vulnerable adults, end up as either domestic slaves or as victims of sexual abuse and exploitation.' She nodded. 'Well, that applies to refugees of all ethnic groups, doesn't it?'

She thought for a moment, looking down at her feet as she walked slowly on. When she looked up, he could see that her eyes were moist. 'Yes,' she said, very quietly.

He stopped and took hold of her forearm, gripping it slightly more tightly than he'd intended and forcing her to stop alongside him. 'Yes, what?' he asked.

'You're right. I'm sorry. I suppose when I said I accepted that Zahra was almost certainly dead, I wasn't really telling the truth… I don't mean I was lying – not deliberately anyway – or if I was, I was lying to myself rather than lying to you and Luana. I know logic says that Zahra's gone and… and I really do feel that I should carry on for Coulibaly's sake, but…'

'But,' continued Luke in a much softer tone than before, 'It's must be very hard to completely give up on someone when they're probably the only family you have left. It's alright, I understand – or at least I think I do – and I'm not blaming you for it at all. I'm just saying that I don't necessarily think we should limit ourselves to a single ethnic group. Whatever has happened to Zahra, has almost certainly happened to Ghanaians, Sudanese, Syrians and everyone else, so I don't think we should rule them out – and don't forget, some of them will speak pretty good English, which will make communication a lot easier.'

She was silent for a few seconds, digesting what he had said and he thought she was about to object, but then she looked up again and gave a little smile. 'Thankyou. I'm really glad that you're here to explain to me when I'm getting things wrong,' and she turned and began walking again.

She agreed with a nod of the head when he suggested that they take a roundabout route back to Grammichele and drive past the camp on the way, just to get a rough idea of the lie of the land and help them plan their next step.

A fairly narrow road, in need of resurfacing, dropped northwards out of the town towards the extensive plain that separated them the distant slopes of the volcano which now appeared less distinct as the leaden sky against which it had previously been set had now softened, while the air in front of them appeared to have thickened. After a while, they turned left onto a slightly wider, better maintained road that continued to snake its way down the hillside towards the plane between a retaining wall on one side and a crash barrier on the other. There were occasional small clusters of olive trees, and at times the road was fringed by individual olives that had been allowed to grow tall and were obviously uncared for but which, suggested to Luke that the entire hillside must once have been covered with olives.

As they approached the plain, the land below them and to their right, which had previously seemed a sea of a richer green, resolved itself into individual trees, carefully planted in evenly spaced rows and covering several square kilometres of land. These, he realised were citrus plantations, producing many of the oranges for which the island was famous, and this was confirmed as they approached the bottom of the hill and found themselves surrounded by orange trees on both sides. There were still occasional olives left growing by the side of the road together with the odd clump of prickly pears which added variety to the scene. Once they had crossed the main Caltagirone-Catania road, they were again immersed in rich agricultural land. In several of the orange groves they could see figures hard at work snipping the stems of oranges and placing them carefully in blue plastic trays while at the gateway to one of the groves a fork-lift truck was loading a pallet full of the plastic trays onto the back of a lorry. Although they could see the occasional white face amongst the workers, the impression was that most of the labour force was composed of immigrants and Luke wondered how many of them were from the camp.

They also passed several small groups of migrants walking slowly along the road, mainly in the direction they were going. It was noticeable that the groups were either made up of men or of women, never, as far as they could tell, of both. Several of the women were carrying bags, sometimes in their hands but mainly balanced on their heads. 'I hope they haven't carried those all the way from Mineo; it's more than five miles,' commented Luke.

'I'm pretty sure they have,' said Layla, 'the women from some of the tribes in Central Africa have to walk for miles each day carrying provisions. You can't expect the men to do it, can you? Even if they've got nothing else to do.' Luke decided that it was better not to reply to this, but instead, as they rounded a bend, indicated a large area full of modern buildings ahead of them.

'That must be the centre.'

Although, as far as they could see, every building was the same, arranged in neat straight rows, superficially, and from a few hundred metres away, the centre did not appear unpleasant. It was almost entirely surrounded by a screen of orange trees which distracted one's eyes from the security fence that ran all the way round, and the hills to the North also helped soften the sharp contours of the buildings. As they got nearer, the security fence became more noticeable and, although he didn't slow down too much, Luke was sure that the fence was made of razor-wire, while lamps were positioned so that the fence could be illuminated at night.

In the car-park outside the main entrance, two military troop carriers were parked along with two *carabinieri* jeeps and several other official looking vehicles. A small group of people was collected outside the main entrance where two soldiers, loosely holding sub-machine guns and wearing flak jackets seemed to be in control of a heavy barrier at the gate. Through the gate they caught a glimpse of the start of one of the streets; although the buildings were clearly modern, the kind of cloned semi-detached dwellings that could be found on many suburban housing estates, each was almost covered with drying washing and the intended front gardens were crammed full with a variety of objects.

Neither spoke until they had turned left at a junction just after the centre and taken the general direction of Grammichele. 'It reminds me of open-prison… except that the prison officers weren't armed.'

'You're the expert… but it made me think of the descriptions I've read of the ghettos that Jews were forced to live in during the war. What purpose can it possible serve to cram together several thousand, mainly young people, in the middle of nowhere? People who've made it this far are some of the most resourceful and enterprising people you could hope to meet, and they're just being hidden away and forgotten about.' She shook her head, sadly.

'One of the articles I read on the internet last night was saying that it was the idea of Berlusconi's Home Secretary Roberto Maroni under the last government. It had been built and managed by a big Parma based construction company and rented out to the American Forces for several years for an enormous amount of money. When the Americans pulled out, they agreed an even more lucrative contract with Maroni who saw it as an opportunity to gather most of the asylum seekers in Italy all together in one place. An isolated location had suited the Americans because, after 9/11 they were very security conscious while it suited Maroni because it meant that, as far as possible, the immigrants were out of sight and out of mind. He claimed that because it had been an American base it had all the facilities necessary to ensure that the refugees could live with dignity, instead, most of the charities and aid agencies warned that it would soon become over-crowded and be used as a dumping ground, but the opposition couldn't agree a united approach amongst themselves so Maroni's proposal went through.'

'And now?'

Luke gave a humourless laugh. 'And now… it's a mess. You know what that girl told you about conditions inside. The government recognises that it's a mess but hasn't got the money, or the political capital, to do anything about it. A lot less immigrants risk the journey over from Libya during the winter, so the world's media are ignoring Italy for the moment and making everyone think that the only refugee route is now the overland route through the Balkans, or the much shorter sea-crossing from Turkey to Kos. As soon as the weather warms up and more people start to risk the longer sea-crossing, they'll turn their attention back to Italy. Funnily enough, most journalists seem to prefer to spend their summers reporting from sunny islands with nice beaches, rather than from muddy fields on the borders of Austria, Hungary and Slovakia.'

They bought a large, firm white fish at the supermarket, which Luke then roasted on a bed of potatoes, leeks and carrots, liberally drizzled with local olive oil and white wine and sprinkled with parsley; the rest of the bottle of wine, they drank.

When Luke logged onto his computer while Layla washed the pots, he saw that he had a message from Luana – 'Ring me, as soon as possible.'

'I think I've found something that will interest you… it may or may not be relevant… but it's definitely interesting.'

'OK. I'm all ears.'

What she said next made him breathe in sharply and his nostrils flare with anger.

'You know that the centres for refugees and asylum seekers are run by groups known as co-operatives which have been approved as providers of assistance on behalf of, but not technically part of government, don't you?'

'Uh huh.'

'Well, the C.A.R.A at Mineo is run by a consortium of these co-operatives, as is the first response centre on Lampedusa. Some of the leading co-operatives are involved in both consortia and one of these, is very closely linked to a company controlled by Giacinto Marelli.' Luana stopped and waited.

'The Giacinto Marelli? The former Interior Minister who avoided prison but who had to step down from public life ten years ago?'

'The very same. He got away with it then partly because of his network of influential friends and partly because the then President was insistent on limiting the bad publicity. He's been out of the public eye for the last few years but he's been busy building up his financial and business interests.'

'OK,' he took a deep breath. He knew that he would love to see Marelli behind bars but he also knew that he mustn't let that cloud his judgement: he might not have taken much away from his time with the police, but not getting emotionally involved had been one thing that had been drummed into them from the first day of training onwards. 'Are we sure that this helps us rather than just being "interesting" information?'

'Can you come to Catania tomorrow afternoon – there's someone I'd like you to talk to? He should be able to help us decide whether Marelli's involvement is significant or not.'

'Alright. I can't think of any reason why not. What time do you need us there? And where should we meet?'

Luana suggested that the best place would probably be at her apartment as they could be sure of privacy and they arranged to meet there at around five o'clock.

When he informed Layla of the arrangement, she said that it was probably a better use of time if he went alone as she thought that she would have a better chance of making contact with some of the women from the camp if she were on her own. As that seemed reasonable, he agreed.

In the morning they drove the ten miles to Caltagirone, partly because they wanted to get an idea whether any of the residents from the centre were travelling that way to find work each day, and partly because Luke felt that he couldn't miss the opportunity of seeing the magnificent tiled steps that ran up the hill at the centre of the old town. They parked in a large, almost deserted multi-storey car park on the south-western edge of the city where the built up area came to a sudden end as the ground fell away steeply into a wide valley. Only the top floor of the car-park protruded above the road with the rest being built into the hillside below.

As they walked from the car-park towards the centre they came to a junction where a sign indicated that the steps to Santa Maria del Monte were in one direction and that there was a market in the other. Layla told Luke to go ahead and that she would either catch up with him at the top of the steps or, give him a ring in about an hour to find out where was the best place to meet up again. Luke agreed, pleased that he would be able to take as much time as he wished to view the glazed terracotta tiles that, if his guidebook was to be believed, had no equal anywhere else in the world and were the best and most potent reminder of the island's Moorish history.

The whole of the old centre was in a harmonious baroque style, having been almost completely reconstructed after the devastating earthquake of 1693 that had destroyed many of the old Sicilian towns, and the steps, or staircase as the guidebook referred to it, was certainly the highlight. He was lucky that when he arrived the steps were facing the sun bringing out all the brightness of the glazed colours. The tiles lining each of the one hundred and forty steps had a different design although the whole sight was unified as the dominant colours on each row of tiles were blue and yellow. To each side of the steps there were several ceramics shops and ceramics workshops producing every conceivable brightly-coloured ceramic product from spoon-rests to dining tables big enough to seat eight people in comfort. Most of the shops and ateliers sported signs proudly proclaiming "English spoken here – *Mann sprecht Deutsch – En parle Francais*" with occasional examples of other languages, making it very clear that, as much as ceramics, the key industry in Caltagirone was tourism. Several of the shops also had signs offering goods at sale prices although he noticed that only a handful of shops actually had prices on display and he assumed that the sale prices offered by the keen-eyed shop-keepers may well depend on how affluent they judged each client to be. Despite being sure that the larger products would be far beyond his price range he could not help admiring their beauty and the craftsmanship that had gone into them.

When he had finally looked carefully at every step and visited several of the shops and workshops, he crossed the road that ran across the top of the steps and looked at the large tiled panel depicting what he assumed was a key moment from the town's history, as a sign to one side informed him that the scene represented the "Deliverance of the Bell of Altavilla to Caltagirone" - he promised himself that he would look it up on the internet later. After studying the panel, he sat down on the step in front of it and leaned back against the plinth, closing his eyes and letting the sun fall on his face.

'Hey! Wake up!' came a voice containing a hint of amusement. 'You didn't answer your phone.'

He stretched and then reached into his pocket for the offending implement. "2 Missed Calls". 'Sorry. I had a look in some of the pottery shops and there must have been a poor signal. Never mind. You've found me now... time for a *caffè*... I know I could do with one... What have you been buying?' he added, noticing the bag she was carrying.

She raised a shoulder dismissively, 'Nothing much. Toiletries and a change of clothes so I look less like a tourist when I try and make contact with some of the women from the camp later.'

'I noticed a bar just down one of the little side streets off the steps', he said, his conversational resources regarding shopping for clothes and toiletries being virtually non-existent.

'OK. Lead the way. You're buying after making me walk all the way up those steps while you were having a rest.'

'Fair enough. I think I can manage that.'

After Caltagirone, they had time for a quick *spaghetti alla Norma* back at the house and then Layla gave him a lift to Grammichele station. 'I should be back by about eight tomorrow morning. It doesn't look as if there's a train I can get back tonight, but there's one about half past five in the morning. Let me know if you discover anything useful and I'll do the same...OK?' In reply, he received a casual wave and what appeared to be a nod of the head as she pulled away from the front of the station.

The train was almost on time, getting into Catania just after ten past four and giving him enough time to walk to Luana's and pick up a bunch of flowers on the way. *'Ciao,'* she said, taking the flowers at the door, 'No Layla?'

He shook his head, 'Not this time. There were things she wanted to do… I've come by train so, if you don't mind, I'll need to kip on your sofa. I'll be away before five to get the first train back, so if I'm nice and quiet you won't notice I'm here.'

She gave a little smile. 'That's OK. The bed that Layla slept in is still made up. You may as well sleep there. Go through to the living room while I put these in some water. The person I want you to meet should be here anytime now.' In fact, hardly had he sat down when there were two short rings on the doorbell, and a minute later, Luana showed in a tallish man, in his late thirties and dressed in jeans and a jeans jacket and with an upright purposeful stance and air of authority. He stood up.

'Giò, this is Luke, the person I was telling you about. Luke, this is Giò; Giò and I did our initial training together, many years ago.'

'Steady on, Lu. It's not that long ago.'

She gave another smile, and Luke noticed that this one was a much warmer one than the one he'd been treated to on his arrival. He sat down again as did the newcomer. 'Are you still with the force?' he asked to help break the ice.

'I am, and thanks to the *Legge Fornero*, I will be for the next thirty-two years – if I survive that long.'

'Legge Fornero?'

'Changes to pension ages, brought in in 2012', he explained. 'No jobs for young people, but save money on pensions by making people work much longer. It's almost impossible to get round it.'

'It's incredible. All over Europe, governments of all sorts seem to think that they can save money by making everyone work longer, except the very rich, of course, who only have to work if they feel the need to make even more money that they'll never have the opportunity to spend. How they possibly expect people doing hard physical jobs to be able to perform effectively when they're in their sixties, I've no idea.'

The Italian spread his hands wide, 'You're right, although, at least in Italy, the current politicians are not entirely to blame,' Luke raised a quizzical eyebrow, 'before the breakup of the communist block, when the west's main concern was to stop the spread of socialism, other countries were happy for Italian governments to run up massive deficits to convince people of the benefits of capitalism, and part of that was by paying out some of the most generous pensions in the world, and people came to expect that as their right. I have a relative, not, I'm afraid to say, a particularly bright one, who, because she married the son of a bank manager, walked into an undemanding job as a bank clerk when she was nineteen, and was then able to retire on a 'baby pension' when she was thirty nine. There are over half a million "baby pensioners" who receive an average of seventeen and a half thousand euros a year, usually for over forty years, without doing anything, and then you've got all the "normal" pensioners who get a pension equal to their final salary. And all these people are respectable voters, so no political party can ever get a mandate to solve the problem and they hope to get away with it by just making those who don't yet have problems work longer and longer. We're an economically illiterate population I'm afraid.'

'I see you didn't waste any time in getting onto your favourite hobby-horse,' said Luana, who had slipped back into the room unnoticed carrying a small maiolica tray bearing three coffees and a sugar bowl.

'Sorry,' said Giò, with an apologetic look, 'We had another memo this morning about reducing our use of official pens and needing to be aware of budget pressures.' He shook his head resignedly. 'Anyway, you didn't ask me along to talk to Luke about economics, did you?'

'Not directly,' replied Luana, 'but most things are linked to economics, at least in the broader sense of money, aren't they?' He gave a small nod in agreement. 'Right,' said Luana, in a more business-like tone, turning towards Luke, 'As I said, Giò and I have known each other, and been friends for a long time and I approached him because I thought he might be able to help. Giò is a *vice commissario* stationed in Caltagirone, so he's fairly well informed on everything to do with the CARA Mineo. Giò...'

Giò sighed and then sat upright and breathed in. 'I take it that you've seen the CARA and have an idea of the layout,' Luke inclined his head in confirmation, 'OK. You will have seen then, that there's always a *Carabinieri* vehicle and a couple of military vehicles outside the main gate... The *Carabinieri* presence is mainly a symbolic one as the authorities are very sensitive to accusations from civil rights and anti-racism groups that the CARA is just a concentration camp run by the military. The officers who are there, don't want to be there; the *Maresciallo* in Caltagirone is furious because he's understaffed and he has to use three men for purely decorative purposes. Whenever there's any trouble in the camp – and we always see more when the weather gets very hot – and the migrants are feeling particularly bored and frustrated – they have to rely on the regular army troops who're there to restore order. Day to day security within the camp, including ID checks at the gate are carried out by private security contractors employed directly by one of the co-operatives forming part of the consortium that has the contract to run the centre. In the state police force, we have little regular involvement with the camp except when specific crimes are reported to us for investigation.

'However, not only do we have a good working relationship with the *Comando dei Carabinieri* locally – despite the commonly believed myth that we're in direct competition – but we also share some of our office space with some of the officers from the *Guardia di Finanza* who've been posted here as part of the ongoing *Mafia Capitale* investigations.' Luke gave an enquiring look.

'Don't worry,' said Luana, 'it's not something you need to know the details of; suffice it to say that an enquiry was set up two years ago to look into alleged links between the Mafia and some of the co-operatives involved in managing the refugee crisis.'

'OK. I'll try to avoid unnecessary details. Anyway, although what happens in the camp is not our business, we do have to deal with what happens outside the camp. Each evening, groups of young women are picked up by vans on the road outside the camp and taken to various places to work as prostitutes, before being picked up again and taken back to the camp at dawn. When we stop the vans, the drivers insist that they're just doing a good deed in taking the girls out to enjoy themselves; the girls refuse to say anything and the drivers claim not to know what the girls do when they leave them, so we can't do anything. Occasionally, those who control the prostitutes from the camp, stray into areas where prostitution and other rackets are controlled by local gangs, and we end up with violence, which is how we get involved. The prostitutes run by gangs within the camp are only really relevant because it shows you how easy it is for inmates to come and go from the camp.

'What really interested Luana when she applied the thumb screws to get information out of me, 'he flashed a smile at her, 'is what the *Guardia di Finanza* are looking at. The consortium administering the centre is paid between thirty and thirty five euros per day for each inmate, depending on various factors to do with age, provenance, length of stay and so on, that we don't need to go into. Each member of the consortium has its own responsibilities and area of expertise and the money is divided amongst them on a formula they've come up with themselves. Obviously, the more refugees there are, the more money is paid to the consortium, so the Regional authorities insist that they have an accurate, robust system for controlling the numbers and ensuring that payments are accurate. Now… when inmates arrive, they are fingerprinted and given a chipped "badge" that has to be swiped each time they leave or enter the centre, whenever they eat in the refectory and whenever they purchase anything in the official on-site shop. If a badge is not used for forty eight hours, it flashes up a warning and then, if it's not used in the next twenty-four hours the chip is cancelled and the person to whom it was issued is presumed to have left and no further payment on their account is made.'

'Told straight, it sounds like an effective system. There'll be small overpayments relating to the seventy-two hour periods but these presumably balance out against the cost and hassle of reinstating someone if their badge is cancelled too soon… But, I suspect you're going to tell me that the system doesn't work as well as it should.'

Giò smiled, 'Luana told me that you used to be with the police. If I hadn't known, I'd have assumed you had a devious mind. As I'm sure you can see, the system only works effectively if those who are administering it are doing so honestly. The central computer that registers the badges' usage is inside the centre, under the control of one of the co-operatives. Every day they submit a report to the regional Prefecture in Catania showing the number of refugees present and the payments to them are calculated weekly on the basis of these figures. What the *Guardia di Finanza* believe, and are currently trying to prove is that the figures are falsified and that the centre continues to claim its daily thirty-five euros for inmates for weeks, maybe even months after they have left. One estimate I heard was that in the last two years over a million euros has been paid over to fund the care of migrants who have left. Some of the migrants who've disappeared will have fled of their own accord, frustrated by the long waits to be processed and determined to make their own way towards Northern Europe, but mainly it seems as if there are people within the co-operatives who, for a price, will arrange for migrants to bypass the official processes and set them on their way.'

'A million euros! That's not a bad bonus from a business where you're already making a reasonable amount of profit. Are we talking about a scam organised by local employees and managers, or does this go higher?'

'*Bravo!* Exactly the right question. If the *Guardia di Finanza* thought it was just a few local employees they'd have swooped already and arrested those responsible but, from what I hear, they're fairly sure that at least one of the co-operatives sees it as a core part of their business. If you think about it, and think about the recent Volkswagen emissions scandal, there have to be people high up who can make the system work – making sure the computer software doesn't create problems, arranging onward transfers and building up political connections to protect themselves.'

This was going to get far more complicated than they'd anticipated thought Luke. 'Luana mentioned a connection to Giacinto Marelli when she rang me yesterday; I assume that he still has very influential political friends.'

'You could say that,' responded Giò drily. 'Since his "retirement" from politics, he's been developing his business interests and rebuilding his reputation by getting involved in a number of "good-works" and helping set up co-operatives to carry out "projects of social value". He's been very clever about it; he manages to give the appearance of wanting to avoid publicity, while at the same time allowing friendly right wing journalists to drop veiled hints about how much good he continues to do for the country, even in retirement.'

'I don't suppose by any chance that one of the co-operatives with which he is involved is the one monitoring the number of presences in the CARA di Mineo is it?' Giò's little smile confirmed that Luke had understood exactly what Marelli's involvement was.

Unfortunately, both Giò and Luana were sure that the control structures of the organisation would be so intricate that it would be impossible to trace a direct chain of responsibility all the way up to Marelli, so that even when the *Guardia di Finanza* swooped to close down the operation and arrests were made, they would be unable to touch Marelli and other shady figures who undoubtedly were the ultimate beneficiaries of the fraud.

Luke expressed surprise that Giò had been able to obtain so much information about the investigation even though the state police were not involved. The *Guardia di Finanza*'s security couldn't be up to much if he had been able to find out as much as he had just because they were sharing the same building.

'I'd like to take the credit for my superb detecting skills but my conscience won't let me. I was contacted by colleagues in Porto Empedocle, as they came across evidence suggesting that a group of traffickers that they were investigating had links to the CARA di Mineo. Unlike in Caltagirone, the Police in Porto Empedocle have a less trusting relationship with the *Carabinieri*, so they contacted my office instead... What we are fairly sure is happening is that traffickers who manage to land refugees who don't get picked up by the system, are bringing them to Mineo, issuing them with the badges of people who have left without their departures being recorded and effectively having their clients housed and fed by the state while they organise the next stage of their journey. We could prove this and shut the route down very quickly with a raid on the CARA but, when I went to the *Questore* for authorisation, permission was denied. Later that day, a captain from the *Guardia di Finanza* came into my office, shut the door, and explained how my operation had to be placed on hold until they were ready to move on theirs. He pointed out that as the money being paid out for the recycled badges obviously overlapped with the money trail they were following, it couldn't be seen as a separate operation and that it therefore fell under their overall control'.

After Giò had finished explaining, he didn't stay much longer and left after wishing Luke luck and pointing out that everything was completely off the record and that the meeting had never taken place.

Luana suggested that they ate in a pleasant *pizzeria* she knew where the windows faced out towards the gardens of the Villa Bellini. It would be fairly busy, she said, but she was known there so there would be no difficulty in getting a table and the chatter of the other customers would mean that their own conversation wouldn't be overheard. Luana advised Luke to try the *pizza con zucchina e caciotta affumicata* although she herself chose a salad. The *pizza* was cooked perfectly and the *caciotta* made a change from the more usual toppings although he did find that it was a little smaller than the ones he was used to eating on Lipari.

He set out to her what they had done so far and explained how they hoped to make contact with some of the residents and try to get more details of what happened to unaccompanied minors in the camp. Now that he had met Giò, he hoped that they may be able to take a more focussed approach when they made contact; it seemed unlikely that the large numbers of unaccompanied minors who were unaccounted for were being taken out singly, so their disappearances were almost certainly linked to the groups who were being moved on by the traffickers.

'Be very careful. Most of the refugees are fantastic people who've overcome all sorts of obstacles, risking their lives, just to get this far, and all they want to do is fit in and have the opportunity to make some sort of decent life for themselves and their families. The problem is that there are a few bad apples in there, traffickers who make money by exploiting human misery and vulnerability, and they gather around them some of the disaffected young men who've become frustrated by the lack of progress with their applications, who feel that Italy and Europe have let them down. And remember, we're not just talking about third world peasants who've been displaced from their fields: we're talking about well-educated, resourceful young people who have a lot to contribute to society. There are trained lawyers, doctors, accountants, teachers, any profession you care to mention amongst the refugees and, because we're overwhelmed by the numbers and underwhelmed by the lack of meaningful support from some of the other European countries, we don't manage to process them effectively, or even humanely.'

'And that makes them dangerous.' It wasn't a question but she treated it as though it was.

'It does. The traffickers are dangerous anyway; they put profits before people and have no loyalty to anyone other than themselves – get in their way and they'll kill you without a second thought. The others have come to believe that the traffickers and the people they're working with outside the camp, are the people who can get them out of there. They might not like them but, when you've made it so far, almost certainly having had to make use of unscrupulous individuals and organisations on the way, why stop now when they see freedom as within touching distance. Once they're away from here and finally settled in Germany or Sweden, they'll put all this behind them and be model citizens – but until then…'

He smiled and reaching out, placed a hand on top of hers as he said, 'Don't worry. I've no intention of putting myself in any danger, and I can't imagine that Layla has either.'

She withdrew her hand from underneath his and looked him in the eye. 'Layla. I think it's about time that we had a talk about Layla.'

Chapter Eight

He bought copies of both the *Gazzetta di Sicilia* and *Espresso* magazine at the station to read during the slow train journey back to Grammichele, but found that the effect of having got up just before five added to the rhythmic rocking and clacking of the slow train meant that he couldn't read more than two paragraphs without falling into a doze. By the time he stepped out onto the platform at Grammichele, he felt stiff and far more tired and irritable than when he'd set off. It didn't help that he knew that Luana's criticisms of him the previous evening had been mainly justified, even if he hadn't accepted it at the time. Before he set off walking back to the house, he took out his phone and composed a text - "Thanks for hospitality. Agree you were right. Not sure can change. Will try" - then sent it to Luana and sighed.

When he let himself in the house just before eight, he hoped that Layla would be up and that he'd timed it right for a coffee, but the house was in silence. The car keys were on the kitchen table and the door to the main bedroom was closed so he quietly prepared the *macchinetta del caffè* himself and then sat down on a more comfortable chair to browse through *Espresso*.

After reading through a long article explaining the dangers and ramification of the referendum on constitutional reform that Prime Minister Matteo Renzi had called for later in the year, he looked at his watch and saw that it was just after nine. He knocked on the bedroom door, *'Caffè?'*

There was no reply so he knocked again, a little harder, 'Morning!'

There was still no sound so, frowning slightly and suddenly finding that he was holding his breath, he turned the handle and pushed the door open. There was no-one there. The bed had been made but there was nothing to tell him whether it had been made that morning or the day before. He was fairly sure that the top hanging on the back of the chair was the one that she had been wearing when she dropped him off at the station the previous afternoon – but he wasn't sure. There was nothing to give him a clue to where she had gone.

Aware that his heart was beating faster than it normally did, he returned to the main room and looked around to see if there was a message he'd missed, but there wasn't.

When he'd checked that there wasn't a note under the bag he dropped onto the sofa when he'd arrived, he opened his bedroom door to throw the bag in rather than put it down again in the main room. There was a sheet of printer paper on his bed. "Ciao. Hope everything went well in Catania last night. Look forward to hearing about it. I'm going into the camp. I have got my phone – just in case – but it will be switched off most of the time. I don't think I'll be back until tomorrow afternoon or maybe the following morning. Should be fun ;-) Layla" and then the previous day's date.

'Damn!' and he screwed the paper up and threw it on the floor, giving it a kick for good measure as he went back through to the main room. 'Now what?' he said to himself angrily.

When he had calmed down, he decided that there was no point waiting in the house; she had her phone and, if she needed a lift back at some point, it was probably more sensible if he were nearer to the centre. He supposed that he might as well go back to Mineo and see if he could make contact with anyone from the centre who went over to use the shops.

His day was very unproductive: he tried to approach several young men to draw them into conversation, but it was clear that they viewed him with distrust and lost interest in him when they discovered he was unable to give them money or offer them a lift off the island. Some of them spoke some Italian, clearly having spent some time in the refugee camps, but mainly it was far easier to speak in English, or even French. One group of young men asked him how long it would take to get from France to England, but clearly didn't believe him when he tried to describe what he'd heard about the appalling conditions in Calais's jungle, and the intransigence of the British authorities even where there were clearly justified asylum claims and where refugees had relatives already established in Britain which should have allowed them to be fast tracked. The main speaker in the group said that he must be lying as the queen would not allow such things. He gave up trying to explain.

He stayed in Mineo until he judged that there was only about half an hour's daylight left, and then drove home, going slowly past the gates of the refugee village on his way, but without seeing any sign of Layla. Not feeling like eating out or cooking, he bought half a roast chicken from a *rosticceria* and devoured it as soon as he got home almost without registering the flavour. He reached for the bottle of *grappa* but then, when he already had his hand on the stopper, changed his mind, aware that he might have to drive later. He put the television on and surfed through the channels, mainly because he could think of nothing else to do, but found nothing to distract his thoughts from worrying about Layla.

There was no point going to bed as he knew he wouldn't be able to sleep, so he lay on the sofa, dozing for a few minutes every now and again but waking with a start if his phone fell out of his hand or if there was the slightest noise inside or outside the house.

By six in the morning he could stand it no longer. The larger of the two *macchinette* in the house was designed to make four *caffés* and he used it to make a very large cup of *espresso* into which he stirred three spoonfuls of sugar before knocking it back with a grimace. Then he went out.

He had just pointed the car in the direction of the refugee centre when his phone buzzed to announce an incoming message. Grabbing the phone from the passenger seat as he checked the rear-view mirror, he pulled the car untidily to the side of the road. On his first attempt to unlock the handset, he keyed in the code incorrectly in his haste and had to start again, forcing himself to keep calm. 'Junction SS417 with road to Gram. 20 minutes if poss – if not will walk'.

When he got there, it appeared to be quite a complicated junction but he soon realised that appearances were deceptive as two of the roads were slip-roads that had never been completed, and he reversed into one of these before getting out of the car to wait.

After a few minutes he saw a bus coming from the direction of Catania stop about a quarter of a mile down the road before setting off again and continuing along the road until it passed him heading towards Caltagirone. He could see that one person had got off the bus and was making their way in his direction. As the person came closer and the outlines became clearer, the figure resolved itself into that of an old, slightly hunchbacked woman with a significant stoop and a limp, dressed in a long brownish chador, that he suspected may once have been red, which was raised so that it covered most of a black *hijab*.

Aware of the impropriety if he appeared to be staring, he turned slightly to one side and lowered his eyes as the woman approached, hoping that Layla would be there soon.

When she was within ten metres of him, the woman stopped and straightened, the stoop suddenly disappearing. 'Good morning!'

He was unable to move for a moment, unable to sort out what he felt as she stood smiling at him as if they were playing a game, then a sense of anger got the upper hand and he strode forward and gripped her shoulders tightly. The smile disappeared from her face. 'Do you have any idea how much danger you've put yourself in? How stupid and irresponsible this crazy adventure of yours was? It's not a game. The people behind the trafficking and all the rest of it have got too much to lose to allow some bloody amateur to just wander in thinking they can solve all the world's problems. It's just unbelievable.' he almost shouted.

Although there were tears in her eyes, her face had set hard and she jerked her right arm up against his forearm to knock his hand off one shoulder and then pushed past him and headed in the direction of Grammichele.

Still fuming, he watched her walk into the distance, not stooping any more but with a limp. She didn't look back.

After nearly five minutes, he felt slightly calmer, although not, he realised, in any state to have a rational conversation. 'Fuck, fuck, fuck, fuck, fuck,' he shouted and kicked the side of the car, which caused him enough pain to give him something else to think about. He slid into the car, breathed deeply for a few seconds and then turned the key.

She had covered about six hundred metres when he caught up with her and then stopped the car about thirty metres beyond. He got out as she approached and, leaving the door open, placed the keys on top of the car and said, 'Take the car. I'd rather walk,' before turning and setting off without waiting for a reply.

The little Mercedes accelerated past him almost immediately and he winced as he heard the gearbox protest at a mistimed change.

The forty minutes it took him to get back to the house helped him get a better sense of perspective and even to feel ashamed of his reaction to her reappearance. He told himself he had always made it clear that they were only co-operating because they both felt strongly about what was happening to the refugees. She had her own strong reasons because of Zahra and because she had been affected by Coulibaly's experiences. He'd agreed to help because if he did so she would keep away from him in future and he could move on from his past, so if she chose to put herself in danger, it didn't really matter to him. He told himself this several times, but each time he repeated it to himself he found it less convincing. His reaction had been over the top; it was entirely her own business whether she put herself in danger or not, wasn't it? What difference did it make to him if she got herself killed? That would get her off his back wouldn't it? But still he failed to convince himself with his own arguments; he remembered how he'd felt when he'd returned home the previous morning and not been able to find her; he knew how he'd felt during the night when she still hadn't come home and he hadn't heard anything. He thought about what Luana had said to him.

She had showered and changed into a loose fitting pyjama bottom below one of his t-shirts and was sitting on a chair with her legs pulled up beneath her and cradling a cup of peppermint tea between her hands. She looked at him with trepidation in her eyes which were red and slightly swollen, but remained silent as if waiting for him to establish the tone. Suddenly, it was as if a wall of tiredness hit him. He steadied himself by leaning against the doorframe, and then, pushing himself upright with an effort, muttered, 'Give me five minutes,' and disappeared into the bathroom.

When he re-emerged, wearing a towelling bath-robe and with tousled, towel-dried hair, there was a cup of tea waiting on the table for him. He placed his hands around it without thinking to raise it to his lips. 'I'm sorry… I over-reacted.'

She had moved almost imperceptibly towards him when he'd said he was sorry, but seemed to sway back as he said he had over-reacted. She uncoiled her legs, stood up and moved over to the window where she rested her head against the glass apparently undergoing some internal struggle.

When she turned to face him, there were tears flowing down her cheeks again, although she seemed oblivious to them. '"Over-reacted" - but you still feel that a reaction was needed – that it's up to you to decide what I should do.'

He closed his eyes and let the air in his lungs escape through his nose. Then, opening his eyes again, he said quietly, 'That's not what I meant. What I'm trying to say is that I was really, really worried about you and what could have happened to you. I know that it's not really any of my business but I couldn't stand the idea of you being in danger – especially when I couldn't do anything about it.' She looked at him for a moment and then came over and sat down again.

'Drink your tea, before it goes cold,' she said gently, nodding towards the cup that was clasped tightly between his hands. 'I'm sorry you were worried about me. It just hadn't crossed my mind that you'd be worried.' She raised her hands in a calming gesture to pre-empt the objection that she could see he was about to make, 'No. Don't misunderstand me. I don't mean that I thought you couldn't care less, it's more that I just didn't think at all. Remember, I've spent most of the last few years reporting from the Middle-East on the Arab-Spring and everything that followed on from that. I seem to have spent half my time trying to get as close as possible to freedom fighters, or *jihadis*, so that I could understand them better. I've had to run for cover to avoid snipers, I've been showered by debris from bomb blasts and I've seen people beheaded for saying the wrong thing… What I'm trying to say is that going into the camp didn't seem like such a big deal and I just didn't think.' She stretched a hand out across the table, 'I'm sorry. I was wrong. I've seen others in the Middle-East get blasé about the risks and end up dead because of it. You were right to be angry.'

'But not like that, and not then... Can we try and forget about it?' he stretched out a hand which she took and gripped tightly.

She insisted that he went first in recounting what he had learnt while he was in Catania, listening attentively throughout and nodding when the things he was describing agreed with what she herself had witnessed in the camp.

'A lot of that agrees with things I was told or saw for myself, and helps to explain some of the other things that I didn't quite understand at the time.'

Layla explained how, when she had bought the clothes at the market in Caltagirone, she had only been planning to use them so that she could make contact with some of the women making purchases at the shops on the edge of Mineo. It had been later, as a result of what she had heard there that she had decided to go inside herself. One of the women had told her how they had been told that they needed to make room for a large group of new arrivals who were due later that evening and how, as a result of people moving around, life in the camp was even more chaotic than usual. She had told two of the women that she was a journalist and that, if she could get inside the camp, she could write articles that might lead to the process being speeded up, or at least shame the authorities into forcing those running the camps to provide the services they were meant to be providing.' She saw Luke raise an eyebrow at this and added defensively, 'I am going to write articles, and you never know, they might have some effect.'

He shook his head, 'It wasn't that. I was just wondering what services you think they might provide.'

'Well. There are some pretty well educated people amongst the refugees, and some of them know what rights they have – in theory anyway. Did you know that amongst other things, the people running the camp are meant to provide Italian lessons to all the residents as well as offering free legal advice and help in filling in all the forms that they have to fill in?'

He snorted, 'Fat chance of that! Even if they wanted to it would be logistically impossible: the numbers are just too big.'

'Maybe,' she retorted, 'but they could at least make the effort.... Anyway, the women agreed that one of them would meet me about half a mile from the camp, just before it went dark, and I could use the other one's identity badge to sign my way in. When the badge is swiped, the badge-holder's photograph and fingerprints show up on the screen by the gate, but she assured me that they never bother looking at them, and they only make very casual searches of people's bags as they go in and out.'

'Looking for?'

'Arms and drugs, I think. The women told me that they weren't bothered about anything else, and even then, it's just for show. Some of the ones who hang around the kapos are quite clearly armed and it's best to keep well out of their way.'

'How did you eat? Aren't they supposed to only serve food to people with badges?'

'There are plenty of unofficial shops in the camp selling things that have been smuggled in from outside, so I bought some bottled water and some fruit there. Only a small amount because I wanted to draw as little attention to myself as possible. For the rest, I'd made sure I'd taken some bread with me when I went in. There are plenty of families who cook their own food, as often as possible, on camping stoves in the gardens; it's very hot and crowded in the official refectory and, from what I'm told, the food is very bland and doesn't vary from day to day. Again, that's not something that's supposed to happen.

'The really interesting thing that I saw was when the four coaches carrying the new arrivals appeared. Each of the kapos was there waiting, so that the new arrivals could be split up by nationality and sent to the right area of the camp, but eight of them: six girls and two teenage boys were separated out and then led off by two men who'd been lurking behind the kapos,' she paused.

'Let me guess. They were all unaccompanied and all attractive.'

'They were, and I very much doubt that any of them was older than fifteen. I asked one of the women who'd helped get me in about them, but she was obviously far too frightened to speak, even though I promised that there was no way that anyone would even know that she'd been talking to me.

'There wasn't much I could do about that but I managed to see the direction they were taken in and, by slipping away as soon as I could, got within sight of them again a few minutes later. They were taken to a house on the northern edge of the village and taken inside straight away. I didn't want to risk getting close enough to have a good look at the house because there were a couple of heavies sitting outside the door, so I thought it was best to turn down a side street rather than get anywhere near. What I did notice was that, whereas most of the other houses had open windows with washing hanging out, the windows of this house were heavily curtained so that it was impossible to see in or out. I hung around as long as I dared then went back towards the house where I knew that the women I'd met earlier were staying. Most of the time the women sit apart from the men – at least in that house, anyway – so they were able to talk to me reasonably openly. Some of them were telling me that they and their husbands were saving up, because if you had a thousand euros each, there were people who could arrange for you to get out sooner and then you could apply for asylum again when you got to another country without as much bureaucracy – Yes, I know, I should really have told them it wasn't true, but I couldn't could I? If I'd told them and they'd believed me, they'd have gone to tell their husbands and I've have found myself right in the middle of the trouble that would have followed. If I'd told them and they didn't believe me, they wouldn't have told me anything else and anyway, apart from the loss of a thousand euros, they might even be better off out of the camp.' She looked at him for approval and he raised a shoulder resignedly.

'How could they possibly get that amount of money together? From what I saw in Lampedusa, most of them arrive with nothing.'

'There are ways. Each refugee is given two euros fifty a day as pocket money, and even if it doesn't always get paid, most of the time it does. Some of the men manage to earn twenty to twenty five euros a day working ten hours a day on local farms, or in factories a bit further afield and some…'

'Twenty euros a day for ten hours!' he exclaimed. 'That's disgraceful.'

'The farmers pay more than that, but it gets paid to the gangmasters and, after they've taken their cut, the rest is given to the kapos to distribute, and they obviously have to take their share out first. The other way of earning money, as I was about to say, is money that the women can earn, if they're prepared to make the sacrifice.'

He thought for a moment, considering what she'd said. 'You mean...' She thought he looked even more shocked than he had been over the twenty euro wages.

'Why not? We're not talking blushing virgins. Many of the women have been through brutal rapes or been forced to submit to exploitation to pay the passage for themselves and their husbands; at least this way, they have an element of control and most of them have reached the stage where they can just switch off mentally: make the appropriate noises then take the money and blank it out.' He had no response to this except to shake his head sadly.

'Anyway. The last useful bit of information I got was at about ten o'clock. Many people had already gone to bed as they tend to get up early in the morning, when one of the younger women, who'd almost qualified as a lawyer before she had to flee, tugged my sleeve and indicated that I should go with her. She didn't speak but led me back to not far from the house where the eight teenagers had been taken earlier on. There was a patch of deep shade by the rear corner of one of the other houses, out of reach of the perimeter lights, and she pulled me in there and put a finger on her lips to warn me to keep quiet. After about five minutes, a large dark coloured van pulled up on the road outside, opposite a point where two of the lights, on either side of an emergency gate, weren't working. A few seconds after the van had pulled up, the back door of the house opened and four men brought out sixteen women and walked them over to the van. The driver opened the back door of the van; the women were shown inside and two of the men who'd brought them out of the house got in with them. The driver gave each of the other two men a cigarette, shook hands with them and then drove off towards Catania. The men stayed outside until they'd finished their smokes then ground the last little bit under their heels and went back inside. We stayed there for at least another five minutes then she led me back.'

'Prostitution?'

'What else? She told me that they were usually brought back about five in the morning but that they were never seen outside the house during the day.'

Luke stretched and put his hands on his head as he thought it through. 'Presumably, as they seem to make a new selection when a new batch of refugees arrives in the camp, the originals are moved on elsewhere to make room for them.'

'A constant supply of fresh meat,' she said bitterly. He declined to comment.

Chapter Nine

As they were both exhausted, they spend most of the day resting and it was only towards evening that they felt able to plan their next moves. Luke pointed out that as the prostitution ring had a new supply of girls, it might be the ideal opportunity to find out where they were being sent to. Consequently, later that evening, he parked the car about a hundred metres down a side road, a couple of kilometres along the road between the CARA and Catania, and then walked back along the road until he could see the perimeter lights around the centre.

He could see clearly where the two lights had been de-activated near the service entrance and he settled down to await developments. Just after ten past ten, he saw a dark vehicle pull up outside the entrance and turn its lights off. If things proceeded as they had done the previous evening he had about five minutes to get back to the car before the van reached the junction with the side road.

He was in place before he saw the glow caused by the van's lights in the distance and, after a minute, he started the car up and moved slowly towards the junction. He was too far back when the van passed the end of the road for the driver to get any sort of good look at him or the Mercedes, and he knew that his lights would make it impossible for the van driver to get a good look at him in his mirrors, at least until they were under streetlights. His phone was on the passenger seat and he picked it up as he drove and pressed 'Send', so the message he'd prepared earlier was transmitted to both Layla and Luana.

Thirty five minutes later, as the two vehicles approached the entrance to the A19 Motorway, his phone started to ring but stopped almost immediately. He indicated right and turned onto the access road for the motorway; as he did so a Fiat Bravo turned onto the main road and replaced him behind the van. He waited until both vehicles were well out of sight and then reversed back onto the main road and continued until he reached the edge of the city where he pulled over to await further instructions.

It was less than ten minutes later when he got the call from Luana. She explained that the van had pulled over less than two kilometres further on where the driver had gone round the back and let one of the girls out before leaving her at the side of the road. He had then let two more girls out, who had stayed together, roughly fifty metres further along the road. Luana had driven past so as not to arouse suspicion and continued until she was out of sight beyond the next roundabout where she had turned round and parked facing back the way she had come. She was not sure how many more girls had been left before the roundabout but she had seen five girls dropped off at the roundabout so that, between them, they were able to establish either a single or double presence at each of the three roads leading off. The van had taken the road to the north and, although she only had a limited view, she was sure that it had stopped at least twice more before disappearing. 'There's a big supermarket close to the roundabout – you can't miss it if you carry on the road you were on before – It's closed, but I'll meet you just this side of the barrier in the entrance to the carpark – if anyone notices us there it will just look like a clandestine assignation and no-one will take any notice.'

When he got there, she had already arrived and was waiting in her car. He pulled in alongside and got into the passenger seat of her Punto. They exchanged a brief hug before speaking.

'Thanks for this. It would have been much more difficult keeping tabs on them at night without being spotted if I'd been on my own. I don't really have a clue where we are.'

'Not really where I'd expected to be,' she replied, 'I don't know whether you know but historically the main area for prostitution in Catania is the old San Berillo quarter. I'd assumed that they'd be going there, especially as there's a strong Senegalese presence there now. I hadn't heard that this area, not far from the airport, is now being used… Did you see the girls along the roadside as you drove along?'

'I did and, unless I'm much mistaken, they've changed their clothes, or been made to change their clothes, while they were in the back of the van.' They lapsed into silence.

'So, what's the next move?' she asked after a while.

'I think you need to be here with me, as a lone man would stand out like a sore thumb – but that doesn't mean you need to be awake; if you want to lean your head on my shoulder and try and get some sleep, that's fine by me. I assume you've got to go to work tomorrow.'

She insisted she would be fine but twenty minutes later her head was on his shoulder and he was able to listen to the sound of her regular breathing as he continued to watch the first hundred metres or so of two of the roads that ran off the roundabout.

It wasn't long before the first car, a Volkswagen Golf, drew up alongside one of the girls who rested her hand on the roof of the car and leant down towards the driver's window. Even though Luke's view was obscured by the car, having seen the top that the girl was wearing before the car had pulled alongside, it wasn't hard to imagine the view the driver was getting as she bent towards him. After a brief negotiation, the girl stepped back and the car pulled away, making its way to the roundabout where it went slowly round one and a quarter times, clearly window shopping before deciding on a purchase. Luke could just see the rear-lights of the car as it pulled over and another negotiation must have taken place.

Again, Luke could only assume that agreement had not been reached, as it wasn't long before the car set off again and returned to the first girl who had been approached, This time, the girl got in the car almost immediately. The driver performed a u-turn and drove back down the road away from the street lights.

Over the next three and a half hours, Luke witnessed several similar performances, and he could only imagine that the girls he couldn't see from his position were meeting similar success. The first girl was returned by the car after twenty minutes and he watched her retch after the car had pulled away. Although he was too far away to get a good look at the girl, she must have been one of the most marketable as, after the driver of the Golf, she was picked up three more times before the night was over, more than any of the other girls he could see. Twice, cars belonging to the *Polizia Municipale* passed slowly by, as did a *carabinieri* vehicle but, other than looking, none of them took any further interest or action.

Luana woke up not long before the second of the cars belonging to the Municipal Police passed. Both officers in the car had their eyes fixed on them as they drove slowly past and she surprised him by leaning across, pulling his head down towards her and kissing him. She pulled away sharply after they gone, just as Luke was opening his mouth to participate fully. 'Voyeurs,' she said contemptuously, looking down the road where the police-car's tail-lights were still visible.

Sometime later, the van reappeared and the girls, after a brief conversation with the driver, during which, Luke assumed, they had to hand over their takings, each was loaded into the back of the van.

'So. At least now we've got confirmation that there's a prostitution ring being run from the C.A.R.A,' said Luke, yawning.

'We do. But it's not enough, is it?'

Luke closed his tired eyes for a moment and tried to think, but he felt exhausted and could only encourage her to continue rather than thinking it through himself.

'You saw how the local police turn a blind-eye. Giò told us that prostitutes were being taken out of the centre each night. Unfortunately, not many people are really going to be shocked that a handful of girls are making money from prostituting themselves, are they? We don't even have any evidence that they're being forced into it… At the moment, what we know could just be used by those who don't want refugees to back up their claims that the camps are just breeding grounds for disease and criminality.'

He leaned his head back and sighed.

She gave a little laugh. 'Don't worry. I'm just playing Devil's advocate. I don't want to be too negative, but you need to realise that we need more than this. We need to know what happens to the girls after they've done this for a while – and the longer we have to watch them, the harder it's going to be – I don't think we can become a regular feature in the entrance to this carpark.'

'OK. I'm sure you're right. I just feel absolutely shattered at the moment. Let me get back, get some sleep and then ring you.' He placed a hand on hers, squeezed, and then gave her a peck on the cheek and got out of the car.'

They decided that they had no choice but to carry on watching until something happened as none of them was able to offer any realistic alternative. A friend of Luana's was able to confirm that the van belonged to a Caltagirone based firm, nominally dealing in electrical goods but whose owner had a string of convictions for minor offences stretching back over a number of years. It would have been easy for Luana to speak to friends in the police and have the van stopped but, as she pointed out, there would be others that would replace it, and at least at the moment they knew who to keep an eye on.

For three nights they parked one or other of the cars in a position from where they could keep an eye on what was happening, being careful to vary their routine so avoid arousing suspicion.

On the fourth night Luke and Layla were waiting before the C.A.R.A. so as not to pull out from the same lane each night. Luckily they were in place early as the van came past ten minutes before its usual time. As it pulled in alongside the service gate, Layla took the binoculars out of the glove compartment and stepped out to watch the loading of the van while Luke leaned his head back on the head-rest and closed his eyes while he waited.

'Drive,' said Layla, with a touch of excitement in her voice as she slipped back into her seat and pulled her phone out of her pocket.

'Luana? It's me….. Yes. I think we might be in luck….. twelve extra girls packed into the van tonight.. I think they're all girls, anyway…. No. They've just set off now…..OK. We'll hang back until we get nearer the city then we'll have to get closer to make sure we don't lose them….. You will?….. OK. I'm listening….. Right. I'll tell him….. Talk to you later.'

'Well?' said Luke, impatiently, as she ended the call.

'You got the gist. It looks as if they're not just delivering girls to the side of the road tonight, but they're also moving some girls on.'

'How can you be sure that they're not just getting more ambitious and using more girls tonight? There doesn't seem to be a shortage of customers'

'I'm sure. Trust me. There was something about the way some of them were dressed. I know that they usually change in the back of the van, but some of them didn't look as if they were prepared to do a quick change'

'Alright. So what did she suggest?'

'She said that if they don't turn off first, she'll take over tailing them at the same point as she did on the first night. We're to let her get out of sight and then continue. If the girls who're working get out in the same area, she'll follow the van – unless it has dropped all the girls off. We should have time to pass them while they're dropping the girls off and then be ready to head back to the roundabout from the other direction.'

'And then?'

Although he was watching the road and the distant tail-lights of the van, he could sense her raise her shoulders next to him. 'We play it by ear,' she said.

Playing it by ear turned out to be far more complicated than either of them had anticipated. The van made its regular drop offs but then, instead of parking up in one of the suburbs, as they had ascertained was normally the case, and where they assumed that the driver either lived or had friends, its driver pointed it back in the direction from which it had arrived, until reaching the entrance to the motorway.

The van took the north bound side and immediately accelerated up to a hundred and forty which Luke's little old Mercedes could just about manage. Layla took a call from Luana and listened attentively for a few seconds before saying 'OK.' and ending the call.

'Luana says that they could be heading for either Messina or Palermo. Probably Messina as they can get them onto the mainland sooner. If it's Palermo, she says she doesn't have enough fuel to get there so she's going to put some in at the first service area. That way, she might just manage to catch up again before we get to Messina... How are we for diesel?'

He shrugged. 'Messina won't be a problem. If they go further than that, let's just hope that they need to make a stop too.'

There was plenty of traffic about and Luke was glad that the van they were following was fairly large as it made it much easier to keep in sight while he was certain that their car would just blend in with all the others. As well as keeping an eye on the van, he also kept half an eye almost permanently on the rear view mirror hoping, each time he saw faster lights coming up behind, that it would be Luana and that she would settle in behind them – but each time he was disappointed.

The van slowed as it approached the Messina-Boccetta exit, which was also signed as the last exit for the ferries. Luke drew closer.

'Don't get too close. We don't want to be spotted now.' She sounded worried.

'No choice. If I drop back, we'll almost certainly be separated by traffic lights and we can't risk that now. Even though it's fairly certain that they're going to cross over, there's more than one ferry port in Messina. Let Luana know that we've come off at Messina-Boccetta and are heading down towards the sea, but don't hang-up, she'll need to know whether we turn left or right when we get to the bottom.'

The van driver chose to go right, as Luke had feared he would. 'Pity,' he muttered as he indicated to follow. Layla gave him an enquiring glance which, as he was concentrating on both the van and the road layout, he sensed rather than saw. 'As far as I know, the northern port is nice and straightforward and pretty simple. The southern port has at least three car-ferry departure points and is surrounded by industrial buildings, some of which may have their own private docks.'

His worst fears were realised; their quarry headed round the edge of the port, past the Maritime Station where a large overhead sign advised everyone that they were in the right place to embark for Villa San Giovanni, and then round a large square and into a maze of backstreets.

Suddenly, just as he was beginning to think that they were bound to be spotted tailing the van through these streets, the maze ended and they saw the van turn left onto a larger road. 'We're heading up the strip of land that forms the eastern side of the port, making Messina a natural harbour; I've never been here before.' Layla said nothing.

They soon passed a turn off to another Messina-Villa San Giovanni ferry port and one which indicated that it was the right place to be for those heading towards Salerno, but the van showed no signs of turning. The road was fringed by the ugly backs of port buildings on their left and on their right by high walls topped with barbed wire, and sporting yellow signs advising passers by that they enclosed property belonging to the military, and that there would be dire consequences for any intruders. Eventually, there was a similar stretch of wall, but without the military signage, and here the van stopped near a gate and sounded its horn twice. Luke went past and continued, as slowly as he dared, while Layla watched out of the rear window.

'Its going inside! Stop!'

'I can't stop here. It's too obvious... I'll turn round as soon as I can and then find somewhere to pull over.'

'This is a complete waste of time. We've been here for over an hour now and we have no idea what's going on behind that wall. Let's hope Luana's had more luck, trying to find a vantage point where she can see the coastline.' Luke banged the side of his fist on the dashboard in frustration.'

'Just a bit longer... they can't stay here all night, they must have to pick the other girls up again and get them back to the camp.'

He exhaled noisily and shook his head, 'And that gets us right back where we started. We might as well as have caught up with some sleep.'

Layla's phone brought the conversation to an end by lighting up and vibrating. She reached for it quickly and opened the message.

'She says that she's too far away to get a good look - even with the binoculars – but that a covered boat has just pulled away from the shore and is heading out across the Strait.'

'From here?'

'Here or very close to here. Like I said, she's a fair distance away. But why else would a boat be slipping out at this time of the night? It's got to be carrying the girls.... The gates!'

The gates through which the van had earlier disappeared were opening and the headlights announced its imminent reappearance.

'Let Luana know. I'm going to wait a couple of minutes before I set off, just in case anyone inside is keeping an eye on the road. We're pretty certain that we know where it's headed, so we should be able to catch up with it on the motorway.'

'Luana... The van's just come out... We're going to give it a couple of minutes start.... Where are you?.... Alright. Let us know... We'll meet up tomorrow... Ciao, ciao.' She looked across at Luke, 'She's staying put for a while, hoping to get at least a rough idea where the boat makes landfall on the other side.'

His expression suggested that he wasn't convinced that they would learn much from this, but he didn't comment and just turned the key in the ignition.

Despite pushing the Mercedes to its limits, they didn't catch the van before Catania, and were doubly concerned to note that the girls who had been dropped off were still there.

'Maybe Luana was wrong about the boat. The van might have gone the other way and headed for Palermo.'

'Or maybe,' said Layla, 'we missed them because they stopped at one of the service stations on the way.' She gave a smile of relief as the van came into view and pulled over to collect the first of the girls.

'Why aren't they moving? It must be more than five minutes since they made the last pickup. What are they waiting for?' Just then a fairly new looking BMW with tinted glass and stereo blaring, roared up to the roundabout and screeched to a halt. The passenger door opened immediately and a dishevelled girl with what appeared in the sodium glare of a nearby street-light to be coal black skin, staggered out, clearly helped on her way by a push – or worse. A hand reached across, the door was pulled closed and, with an extravagant wheel-spin, the BMW sped off again.

Luke's eyes initially followed the rapidly receding car, but Layla's had immediately fixed on the girl.

'*Al'awghad!*' she said, with disgust in her voice. 'She can't be more than fourteen!'

'What?'

'Just look at her. She can't be more than fourteen. What sort of people would force young girls like that to do these sorts of things?'

'No... I meant, what did you say before that?'

'Oh that. It's arabic. It's what my mother used to call people she really disliked.'

'Anyway. She's the one they must have been waiting for. We may as well go. We know where they're going so there's nothing to be gained by following them.'

'You've done fantastically. But I don't really see how you can take it forward from here, and now that you know how they're getting the girls off the island, I really think you ought to let the authorities know. They've got the resources to follow it up, and they can hardly refuse to do anything now that you've got proof.'

Layla leaned forward and, placing her elbows on the edge of the table, rested her face in her hands and closed her eyes. Luana waited patiently, knowing how difficult it would be for her. Handing everything over to the authorities meant impicitly accepting that she no longer had any realistic hope of tracking down Zahra – accepting that the girl was beyond her reach, even if, by some chance, she were still alive.

'I can't... If the police take over, they'll insist that I keep out of their way: that I don't interfere with their investigation and... no offence, but I don't have much faith in the police's capacity or motivation to see this through.'

Luana reached a hand out across the table in a conciliatory gesture. 'No offence taken; I know as well as anyone that the police are under-resourced and often forced to make harsh choices about where to deploy their resources. On one level I'm sure that there are people in the police both here and across the straits in Reggio Calabria who are secretly delighted that some of the immigrants are being moved

North, where they'll be someone else's problem... but... where they're presented with clear evidence of a crime being committed, they have to take some action.'

'Yes. I know that. But what does that mean? What action are they going to take? And what real difference will it make? It's not as if they didn't already know that refugees were working as prostitutes, did they?'

'I know,' said Luana soothingly, 'but at least now that we're pretty sure that at least one of the new batch is underage and that there's a direct link to people being illegally removed from the island; they can't ignore that; they have to step in and put an end to it – arrest the ones who're organising them, and hopefully deport them. Think about the girl you saw last night.. could you live with yourself knowing that you'd turned a blind eye and not tried to save her? Luke; I'm right aren't I? You know I am.'

Luke sighed. He'd been sitting to one side on a chair by the window, appearing to be giving all his attention to the busy street below, but in reality taking in every word they said. He turned to face them. 'You're right about the girl. What's happening to her has got to be stopped, even though she'll be replaced by others who're just a bit older and, while there's obviously a legal difference, I'm not sure that there's much of a moral difference between exploiting a fifteen year old and exploiting an eighteen year old under these circumstances. We have to report what we know about the girl but I'm not sure we need to report what we know about the onward movements.'

'But surely, it's all tied in together, and I'm sure there are plenty of other young girls who've already been moved off the island.'

'So am I, but I'm pretty sure that they also know that and, if they haven't managed to do anything about it so far. Why should things change now?'

'Because now, we know how they're getting them off the island and where from.'

'OK. Although I'm pretty sure the police could have found that out for themselves if they'd really wanted to – but what's it going to lead to? The arrest of the van driver and, if you're lucky, a couple of people at the dock? You know as well as I do that these people are expendable and will just be replaced by others who'll use a slightly different route... It's your call... it's your country after all... but my advice would be to just let them save the girl we saw last night, and leave Layla free to carry on looking.'

'Tell me, Luke, do you honestly thing that there is any chance of Zahra still being alive, and if there is, of finding her?' She looked at him with a steady but challenging gaze, and he knew that Layla's eyes were also on him, awaiting his response.

'When we started looking, what now seems like ages ago, I'd have said there was a reasonable chance... but that was when I only thought I knew about the refugees' situation, before I'd been to Lampedusa, before I'd talked to people who were directly involved, and before I really knew anything about the camp at Mineo.' He paused.

'And now?' Luana prompted. He felt as if Layla's eyes were burning into him.

'Now... I don't really think that there's any realistic hope of finding her, or even of finding out what happened to her.' He turned towards Layla whose tear filled eyes met his for a moment before she turned away. 'I'm sorry.'

There was an awkward silence which both Luke and Luana were reluctant to break, both anxious to see how Layla reacted.

'So that's it then,' she said flatly, eventually taking them both by surprise, 'You've given up.'

'Layla…' said Luke.

'It's alright. Really. You can go back to your island and forget about it. I promise I won't bother you again. Thanks for all the help you've given so far.' There was a forced casualness to her voice and she managed to keep her eyes expressionless as she looked at Luke.

He had a hollow feeling behind his ribs and it seemed as if there were a low buzzing in his ears. 'I… Listen…. I don't..' Luana put a hand on his forearm to silence him and then stepped over to put her arms around the younger woman.

'What are you going to do?' she asked, gently.

'I don't know… I suppose I'll go back to Britain and think things over. I need to raise some money, but if I can, I'm coming back to

Italy. Even if I can't do anything else, I can write about what's going on so that eventually someone will have to do something about it.'

'That's good. And you know you can rely on me – and on Luke – if you need any help.'

Layla gave a little smile. 'Thankyou, but Luke's already done more than enough; it was a mistake getting him involved. I'm sorry, Luke. I shouldn't have come looking for you.'

'Hang on a minute,' said Luke, feeling somewhat affronted, 'you may be sorry, but I'm not.'

'Leave it.' said Layla, shaking her head, 'Just forget about everything – we're straight now – and if you don't mind, I think I'll go to bed; I can feel another one of my headaches coming on.' and, after hugging Luana tightly, she left the room.

'You didn't talk to her, did you?' said Luana accusingly.

Luke ignored the question. 'Should I go after her?' He took a step towards the door.

'No!' said Luana sharply. 'It would only make matters worse. If you'd told her how you really feel about what she did before, it would have been different, but it's out of your hands now. You need to give her time and then let her decide. But now… well. Now you're no good to her if she doesn't think you believe in what she's doing.'

'So what do I do? Shall I talk to her in the morning?'

'No. She's not going to change her mind like that. Surely you've noticed that she's almost as stubborn as you.' She gave a little smile. 'Do what she said; go back to Lipari; see if you can settle down again; see if you can move on. Both of you need space.'

'And if I can't move on? Won't I have burnt my boats by just disappearing back to Lipari now? What's she going to think?'

'I'll talk to her in the morning. I'll tell her that I told you to give her space, and I'll try and convince her to keep an open mind.'

Part Two – Tuscany

Chapter Ten

Luke had always got on well with Mati despite the age difference. As a teenager, he'd spent almost every school-holiday with his aunt and uncle in Florence, either visiting with his parents, with just his mother or, as soon as he was allowed, on his own. A couple of times he'd bowed to pressure from his mother and invited a school-friend along but he'd soon discovered that even the most enlightened of them were only interested in seeing the main tourist sights and then making the most of the absence of parental supervision and becoming the stereotypical young English tourists abroad. It wasn't that he particularly minded sitting on a park bench sharing a bottle of wine, or a few cans of beer that they'd managed to buy in one of the many shops that weren't too particular about selling alcohol to minors, but his friends only seemed to care about price and not about quality.

In the summer of 2000, Alessio had had his appendix removed while Luke was visiting and, as Paul and Rosa were rushing around, visiting Alessio, visiting Rosa's mother who was also unwell, as well as trying to earn a living, he had not only been left largely to his own devices but had also found that nine-year-old Mati also seemed to have become his responsibility during the day. At first, this had seemed a somewhat onerous responsibility that was likely to seriously impinge on his freedom and he had resigned himself to being dragged into Barbie based fantasies and inane conversations about Italian soaps and reality TV shows. Instead, he had been pleasantly surprised.

After an excruciatingly dull morning in the apartment, Mati had suggested that they went out after they'd eaten the lunch that Rosa had left for them and, rather than suggesting a visit to various clothes shops, she had suggested that they visited the *Bargello*. She had been to the old prison on a visit with school some months before and had been wanting to go back for a longer visit ever since. Paul and Rosa, who were both artistic, had promised to take her but just hadn't found the time; Luke was only too happy to oblige.

Once inside the museum, Mati had told him as much as she could remember about the building's long history and shown him the most famous exhibits which were the ones her teacher had shown the class. Luke was impressed, not only by the sculptures and the details she remembered about them but also, by the way, when she moved on to the lesser known pieces that her teacher had ignored, she was able to make what, at least to him, sounded intelligent observations about the similarities some of them had to the better known works. Although he didn't know a lot about sculpture, the points she was making seemed intelligent and he liked the way she gave reasons for all her opinions rather than just saying whether or not she liked pieces. Despite his admitting that his own knowledge of sculpture was very limited, she regularly asked his opinion and he soon realised that she always wanted to know why he thought something, forcing him to consider each of the sculptures very carefully before he gave an answer.

They were in the *Bargello* for almost four hours although the time seemed to pass much more quickly. Twice, security guards approached them, concerned by why the two kids were hanging around in the museum for so long, but each time they veered away when they heard the animated discussions about the articulation of a marble arm, or the unnatural protrusion of a bronze neck muscle. Over the next few days they had returned to the *Bargello* twice to argue out disagreements over the qualities of particular sculptures, and begun to seek out other noteworthy pieces around the city, whether famous or not. By the time Luke had to return to England and to school there was a firm friendship between the two cousins and each looked forward to their next meeting.

As each grew up, they had confided in each other about almost everything and still, as adults, they remained very close. Luke had taught Mati everything he knew about computers and she had proved an exceptionally quick learner, particularly after he had joined the police force and begun to specialise in cyber-crime. When Mati's grandmother, Maddi, had set out to track down the elusive distant relative who she was sure was behind the deaths of Paul and Rosa and the terrible injuries suffered by Rosa's younger sister, Francesca,

Mati had been able to sift through and categorise the masses of information that Luke had managed to extract from 'secure' computer files held by Europol, Interpol and various official Italian organisations. When Luke's part in this came to light, after Maddi had ensured that the relative would no longer evade justice, he had insisted on shielding Mati from any of the repercussions, assuring her that if she confessed it would not make any difference to his own sentence.

Now, as he finally finished his account of what he'd been doing for the last few weeks of April, he glanced across her grandparents' sitting-room to where she was curled up in an armchair, her forehead resting on her forearms which in turn were folded on the knees she had gathered up in front of her. For a few moments, that seemed to last much longer than they really did, she said nothing and he wondered if she'd dropped off to sleep – then she raised her head and looked at him with eyes that were drawn together in a frown.

He'd expected sympathy for all the time he'd wasted and for having heard that Judi was now with someone he'd thought of as one of his best friends, maybe shock at what he'd told her about the conditions faced by the refugees, maybe some disappointment that he'd been talked into helping the woman who they both felt had been instrumental in his conviction. What he didn't expect was the anger, bordering on contempt, with which his cousin addressed him.

'*Cretino!* You idiot! How could you possibly be so stupid? So blind? You're supposed to be intelligent – not just clever intelligent, but emotionally intelligent as well.'

'Hang on a…'

'Shut up and listen,' she interrupted in a tone he'd never heard her use before. 'Don't you realise, she's been desperate to make it up with you? And, what's more, if you could only see past your stupid pride, you'd pretty soon realise that it's what you want too!'

'I think you're…'

'I said, "shut up and listen". Do you really think that she'd go to all the trouble to track you down to Lipari, just because she wanted your help in finding this girl?.. It's rhetorical – don't bother answering.' She spat out as he gathered himself to argue. '"Use your policing and

Italian language skills to help me track someone down and then I'll never bother you again", do me a favour!' she said contemptuously and shook her head. 'You were a police computer analyst! How much use were your computer skills while you were helping her?' She raised a finger, again warning him to keep quiet as he was about to respond. If she's as good-looking as you say she is, she could have easily found someone far more qualified to help her, without having to enlist someone who had a grudge against her.

'She came to you because she wanted to prove to you that she's not the heartless, career-driven hack that you thought she was. From what you say, it seems that she did her best not just to apologise, but also to explain- to demonstrate that it wasn't her fault. If she'd wanted to hurt you, she could have told you about Judi and Cameron, and when you say she was trying to tempt you in to bed just so that that she could show that she was completely dominant, I don't think I've ever heard anything so stupid. Do you really think that she couldn't have got you into her bed if that had been her intention? It seems to me that she gave you the opportunity to either punish and humiliate her if that was what you felt you needed to do or, to come together as friends, only you were too pig-headed and prejudiced to understand.'

'But she's still the woman who broke up my marriage,' he offered almost apologetically.

Mati emitted a sound between a groan and a growl. 'I always looked up to you and thought you were bright, but you still don't get it, do you? Luana told you that Judi was already seeing McCreggan before Layla did the interview with you, so it wasn't Layla who caused your marriage to break up; that's something that you and Judi managed between you. A few hours ago, I'd have automatically blamed Judi, who I never really trusted, but now that I've heard how insensitive you can be, I'm not quite sure.'

'That's a bit harsh.'

She finally gave a small smile, 'You deserve it. Although, if it's any consolation, I never really liked Judi anyway.'

'You never said, or gave any sign!'

She rolled her eyes, 'Well, of course I didn't. I didn't really have a reason for not liking her; it was just a feeling- and I was always aware that it might just have been a bit of jealousy. So long as you were happy, that was all that mattered really... If you really want to know, I think you're better off without her - or you would be if you were capable of recognising when other people really like you.' Suddenly, she uncoiled herself from the armchair and made her way over to the full length windows where the shutters had been left partly open. She opened one side of the window and stepped through, pushing the shutters back to allow her to access the balcony.

When he gingerly followed her after a couple of minutes, he found her leaning on the balustrade, looking out silently across the city. He took up a similar position, deciding it was better not to speak, after a quick glance showed him a face that could have been carved out of granite.

'Well?' she said finally. Now it was his turn to pause.

'Even if you're right - and I'm not agreeing that you are - it's done now and there's no going back.'

'What!' she responded sharply, and clearly louder than she'd intended. A faint glow behind the shutters further along the wall showed that one of her grandparents had woken up and turned the bedside light on. Luke put a finger to his lips and with his other hand indicated the faint glow behind and beyond her. She glanced round quickly, nodded curtly to show that she had understood, then jerked her head towards the window they had stepped out of, indicating that it would be better to go inside.

'Find her, and sort things out.'

'That's easier to say than do.'

Mati shook her head decisively. 'No. You can find her quite easily, and you know it. If she's stayed in England, you know who she writes for, and if she's come back to Italy, she'll have been in touch with Luana. She has to, to find out more about where that boat went.'

He knew she was right, but he also knew he didn't want to admit it – at least not straight away. 'I'll think about what you've said... but now... I suddenly feel really tired. I'm going to get some sleep. *Buonanotte.*'

'*Buonanotte,*' she responded tonelessly.

She was sitting at the table, spooning her grandmother's home-made fig jam onto a biscuit that looked a bit like a ryvita when he came into the kitchen in the morning. *'Buongiorno,'* he said, encompassing both Mati and her grandmother with the greeting. Her grandmother, who was unloading the dishwasher and had her back to him, responded in kind, while Mati raised an enquiring eyebrow. He gave a little nod and then she smiled, *'Buongiorno.'*

'Is there any proper bread, or do I have to pretend I'm concerned about my waist while I pour your deliciously sweet jam onto a low-fat, high-fibre cracker?'

'There's bread in the cupboard on your left,' said Lia, as she turned with a smile, just too late to see her grand-daughter pull a face and jab out her tongue at Luke. 'I'm going to go and get some *trippa* later to cook for you for tonight; I know it's your favourite and I'm sure they have no idea how to prepare *trippa alla fiorentina* down in Sicily.'

He went over and gave the handsome old lady a hug, 'That's really sweet of you, Lia, but I'm afraid I'm going to have to leave early this afternoon. I have to attend a meeting with someone related to my conviction, which I'd completely forgotten about.'

'Ohhh'.

'I'm sorry. I really am. I promise I won't eat *trippa* cooked by anyone else before I come back and see you again – and I won't let as long pass between visits this time.' He could feel Mati's eyes burning into his back, but chose to ignore them.

Her patience lasted less than five minutes before she sought further information. 'Is the person you're meeting, the person you mentioned last night?' she asked, making an effort to make it seem a matter of little importance.

'Uh huh,' he said, as he slipped another piece of bread and jam into his mouth, and then after a few seconds, relenting slightly, 'I need to ring them after breakfast to set up the details, but it's a meeting that needs to happen sooner rather than later.'

'Keep hold of the car – at least for now,' she said, catching his eye, and he smiled, wondering if there was an implied threat in the second clause.

'Are you sure? I came up here in it, thinking you'd be needing it up in Geneva.

She pulled a face for the benefit of her grandmother. 'It would be more trouble than it's worth if I took it now. I haven't got round to applying for a parking permit yet, and the Swiss are quite hot on illegal parking – especially by foreign registered cars.'

'That's very good of you. Thankyou.'

She gave Luke a smile that conveyed far more than her words, 'You can chauffeur me around and introduce me to your friends when I fly down to see you in a few days.'

'Are you really sure it's a good idea for you to meet her? She's convinced that what I did, I didn't do alone and, from things she's said, it's fairly clear that she thinks it was you who helped me… Remember she's a journalist.'

He'd had to restrain himself from asking the question until Lia was out of earshot, but now he couldn't bear it any longer. He hoped that Mati was right about how Layla thought about him; knew deep down that she was right about his own feelings for Layla; reluctant to admit that Mati was right and that he'd been a complete idiot and genuinely concerned that it was not wise that anyone else, particularly a journalist, should know the part his cousin had played in the crime for which he'd served time in prison. While he was fairly sure that it would be impossible at this stage to find enough proof to convict her, even just the suggestion that she had been involved in a criminal conspiracy would be enough to cost her her job.

Mati gave a slight, but infuriating shrug, 'She's a journalist, and probably a very good one, but she's also a woman – and that means a lot.'

'And, if I'd said that, you'd have dragged me down to the nearest tattoo parlour and had "misogynist" tattooed across my forehead! What do you mean, "she's a woman"?'

As a reply, he only received a smile and then Lia's return prevented him from pushing any further.

Not wanting to make the call from the house, he walked up into the peaceful wood behind San Miniato, followed the deserted path until he found a bench and then sat down and took his phone out. There was no reply from Layla's phone and he decided not to leave a message. Hopefully, when she checked her phone, it would tell her that she had a missed call from him, and that would be as eloquent as any message he could think up on the spur of the moment.

Next he called Luana, who was at work and unable to talk freely and suggested that they should speak on Skype that evening. She did, however, say that Layla either was, or would soon be, in Rome and Luke decided that, as he had already told Lia he would be leaving, he might as well catch a train to the capital as he had several hours to fill before he could have the conversation he needed to have with Luana.

'Remember, I want to meet her – and the sooner the better,' said Mati as she placed her coffee cup down on the counter, 'No excuses.'

'I know. I'll ring you after I've spoken to Luana tonight… Promise.'

'Make sure you do. I've got four more days before I need to fly back to Geneva, and it's just as easy – probably easier – to get a flight from Rome as it is from Florence or Pisa. Now, you can pay for these and go and get your train; I've got shopping to do.'

Chapter Eleven

When he arrived in Rome, he turned right at the end of the platforms in Termini Station and, in less than ten minutes, made his way to the Funny Palace Hostel in Via Varese where he was able to secure a place in a six-bed dormitory room for twelve euros including breakfast.

Once he'd stowed away his travelling bag in the locker he'd been allocated, he decided to make the most of the good weather and the three hours he still had to spare before the earliest he could call Luana by taking a walk. His first destination allowed him to revisit Bernini's sculpture of Santa Teresa in the Church of Santa Maria della Vittoria, and then he moved on to the Borghese gardens and the Borghese Gallery, which held the world's finest collection of Bernini statues as well as masterpieces by Canova and others.

Inside the gallery, which fortunately was relatively free of organized groups of tourists, he slowly made his way to the main room where the finest sculptures were collected together. He admired the graceful figure of Napoleon's sister, Pauline Borghese, stretched out elegantly on her chaise-longue, with a smile, wondering how much artistic licence Canova had been obliged to use to flatter his powerful patron. While Canova's sculpture was impressive, the two pieces by Bernini that dominated the centre of the room were breathtaking. *"The Abduction of Prosperine"* never failed to amaze him with its vivacity and sense of life. In both Pluto and Prosperine, every muscle and every fold of sculpted skin seemed perfect and he wondered whether William Gilbert had been inspired by this piece when he wrote his *"Pygmalion and Galatea"* back in the nineteenth century.

As he thought of the legend of Prosperine, his mood darkened as the thought of the goddess being forcibly carried off by Pluto to be his bride in the underworld, reminded him of the likely fate of Zahra who, if by some miracle she were still alive was almost certainly living a life far worse than that endured by Prosperine.

Once his thoughts had returned to the plight of the refugees, it was difficult to think only about the sculptures again although, when he moved on to *"Apollo and Daphne"*, it was not Zahra who it brought to mind but Layla. The graceful figure of the nymph brought back memories of her diving into the sea on Lipari and his mind's eye saw the water splashing up around her where Bernini had sculpted the fronds emerging as the naiad began to transform into a laurel tree. Daphne's transformation had thwarted Apollo's desires and, as he thought of that, he hoped that it wasn't an omen.

The thoughts that the sculpture inspired in him reminded him of another of his favourite Bernini sculptures – one that Mati had shown him on a visit to Rome when she'd insisted he accompany her there after reading *"Angels and Demons"*. After checking his watch to make sure there was time, he left the gallery and after hurrying back to Termini, which he thought was the nearest Metro station, hopped on the first train to Piramidi and then scurried across the river and made his way to The Basilica of San Francesco a Ripa on the other side of the Tiber.

Inside the Basilica, he acknowledged an aged sacristan who advised him that a service would be beginning in fifteen minutes and that tourists should leave before that, and made his way straight to the chapel in the left transept which housed Bernini's stunning and unashamedly erotic funerary monument to the Blessed Ludovica Albertoni. A printed notice, next to the monument, advised "the faithful" that the reclining statue showed the dying Albertoni, who lived from 1473 to 1533, as she reached a moment of magical communion with God. Not counting himself as one of 'the faithful', Luke found it impossible to see it as a sixty-year old on her deathbed and instead, could not see it as other than a faithful representation of a much younger, really beautiful woman having the biggest orgasm ever.

Looking at the expressive sculpted face, he realised why he had suddenly thought of the sculpture and felt the need to see it. Whoever had modelled for the monument must have borne a strong facial resemblance to Layla and, as he studied the monument again, he allowed his imagination free rein.

It is always difficult to spot people when one emerges from the 'Nothing to Declare' channel into the busy arrival hall of an international airport. Even when you are looking for a specific face they tend to merge into a sea of happy but anxious visages interspersed with signs being held up showing the names of business passengers or hotel destinations by anonymous taxi-drivers wearing deadpan expressions. It was, therefore, no surprise that Layla didn't notice him until he came alongside her and gently took hold of her arm just above the elbow.

'Luke!'

'Hi,'

'But what are you doing here? How did you know…?'

He still had hold of her arm and now applied a light pressure to steer her towards the slightly garish Spizzico outlet where he was sure there would be a free table. She allowed herself to be guided without protesting until she could slip into an orange plastic seat at one of the tables.

'I'll get a couple of coffees, to justify occupying the table,' said Luke, making his way over to the counter, without looking at her.

When he returned, she looked directly at him without revealing anything of what she was feeling in her expression. Feeling nervous, he sipped the bitter coffee to gain a few moments.

'Well?' she said, still not allowing him any clues about how she felt.

He cleared his throat nervously. 'I was wrong… It doesn't matter whether I think there's any chance of finding Zahra or not, for as long as you want to go on looking, I want to be by your side and help.'

She still didn't smile, but in some way he would have found hard to describe, it was as if her face had softened; the brittle protective mask she had constructed to hide her feelings had melted away. He was almost certain that the hand she raised to sweep her hair back was really a way of brushing a nascent tear away from the corner of her eye with the heel of her hand. 'Why?'

Now it was his turn to be taken aback. He wasn't sure he was quite ready to answer the question. 'Why?' he repeated, as if it were a question he hadn't considered.

'Yes. Why have you changed your mind? Why should I believe you? And how do I know that you're not going to change your mind again as soon as things get difficult or you lose interest?'

Although slightly stung by the implications of the last part of her question, the last thing he wanted to do was to disagree with her. 'OK. I don't want to avoid your questions; you've got every right to ask those and more, but I'm not sure that this is the ideal place to have the discussion. Can I suggest that we go into the centre of Rome and then find somewhere more suitable to talk?' She indicated her agreement and they stood up. He picked her bag up and slung it over his shoulder before making for the exit.

He ignored the stop for the dedicated airport buses just outside the terminal and walked for five minutes to the main road before stopping at a standard bus-stop. 'Less than a third of the price, less crowded and much more frequent,' he explained when she gave him an inquiring look. After that, they spoke little during the journey to the edge of the city where they switched to the Metro at Laurentina station, although he occasionally pointed out some of the lesser known landmarks along the route.

When they arrived at Termini she said she needed some time to book into a nearby hotel and freshen up and suggested they meet in a couple of hours to talk and eat. Luke felt slightly disappointed that she courteously declined to see if there was a bed free in his hostel but tried not to show it. He pointed out that often the hotels and *pensioni* very close to central stations in capital cities tended to attract a fairly dubious clientele and, to help her find one that was suitable, led her down a side road on the southern side of the station until he judged that hotels were likely to be respectable. The first he tried was full, but they recommended another just round the corner in Via Amedeo. The reception area and receptionist created a positive impression so he left her there after arranging to pass by and meet her at the main entrance at quarter past seven.

He filled up the time by returning to his hostel, showering and changing and then surfing the internet to identify a suitable place to eat before, at half past six, leaving the hostel. As he still had plenty of time, he didn't take the direct route to Layla's hotel but instead headed to the restaurant he'd identified, both to check that, at least appearance wise, it lived up to expectations and to book a table. When he got there, he was pleased to see that the restaurant did seem to offer the ambience he wanted and, although the barman said that it wouldn't be necessary to reserve a table, he agreed to hold a more secluded table for two that nestled in one corner for them.

Satisfied with his efforts, Luke then made his way towards Layla's hotel, pausing for five minutes to admire the imposing Basilica of Santa Maria Maggiore. He would have liked to have gone inside to see the famous mosaics which he had heard to be the equal of, if not better than, any others in Italy, but he knew that there was too much to see in a few minutes. Instead, after admiring the architectural features of the façade, he made his way down Via Amedeo to arrive just before the appointed time.

She was dressed fairly simply in figure-hugging blue jeans and a white blouse under a denim jacket and a burnt-orange foulard enhanced with black, possibly Arabic, flowing motifs that blended in with her hair which she wore loosely except for a discreet orange hair-slide that kept it back from the left side of her face.

'Ciao... New outfit?' She smiled. 'It looks really good on you.' Then, conscious that he was rambling. 'I've booked a table at a little restaurant about ten minutes' walk away. I haven't eaten there before but it looks good.'

'That's fine by me. Lead the way.'

He offered his arm and, after a moment's hesitation, she slipped hers through his and they set off.

Three of the tables were occupied when they got to the restaurant: a family of Germans and, he was pleased to note, two Italian couples, which gave him hope that the food would be as good as the ambience. Luke explained to the waiter who greeted them that he'd reserved the table in the corner earlier, which the barman confirmed with a nod when the waiter looked over at him. As soon as they were seated, they were given menus and offered the choice of still or sparkling water. 'Naturale,' Luke responded, knowing that Layla never went for sparkling.

She had said, just before they entered, that she didn't feel particularly hungry and Luke had shrugged and said she could eat as much or as little as she liked. The menu, however, seemed to drive all thoughts of not being hungry out of her mind and he metaphorically crossed his fingers and hoped that the food was as good as it sounded.

'I don't know whether to have an *antipasto* or a *primo* to start with... there are so many things I want to try.'

'You could have both,' he suggested, half in jest.

'Tempting – but probably not a good idea. I want to be able to give myself some chance of having room for a dessert later.'

When the waiter came over and positioned himself to his right, facing Layla, Luke looked at her and said 'Ready?'

She gave him a little smile and then turned to the waiter, 'I'd like to start with the *seppie locali con lenticchie bio mozzarella e boragine* and then I'd like *the coscio di pollo bio con castagne, puntarelle e salsa di cachi.'* Luke saw the waiter jot down *'Seppie'* and *'Pollo'* and smiled at the effort Layla had made to read out the full name of the dishes, although he realised she had done it to practise her Italian. To help her feel at ease, he decided that he too would give his order in full, although first he needed to check just what one of the ingredients was.

'Could I just ask what *"berberè"* is, please." To his surprise Layla provided him with the answer before the waiter could speak.

'It's a very spicy seasoning from Ethiopia made by blending: peppers, chilis, ginger, coriander, nigella and several other spices.' The waiter inclined his head in admiration at her knowledge.

'In that case,' said Luke, 'I'll start with the *strozzapreti con sugo di agnello bio, berberè e cime di broccoli romane*, then I'll have the *straccetti di manzo brado alla birra, verdure e pilaf di farro.'*

'Very good, sir. And to drink?'

'A bottle of *Cesanese di Affile*.'

'Certainly', and he moved away.

'Very impressive.'

She gave a half smile, 'I came across it regularly when I was working in the middle-east.'

'I was thinking more about the way your Italian is improving.'

'The starter was pretty easy as restaurants in England that want to be pretentious, sometimes write *seppie* on the menu instead of cuttlefish; lentils, mozzarella and borage are pretty much the same, and as for the second course, I know I'm getting chicken thigh with chestnuts, a sauce made of kaki and, I think, mushrooms.'

'Almost, but not quite. *'Puntarelle'* is a sort of chicory, not a mushroom.'

'That'll be fine. but we didn't come here to talk about food, did we?'

'No, we didn't. You asked me, quite reasonably, why I'd come back - although I suppose that an even better question might have been to ask me why I'd left in the first place.'

'And...?

He paused before replying as the waiter arrived with the wine and tilted it so that he could see the label. He nodded to confirm that it was the correct one and the waiter skilfully inserted a corkscrew, twisted and pulled in what appeared to be one swift movement before sniffing the cork. He poured a small amount in Luke's glass and then stepped back respectfully as Luke rolled the glass to study the wine's legs, sniffed and then took a sip which he allowed to rotate around his mouth while he savoured the complex flavours of blueberry, violet and juniper.'

'Buono,' he said appreciatively to the waiter after he had swallowed. The waiter half-filled Layla's glass and then topped up Luke's to the same level before moving away.

'If you think back to when you found me on Lipari, you said that if I could use the skills I'd picked up while I was in the Police, to help you try and find Zahra, you'd never bother me again.'

'I...' He silenced her with a gesture.

'I know. On any rational level, it was a pretty meaningless bluff and, if I'd wanted to, I could have laughed in your face. People have short memories – especially tabloid readers – and realistically, only tabloids could ever have shown any interest in a story about an ex-cop who was living the good life on an idyllic Mediterranean island after spending time in prison at the taxpayer's expense. I think I allowed myself to believe that it was a real threat and that I didn't have any choice, because that was what I wanted to believe.'

'I don't understand.'

'Look. I'd spent five years blaming you for the breakup of what I thought was a happy marriage; for getting me sent to prison and ruining my career. Five years is a long time; you can build up a lot of hatred in five years – but then you turned up.'

'I turned up and threatened you!'

'You turned up and when I showed you the scars on my back, instead of telling me I'd only got what I deserved, you brushed your lips over them. From that moment on, I didn't really have a choice. It had nothing to do with your threat – all that did was allow me to convince myself that being with you wasn't a betrayal of everything I'd thought was important before.'

The starters arrived at that point and by tacit agreement they concentrated on the rich but delicately balanced flavours of the food for the next quarter of an hour until both plates had been finished and collected by the waiter.

'I felt bad about having made you come with me, as soon as we were on mainland Sicily. I tried to work up the courage to apologise and tell you to forget about me a few times, but I couldn't bear the thought that, if I did, you'd just walk out and I'd never see you again. I tried to be as nice as I could to you, to sort of make up for it, but you always seemed to tense up and push me away if I tried to be nice – I suppose it's what I deserved really.'

'Like an idiot, I convinced myself that if I let myself get close to you, it would be reinforcing the break-up of my marriage. I found it hard to believe that things wouldn't go back to how I thought they used to be, if only I could resist temptation in the meantime.'

'It sounds as if you've been reading the Bible.'

'Ha ha, very funny. You know what I mean.' She nodded apologetically. 'I should have realised a long time ago that, not only was it over with Judi, but that it was better for both of us that way. You knew, didn't you?'

She nodded and stretched out a hand, which he took. 'I'm sorry. I found out when I was preparing for the interview, doing my research. Whenever you mentioned her as we were talking, I was dying to tell you that she was cheating on you, even before you were arrested, but I couldn't. I remember, I really wanted to tell and then put my arms around you and comfort you – but that wouldn't have been very professional, would it?'

'It certainly wouldn't have gone down very well with the guards in the prison. As far as professional ethics go, I didn't think they existed any more in this tabloid age.'

'I think it's probably better if we don't go there.' He nodded his agreement.

'What I do need to do, at some point, is to have a talk with Cam McCreggan - No, don't worry. I'm not going to do anything stupid. Like I said, I now realise that I'm better off without her, but I'm disappointed by Cam. I thought he was honest enough to come and talk to me and be straight about things – maybe there's a lesson there about what happens when you trust a LibDem. I want him to do me the courtesy of telling me his side of the story and apologise for going behind my back - If he can do that, we can shake hands and forget about it.'

'Hmmm,' she said, doubtfully, and then, after a pause, 'So, why the Damascene conversion? Why come back?'

He didn't have to answer the question immediately, as the waiter arrived with their main courses. They thanked him as he set the plates down in front of them and wished them *'Buon appetito'*. Layla raised her left shoulder slightly and then let it fall again while making a gesture with her right hand which he interpreted as indicating that his answer could wait until after they had eaten.

'The first day back on Lipari, I had plenty to do: the hut to clean; the water system to service; catching up with people I know; getting a bit of shopping in; anything except think, really. But from the second day, I started to feel restless; the place was still idyllic and I had plenty of ideas for new stories to write but, even though there were plenty more tourists around, lots of whom were happy to chat, it felt as if there was something missing. Anyway, on my third day there, I got a message from my cousin to say that she was due for a few days' holiday and was thinking of spending most of it at her grandparents in Florence and was wondering if I'd be able to go up while she was there. There have been a couple of other occasions when I've had similar invitations since I moved onto the island and I've always turned them down - but this time...' He held his hands out, turning the palms upward as if to say, 'Well, what could I do.'

Layla indicated that he should continue.

'What I thought I needed was to get you out of my system, so I could move on. And talking through everything with Mati seemed like a good way of doing it. I knew that she detested you for the damage your interview had done and expected her to be outraged at how you'd forced me to help you, but...'

'But?'

'But that's not quite how it went. I told her everything – well, almost everything – and she listened to it all, very carefully and without interrupting. I assumed, as I told her, that she was getting angrier and angrier – and she was – but not with you.' He gave her a half smile, 'When I'd finished, she really had a go at me, called me an emotionally illiterate idiot, amongst other things. It turns out that she'd never really liked Judi anyway, so even there, she thought that you'd done me a good turn... anyway...'

Layla fixed her eyes on his, 'Anyway...?'

'Anyway. As everyone I know who's got any sense, seems to think that I'm really dumb for not forgiving you and trusting you, and my heart keeps telling me that my head doesn't know what it's doing, I decided I'd better find you and see if I can do better this time. So here I am.'

'So you are. Let's get a coffee, then I need to walk while I think.'

Outside, she put her arm through his although without getting too close, and they walked, without talking for the whole of the twenty minutes it took them to arrive at the Trevi Fountain. When they reached the railing, erected to discourage tourists from imitating Anita Ekberg and paddling in the water, Luke dipped a hand in to his back pocket and then, turning away from the water, threw a coin with his right hand, over his left shoulder and into the fountain.

'Doesn't that guarantee that you'll come back to Rome?' asked Layla.

'You watch too much television,' he replied with a smile. 'People say that because that's what was wished for in a film called *"three coins in the fountain"*, back in the 1950s. But that's just Hollywood; everyone knows that really, it applies to any wish you make.'

'And what did you wish for?'

He shook his head, 'The wish has to be a secret. If I say it out loud, it won't come true.'

'Aah, I see.' She opened her bag and took out a two euro coin.

'Any coin will do,' he said.

She smiled, 'I want to make sure that old Triton over there, knows that this is important.' She turned and threw her coin after his. 'Done it! Now we'll wait and see.'

They stopped on the pavement outside her hotel. He turned to face her and looked into her face which had become serious.

'Am I forgiven? He asked quietly.

She nodded. 'Let's say "on parole". But, Luke, how do I know you won't just walk out on me again when things get difficult?'

'We're trying to find a single girl amongst thousands, who could be dead, or in almost any country in Europe – possibly beyond. Just how much more difficult do you think things can get?'

'That's not what I meant.'

He sighed. 'I know'. He took her hands in his and squeezed as he looked into her dark eyes. 'You have to decide whether you can trust me – as I've decided I trust you. Without trust there can be nothing; it's like building a house on sand. It doesn't matter how good it looks, it's not going to last.'

She opened her mouth to speak, but he was quicker and, letting go of one of her hands, he placed the tips of his fingers on her lips. 'Goodnight. Think about it and, if you want me to hang around, meet me in the big Church we passed at the end of the road at half past nine. There's a famous chapel in there, the Borghese Chapel, where

Napoleon's sister is buried. I'll be there.' He leaned forwards and, removing his fingers, gave her the slightest of kisses on her cheek and then turned and walked away without looking back.

Although he was fairly sure that she would say "yes", his brain was so full of thoughts and possible scenarios that he found it difficult to get to sleep and, when some external noise woke him just before five, it was impossible to drop off again. He did his best to distract himself, mentally listing as many footballers as he could remember, going through the English football teams division by division and club by club. Even so, he had great difficulty in forcing himself to remain in bed until his watch told him it was half past six.

After showering and dressing, he left the hostel and slipped into a bar opposite the *Ministero dell'Interno* to consume a light breakfast. The bar's copy of the *Corriere dello Sport* was already being read on another table, so he picked up a copy of *Il Messaggero* to peruse while he ate his chocolate filled doughnut and sipped his *latte macchiato*. A link on the front page directed him to page seven and an article about the forthcoming referendum back in Britain. It was obviously a massive waste of money as no-one in their right mind could possibly think of voting to leave the European Union, but even so, the paper's London correspondent seemed to think that there would be quite a high anti-establishment protest vote. He realised that he'd have to make sure he was registered to vote; he couldn't remember whether he'd reregistered after leaving prison and before coming over to Italy.

After breakfasting, he made his way to the Basilica where he knew there would be enough artwork to allow him to while away the forty minutes that separated him from nine-thirty.

He didn't get as far as the Borghese Chapel as he saw Layla enter the church just before quarter past. She looked round as her eyes became accustomed to the light and he saw her look for a few seconds at the high ceiling of the nave before starting to move directly towards the chapel. He imagined that she had looked at the layout of the church on the internet before coming. The mosaic he was admiring was nearly forty metres further down the church and he quickly stepped out into the light and moved to intercept her.

She heard his footsteps and, somehow aware that it was him, turned with a broad smile on her face. 'You're early.'

'So are you. Do you mind?'

She shook her head. 'Do you really want to visit the chapel, or can we go outside?' His smile was all the response she needed.

'I'm glad you came,' he said as they came out into the bright sunshine.

'We've still got a lot we need to talk about - but that will have to wait until later.' He looked at her enquiringly. 'I have an appointment with a human rights lawyer at eleven; Luana set it up. I'll tell you about it on the way.'

'Whatever you say. Whereabouts are we - or you - meeting this lawyer?'

She pulled a phone out of her back pocket and pressed the button on the side. 'I've saved the address, and the directions for getting there on here. We need to go back to Termini and get the *Metro* as far as Marconi and the lawyer's studio is about five minutes' walk from there.'

The underground was crowded and it was difficult to conduct a conversation on the way but, as they located the lawyer's office with twenty minutes to spare, they decided they had time for a coffee in a nearby bar before ringing the bell by the brass nameplate.

Layla explained that Luana knew the lawyer slightly as a woman under her supervision in Catania had been called as a witness in a case that the lawyer had been dealing with a few months previously. She had not specified what that case had been about but she had said that the lawyer had a good reputation amongst social workers for being prepared to take on cases where she believed that discrimination was involved or where it appeared that refugees or other less fortunate members of society were being used as convenient scapegoats. Apparently, the lawyer had also written an article about the exploitation of refugees calling on government ministers to impose measures to improve the situation. The lawyer had agreed to set aside half an hour to talk to Layla.

The nameplate informed visitors that they were at the office of advocates Orlando and Giuliana Pusceddu. 'Husband and wife?' suggested Layla as she pushed the bell.

Luke shook his head, 'Not unless they were related before they married; women keep their surnames in Italy.'

'Desidera?' came a slightly metallic, but clearly female voice from the small grill beneath the bell-push.

Layla leaned forwards and said slowly and clearly, *'Signorina Layla Simons per vedere l'avvocato Pusceddu.'*

'Entra. Terzo piano.' And there was a click as the lock on the door disengaged. Luke pushed the door open and stepped slightly to the side to allow Layla to precede him. 'Third floor.'

She nodded, 'I got that,' and then added, 'but thanks anyway.' He suppressed a smile at the unnecessary politeness.

They took the lift as it wasn't immediately obvious which of the other doors led to the stairs. When they emerged on the third floor, a motion activated sensor turned on the light in the corridor and they found themselves faced with three strong looking doors. Two were closed, but the third was ajar. Luke tapped and opened the door saying, *'permesso'* as he allowed Layla to step past him.

A woman in her mid to late forties smiled at them from behind a very tidy desk where a central working space was surrounded by three neat piles of papers and an intercom system. *'Signorina* Simons?' she said with a welcoming smile, and glanced from Layla to Luke.

'Si,' said Layla, *'e questo é...'* she paused searching for the right words.

Luke stepped in with his more polished Italian, 'My name is Luke Garvey. I'm a friend of Miss Simons and I've been working with her on the case she's here to discuss.'

Still smiling, the secretary gestured them towards a well-worn settee with an *'Accomodatevi, prego.'* They sat, as directed.

After a short time, there was a buzzing on the intercom system. The secretary pressed a button and said, *'Dottoressa,* I have Signorina Simons and a friend here to see you.'

A soft voice said something in reply that Luke didn't catch and the secretary said 'OK' and then removed her finger from the button. She looked over at them, smiled and then, after carefully straightening the document she' been reading and placing her pen on top of it, stood up and said, in English, 'This way, please.'

They stood and followed her through the frosted glass door to one side of her desk.

A slightly built woman wearing a plain grey trouser suit over a white blouse with its collar buttoned right up to her neck, was already on her feet behind a large desk and, as they entered, moved from behind it to greet them. Luke observed her as she turned to Layla, with grey hair tied back in a simple pony-tail and apparently not wearing any make up, she seemed very plain and did not immediately inspire confidence. When she turned towards him, however, he was struck by the intensity of her grey-green eyes that seemed to penetrate as if carrying out a brain scan.

'This is Luke Garvey, a very good friend of mine who's helped me get as far as I have. It was Luke who introduced me to Luana Capezzi, who put me in touch with you.'

'Please, take a seat,' said the lawyer, gesturing toward one side of the room where six chairs were arranged around a conference table.'

When they were seated, it was the lawyer who began. 'Now. I hope you don't mind but I telephoned *la* Capezzi last night, so that I could get as much background information as possible before our meeting. She did mention that you would probably be accompanying Miss Simons, Mr Garvey - If I understand correctly, you are trying to trace a fourteen year old Libyan relative who you believe was smuggled over to Italy round about a year ago, and since then there has been no trace.' She looked at Layla, who indicated that that was correct. 'OK. I also understand that you managed to see conditions inside the camp at Mineo, and then to discover how the Sicilian section of the trafficking trade works.'

'Almost,' said Luke, 'although we only have circumstantial evidence that the girls, and occasionally boys, are being taken out of Sicily by traffickers and not moving of their own free will.'

'You're right, Mr Garvey; an important legal distinction but, although it may not stand up in court, I think we're fairly safe in basing future suppositions on that premise.' Luke nodded and the lawyer gave a grim smile. 'Now, *la* Capezzi has looked into the ownership of the lorry that was used and the sea-front warehouse where the girls were transferred to the boat. As I'm sure you can imagine, the traffickers have done their best to muddy the waters and make it very difficult to pick up the trail on the mainland. Or at least, it would be, if we weren't able to cross reference the information you provided with suspicious information that we've put together over the last year or so from other sources.'

Luke saw Layla's knuckles whiten as she gripped the arms of her chair tightly. 'So we'll be able to trace Zahra!' He reached over and gently placed his hand on top of one of hers.

An apologetic smile accompanied a shake of the head from the lawyer. 'That wasn't exactly what I meant, and I'm sorry if I gave that impression… There are a number of powerful people or organisations that we've suspected are involved in the trafficking trade, but so far, we've only had fairly limited circumstantial evidence. Now we believe that we've established definite connections between two of these people and what you've discovered in Sicily.'

'How definite is definite?' asked Luke.

'Not definite enough to lead to prosecutions, or even to make allegations without being prosecuted for defamation, but definite enough to make it improbable that we're barking up the wrong tree.'

'Go on.'

'As you may know, company ownership structures and cross-holdings can be very complex in Italy. Italy doesn't have its own offshore tax havens like Britain does, so instead, our corporate lawyers and accountants have developed extremely complicated structures which are almost impossible to understand. I won't bore you with details of all the work we've done trying to unravel some of these devices but, suffice it to say that we've managed to link the company that owns the warehouse to a former government minister and the company that leased the van used in the operation to a Milanese company, the beneficial owners of which also have interests in some of the co-operatives 'helping' refugees.' The contempt that she managed to express when she used the word "helping" was unmistakeable.

'So you think that the trail leads to Milan?' asked Layla, whose hopes had clearly been raised.

'Not necessarily, and for your sake, I hope not.'

Layla looked puzzled, and Luke, while remaining focused on the lawyer, increased the comforting pressure on her hand.

'As far as my associates in Milan have been able to ascertain, the mafia style gangs putting refugees on the streets in Milan and nearby provinces, tend to use mainly Nigerian girls. Depending on the area, the vast majority of girls tend to be either Nigerian, Albanian or Rumanian. Nearer the centre of the city, one finds a more upmarket type of prostitute, either Italian or Eastern Europeans who've been in the country for some time.'

'But what about girls from other countries? What happens to them?'

Pusceddu breathed out somewhat noisily through her nose as she gave a slight shake of her head.

'Girls of other – rarer – nationalities, tend to be kept together and sent to smaller towns or, treated as exotic goods and sold to individuals on a permanent basis.'

'Modern slavery,' said Layla.

'Almost certainly sex slaves,' added Luke. The lawyer nodded her head in agreement. 'And what happens to these girls when their new owners tire of them? Passed down the line until no-one has any use for them anymore and then killed?'

Pusceddu didn't respond immediately, but then said, 'As I said, we have two possible trails. However you look at the Milanese trail, it's difficult to see any possible positive outcome, but there just might be if you focus on the former government minister who, if our suspicions are correct, controls either directly or indirectly, much of the prostitution in Northern Tuscany.'

'By "Northern Tuscany" you mean...?'

'I'm excluding the Province of Arezzo which seems to be controlled from Perugia and the Province of Grosseto and the area to the south of Siena which we have reason to believe is controlled from Rome.'

'Sorry,' said Layla, who was struggling to keep up with the conversation, 'Remind me. Why are we excluding areas controlled by Rome and Perugia? Couldn't my cousin have been trafficked there?'

'She could. But at the moment, the only links we have, are to northern Tuscany and Milan. If your cousin is still alive, it's possible she could be anywhere in Western Europe – if not beyond. My suggestion would be that if you want to pursue your search, you go to Tuscany.

'Tuscany - whereabouts in Tuscany? It's quite a big place!'

The lawyer assented, 'It is, but some parts are more known for prostitution than others. As the region's capital, Florence has more than its fair share but the information we have suggests that much of the organized activity there is controlled outside the city where the police and *carabinieri* tend to be underfunded and overstretched, and where there are less likely to be complaints from tourists.'

'Montecatini?' he said quizzically, and this time it was the lawyer's turn to look surprised.

'My aunt's father had a friend who lived in the hills above Pescia. I went with him to visit a few times and I was always amazed when we drove through the outskirts of Montecatini on the way back. I doubt if there were ever less than ten, spread out over a two or three kilometre stretch of road.'

'Our information indicates that there are usually far more than that,' said the lawyer drily.

Out of the corner of his eye, he saw Layla raise a hand to her forehead and rub it gently – It must be terrible to think that Zahra could have been forced into that kind of life. He looked at the lawyer, trying not to lose focus on the practical aspects of the situation. 'How do we move forward from here? I mean, is there any practical information you can give us, so that we know where to start looking?'

'Not much, I'm afraid. We've just been keeping an eye on Tuscany while our main efforts have been directed at Milan. But I can give you the names of a couple of contacts in the area whom you can trust.'

He nodded, and she pulled a block of post-it notes towards her. 'Before I do, however, I need your written agreement that no information you gather, either here or in Tuscany, will ever find its way into print without first being approved by this office.' She smiled.

Luke glanced across at Layla who had her hand on her forehead again and was looking a little dazed. He looked back at the lawyer, 'That's a very wide ranging agreement. I think we would prefer just to give you our word that we would never do anything that would endanger your work and the people working with you, in any way.'

'I need more than that, I'm afraid, Signor Garvey... particularly in view of Signorina Simons' profession as a journalist. In this country, we've learnt to be very wary of journalists.'

'As we have in England, but sometimes you have to rely on instinct,' he said, hoping that there was no trace of bitterness in his voice.

'I do, Signor Garvey. I've heard of Luana Capezzi and I was prepared to rely on her judgement in agreeing to meet Signorina Simons, and my own judgement allowed me to give you the information I already have but, at the moment, I have to protect the people who are already helping me, sometimes at risk of their lives, above all else. So I'm afraid that, without having something in writing, I'm unable to release any further information.' Luke shook his head with a wry smile. 'In that case,' she said, rising, 'as you are unable to provide the assurances I need, you'll have to excuse me as I have another appointment.'

Luke also rose, stretching out his right hand as he did so, while putting gentle pressure on Layla's right elbow with his left hand to indicate that she too should rise. He looked the lawyer in the eye, 'You said, "at the moment".' For the first time, her slight smile reached her eyes.

'I did Signor Garvey. I did.'

'In that case then, I'll say *arriverderci,* rather than *addio.*'

'Arriverderci, Signor Garvey, Signorina Simons.'

'Arriverderci,' repeated Layla, although Luke was fairly sure that she wouldn't have picked up on the subtle choice of salutation – he'd have to explain to her later how *addio* would have indicated finality while the less formal *arrivederci* didn't.

'Are you OK?' he asked, as they stepped out onto the street. 'You were very quiet in there.'

'I'm sorry,' she said, breathing in deeply, 'A headache came on and, because of that, I lost track of the conversation completely.'

He looked at her with concern, 'You do look a bit pale. Shall we find a bar and order the strongest cup of tea they can make.'

'Mum always used to say that the most important thing that she'd learnt in England was that a good cup of tea will always make you feel better. Thanks for the suggestion, but I'm feeling a bit better now that we're out in the fresh air. I think that a bit of a walk would do me more good than anything else.'

'Whatever you think best.' he said, as he looked round to get his bearings. 'I think that if we go in that general direction, it should take us to the river.' He held his arm out for her to take.

'Do you often get these headaches?'

She leaned her head against his shoulder as they sat on the bench by the Tiber. I've been having them on and off since around the time when I first found out about Aida; usually they're fairly light, sometimes, like this morning, they make it more difficult to concentrate for a bit, but then they pass.' She looked up and smiled at him.

He wasn't to be distracted so easily. 'Have you told anyone about them? Apart from me, I mean - like a doctor?'

'It's nothing to worry about. I mentioned them to a friend who did Psychology at Uni, and she said that they'll be stress related and that they'll pass eventually – especially if I can get rid of the causes of the stress – and that's what we're trying to do, isn't it?'

'I suppose so. But, if they continue, or get worse, I want you to promise that you'll see a proper doctor.'

'Mmmm. You're so masterful. I hope you're not masking your insecurities like the male character in *"Fifty Shades"*,' she laughed.

'I'm afraid I haven't read it. I've only seen the trailer for the film, and that was bad enough.'

Luke suddenly remembered Mati. 'Oh, bugger. I forgot.' Layla looked up at him. 'My cousin, Matilde, is going to be in Rome tonight, and she wants to meet you.'

'Why?' she said, lifting her head off his shoulder and sitting upright.

'Well... If she'd said she wanted to see you a week ago, you'd probably have been better off avoiding her but, since I told her your side of the story and let her know what we've been doing for the last few weeks, she now seems to be under the impression that you're the one whose been hard done by in all this.'

'I'm not sure about it. You can't spend five years hating someone and then just forget all about it overnight.'

'I did tell her that I didn't think it was a good idea, and warned her not to forget that you're a journalist and that makes you dangerous – but you females are pretty stubborn when you set your mind to it.'

'That's a typically sexist male comment. From personal experience, I'd say that you more often find men with fixed ideas.'

'So, should I send her a message and tell her you can't make it? I won't ring her as it's easier to say no to her in a text message.'

'Coward!' She sighed, then said, 'No. I'll do it. If she wants to have a go at me then I completely understand.'

'Thankyou. I'm sure she doesn't want to have a go at you, and I'd be really pleased if the two of you like each other.' She squeezed his arm and then leaned her head back and closed her eyes.

They met Mati by the fountain at the foot of the Spanish Steps at eight o'clock and, after Luke and Mati had briefly embraced, he presented her somewhat awkwardly to Layla. Layla extended a hand in greeting but Mati ignored it and stepped forward to kiss Layla on both cheeks and give her a hug.

When they separated, Mati turned to Luke and, with a stern look said, 'Luke, go and find somewhere decent for us to eat, and don't come back for at least half an hour. Layla and I have got things to talk about. Make sure it's a nice restaurant; I'm paying.'

Layla looked at him, her eyes pleading with him to stay but he gave her a little smile and shrugged resignedly before turning away and heading off without looking back.

He avoided the roads leading back towards the main tourist attractions and likewise Via dei Condotti with its expensive boutiques, instead directing his steps westwards hoping that the restaurants he would stumble across would be more genuine and less focussed on giving tourists the 'traditional' Italian-eating experience they expected; on one of his first visits to Italy, when he had expressed a desire for *spaghetti bolognese*, his uncle had given him some good advice that he'd never forgotten: 'If ever you see *"Spaghetti Bolognese"* written on a restaurant menu in Italy, run a mile. No-one in Italy would ever refer to it by that name unless they're only interested in cooking for the English and Americans. You'd almost be better off eating at MacDonald's; at least you'd know what you were eating'.

Although he'd been ordered to go away for half an hour, he was anxious to know how it was going in the square and determined to reserve a table at the first reasonable restaurant or trattoria that he found. The first he came across was only two minutes' walk from where he'd left the others and looked reasonable from the outside. Before going in, however, he pulled out his phone and looked for reviews. Every single review he found on TripAdvisor was by a native English speaker, which didn't fill him with confidence and the ratings covered the whole spectrum from excellent to terrible and were fairly evenly spread. Reluctantly, he put his phone away and hurried along to the next restaurant another two minutes' walk away. This time, there was something about the understated exterior of the restaurant that inspired confidence and he didn't bother to check the reviews, preferring to trust his instinct.

Once through the door, he descended a flight of well illuminated stone steps that descended in a slight curve between beige plastered walls, tastefully decorated with unusual photographs of icons from the golden age of Italian cinema. He recognised the better known actors such as Loren, Magnani, Cardinale and Mastroianni but several others were unfamiliar to him. At the bottom of the steps, an immaculately turned-out waiter greeted him with a formality that was softened by a smile.

Luke glanced around and saw that the restaurant was in what must once have been the cellars of a large house, but which had now been tastefully restored with several brick archways dividing the eating area up to give all diners a degree of privacy. He could see that two tables were already occupied and all the others appeared to have *'riservato'* signs on them; he resigned himself to having to continue his search.

'I was wondering, if you might have a table available for three people in about forty-five minutes,' he said, without much hope.

The waiter smiled, 'That will be no problem, sir. We were fully booked, but we've just had a cancellation. May I take your name?'

'Garvey; that's, gee – ah – erre – vu – ay – e-greca.' He said, glad he could remember how to pronounce the letters in Italian.

'Very good, sir. We look forward to seeing you later.'

At the beginning of Piazza di Spagna, he cut off to his left and, after cutting up a side-street, took the steps by the Bottino Fountain to reach the obelisk in front of the Church of Santa Trinitá al Monte from where he had a good view over the Spanish Steps and Piazza di Spagna.

As usual, there were plenty of people in the piazza and it took him a couple of minutes to locate the two women who were sitting on one of the steps talking animatedly. He tried to work out how they were getting on from their body language but found it too difficult as his view was regularly obscured as groups of tourists ascended or descended the steps. The best he could manage was to feel fairly confident that they weren't arguing.

After watching them for ten minutes, he made his way down the steps to join them.

'Hi!' he said cheerfully. 'Hope I haven't kept you waiting.'

'No problem. We girls can always find plenty to talk about. Did you find somewhere decent to eat? I could eat a horse.'

'You should have said. I'm sure I could have found somewhere that does horse if I'd known about your new dietary requirements. Is that something you've developed in Switzerland?'

Luke was burning with curiosity to find out how their talk had gone but, both on their way to the restaurant and while they were eating, it was clear that there was a tacit agreement between them to give nothing away and only talk about the food, which was excellent. The waiter, after establishing that there were no food allergies to worry about, suggested that they try the taster menu, which removed the problem of having to take decisions, other than the choice of wine, and even there, the waiter was able to make helpful suggestions.

He knew he was being teased, and was fairly certain that Mati was to blame, but he was not prepared to give them the satisfaction of asking until he was in a position to ask them separately. After the meal and a *caffé*, Mati placed herself between the two of them as they walked back towards Layla's hotel, and it was only at the last minute that she relented, stopping to look in a shop window just before the hotel. She gave Layla a hug and said something that Luke didn't catch before moving over to the window. Layla moved closer to him and put her arm through his for the last few metres.

'Well?' he asked, unable to restrain himself any longer as they came to a halt in front of the entrance and she turned towards him, taking a step closer and offering her cheek for a goodnight kiss.

'I haven't changed my mind about you,' she said, with a smile, and he gave her a brief kiss.

'And did you get on with Mati.'

'I think so; I liked her - and she seemed friendly. Does it make a big difference to you?'

He smiled, 'I'm really glad you got on; it makes life a lot easier, but,' he paused and she looked up at him with a slight look of anxiety in her eyes. 'But, if I had to choose...' He raised his hand and gently stroked her cheek with one finger, 'I've already made my decision, and I'm sticking with it.'

She leaned in quickly, gave him a brief kiss that seemed to have a lingering afterglow, slipped away from his hand and almost ran into her hotel, calling, 'Goodnight,' as she did.

'*Andiamo*. Time to go,' came Mati's voice from behind him. 'Everything OK?'

He was about to give an enthusiastic affirmative when he remembered that Mati had admitted to never having told him what she really thought of Judi, and instead attempted a non-committal shrug.

'What did you think of her?' he asked, forcing his voice to sound neutral, although he was fairly sure she'd see through it.

'Does it make any difference?' she responded with a smile.

Luke avoided answering the question as she had with his. 'You know I value your opinion – and I'm still not sure I've forgiven you for not telling me what you really thought about Judi.'

She laughed and slipped an arm through his, 'I don't think it would change your mind if I said I didn't like her but,' she hurried to continue, 'I really liked her and, if you don't make the most of your time with her, I'll never forgive you,' she finished with a note of mock severity.

'*Grazie.*'

Chapter Twelve

Luke didn't see Mati the following morning as her flight to Geneva was an early one, but he received a text from her as he was getting ready to leave the hostel.

<Suggest you take 9.57 to Viareggio then 13.15 to Florence via Montecatini. Have booked hotel for two nights outside Montecatini –confirmation to your e-mail - Why not borrow Francesca's old Ducati as well as car? Speak tonight.>

Layla had also checked out of her hotel and they had time to grab a light breakfast in the station buffet between purchasing their tickets and catching the train.

Luke was slightly surprised to see that their hotel was in Borgo a Buggiano, a couple of miles outside Montecatini, rather than in the town itself. 'Surely, a place like Montecatini must have loads of hotel rooms free so early in the season.'

'It probably does. But if you think about it, it makes more sense to be outside the town – we can't afford a long stay in the more upmarket hotels and we don't know which ones at the cheaper end of the spectrum might be being used by the prostitutes – or even worse by those who're controlling them.'

They agreed that if Layla came with Luke to Florence to pick up the car from Mati's grandparents' house near San Miniato it would require too many complicated introductions and explanations. Meeting them would be better if put off until another day and Luke, on his own, could have a coffee with them, express his regrets at not being able to stay longer, promise to see them again soon and leave with the car and with the bike keys which he knew were kept in Mati's room. In the meantime, Layla could get off the train at Borgo a Buggiano, check into their hotel and then catch a bus into Montecatini.

It was early evening when they were able to meet up again after Layla had sent him a text with the name and location of a piano-bar just north of Montecatini's central square.

'Been waiting long?' he asked, as he slid into a chair at ninety degrees to hers, looking round at the expensive décor. 'Last night must have given you a taste for luxury.'

'Only a few minutes and, it may be a bit over the top but, and I know it's silly, I felt a bit self-conscious as a single woman going into some of the other bars.' He gave a quizzical frown.

'That doesn't sound like the intrepid reporter who's spent the last few years exploring some of the most dangerous places in the middle-east.'

She reached out and put her hand on his, 'I had a walk round the edge of the town earlier. There's quite a long road that takes traffic round the southern edge of the town – seems to be traffic to and from the motorway. Well, even though it's still early, there are girls every fifty metres or so, usually alone but occasionally in pairs. As you walk past, they either turn away or stare at you with a sort of contempt, almost daring you to say something. And the cars that drive past...' she shuddered, 'I know what cattle must feel like when they're in the ring at an auction, being weighed up by everyone and knowing that they all think they can buy you as a piece of meat. They almost all slow down and it's as if they're peeling your clothes off and violating you with their eyes.'

He rotated his hand under hers so that he could grip it and give it a reassuring squeeze. 'Was there any sign of who was controlling the girls?'

She shook her head. 'None that I saw, although I was trying to look nonchalant and didn't dare look round too much. There were a couple of bars that seemed fairly well populated but I didn't feel up to going in.' She smiled. 'And I did notice a couple of girls disappear up one of the side streets, but again, I didn't feel it was sensible to follow them.'

'No. I'm glad you didn't. I suppose that at some point, I'm going to have to play the part of a punter, if we think these girls may be able to give us any information.'

'Hmmm. You'd better be careful and make sure you've got your EHIC card handy!'

He gave her a gentle smile and leaned closer to her, 'Weren't we talking about the need for mutual trust a couple of days ago?'

The Hotel was reasonably comfortable with free Wi-Fi, free parking and what seemed to be a reasonably new mattress on the bed, but the limited breakfast choices, the main feature of which seemed to be cellophane wrapped plain sponge cakes was a perfect metaphor for its overall blandness. Even the pleasure that they had found in finally being able to speak openly, without pretence and without reserve, was not enough to blind them to the hotel's lack of character.

Over their uninspiring breakfast, they agreed that finding somewhere they felt more comfortable in should be a priority as the time it took to locate would be more than compensated for by the advantages to be gained. Layla suggested checking the small-ads but Luke was adamant that they were far more likely to find somewhere by just asking around, and so, as soon as both were ready, they began a tour of the bars of Borgo a Buggiano.

'Buongiorno,'

'Buongiorno. What can I get you?'

'Un caffé and a *té caldo* please.'

…. 'Here they are.'

'Grazie.'

'Prego.'

…. 'I don't suppose you know of anyone in, or near, Buggiano who might have a small apartment or a *rustico* that they'd be interested to rent out for a month, do you?'

'I can't think of anyone offhand. Have you tried asking in the estate agency?'

'Not yet. As it's only for a short period, I was hoping for something a bit more informal. There's no point paying agency fees if it's possible to avoid them, is there?' A look of understanding passed between them.

'Leave me your number and I'll ask around – although, as I said, I'm not aware of anyone.'

'That's great, thanks. Here you are.'

The same, or very similar conversations, took place in four bars during the morning, while in two others Luke decided that those serving behind the counters inspired no confidence and he didn't bother. The result of all this was that by the time they decided to lunch in a small and very basic looking *trattoria* by the market place, they were feeling a little dispirited and somewhat thick-headed with all the caffeine.

The tables and chairs in the trattoria were very plain with blue and white check tablecloths that could be wiped down with a cloth between customers. Old photographs of the area covered much of the wall-space, although in a fairly haphazard way and without any attempt to use similar types of framing. They paused and looked round as they went through the door then a large man who had been leaning over the little desk part way down the left hand side of the room, raised his head and gestured towards an empty table set for two.

A couple of minutes later, the man came over and placed a basket of bread in the middle of their table.

'*Acqua? Vino?*'

'A jug of tap-water if that's possible and some *vino rosso.*'

'OK. To start, we've got penne or *spaghetti* with *ragu*, tomato or *amatriciana*. Then for secondo we've got spare-ribs, *salsiccie* or *trippa.*'

'What is *amatriciana*?' Layla asked.

'It's basically: tomato, bacon, garlic, basil and seasoning', replied Luke, and then to the waiter, 'That's right isn't it: *pomodoro, pancetta, aglio e basilico?*'

'Not *pancetta*; we use *guanciale*, pig's cheek, instead. My mother-in-law was from Norcia which is not far from Amatrice, and she insisted we follow the original recipe.'

'In that case, I'll definitely have *spaghetti all'amatriciana* and then the *trippa.*'

'I'll have the *amatriciana* as well and then the *salsicce.*'

'*Contorno?*'

'Can you bring us some chips, please.'

The waiter nodded and then disappeared for a minute or so through a door at the back of the room.

'I hope it's alright,' said Layla, 'it's a bit different to the restaurant in Rome, isn't it?'

'It will be. Places like this will hardly ever see a tourist; they rely on locals and local workers for their custom, so even if the food's simple, it has to be made of quality ingredients cooked well - otherwise custom would just dry up straight away.'

The man returned with a jug of water and a two litre flask of red wine into which a cork had been pushed by hand. Layla's eyes opened wide at the sight of the wine.

'Excuse me,' said Luke, touching the man briefly on the forearm, preventing him from moving away, 'I don't suppose you know of anyone with a small apartment or a *rustico* that they'd be willing to rent out for a couple of months, do you?'

The man glanced around and then shook his head.

'OK. Not to worry.'

'Let's worry about it after lunch,' said Layla, 'My head's starting to ache again; I think it must be the effect of an empty stomach and too many coffees.' Luke gave her a concerned look. 'Don't worry, It'll be OK when I've had something to eat and drunk some water... but I'm not sure I'll be able to manage my half of the wine.'

He laughed. 'Don't worry, I'll drink your share as well... No. Not really. We'll only be charged for the amount we actually drink, so we can drink as much, or as little as we like. Oh, a text,' he said as his phone vibrated in his pocket. He pulled it out and looked at it. 'It's from my other Italian cousin, Alessio.'

She tilted her head back and raised her eyes, 'I don't have to be inspected and approved by every member of your family, do I? No wonder I've got a head-ache.'

'I don't think so. He wants me to give him a ring after five; says he may be able to help me; I assume he must have been talking to Mati.'

The food was as simple and as good as Luke had hoped and he finished it off with a coffee, although Layla declined to join him, giving a slight shake of her head and a wan smile. He realised that her headache had not yet left her and looked at her with concern.

'Don't worry,' she said, noticing his look, 'I'll be fine soon.'

Layla was right. Once they were outside in the crisp spring air, her headache disappeared. They stood for a minute discussing, without much enthusiasm, which direction to go in to continue their trail around the bars when a white Nissan Qashqai pulled into a space a few metres from them and a balding man in his thirties wearing a well-worn grey suit got out and, without bothering to lock the car, hurried into the trattoria from which they had recently emerged.

He came out again almost immediately accompanied by the proprietor who looked around and them waved an arm in their direction before retreating back through the door. The man turned towards them and approached, extending his right hand towards Luke as he did so.

'Pasquale,' he said, introducing himself. 'I believe you're interested in a short term rental.'

'We are,' said Luke, taking the other man's hand. 'Garvey, Luke Garvey and this is my...' he glanced at Layla, 'my wife.'

The man inclined his head towards Layla, acknowledging her existence, but continued to direct his attention towards Luke. 'I have a small house in a village about four kilometres from here that might suit your purposes. It hasn't been modernised but it has everything you should need. If you'd like to come up and see it now, I can take you up there.' Luke glanced towards Layla who gave a shrug of acquiescence.

'OK. Thankyou.'

The four kilometres seemed somewhat of an understatement to Luke, and the narrow twisting lanes made it seem even longer than it actually was, but he liked the look of the village when got there. He could see that the road finished by the village church but Pasquale turned off the road onto a steep track just at the start of the houses and Luke thought that they were going to end up in the middle of the woods. However, the track, after initially taking them away from the buildings, looped back to bring them into the top of the village where they pulled up in a slightly wider area enclosed on three sides by the buildings at the top of the village.

At the far end of the square, as he euphemistically thought of it, was what appeared to be the rear of one of the village's original medieval buildings while the five buildings which formed the other two built-up sides appeared to be later additions. To their right was a large dilapidated house with the appearance of having been uninhabited for years and which had a handwritten 'for sale' notice attached to the door with drawing pins. Next to that was a smaller but immaculately maintained house covered in white stucco and with a vine-shaded terrace alongside where the inhabitants obviously ate outside when the weather allowed. The first building on the left-hand side was also clearly inhabited and a mini-tractor with a trailer full of logs parked between the side of the house and a thriving vegetable plot indicated that its owners were well established and active. At the far end of the left-hand side, facing the white house with the terrace, was another that could have been its twin had it not been for the large terracotta vases full of flowering shrubs that flanked the door.

The middle house on the left-hand side was much smaller. It appeared to be in good condition with the traditional wooden green shutters that covered the single window on the ground floor and the two above having been replaced with green aluminium ones, probably at the same time as a sturdy new door had been installed. A 'for sale' notice with two telephone numbers to call had been attached to one side of the shutters over the ground floor window.

Pasquale extracted a bunch of keys from the glove box in the car and selected the right ones to unlock the two locks on the door before preceding them in so that he could turn on the electricity and open the shutters to allow light to flood in. The entrance gave directly onto a combined kitchen and utility room that stretched the full length of the ground floor. In front of them was a marble tiled staircase that led to the upper floor turning at ninety degrees for the last few steps. Most of the room, and the window were to their right with the far wall being covered by high storage cupboards above an old fashioned sink and draining board. Between the window and the door was a free-standing gas cooker similar to one that Luke could just about remember in his grandparents' house. The only other item of furniture occupying part of the terracotta tiled floor was a simple formica-topped table with three chairs.

'There's a cloakroom under the stairs,' said Pasquale, opening a narrow door beside the stairs and stepping aside to allow Layla to go in and look. 'It was the original bathroom but, when my grandparents moved in after they inherited the house back in the early seventies they sacrificed one of the bedrooms and had a proper bathroom put in upstairs'. He stepped back and, after Layla rejoined them, said, 'But the best room downstairs is this one,' and he opened another door, allowing them to step into a trapezoid shaped living room with two windows giving spectacular views across the valley and towards Montecatini. 'I'm afraid there's no furniture as my grandmother slept in here during the last few months of her life when the stairs were too much for her. The bed and most of the other things were orthopaedic ones provided by social services and the hospital. Everything in here, either went back, or was thrown out after she died but, if you decide you're interested, I've got a few bits in my cellar that I could move in.'

'OK,' said Luke, 'it's looking like a possibility so far. Can we see upstairs?'

'Of course.'

Three doors led off a small landing at the top of the stairs. Two led to bedrooms that faced out over the square. Each contained a double bed and a wardrobe, which didn't leave much space for anything else; in one of the rooms, a piece had been cut out of the top of the wardrobe to allow an exposed chestnut beam to pass over the top.

'It must get pretty hot in summer,' said Luke, looking up at the terracotta under- tiles between the beams, 'I don't imagine they put in much insulation when these were built.'

Pasquale shrugged, 'Most people – except for the young ones who have air conditioning fitted – keep the shutters closed during the day and then open everything up as soon as it goes dark, so that air passes through the house. The important thing is to remember not to turn the lights on so you don't attract insects.'

The third door led to a bathroom that was surprisingly modern with a walk-in shower as well as a bath. As it faced in the same direction as the living room, it enjoyed the same panoramic views with the extra advantage conferred by being slightly higher up.

'Impressive!.. You wouldn't think that that was fitted in the seventies.'

Pasquale smiled and shook his head. 'No. About eight years ago, my father was thinking of moving in with my grandparents so he could keep an eye on them, and he got as far as having the bathroom redone, but then... it didn't happen.'

'You never thought of living here yourself?' asked Luke.

'I would have liked to; I spent a lot of time here when I was growing up, but my wife has never liked it.'

Luke nodded and Pasquale looked at him expectantly.

'Can we have a few minutes to think about it?'

'No problem. I want to call in and see an old friend so feel free to have another look without me and discuss it between you. I'll be back in about ten minutes.'

'That's great. Thanks.'

'Well... What do you think?'

'I like it. Although, is it a bit far from Montecatini? Remember, we'll probably need to be down there quite late at night, and it'll take at least twenty minutes, probably half an hour.'

'On the other hand, we don't need to be up early in the mornings and, if it might be an advantage living out of sight of the people we're trying to find out about. It doesn't seem like the sort of place where you need to worry about someone sticking a knife in you.'

'Alright,' said Layla. 'See how much it's going to cost. If we can afford it, then fine.'

'What sort of amount were you thinking of?' asked Luke.

'How about a hundred a week?'

Luke shook his head. 'We like it but it's not all that convenient. We're going to need to go down to Montecatini or Pistoia most days.

For that price we could find somewhere in one of the bigger towns. It probably wouldn't be as nice but it would save us a lot of time.'

'So how much would you be willing to pay?'

'Well, I was hoping you'd be asking about half that - Cash in hand, of course.'

Shortly after they settled on sixty euros a week and Pasquale got one of their new neighbours to agree to allow them to use the password for their wireless internet connection. Luke handed over two hundred and forty euros when Pasquale dropped them off by a cash-point back in Borgo a Buggiano half an hour later with an agreement that he would pay over another hundred and twenty in two weeks' time, so that they remained a month in advance.

As soon as Pasquale had driven off, Layla punched him hard on his arm.

'Ow!' he said, rubbing his arm, 'What was that for?'

She glared at him, 'my wife!'

He grinned, 'Oh that. You need to remember that in a lot of ways people here are very conservative. Some people wouldn't be all that keen on allowing unmarried couples to live in their houses; I thought it best to pretend you were a respectable woman.'

She rolled her eyes and then waved her left hand in front of him. 'And how do we explain this when we meet the neighbours?'

'Good point. I hadn't thought about that. Come on!' and he took hold of her hand and set off down the street.

'Choose.'

'It had better be the cheapest, hadn't it?'

'No,' he said, looking at the tray of wedding rings that the assistant had pulled out of the display case, 'Choose whichever you think best suits you.'

'But that's silly.'

'No, it isn't, and anyway, gold holds it value, doesn't it?'

As it happened, the ring Layla preferred, a simple gold band, while not the cheapest was towards the lower end of the price spectrum. It needed to be adjusted slightly but the assistant promised them it would be ready for the following afternoon.

They were silent for a while as they walked back towards their hotel then, as they waited to cross the main road, she said, 'I never thought I'd ever have one of those on my finger.'

'And I never thought I'd be buying one again - life's full of surprises isn't it?'

Luke rang Alessio just before six and, after a couple of minutes light hearted banter, as if by mutual agreement, they moved on to the real reason for the call.

'Mati called me last night and told me what you're trying to do over in Montecatini; it may surprise you, but I think I may be able to help.'

'Go on. I'm listening.'

'OK. The elder brother of an old school friend amazed all his family one day by announcing he'd decided to become a priest, after several years of saying he wanted to train to be a social worker after university. Anyway, despite his parents – particularly his father – being unhappy about it, and constant teasing from my friend and his sister, he went ahead with it. I saw Lorenzo – my friend – last week, and he was telling me that Simone finished at the seminary last year and has been sent as an assistant Priest to a church in Montecatini. I thought he might be able to help you.'

Luke thought for a moment. 'It's a good idea, although I'm not sure how closely involved the local churches would be with the prostitution and trafficking scenes.'

'You're probably right about the trafficking but I would have thought that prostitution would be one of their concerns. Apart from the fact that a lot of the clients will go along to confession every now and again to get a slap on the wrist that wipes the slate clean, from what I've read, there are a lot of prostitutes from Eastern Europe, and some of them will be Catholic.'

'But, even if they are, surely anything they reveal in the confessional has to stay secret, doesn't it?'

'It does. But only if the person wants it to stay secret, and also, I would have thought that most contact would take place outside the confessional.'

'What? You mean the priests…'

'No. That's not what I mean. If I were a priest, I imagine that I would see a big part of my role as getting out in the community and helping people – and, in Montecatini, can you think of any group of people more obviously in need of help?'

'OK. I see what you mean - and you think that this priest friend of yours will have contacts with…'

'Not so fast'. Alessio interrupted him. 'He's only been there a few months and I've no idea how busy his regular church duties keep him but, I thought, he may well be aware if there is any church initiative, or if any individuals in any of the other churches in Montecatini take an interest.'

'It's an idea - and probably a good one. If you can give me his name and let me know what church he's attached to, I'll look him up tomorrow.'

'It might be better if you leave it to me to contact him; even though he's a few years older than me, he'll remember me because I used to go round quite often to do homework together with Lorenzo.'

'That'd be great. But probably best not to give him too many details before I meet him - if he's prepared to meet me, of course.'

'You can rely on me.'

'So he agreed to contact this Don Simone, and he'll let me know tomorrow, or as soon as he's been able to fix something up.'

'That's great. It sounds much more promising than just spending our evenings sitting around watching prostitutes,' said Layla enthusiastically.

'Maybe,' said Luke, without anything like the same enthusiasm, 'I'm just not sure how much faith I've got in priests to help.'

Layla put her hand on his, 'Don't be so judgemental. From what I saw down in Sicily, there are all sorts. If either this priest, or any others he knows, are anything like the two nuns who ran the refuge at Poggio al Vento, it'll be a big help. If not...' she raised a shoulder. 'nothing ventured, nothing gained.'

'OK,' he sighed, 'but don't get your hopes up too high.'

Alessio rang early the following morning just as Luke was stepping out of a lukewarm shower. 'Tomorrow evening, about eight-thirty in the bar and *gelateria* on Via Verdi,' he repeated. 'Will that be easy to find? Aren't there a lot of ice-cream places in Montecatini?'......... 'OK. Got that... brightly coloured tables outside... yes, I'm making notes.' He glanced across at Layla and she nodded as she clicked onto Google Maps. 'Bringing someone with him. Who?'......... 'Alright. What did you tell him?' .... 'And he didn't want to know any more?'........... 'OK. Understood. Found it!' he said as Layla passed him the tablet. 'Layla, just found the ice-cream place on Google Streetview.'........ 'I know. The wonders of modern technology.'......... He laughed, 'I do, don't I? I'll let you know how it goes, and we'll see you on Wednesday when we come over to pick up the Ducati.'...... 'Yes. Same to you. *Ciao. A presto.*'

'So. Tomorrow evening,' said Layla.

'Yes. And he's bringing along another priest who he thinks may be of more use to us.'

'I thought you asked your cousin not to tell him too much.'

'He didn't. He only told him that we were trying to trace someone from Africa, and this other priest happens to be from Africa, so he thought he might be of more use to us. You never know.'

'And what do you think?'

'I really don't know,' responded Luke, 'It could work either way. I'd heard that there are more and more priests coming into Italy from Catholic countries around the world, because they're struggling to find enough Italians who're interested – one effect of a falling birth-rate, I suppose; if you're an only child, in line to inherit anything that's going, then people are less likely to suggest the church as a career for you.'

'Isn't it supposed to be about vocation?' asked Layla with a smile.

'Of course,' said Luke adopting a pious expression, 'And in the past, when families were bigger, a surprising number of younger sons got the call, leaving their older brothers to inherit their parents' estate.'

'Cynic,' said Layla, punching him lightly on the arm.

Despite being more hopeful about the meeting with the priests than Luke was, Layla agreed that it wasn't sensible to waste the time before then. Stocking up the food cupboards in their new home and working out how to improve the water temperature took up most of the daylight hours and they determined to use the evening to try an alternative approach.

Having driven to the far end of the long road that took traffic around the southern edge of the town centre, and which was the axis around which the red-light area revolved, Luke parked the car in the near deserted car-park by the basketball arena.

'Ready?'

She smiled. 'I went to far more dangerous places during the Arab Spring and, as far as I'm aware, this time I'm not breaking any laws. Come on; you're meant to be my cameraman.' She opened the door and got out. He followed, and locked the car manually as the remote had stopped working.

'You might get an offer as we walk along.'

'Not dressed like this I won't,' she said, giving him a little twirl to illustrate the fact that she had put on the most sober and serious clothes available in the somewhat limited wardrobe she had with her.

'I don't know. You hear about people dressing us as nurses or nuns – why not as business women.' She thumped him on his arm and then, when he added, 'good idea; add in a bit of S and M as well,' she followed up by sticking her tongue out at him.

They had noticed from the car that the first stretch of the road was only occupied by two girls with about fifty metres between them, both, fortunately, on the same side of the road, allowing them to pass by on the other. As they did so, they were careful not to look across, and to keep their heads down to make it less likely to be recognised if they came across the girls at a later date.

After two hundred metres they came to a small roundabout where they had noticed a police car parked. The car was still there as they had thought it would be. They could see that beginning immediately after the roundabout, the number of girls increased dramatically and Luke could clearly distinguish as least seven, three of whom held cigarettes either in between their fingers or pressed nervously into their mouths, while another three held mobiles. All were dressed in very short skirts and one of them had one foot resting on the top of a low bollard which drew even more attention to her legs and the beginning of the curve above where the tight skirt had begun to ride up. At least two of the girls wore skimpy crop-tops under light unzipped jackets while the closest girl, who was also the nearest to the police car, wore a blouse that was so sheer that it left nothing to the imagination.

Luke stopped five metres before the police car and leaned casually against a lamp-post, camera in hand, as he'd been instructed. Layla continued on to the car where two officers sat chatting casually. Although the window was open and one of the officers had his arm resting on the top with an unlit cigarette between his fingers, both officers were turned slightly towards the stretch of road where the seven girls were standing.

'*Mi scusi.*' The officers turned.

'I wonder if you could give me some information.' Luke saw the nearest officer look her up and down and then change his expression slightly as he realised she was not a working girl.

'How can we help you?' asked the officer, clearly expecting to be asked directions and assuming that she was asking because she, rather than Luke, who he could see behind, was able to speak Italian.'

Layla gave her most ingratiating smile and Luke saw the officer's look travel quickly over her again before returning to her face, although his expression changed rapidly as she continued; 'I'm an English journalist researching for an article on Montecatini. I was hoping you'd be able to give me the perspective of someone on the front line.'

The officer's head turned slightly as his colleague said something, although Luke couldn't catch what it was.

'I'm sorry, *Signorina,* I'm afraid we're unable to help you. We have work to do. I'm afraid you'll have to ask in the *Questura.*' He moved his arm inside and obviously put a finger on the button to close the window. Unperturbed, Layla leaned forward and placed an elbow on top of the glass.

'Are you sent here to make sure that there's no violence towards the girls, or are you here to put off kerb crawlers... or is it to find out who's controlling the girls?'

The nearest officer had given up trying to raise the window and looked very discomfited; he looked to his colleague for assistance. The other officer got out of the other side of the car and took a couple of steps away, taking a mobile out of his pocket. Luke remembered he needed to be seen taking photographs and stepped to one side so that he had a clearer view of the two officers.

The second officer finished his brief call and stepped around the car to where Layla was repeating her questions to his red-faced colleague. He took hold of her arm and firmly pulled it away from the window, allowing his colleague to close it, then he noticed Luke and, releasing Layla's arm stepped towards him, reaching out towards the camera.

'That's not allowed. You'll have to hand the camera over.' The first officer got out of the car to join his colleague. Luke lifted his hands part way up in a gesture of surrender.

'*Calmi, calmi*', said Layla, 'We'll delete them.' And then, in English to Luke, 'Give me the camera. We need to delete the photos.' Luke ignored the policeman's outstretched arm and passed the camera to Layla. She turned the camera around and pressed a button so that the last photo Luke had taken appeared on screen. She held it so that the officer could see her and pressed the delete button and then repeated the process for the next three pictures until a picture of Montecatini's central square appeared. 'OK? Satisfied?'

'Show me the camera,' said the officer.

She moved the camera closer to him although without letting go. 'Look,' she pressed the review button and the picture of the square appeared again. She showed him she was pressing the forward button and the screen went blank. She pressed back and the picture of the square appeared again then back again and the picture was replaced with one of the fountain in the central square. *'Va bene?'* she said and, still ignoring his outstretched hand, passed the camera back to Luke and said, 'Come on. Let's go.'

She put her arm through Luke's, turning him round, as she began walking away from the two officers. He could feel that despite the relaxed look on her face, she was tense until, as they crossed the road without being ordered back, she relaxed.

They didn't take the road that led directly back to the car, but instead headed towards the centre of the town where it would be easier to disappear. 'Did you get pictures?' she asked, when she was sure they were well out of the line of sight of the two officers.

'Of course,' he replied pulling out what appeared to be a fountain pen from where it had been protruding from the breast pocket of his jacket. 'When I did the basic training, we were told to always check how many cameras there were, if ever we had to stop someone filming. That's obviously not included in the training here.'

'And did you?'

'Did I what?'

'Always check if there was more than one camera.'

He laughed, 'I never had to. Once they found I was good with computers, I never had to do any face-to-face policing.'

'But, of course, you would have remembered if the situation had ever arisen.'

He smiled ruefully, 'Probably not.'

'So don't be so smugly superior then,' and she squeezed his arm to show that she was only teasing.

'I'm not sure we really learnt much of any use,' she said as he placed a cup of hot chocolate topped with cream in-front of her and sat beside her with his own.

'Oh, I don't know. I think we learnt a few useful things.;

'Such as?'

'Such as; did you see what he did when he got out of the car, before he came round to you?'

'I was concentrating on the other one but - he radioed through didn't he?'

'Almost, but not quite. The radio is in the car; he made a quick call on his mobile when he got out, and why would he do that?'

'To let the control room know what was going on, I suppose.'

Luke shook his head. 'No. If he'd wanted to do that, he'd have used the radio in the car. If he was using his mobile, he was calling someone else – and why do that if he was in a hurry to come round the car and help his mate?' He raised an eyebrow and inclined his head slightly to one side.

'So he might have been letting someone else – outside the police force – know that there was a journalist sniffing around the prostitutes.'

'I'm not sure that that's the best metaphor you could have chosen, but yes, that's exactly what I mean, although he wasn't necessarily calling someone outside the force – it could have been someone inside who doesn't want some things to go through official channels.'

She was silent as she thought about what he'd said, so he added, 'And it's fairly clear that they're not there to deter kerb-crawlers, otherwise the girls would move somewhere else.'

'So what next? Do we just forget about the police?'

He thought…. 'No,' he said at last, 'but we do need to tread very carefully. We told them that you're a journalist and that you're doing an article about the town. It's going to look odd if you just disappear now, so why not do as he suggested and ask for information in the *Questura*. They'll let their superiors know what happened, so it will look suspicious if you don't.'

When they checked the internet, they discovered that the town did not have its own *Questura*, being situated roughly half way between the *Questura*s in Pescia and Pistoia. The Police in Montecatini were based in a *Commissariato* a few hundred metres to the north of the centre, closer to the famous spas that gave the town its name, and also to the more upmarket residential areas, at a comfortable distance from the less salubrious aspects of the town's nightlife. Luke shook his head and sighed as he read that there had been regular complaints by the Police officer's union about understaffing in Montecatini and wondered if the decision to deny the town's *Commissario* greater resources had any influence on the apparent impunity of the sex industry. The lower status of the police headquarters did, however, give them some hope that staff there might be slightly more approachable than in a larger centre.

They decided that it would be better if Layla were unaccompanied on her visit to the *Commissariato*. As her credentials as an experienced professional journalist could by verified in a few seconds by a few clicks on a keyboard, there would be no reason for her claim to be working on an article about Montecatini to be doubted, while it did not seem sensible to draw attention to the presence of Luke.

The next morning she confidently walked into the pleasant three storey building on the corner of two quiet tree-lined roads which proudly flew the Italian and European flags. There were three people waiting on chairs by the side wall of the reception area but no obvious signage asking people to wait or follow any particular procedure to make themselves known. After a slight hesitation during which she wondered if she too should take a seat, she decided to push herself forward and walked over to a glass partition behind which a shirt-sleeved officer in his mid-to-late forties sat tapping at a computer keyboard.

Layla stood by a section of the partition where one of the glass panels was clearly intended to be slid open to allow officers to speak to the public. The officer didn't look up from his keyboard. Wondering whether she was being deliberately ignored or if the officer was completely immersed in what he was writing she waited for about thirty seconds before giving two light taps on the glass. The officer looked up startled and pushed his chair back.

'*Buongiorno,*' said Layla with a smile.

'*Buongiorno*. How can I help you?' said the officer, straightening his tie as he did so.

~ 242 ~

'I'd like to speak to your media-relations officer, if that's possible.'
The officer looked confused. *'Ma…'*

'I'm a journalist from England, writing an article on Montecatini, and I thought it would be helpful to get the Police's official perspective on the area.'

The officer still looked confused but seemed to have regained some composure. 'If you'd like to take a seat Miss…?'

'Simons. Layla Simons.'

'Signorina Simons – I'll find out if there is someone able to speak to you.'

She smiled again and nodded before retreating towards the seats while he slid the glass panel closed again and picked up the telephone by his computer. She watched him, trying to look as casual and unconcerned as possible. He occasionally glanced over in her direction as he spoke and she smiled as she caught his eye.'

When he put the phone down he moved over to the partition and slid the panel open again. *'Signorina* Simons.'

She stood and moved back to the panel. *'Ispettore* Tardelli will be through to see you in a few minutes. If you'd like to take a seat again, he won't be long.'

Layla sat again, resigned to a wait of at least half an hour, but was pleasantly surprised when, less than five minutes later, a young man wearing jeans and a light brown-leather jacket, came through a door to one side of the reception area and, after a quick glance at the other people waiting, made his way towards her, extending his hand as he did so.

'Miss Simons?' he asked and, on receiving her answering smile but before giving her time to speak, 'If you'd like to come this way, we'll be more comfortable in my office.'

He ushered her through the door at the side, down a short corridor and through a door into a sparsely furnished office where he gestured towards a chair.

'Now, Miss Simons,' he said in English, 'In what way can I be of assistance to you?'

'As I told your colleague, I'm an English journalist. I work as a freelance although my main pieces over the past three or four years have been either for the Huffington Post or for the Al Jazeera website. Most of what I've written has been reporting on uprisings and revolutions but, as I've travelled about, I've made smaller contributions to travel sections and, as a result, I've now been asked to write an article about Montecatini.'

Tardelli looked at her quizzically. 'It's not for me to tell you how to do your job, but shouldn't you be at the Tourist Information Office on Viale Verdi, rather than in the Police Station? I would have thought that they would be able to help you much better than we can.'

She met his look. 'From what I've seen so far, there is a lot more to Montecatini than the Tourist Board is likely to give me leaflets about. My article will, hopefully, cover all aspects of Montecatini – the good - and the not so good.'

'Aah! I see.' He looked at his watch. 'I don't think that this is something we can cover effectively in ten minutes, which is all I have available at the moment. May I ask what you're doing for lunch?'

She was surprised; she'd though it was only fictional detectives such as Montalbano and Bordelli who did their business with the public over lunch. Apparently not. 'I hadn't got anything planned. I was just going to wander round today and get to see as much of the town as I could.'

'Then that's settled,' said Tardelli with an engaging smile. There's a pizzeria near the Hippodrome called Z Point. Cheap and cheerful, I think you'd say in English. I'll meet you there at one-thirty.'

'And you agreed to go – Just like that?'

'Of course,' said Layla. 'Why shouldn't I?' and then added maliciously, 'he had a lovely smile.'

Luke rolled his eyes. 'Just be very, very careful about who you trust and what you tell them.'

'Don't worry. I know. I'll stick strictly to my story that I'm writing a piece about the town.'

'Hmmm… It'll be interesting to see how much he's prepared to say about the way they police the sex trade. Probably worth trying to get a feel for his views on refugees as well.'

'Right. Yes. Great idea!' she said enthusiastically as she took her phone out and entered her PIN. 'OK Google'. Luke looked at her puzzled. 'What is the meaning of to teach someone to suck eggs?' He leaned back and smiled.

'According to Wikipedia teaching grandmother to suck eggs is an English language saying meaning that a person is giving advice to someone else about a subject of which they are already familiar and probably more so than the first person'.

'OK – I'm sorry. I was only trying to help.' They both laughed.

While Layla went to keep her appointment, Luke grabbed a panino and a caffé in one of the bars in the centre and then went to have a look at the ice-cream parlour where they were due to meet Alessio's priest contact that evening. He was pleased to find that it was quite large and that, while there were very few seats inside, if the weather allowed them to sit outside, it should be possible to find a table where they could talk without being overheard. The rest of the time he filled by wandering around the residential streets to the north of the centre wondering what secrets were hidden behind the respectable façades and how many of the comfortable residents were clients of the girls on the streets.

'According to Roberto - *Ispettore* Tardelli, the local police only get involved with the prostitution rackets when there is an actual crime, like assault or robbery, involved. They have limited resources and they've been told very clearly both by their superiors in Pistoia, and by the leaders of the local council, that their priority is to keep the town centre, the thermal baths and the big hotels safe and crime free. They collaborate with the *Polizia Stradale* which, if I understood correctly, is a more or less separate organisation, to maintain a light-touch presence in the areas where most of the prostitutes tend to work.'

'The *Polizia Stradale*,' the Road Police! What's it got to do with them?'

'That's more or less what I asked after I'd got him explain who the *Polizia Stradale* are. Apparently, kerb-crawling is a violation of the

Italian equivalent of the Highway Code, so they do, technically, have an interest.'

'But that's ridiculous. There were prostitutes operating quite openly less than thirty metres from the police car last night – and there were cars pulling up next to some of the girls while we were approaching the police car. They weren't bothered at all!'

'I know - don't shoot the messenger, I'm only telling you what he told me, and I did say it was a light-touch approach. He said that it's impossible to get a conviction for kerb-crawling and that, as to try would mean a couple of officers having to spend half a day in court waiting for the case to be called and then giving evidence, they just don't bother.'

'And did he think that it was alright? Didn't he think that maybe, just maybe, some of these girls were being exploited?'

'I asked him that, and he said that, as far as they were aware most of the girls are either working on their own, or as part of small groups. Occasionally they find out about some bigger organisation and, when they do, they make sure it gets closed down immediately.'

'What about the nationality of the girls?'

'According to him, the majority of the girls are Eastern European. They're legally allowed to be here, so their papers are in order, and they earn enough to maintain themselves. He said that there are occasionally girls from other places but that they regularly do spot checks, and anyone who doesn't have 'leave to remain' is arrested, processed and then given a notification to leave the EU.'

'And his attitude seemed to be...?'

She thought for a moment. 'Resigned, I'd say. He didn't give the impression that he didn't care, it was just that he seemed to have accepted it as an inescapable fact of life. He accepted that it was "an issue" of sorts but insisted that, as the main residential and tourist areas were separated from the roads where the sex workers operate, it was right not to consider it as a priority.'

'It's only about five minutes' walk from the centre,' commented Luke.

'I know, but he had facts and figures showing that the level of reported crime was very low.'

He shook his head. 'Hardly surprising really if everyone knows that the police aren't interested. Why bother reporting crime if nothing's going to be done about it?'

'He did say that if I needed any more information or assistance, not to hesitate to contact him.'

'I suppose it can't do any harm to have a contact in the police but we need to be very sure about him before we open up too much to him. If this is one of the places where girls are being sent and exploited, then there have to be influential people around to smooth their path.'

'You mean that the Police are deliberately turning a blind eye to what's going on?'

Luke grimaced and gave a slight shake of his head. 'It's more nuanced than that. I'm sure that what Tardelli told you about shortage of resources and the need to prioritise while taking account of local people's concerns is absolutely right but, having said that, there are still decisions that have to be taken, policy decisions that have to be made. I love Italy and the Italians, but I'm not blind to its faults. Although the system is designed so that there are clear rules and open examinations that give people access to professional posts and positions in public services, it can be very easily manipulated.'

'You mean,' said Layla, after a pause, 'that it's still very important who you know as well as what you know.'

'Pretty much. Although, actually, I'd say that in many cases, who you know is the only thing that matters. Italy's still a fairly young country with regional identities being felt as strongly, if not more strongly than national identity, so there's a tendency to mistrust "the State", and it's viewed as perfectly normal to put in a good word on someone's behalf.'

'Alright. I understand that, but how does it work in practice? Let's say I was an Italian and wanted to be a police-woman; I'd just have to sit the same exam as everyone else wouldn't I, and then be ranked depending on how well I did? How can that be manipulated?'

He smiled. 'Well, given that there are likely to be about two thousand of you sitting the exam, there are likely to be about a hundred of you getting the same final mark – that gives a bit of scope for preferential treatment for a start but, more than that, what if someone is able to tip you off about a particular subject that's likely to come up? Or if someone is able to apply a bit of subtle pressure to the people marking the exam? You know, "keep an eye open for candidate number one thousand three hundred and twenty; I've heard that they're absolutely brilliant". A marker who feels that their own career might benefit from giving the candidate the benefit of the doubt, or who thinks that maybe, at some time in the future, they might need to ask a favour, is going to do what's asked of them if at all possible.'

'I never realised you were so cynical.'

'I think I'd call it realism. My uncle used to work at the university in Florence and he had some amazing tales of the way people tried to influence him around exam time.'

'Alright. But where does that leave us? I want as many of these people arrested as possible. Even if we never find out exactly what happened to Zahra or which individuals were responsible, bringing down people like them will be some sort of justice for her, and will make Italy a slightly safer place for girls like Coulibaly. At some point, we have to tell everything to the police and let them do their job.' There was a tremor in her voice as she finished speaking and, as he glanced across the car, he could see that there was a tear in her eye.

He changed gear to slow down for a hairpin bend and allowed his hand to rest on her knee, giving it a quick squeeze before returning it to the wheel.

'Sorry,' he said softly after negotiating the bend, 'I didn't mean to be negative. When we've found something out, of course we'll involve the police, but we need to be absolutely sure that we're dealing with someone we can trust first. Vichi must still have some contacts in the force up here; he'll be able to tell us what's best to do.'

Roberto Tardelli dropped an unopened packet of cigarettes on the desk of the duty admin officer, 'I'll be in my office but if anyone calls in the next twenty minutes, I'm not back yet and you're not sure how to contact me. Understood?'

The admin officer nodded and slipped the cigarettes into his jacket pocket and Tardelli patted him on the shoulder and moved to the door. As the door closed behind the inspector, he took an e-cigarette out of another pocket in his jacket and, after a guilty glance around the room, placed it in his mouth and flicked the on switch.

Tardelli sat down behind his desk and pulled a mobile out of an inner pocket. He glanced across at the obligatory photograph of the current Italian President who seemed to be observing him with disapproval. Looking away from the President again, he entered a number and waited for a response.

'*Pronto*. It's Tardelli from the *Commissariato* in Montecatini. Is it possible to speak with him?' .... 'It could turn out to be important.' .... 'Yes. I'll wait.' .... 'OK Thankyou'........ 'Good afternoon, Sir,' .... 'We have an English journalist in town. She says she's writing a travel article about the town and came to see us to get information so it can be a warts-and-all piece.' .... 'Yes, Sir. She seems to be particularly interested in the prostitution. I took her to lunch and tried to downplay the situation but I got the impression she may well carry on digging.' .... 'I thought you ought to know,' .... 'What! Last night?' .... 'Yes, it sounds like the same woman, But she didn't have a photographer with her today, and she didn't mention that she was not on her own.'..................... 'Yes. Of course. And I'll keep you informed.'.......... '*Grazie*. I won't let you down. *Arrivederci*.'

His eyes narrowed as he sat at his desk thinking, absent-mindedly tapping the end of his pen on his front teeth, then he came to a decision and pressed the intercom button on his desk.

'Gattuso, can you get hold of Capitano Bonetti from the *Stradale* – as soon as possible.'

Releasing the button on the intercom, he dipped a hand into his pocket and pulled out a receipt, across the top of which a telephone number had been written.

With rapid finger movements he entered the number into his mobile.

'*Pronto*. Miss Simons?.... It's Roberto Tardelli here. Do you have a moment? …. Good. I was thinking after I'd left you; I think I could arrange for you to talk to one of the regulars from Viale Foscolo – that's part of the main thoroughfare leading around the southern edge of the centre, towards the motorway….. I'm sure she'll agree. We've had various dealings with her over the years and she owes us a few favours…………… No. that's no problem. I'll get one of my men who's her usual contact to set it up………….. I'll contact you with the details………. You're welcome. Arrivederci.'

He smiled grimly and glanced at the time as he put the phone down. Better not to call Viola just yet in case Bonetti called back. He pulled a file off a pile on the right hand side of his desk and began to study its contents.

Chapter Thirteen

'He's going to arrange for me to talk to one of the girls on the street. What do you make of that?'

'I'm really not sure,' said Luke thoughtfully. 'It seems really helpful and it's obviously an offer you can't turn down but...' he tailed off.

'But?'

'But it just seems almost too good to be true. Being a nark can be a dangerous business and I can't believe anyone would just allow a journalist they've only met once, access to one of their narks.'

'What's a nark?'

'Sorry. Police slang; a nark's an informer. And usually, an informer's identity is a jealously guarded secret.'

'Well, we'll just have to go along with it for now. Hopefully, we'll find out what's going on later.'

'I suppose you're right. Anyway, it can't be tonight; we've got the priests tonight.'

At twenty past seven, after having shown Layla how to make *vitello tonnato*, which they ate with a greek salad, they set off down into Montecatini, parking the car in the residential streets to the north of the park containing most of the spa establishments.

It was a ten minute walk from there to the ice-cream parlour and, after looking at the various flavours of ice-cream on display, they chose an outside table from where they had a good view all around them. 'We're waiting for friends to join us,' said Luke to the waitress who ambled over to their table.

'I'll bring a menu over, so you can be looking while you wait.'

'Thankyou,' said Layla with a warm smile.

The two priests arrived a few minutes after eight and stood looking round near the door. Although they both wore coats and their clerical garb was not immediately noticeable, the appearance of the two men, one black and one white, appearing together at more or less the right time was enough to leave Luke in no doubt as to their identity. He raised an arm in greeting and the two made their way over to the table. Luke stood up and held out a hand, 'Luke – or Luca if you prefer.'

It was the African priest who was the first to take the hand. 'John,' he said, shaking it, 'and Luke will be fine.'

'Thankyou,' said Luke, and turning to the other, 'You must be Don Simone, Alessio's friend.'

'Well, friend might be stretching things a bit. My younger brother and Alessio were very good friends when they were kids, but I was a few years older so didn't take a lot of notice,' he looked at Layla, who smiled.

'This is my friend, Layla.'

'How do you do?' said Simone in heavily accented English.

'Very well, thankyou. But I'm quite happy to speak Italian if you prefer, the more I speak and listen, the better it is for me.'

'I'm sure that the reverse would apply to me but, as we'll clearly make more progress in Italian, perhaps we'd better stick to that.'

'Shall we sit?' said John.

'Now,' said Simone, after the waitress had delivered their ice-creams. 'Alessio rang me and told me that you were in Montecatini and that he thought I might be able to help you. He also said that it had something to do with Africa, which is why I asked Don John to join us.'

'Alright. Let me explain. We have been in Sicily, trying to find a teenage girl – a distant relative of Layla – who we know managed to escape from Libya on a boat bound for Italy last year. We're fairly certain that the boat, or at least the majority of its passengers reached Sicily, but there is no trace of the girl.'

'So what does that have to do with Montecatini?' enquired Simone, puzzled.

'Maybe nothing, but we know that Montecatini is one of main destinations used by one of the organisations that helps refugees avoid the official procedures and start to travel northwards through Europe.'

'Sorry,' said Layla, interrupting. 'Did you say "help"?'

'I did,' said Luke, putting a hand on hers, 'and it was the wrong choice of word. These people take considerable amounts of money off the refugees – money that they've often had to raise either by prostituting themselves or working long days in the fields – and then promise to help them move on to places where they can have a good life.'

'A good life that never arrives,' observed Don John.

'Exactly. They leave Sicily when they can make a downpayment towards the total cost, but they are effectively slaves until such time as the whole debt is paid off.'

'Modern slavery,' added Don Simone, quietly.

'In all its forms. In England, when we think of modern slavery – not that most people do think about it very much – we imagine vulnerable people being exploited for their labour, either in domestic environments or as low-paid unskilled workers. Occasionally, one reads about someone having been exploited for sexual purposes, but the perception, which is probably incorrect, is that it's not frequent. Here though, where the sex-trade is much more out in the open, people are more willing to accept that at least some of the girls involved may be modern slaves.'

'Go on,' said Don Simone.

'We thought,' continued Luke, glancing round to make sure that no-one else was listening, 'or to be more exact, my cousin suggested, that as someone whose role puts them at the heart of the community, you might have some insight into what is happening here. At the moment, while we've been able to follow the trail as far as Montecatini, we have no idea who is involved and aren't sure who we can turn to for help.'

'When you say "the trail", do you mean that you've traced Layla's relative here?' asked Don Simone with an air of surprise.

'Unfortunately not. We've found no trace of her, but we do know that, in general, a lot of girls like her, and who've followed more or less the same path, end up in Montecatini.'

'And what sort of help do you think we might be able to give?' Don John enquired, somewhat defensively.

Layla leaned forward and joined in the conversation, 'From what I've been told, the highest proportions of women being used in the sex trade are Italians and Eastern Europeans. Now, certainly the Italians, but also a fair proportion of the Eastern Europeans will be Catholics prepared to tell things to a priest that they wouldn't necessarily be prepared to tell anyone else.'

'Confessional secrets are inviolable, Layla; surely you're aware of that?'

'I don't think Layla was referring to anything that might be said during confession,' said Luke, hurriedly. 'What we were thinking of was more general conversations, and we've got no interest at all in anything that might incriminate the girls themselves. But anything that's not covered by the seal of the confessional, which might help to identify the people who are exploiting them, would be helpful.'

'Alright,' said Don Simone, who had listened attentively, 'I don't think you're asking us anything that would be against our duty or our faith, but I don't see how it helps you. Italian and Eastern European women have not arrived here as refugees in boats.'

'And the people on the boats are mainly Muslims,' added Don John.

'I've had a look round and checked up as much as I could on the internet, and it seems as if, when the girls are on the street, that different stretches of road are used by different national groups. If that's right, and if we accept that a significant number of them are controlled in some way, whether that be by individual pimps or by bigger criminal organisations, then there must be some kind of agreement about how the territory is divided up.' Luke looked at Don Simone and raised an eyebrow, as if asking for support.

'Like splitting the city into parishes, where each is autonomous but under the overall direction of the Mother Church,' Don Simone smiled, while Don John, who looked surprised, opened his mouth to speak and then thought better and closed it again.

'Exactly. From what I hear, the 'African area' is Via Marruota, just to the south of the main drag although I haven't found out any more yet. There's a chance that whoever is running them is connected to the traffickers, although they're likely to be too scared to talk. It's possible that there may be rivalries and tensions between the different groups, and it's just possible that some of the other girls may know something about the Africans, and be prepared to talk about it'

'To us, you mean,' said Simone.

'Some of them might, and it would also look far less suspicious to any minders who might be hanging about, if a priest is talking to the girls, trying to get them to see the error of their ways.'

'It's possible, although it may be slightly more difficult than you think. I'm attached to the Parish of Saint Anthony at the northern end of the town, while Don John is based in the parish of Saint Francis in Pescia. Neither of us has the authority to take initiatives in either of the two parishes where most of these young women are operating. Unfortunately, I understand that the senior of the two priests most directly affected can be somewhat inflexible in his attitude towards sinners. However,' he gave a little smile, 'I may be able to help you in another way.'

'Go on,' said Luke eagerly, 'We're grateful for any help we can get.'

'OK. But let's get another ice-cream first. I very rarely allow myself to succumb to temptation, but now that I've had one, I may as well make the most of the opportunity.'

When they had re-ordered and were settled again, Don Simone began to explain.

'One of our local Members of Parliament is going to propose an amendment in Parliament to the *Legge Merlin* sometime later this year...'

'What's the Merlin Law?' asked Layla puzzled.

'The main law covering prostitution in Italy; I'll tell you more about it later... Go on,' intervened Luke.

Don Simone nodded his thanks. 'She's been helped in gathering data to support her amendment by the main Scout group in Pistoia. For most of the last year, the older members of the group have been gathering information on levels of prostitution throughout the Province as well as offering girls the opportunity to leave that life behind them.' He glanced at his audience and received a sign of encouragement from Luke who, at the same time put pressure on Layla's hand to indicate that now was not the time to ask questions.

'Well... two weeks ago they turned their attention to Montecatini. About thirty five of them came over and met together on the public area between the hippodrome and the football stadium. They gathered in a circle, sang a couple of songs and said a prayer and then the group leader reminded them what they needed to do and distributed the help packs. Once they were ready, the male scouts took their cars and parked in streets they'd already identified as being close to, but out of sight of, the streets used in the sex trade, while the girls set off on foot in pairs.

Each pair of girls carried a bag with bottles of mineral water, chocolates and cards written in three languages giving the girls a help number to ring if they want to find a new direction. Over the next four hours they approached every woman they could find who was working on the streets, tried to engage them in conversation and, when they could, gave them the cards. Obviously, after sessions like that, they document as much as possible so that it can be used as supporting evidence in Parliament, as well as to better inform future initiatives to help the women.'

'And you have access to this information?' asked Layla, who could no longer restrain herself.

'No, but I do know some of those involved with AGESCI in Pistoia very well.'

'Agesci?' said Luke, puzzled.

'The Associazione Guides e Scouts Cattolici Italiani,' explained Don Simone with a smile. 'Almost all the groups in Italy belong to the association, so you often find that members of the clergy are actively involved. It should be no problem at all to arrange for you to meet one of those who was involved.'

'How old are these scouts? I thought that most guides and scouts tended to drop out by their mid-teens,' asked Layla.

'Not in Italy. Or in Kenya for that matter,' intervened Don John, who had listened quietly to Don Simone's explanation. 'Here, where almost everyone follows the one true faith, being part of an organisation that unites the original principles of Scouting with a

Christian desire to do good, continues to inspire people well into adulthood.'

Normally, Luke would have objected to the wording of the priest's explanation but, after a glance at Layla, he decided to let it pass and addressed Don Simone instead. 'That would be really good if you could. I wasn't really looking forward to trying to make contact with the women myself.'

'No,' said Don Simone with a smile, 'I can imagine that it would be a challenging experience.'

'That was a stroke of luck,' commented Luke, as they were on their way back to the house, 'Who'd have thought that a bunch of Girl Guides would have already done the round of all the girls on the street.'

'Let's just hope that their leader isn't someone like Don John. I can imagine that if it were, most of their good works would have been directed towards those who were, at least nominally, Catholic.'

'The one true faith,' said Luke, mimicking Don John.

'Funny. Every fanatic from every religion or sect is absolutely convinced that theirs is "the one true faith", and anyone who doesn't agree with them will be damned.' Layla laughed. 'Good-job Simone was more open and less judgemental.'

'Hopefully, the scout or scouts that he finds us will be more like him… Anyway, do you still want to know about the Merlin Law? I seem to remember you objecting to my passing on too much information all at once.'

'What?' she said puzzled.

'You objected to my giving you too much information about cetacians when we were on our way to Salina.'

She laughed. 'So I did. Alright, you have my permission to amaze me with your knowledge – but I reserve the right to withdraw it again if you become too dull.'

'OK. Lina Merlin, who was largely responsible for pushing the law through Parliament was probably the most influential Italian woman ever. She qualified as a schoolteacher before the First World War and very soon got involved in arguing for women's rights. She was apparently the sort of person who you'd much rather have on your side than as an opponent, and they say that after the end of the war, the Fascists tried to sign her up to organise their women's section, but she wouldn't have anything to with them. Instead, she ended up joining the Socialist Party and became very close to Matteotti.

After his murder, when the law was changed so that all public employees had to join the Fascist party or be sacked, she refused to sign up and, I believe, spent several years in internal exile in Sardinia.

Later on, she was with the partisans during the war alongside Pertini and others who went on to be national figures after the Second World War. When Italy voted to abolish the monarchy in forty-six, she was elected to the Constituent Assembly that was set up to produce a new Constitution. It's apparently due to her that when the Constitution states that all Italians are equal, it goes on to add, "regardless of gender".

When the Constituent Assembly had done what it had been set up to do, she again stood for election and was the first woman to be voted into the new Senate in forty-eight or forty-nine. Her big thing was always women's rights and she wasn't the sort who'd ever give up until she'd got her own way, no matter how many people she pissed off in the process.

One of the first things the new Government did was to sign up for membership of the United Nations which meant agreeing to do more than just paying lip-service to the various human rights declarations including the one where member states agree to work towards the abolition of the treatment of human beings as saleable commodities – a declaration which makes specific mention of prostitution. Brothels had been legal and widely accepted until then but Merlin argued that by permitting this, and by profiting from it through taxes and licensing laws, the Italian State was in breach of the Human Rights Convention. Eventually, in nineteen-fifty-eight, she managed to get a law passed through Parliament which effectively made brothels illegal overnight along with making money by organising, facilitating or procuring clients for prostitutes.'

'But not prostitution itself?'

'No. They say that that would have been a step too far for a lot of the male members of Parliament.'

'And now they want to amend the law. I wonder in what way.'

Luke shrugged, 'I can't see it being a very dramatic change, if it's going to have a chance of getting through Parliament – but I'm sure Don Simone's scouts will be able to tell us, if we can't find it on the internet first.'

'Maybe,' she replied non-commitally, and then fell silent. 'I got to talk to a few – when I was out in the Middle-East reporting on the Arab Spring. Some people would argue that most of the ones I got to talk to had chosen that way of life, but they hadn't – not really... It was always poverty that lay behind it; they didn't really have a choice, unless it was a choice between doing that or starvation – not just for them, but sometimes for their children as well.'

He parked the car by the side of the track leading to the top of the village, rather than occupying the area between the houses. 'We need to remember though, that this isn't the Middle-East; we're supposed to be in a liberal western democracy where people shouldn't have to make that sort of decision, and that applies to refugees as well as Europeans.'

They received two phone calls in the morning: the first was from Tardelli, telling Layla that he'd persuaded one of the prostitutes to meet her, if she could find her way to an address near the station just before twelve; the second was from Don Simone asking if they could meet two of the scouts who'd been involved in the operation in Montecatini. Both proposals were agreed to immediately and Luke used Google's street-view facility to identify the meeting points.

Layla had expected that the prostitute she was to meet would be living somewhere small and slightly dingy in the sort of dilapidated area that can be found near the railway stations of many provincial towns in European countries. She was surprised to find that the street to which she had been directed had all the appearance of being a very normal residential street with a mixture of individual houses and small condominiums – it was to one of the latter that she'd been directed.

There were six names by the doorbells outside the main entrance and she pressed the top one on the right, as she'd been instructed.

'*Chi è?*' came a crackly voice through the speaker grill.

'Layla Simons. *Giornalista inglese*... I have an appointment.'

There was no reply but, two seconds later, there was a click and she saw the metal edge of the door jump back a couple of millimetres. She pushed and the door swung open revealing an atrium containing six lockable letter boxes and four doors. The floor was covered with large grey ceramic tiles and the walls were clean enough to suggest that they had been re-whitewashed at some time in the past few months. Everything suggested that the residents of the condominium respected the place they lived in.

She passed through the door marked scale and ascended a well-lit ramp of stairs that turned back on itself to bring her onto a small landing. One of the two doors giving onto the landing was open and a woman of about her own age stood waiting for her.

At first glance, the woman could have been any housewife; she was dressed plainly with a simple housecoat protecting her clothes and her hair tied back, slightly off centre as though done in a hurry. It was only her eyes, which had a listless quality to them, and that sat above dark bags, only partially hidden by a layer of foundation, that marked her as anything out of the ordinary.

'Thank you for agreeing to speak to me,' said Layla, not sure whether etiquette required her to offer her hand. The other woman gave a slight grimace that might just have been an attempt at a smile, before turning and retreating into the apartment, leaving Layla to follow her and shut the door as she did so.

The woman sat in a chair when she entered the living room and, despite the lack of a specific invitation to do so, Layla followed suit. 'Well?' she said.

Layla cleared her throat, 'I'm an English journalist, writing an article about all aspects of life in Montecatini. I was hoping you'd be able to tell me something about the sort of work you do.'

'I work in the entertainment industry,' said the woman, 'or I suppose you could call it a public service.'

Layla was silent for a moment as she searched for the right words with which to proceed. 'And do you work alone?' she asked, realising the absurd ambiguity of her words at once, even before she saw the slight flicker of amusement in the other woman's eyes.

'No, I'm always with someone else... occasionally with more than one other.'

'Perhaps I didn't express myself very well. What I meant was... are there many others who do the same work as you? And how do you organise things between you?'

'Have you been in the town at night?' asked the woman rhetorically, with more than a hint of contempt in her voice.

Layla realised that her command of the language was not yet good enough to allow her to direct the conversation as she would have wished, so she took the decision to be more direct.

'Look, I haven't been learning Italian for long so I'll just ask you some direct questions. I apologise if they lack subtlety.'

The woman shrugged a shoulder.

'How long have you been working as a prostitute?'

'I started when I was twenty-two... And I'm thirty-four now.' She looked at Layla as if challenging her to dispute her age.

Layla ignored the challenge. 'And why did you start doing it?'

'My husband lost his job, and because they said he'd been stealing, he wasn't given any pay-off. We had to live.'

'Was it his idea or yours?'

'It was his idea. He said it wouldn't be for long – just until he found another job – but then, when it became clear that I could bring home far more than he ever had, he stopped trying to get another job.'

'So he lives off what you earn and forces you to continue?' asked Layla, trying not to appear shocked.

She laughed, mirthlessly, 'That's what happened for a few months. He said he was taking risks by protecting me; looking after my interests.' Her eyes narrowed, 'But once I started getting regular clients and the risks were less, I decided he had to go.'

'And who protects you now?'

'The people who matter know who my regulars are, so they make sure that nothing happens to me.'

'And who are the people who matter?'

There was a long pause before the woman responded, having clearly considered what it was wise to say. 'All the regular girls have someone who looks after them, makes sure that no-one else takes their spot, and keeps an eye open for violent punters.'

'Would you say that some of these people are exploiting the girls; forcing them to do what they do, and taking most of the money?'

There was another pause. 'It can happen. Especially with some of the Rumanians and Poles; most of them seem to have 'an uncle' who looks after them, but I don't know anything about that.'

'What about the Africans?' asked Layla as if as an afterthought.

The woman looked as if she would have spat on the floor, if it hadn't been that it was her own floor below her. 'They don't count. People here aren't interested. Some might want to try them once as a novelty, but most people know that Africans are full of AIDS and, what's that new one?.... Ebola.'

Layla managed to suppress her anger and maintain her appearance of nonchalance, 'But someone must be organising them and protecting them, mustn't they? Or why would they be here?'

'Who cares? It's what they do isn't it?'

Again, Layla made a great effort to maintain her calm, 'Where do they live? Surely they can't afford housing here.'

The woman shrugged again. 'All together, I suppose. As I said, I don't care.'

'Alright,' said Layla, 'Well, thankyou very much. You've been very helpful,' and she stood up.

'I didn't really have any choice,' relied the woman drily as she got up to show her out.

As Layla stepped out onto the landing she turned to repeat her thanks and the woman said in a low voice, 'Be very careful,' and shut the door behind her.

Odd, thought Layla, as she made her way down the stairs; although the words could be interpreted as a threat, the lowered voice had made the woman seem much more human than when she'd been answering Layla's questions inside.

'You did well,' said Tardelli, emerging from another door that gave on to the living-room, which had been ajar during Layla's meeting with the woman.

'I did what you asked me to do, and only told her what you told me to tell her.'

Tardelli smiled and stepped closer to her. He raised and stretched out a hand as if to caress her face, but his palm glided past her cheek and he twisted his wrist so that a handful of hair was twisted between his fingers. 'And you'll continue to do so, if you know what's good for you.'

Her head tilted back as he continued to twist her hair, leaving her neck exposed. He raised his other hand and dragged a broken fingernail across her neck, leaving a red scratch in its wake. 'I need to know about anything unusual you see or hear, is that clear?' She whimpered. 'Good. I'll be in touch,' and he turned and left.

They had been asked to meet the two scouts in the community centre on the edge of Santomato, a small village a few kilometres east of Pistoia, on a road flanked by olives and vines as well as an extremely ugly orange metal monstrosity which a sign indicated was a memorial to Canadian soldiers killed during the war.

The centre was a large modern building that was obviously well used by the community and there were already several cars in the car-park. Luke pulled in and found a space between a Panda and an ageing Punto.

There were a handful of people sitting or standing smoking by the tables outside; a few of them gave the newcomers look of curiosity but none gave any sign that they were expecting them, so they went inside. Here there were about fifteen people, spread around different tables or table football games. There were three young couples who looked more or less how Luke would have expected young adult scouts to look, but only one of the couples looked at them with anything more than just mild curiosity. Layla spotted them before Luke and gave his arm a little tug to point him in the right direction.

'*Ciao,*' he said with a smile, 'Are you Diletta and Damiano?'

The two stood up and offered their hands; pleasantries were exchanged and Luke went to the counter to order glasses of *spuma* for the two scouts, an orange juice for Layla and a *latte macchiato* for himself.

'We were told you needed to know some information about *operazione donne crocefisse*,' said Damiano when they were all settled.

'That's what we call the research we've been doing for the last few months into the lives of the women on the streets,' explained Diletta.

'That's right. More specifically about what's happening in Montecatini,' replied Luke.

Diletta glanced at Damiano and then turned back so that she was looking Layla in the eyes. 'Do you mind if I ask, why? I mean I know Don Alessandro said it was OK to trust you but…. but I've been out and talked to some of the girls, and I wouldn't want anything I say - or we say - to be used against them.' She looked nervous, as though worried they might take offence.

Layla smiled and reached a hand half-way across the table, 'No. I don't mind at all, and I'm pleased that you want to protect the girls. They're the victims in all this. Luke will tell you everything because he speaks better Italian than I do.' Diletta took hold of the hand and smiled as she gave it a squeeze.

Luke then spent the next forty minutes explaining to the pair, who Zahra was and how looking for her had led them to Montecatini.

'So why Montecatini rather than Milan?' asked Damiano, 'Although Montecatini's busy, they say there are getting on for a thousand sex-workers in and around Milan.'

'It's a good question. And one with several answers, none of which are particularly good ones,' Luke smiled ruefully, 'My uncle used to live in Florence and I visited a lot when I was growing up, so I know this area fairly well, whereas I know very little about Milan - and yes, I know that there are far more prostitutes in Milan, but I wouldn't have a clue where to start.'

'But,' said Diletta, 'if you don't know whether it's Montecatini or Milan aren't you giving yourself very little chance of success by choosing to come here? If there are ten times as many prostitutes in

Milan, surely by coming to Montecatini, you reduce your chances of success by over ninety percent.' She sounded perplexed.

'I did say that there were several reasons for choosing Montecatini,' said Luke, with a grim look on his face, Maybe the best one is that we know that there are connections between an ex-government minister and the groups that have been involved in getting girls out of Sicily - and that ex-government minister is originally from this area.'

'I know,' said Layla, 'that the chances of finding Zahra, or even of finding out what happened to her, are very slim – almost non-existent, but I won't feel as if I've done as much as I can unless I can do something to...' she paused, searching for the right words.

'To get some sort of justice for her,' said Diletta quietly, finishing off the sentence for her. Layla nodded, and there was silence for a moment, the rest of the room momentarily forgotten.

'I'm not sure if it's any consolation or not, but I don't think she would have been put to work on the streets – at least not in Montecatini. As far as possible we spoke to every woman on the streets and there were none of Arabic origin. There were a few black Africans working on one of the roads and we've come across Chinese women in Pistoia and closer to Prato, but not Arabs.'

'So you think that we're wasting our time here – that we should be in Milan?' asked Luke.

'No,' said Diletta quickly, 'That's not what I meant. After what you just told me, I think you were right to come here; Milan is far too big to have any chance of finding what you're looking for. What I was trying to say is that you don't find Arab girls on the streets here, so something else must be happening to them.'

'We know that not all the girls work the streets,' offered Damiano, 'Some work from private houses and clients make appointments.'

Diletta shook her head, 'I don't think so.' She brushed a hand over the back of Damiano's to soften the effect of refuting his suggestion. Luke noticed and gave a cough to hide his smile at the way Damiano was obviously besotted with his companion, and how she was sensitive to this. 'I want to be an economist, so I've done a lot of reading up on supply and demand. Men pay more when they don't have to risk picking girls up on the streets and if some of the girls were Arabs, I'm sure we'd have seen at least some on the streets. I can't imagine that richer men have significantly different tastes.'

'So you think that Italian men prefer white women?' asked Layla.

'I don't know about all Italians, but it seems to be like that in Tuscany. The women on the streets who were prepared, or allowed, to talk to us told us that if you wanted to make much money, you had to be white. The white girls on the street are charging up to eighty euros a time for the basics, but the black girls are lucky if they get thirty.'

Luke was amazed by the calm way in which this determined and precocious young woman was able to set out her ideas so calmly and succinctly. He could understand why Damiano, who had gone from bright red to deathly pale and back again as she spoke, was so in awe of her.

'So, in your view, what do you think might happen to a young Arab girl like Zahra who was brought here? Or do you think that they'd be sent somewhere else before they got here?' asked Layla.

Diletta didn't answer the question directly but responded with one of her own, 'Have you been watching the tv news recently?' Layla shook her head. 'Well: since the weather has improved, the number of people trying to cross over to Sicily has increased massively, and the journalists have put it back at the top of their agenda, so we see loads of refugees being picked up every day – they're almost all black.'

'So you're saying that someone like Zahra would be a rarity and, presumably, that would make her worth a lot more to other people,' said Layla, and Luke noticed an enthusiasm in her voice that he hadn't heard for a while.

'Let's not get ahead of ourselves; it's still more than likely that Zahra never made it this far, and if she did survive the journey, the odds would still favour her having been taken to Milan.'

'I know,' said Layla, thanking Luke with a smile, 'but at least it means we can have something to focus on. Thankyou, Diletta.'

'When you spoke to the Eastern European girls, what did they tell you?' asked Luke.

'There weren't many who were prepared to talk. Most of them either couldn't speak Italian or at pretended not to be able to, so we didn't get much out of them at all. We gave them the card with the contact details on, but a lot of them either refused to take it at all or threw it on the ground,' responded Damiano after receiving a sign of encouragement from Diletta. 'And of the ones who were prepared to talk, most hadn't really got anything to say. It was as if they'd learnt a script off by heart and were determined not to leave it.'

'Determined or scared?' asked Luke.

'The ones I spoke to were scared,' put in Diletta.

Luke nodded then turned back to Damiano, 'You said "most of them". What about the others? Any little thing could be helpful, even if it doesn't seem important. Try and remember – please.'

Damiano shook his head, 'I didn't actually speak with any of the women; it was the girls who did that, in pairs. My job, and that of the other lads was to wait in the cars with our tablets and record everything the girls found out.'

'Everything?'

'I think so – I mean, that's what I did.'

'No,' said Diletta, 'Not absolutely everything. Don't you remember on the way home how Caterina said she was glad she hadn't got as many cousins as the Romanians, that every uncle seemed to have a lot of nieces?' She didn't give him time to answer, 'Nobody wrote down what was said on our way home, but Cat must have picked that up from the girls on the streets, mustn't she? And we have got written down that a couple of the girls said that were only doing the job until they'd paid off their travel debts, and then they'd be moving on.'

'And if some of the Romanians are living together, then it's likely that similar arrangements are in place for the Africans... Do you know if the Africans came up through Sicily?' asked Luke, looking at Diletta.

'I'm sorry. It's not something we were trying to find out so, as far as I know, no-one asked the question or, if they did, I'm fairly sure that they didn't get an answer'.

'Don't worry. What you've been able to tell us so far has really helped. I'm sure we can find another way of talking to the African girls.' Luke avoided looking at Layla, although he could feel her give him a penetrating glance.

'You mentioned an ex-government minister. Are we allowed to know who it was? If he opposes the changes that we want to go through parliament later this year, he won't have a leg to stand on if we can show that he's been involved in trafficking.'

'You probably won't have heard of him. It's over ten years now since he was in government and, if you don't mind me saying so, you probably weren't all that interested in politics ten years ago.'

'That doesn't matter,' said Diletta with a determined look in her eyes, 'I still think that we need to know… and it wouldn't be fair to hold back on us,' she added, sounding, for the first time, slightly querulous.

Luke looked across at Layla and gave an almost imperceptible shrug of the shoulder.

'Look, Diletta, we trust you – and you Damiano – and if you really want to know, we'll tell you but, before we do, just think carefully about whether you really want to know. Although we know that companies and organisations that he's linked to were involved in transporting girls out of Sicily, we have no proof that he was personally involved. It's what, in English, we would call 'a hunch' – I can't think of the Italian word but you could say it's between a suspicion and an idea. If we're wrong, or if we can't get sufficient proof, which amounts to pretty much the same thing, I'm sure he'd be very quick to sue for defamation if word got out. It's also possible that, if he found out he was under suspicion, it would give him the opportunity to destroy any evidence or influence possible witnesses… It's your decision. Do you really want to know?'

The girl leaned back and after a moment's reflection looked across to her companion. 'Damiano?'

The boy, who was now white again, shook his head. 'It's your decision. If you decide we ought to know, you know you can rely on me absolutely not so say a word to anyone else unless you say I can.'

Diletta waited a little longer, then looked Luke directly in the eye, 'Yes. I want to know.'

'Alright.' Luke glanced round to make sure, once again, that they could not be overheard. 'The man who we think is heavily involved, possibly even the person behind most of the trafficking from Sicily, is called Giacinto Marelli. He was Secretary of State for Justice in the Pannunzi government a few years ago. He's from Grosseto originally but he now... what's the matter?'

Diletta's eyes were open wide and she seemed unaware that her lower jaw had dropped leaving her mouth half open. Luke stopped and both he and Layla looked at her curiously. Damiano was also showing signs of alarm.

'What is it?' asked Layla, leaning towards the girl. 'Are you alright?'

She took a deep breath, and her eyes seemed to focus on her companions again. 'It's unbelievable - *Signor* Marelli! There must be some mistake. He can't be like that!'

'Why do you think that, Diletta? What do you know about Marelli?' asked Layla gently.

'*Signor* Marelli is a friend of the Bishop; he makes a large donation every year towards the cost of our summer camp, so that poorer scouts can still join in, and he comes along to support some of our events. He can't be involved in trafficking and exploiting women. He just can't!'

'I'm sorry - and I hope you're right - but sometimes people aren't what they seem. It could be that what he does for the scouts is just to provide himself with a respectable cover, or it could be that he's genuinely enthusiastic about the scouts and wants to support them, but that doesn't exclude him being involved in other activities as well. Usually, even the worst of people have a good side – and often that can blind people to the other things they do,' said Layla, who had taken Diletta's hand again and held it firmly.

'You said that you'd got evidence that organisations he's involved with are involved in smuggling people out of Sicily. What is the evidence?'

Luke looked at his watch. 'Do they do any food here? This could take some time.'

They do pizzas. They don't have a proper oven, so they're bought in and cooked from frozen – but they're OK,' said Damiano.

'Good,' said Layla, 'Do you need to ring home and tell your parents that you'll be late? We don't want them worried.'

Damiano shook his head, 'I told my mum I was going to do something to do with scouts and I quite often go on somewhere with some of the others after we've been to scouts, so they won't be worried if I'm back late.'

'I'll text my mum and tell her I'm eating with Damiano – she thinks he's cute.'

Damiano blushed.

'So,' said Luke, an hour and a half later, 'That's how we tracked them as far as Messina and then friends in the social services with links to the Police, managed to trace the ownership of the warehouse where they were kept temporarily in Villa San Giovanni, as well as finding out which transport companies use the warehouse. All the way along the line, there are companies and people involved who all seem to be connected to Marelli.'

The two youngsters had listened attentively: Damiano wide eyed and Diletta generally with eyes narrowed in concentration, the only interruptions being occasional requests for clarification when Luke had chosen an incorrect word. Now, Diletta took a deep breath. 'But, surely, that doesn't really prove anything about Marelli himself. My father runs a business – nothing like as big as any of the ones that Marelli is involved in – but a lot of the day to day running is done by a couple of managers he employs. Marelli's businesses must be much bigger than my father's, so it could be one of them who's involved in trafficking, couldn't it?' She looked challengingly at Luke.

'If we were talking about almost anyone else, I'd say you were absolutely right but, as it's Marelli, I find it very easy to believe that he's personally responsible.'

Diletta shook her head, and then brushed a stray strand of hair out of her eye, 'Why?'

'How old are you?' asked Luke.

'Seventeen. But I don't see what that's got to do with it. Just because I'm young, it doesn't mean I can't tell the difference between what's fair and what isn't. So far, you haven't told me anything that suggests it's fair to suspect Marelli.'

'Sorry. I didn't mean to imply that you were too young to understand; it was just to help me clarify what you'll know about - I don't suppose you've ever heard of Mauro Rossi, have you?' asked Luke gently.

Diletta frowned, thought for a moment, and then admitted that she hadn't. Damiano was about to offer a suggestion but thought better of it.

'Mauro Rossi was a minister, a very important one, at the time Marelli was Justice Secretary, and both their terms of office came to an end pretty abruptly at the same time, along with a number of other, slightly less prominent politicians. The reason, wasn't because they were defeated politically, it was because they were all deeply involved in a right wing conspiracy to destroy the reputations of leading left wing politicians and, in doing so, subvert the democratic process for their own ends. The conspiracy was uncovered by an investigating magistrate helped by the sister of my Italian aunt and the then President, Innominati, was persuaded to intervene. Some of the conspirators, such as Rossi, were arrested and ended up with long prison sentences. Unfortunately, because Innominati felt that the shock-waves that would be felt if several members of the government were arrested and charged would, in itself, endanger the stability of the state, several conspirators, including Giacinto Marelli, were allowed to resign from office and withdraw from public life. Now, it may be that Marelli was truly penitent and has decided to dedicate himself to helping others, but personally, I find it very hard to believe.'

Diletta stood up, walked over to the window and leaned her forehead against it, the other three all watched her.

After a minute she came back to the table and looked at Luke again, 'How do I know this is all true?'

'Some of it must be on the internet,' offered Damiano hesitantly.

'You'll have to decide who you trust,' said Luke gently, 'but Damiano's right; you won't find everything there, as it was all kept as quiet as possible but, if you look up Marelli, Rossi and several others who were in that last Pannunzi government, you'll find that several of them disappeared suddenly from all forms of politics at the same time. Apart from Rossi and a couple of others who went to prison, you won't find convincing explanations for the others all leaving politics at the same time. Look them up and make your own mind up.'

Diletta sat, deep in thought and drumming her fingers on the edge of the table for a while, then she said, 'All right. I believe you. I will check but I'm sure that you wouldn't have told me to check if it wasn't going to stack up but, there's something I don't understand.'

'Go on.'

'If it was all kept a big secret, and people like Marelli have been able to continue to be involved in the community without anyone talking about it, how come you know about it? I mean, you're not even Italian - either of you.'

'It's a good question,' said Luke with a reassuring smile, 'but if you remember, I said that my aunt's sister was working with the investigating magistrate who discovered the conspiracy and worked to make sure that it didn't succeed.'

Diletta nodded slowly as she thought about his answer. 'So, if we help you, it won't just help the girls who've been trafficked, it will also put Marelli in prison.'

'You've already helped us a lot with what you've told us, and any other information you manage to get will be really useful, and we're really grateful for it,' said Layla.

'But we can do more, can't we? I can't stand the idea that Marelli has taken everyone in, and used the scouts to create an image of himself. Tell me what I can do to help!' insisted Diletta.

'Like Layla said, we need information, particularly about the African girls who're on the streets. If the scouts are planning any more sessions like the one you did in Montecatini, it would be an opportunity to focus on the Africans. But, remember, you need to be very careful. However Marelli may appear, he and others behind this racket are not nice people.'

'And what are you going to do?'

Luke laughed, 'I'm not sure I should really be telling you. I may need to break a few laws to find out the truth, and telling you would make you an accessory, if things don't work out and I get caught,'

Diletta rolled her eyes, 'What was it you said before about trusting you? How are we supposed to do that if you treat us like kids?'

It was on the tip of Luke's tongue to say that they were kids and that they already knew more than was good for them, but he stopped himself. He was sure they weren't going to tell anyone, and no-one would link them to him and Layla if things went wrong, so why not? 'OK. You win. I'm going to have a good look at Marelli's place, to see if I can find anything that links him directly to the people running the girls.'

'How are you going to get in? You can't just knock on the door and ask to be shown round, can you?'

'Don't worry about that. I'll find a way.'

'I could go. I could say it was to do with the scouts.'

'No,' said Luke and Layla in unison.

'Absolutely not. It's out of the question,' said Layla, and then, softening her tone, 'I know you're very mature and sensible but you're only seventeen. Your parents would be furious if we let you put yourself in danger – and they'd be right to be furious. Luke wasn't joking when he said that these people aren't very nice people.'

Damiano had sat listening quietly during this exchange, and his presence had been almost disregarded. Now he surprised them all by saying quietly, 'I'll go.'

'What?' said Diletta.

'I'm eighteen, so I don't need my parents' permission to do anything, and I've been in Marelli's house before,' replied Damiano with more decision.

'When?' asked Diletta, clearly taken aback.

'Do you remember a couple of years ago when Don Sandro set up a film club for scouts who were interested in cinema?... Well, I've always been interested in films, so I went along. Anyway, as well as watching films and discussing them, Don Sandro sometimes invited along experts to come and talk to us, and one of them was Signor Marelli. He came along and talked to us about Luchino Visconti and we watched *'Ossessione'*. Anyway, at the end, he invited us to go to his villa the next weekend, to watch another film. He's got his own little cinema room in the basement and he collects films by directors like Visconti and Flavio Calzavara. Eight of us went, so I'd have a good reason for going back there.'

Layla glanced at Luke and then turned back to Damiano, 'It's a great offer but we can't let you do it. If he finds out why you're really there, there'll be big trouble. It's too risky.'

'He won't find out. I'll only talk about films, so there's no risk at all. I'm going to do it.' He looked across at Diletta searching for approval. She was staring at him, eyes wide open with surprise.

'I suppose it can't really do any harm, so long as you do just talk about films when you're there and don't ask questions about anything else.'

'Luke!' exclaimed Layla.

'He's right. He's eighteen, so we can't prevent him; he's got a valid reason for going there, and even though he'll only be talking about films, he'll be able to at least give us an idea of the layout of the house afterwards.'

Layla looked at Diletta, hoping that she would intervene, but the girl was now looking at Damiano as if seeing him with fresh eyes and it was clear that she was in a minority of one.

Layla hardly spoke as they drove back to the house and when she opened the door, it banged against the wall to the side. Luke entered behind her, took hold of the door and closed it gently.

'Why?' she said, turning towards him and standing glaring, hands on hips. 'How could you agree to let him do it?'

He opened his hands, inviting her to be calm. 'A bit because, if he just goes and asks about something to do with films, he won't be at any risk at all, but mainly because it was something he needed to do.'

'What do you mean, "he needed to do it"?' she asked angrily.

'He needed to do it for Diletta. Didn't you notice, he's mad about her but she hardly notices him – or at least she didn't before tonight - I know, I could have insisted – forced him to back down – but where would that have left him? The Italians have an expression, *"fare brutta figura"* which, more or less means losing face, but it's taken really seriously. If I'd made him back down it would have been a *brutta figura* in front of Diletta, and he'd never have recovered from it.'

'Oh, you men are so stupid sometimes; you think that all women are interested in is super-heroes, and never think that just being nice might be the most important thing,' and she turned and went over to put some water on to boil. Despite her words, the anger had gone out of her voice and Luke knew that the danger of a storm had passed.

Chapter Fourteen

In the morning, Luke was awoken by a stifled groan from Layla and, when he looked into her room, he saw that the tips of her fingers were pressed against her temples and her eyes were screwed tightly closed. He observed her for a moment then went over and gently brushed her side with the back of his hand. 'Hey... Can I get you anything? Glass of water? Tea?'

She opened her eyes and did her best to give him a reassuring smile, although her look was laced with pain. 'Water... be good.'

He nodded and after lightly kissing her cheek, slipped out of the room again, grabbed a t-shirt that had been hanging on the back of his door and went down for the water.

When he got back, she had pulled herself into a sitting position and had her shoulders pressed against the wall behind the bed and her head tilted back so that it felt the cool pressure of the plaster. He stopped for a few seconds in the doorway, unable to take his eyes off her.

She opened her eyes and, aware of his look, modestly pulled the sheet up so that she was mainly covered although not, in Luke's eyes, any less desirable.

'The headache again?' he asked softly as he placed the glass in her free hand and sat down next to her on the edge of the bed.

'Yes. But it's not too bad. It'll pass soon. Sorry if I woke you.'

'Hmmm. I still think you ought to see a doctor about them – just to get them checked out.'

'There's no time. Not until this is over. And they always go away after a bit, so it's got to be psychological rather than physical anyway, hasn't it?'

'I'm not an expert, but you know I'd feel much happier if you saw someone who was.'

'I will... as soon as I've got time...Promise!'

They had decided to spend a few days watching Marelli's house from the hillside behind to try and get a feel for its layout, as well as the number of comings and goings. They also intended to find out where the African girls were living, or being kept, when they weren't working, especially as Luana had contacted them to let them know that there had been another shipment from Sicily.

Luke insisted that Layla stay up in the village for most of the day, pointing out that spending hours peering through binoculars was not likely to help her headaches whereas walking, and hopefully relaxing, in the fresh air, just might. He'd pick some food up in the Co-op at Borgo a Buggiano on his way back, and they would have plenty of time to eat before going out again to watch the girls.

He drove carefully along the winding road that ran along the southern side of the steep hillside to the north of Montecatini until he came to the village of Massa where the carpark offered an excellent view over the valley. Once he'd parked the car, he walked along until he found a suitable place to set up an old easel he'd found in the cellar of the house, on which he placed a large drawing pad he'd bought in the local supermarket and a set of artist's pencils and soft pastels.

It didn't take long to sketch in the outlines of a few key details and it would have been impossible for anyone seeing him to take him as anything other than a dedicated amateur artist, enjoying a holiday in the Tuscan countryside. Whenever, of course, there was any sign of movement in the large house crowning a knoll just off the road down to Montecatini, he was able to study it through his binoculars, as if he needed to see some of the details in front of him in greater detail. The house was perfectly situated; although, from his viewpoint it appeared to stand on the edge of Montecatini, he realised that another rise behind it shielded the villa from the ribbon like sprawl linking Montecatini to Borgo a Buggiano while offering splendid unobstructed views towards the mountains and the string of attractive hill villages that adorned the lower slopes. Most of the sloping grounds were enclosed by an outer wall separating olive trees from the surrounding lanes, while a thick inner hedge around the villa itself acted almost like a moat. It was difficult to judge the age of the villa as a two storey extension appeared to have been built around the four-storey central block. In the middle of the gently sloping roof of the oldest part was a smaller raised section, although he wasn't sure whether this was a truncated medieval tower or a later addition intended to give the villa a more majestic aspect.

Although he soon realised that the binoculars he had were not powerful enough to enable him to pick out fine details like car number plates, they were good enough for him to be able to recognise makes and models, and even to pick out some details of the people getting in and out of them. He had studied all the images of Marelli that he could find and was reasonably sure that he would be able to recognise him if he was in residence and stepped out of the villa. Beyond that, of course, he knew that he was very unlikely to uncover anything that would lead to dramatic progress but, one thing that had always been drummed into them during the basic police training was that if the proper groundwork was not done in any detailed investigation, then that investigation would almost certainly collapse at some point. Lucky breaks only happened in films or novels; real police work, where there was no scientific or electronic procedure that could be utilised was much more mundane and drawn out.

As well as the picture on his easel that gave him his excuse for being there, he also had a smaller pad with him on which he had pre-drawn the general layout of the land, and he annotated this to show the routes of all the vehicles that left the villa during the day, and of as many as possible of those that arrived.

Much of the land within the walls and hedges surrounding the villa was covered with very well-tended olives and other fruit trees and he noticed immediately that these were being tended by three workers, each of whom appeared to have been allocated their own sector of the grounds. He didn't know enough about agriculture to know if this was a normal way of working or not and, other than noting it down, paid little attention to the men until the second time someone came out of the house and held a brief conversation with each one in turn before returning inside. As he added this to his notes, it struck him that the two visits to the gardeners had taken place exactly an hour apart and each had taken place on the hour.

With his binoculars, he looked at every other piece of agricultural land he could see. There were people doing various jobs: strimming grass, burning rubbish, digging, watering vegetables, but nowhere was there anyone working on trees as was the case around Marelli's villa. 'Idiot,' he said to himself. They were far more likely to be security guards than genuine gardeners or agricultural workers; to anyone who just caught a glimpse of them while passing the villa, nothing would appear unusual but, to someone studying the villa from his vantage point, it was clear that they were fulfilling another function and that the gardening was just a cover.

He was surprised by the realisation; there would obviously be a security system at the villa, whether or not Marelli was involved in any criminal activity, but he would have expected it to be far more hi-tech than three people masquerading as gardeners. Unfortunately, there was no more he could tell about the security system without getting much closer.

At lunch time he ate some bread and salami he'd brought along and drank sparingly from a bottle of water; although he didn't expect to see anything particularly important, it would be unfortunate to leave his post for a few minutes and not know whether he'd missed anything or not. Eventually, at about ten past four, he saw what he assumed to be Marelli's chauffeur driven car leaving the villa and taking the road towards Montecatini. Breathing a sigh of relief, he began to pack his things away to return to the village.

Layla was clearly much better. When he parked the car, he saw that she was outside, smiling and talking to one of the neighbours.

'*Ciao,*' she called, waving as he got out of the car, 'This is *Signora* Piramo; she lives in the house down there, facing the church. She brought us some jam and some eggs.'

'That's very kind of you,' he said, extending a hand, 'I'm Luke – or Luca, if you prefer. Pleased to meet you, *Signora.*'

The woman smiled, 'Paola - you can forget about the *Signora*. I was just saying to your wife, how nice it is to have some young blood in the village. Will you be staying here long?'

'It's all very undecided at the moment; it depends how our work goes – but we do like it here – very much.'

'Oh,' said the woman, and then, her curiosity getting the better of her, 'What do you do?'

'We both write,' Luke responded without hesitating. 'Layla's a serious journalist: she writes travel articles and other things, while I write short stories for teen magazines.'

'That's fascinating. What sort of stories?'

He laughed, 'Just silly adventure stories really. I try and take real events, change them a little and then build up stories around them. Unlike real life, however, the good guys always win in the end. You'll have to let me know about any gossip you hear: you never know, it could be the starting point for a story.'

'Just ignore him, Paola,' said Layla, his stories are usually about murderers, kidnappers and criminal gangs, not the sorts of thing that anyone up here would be gossiping about.'

'Maybe not, but there are all sorts of things going on down in the town. You'd be surprised by some of the things we hear about up here.'

'I look forward to it,' said Luke with a smile, 'You'll have to drop in for a coffee some time and tell us all the village secrets.'

The woman smiled, 'I might just take you up on that. Have a nice evening and *buon appetito,*' and she waved a hand as she turned away.

'*Ciao*', responded Layla, while Luke replied with, 'And the same to you.'

'Well?' she asked, as they got inside.

'First of all, I want to know about you,' he said, taking her by the shoulders and holding her at arm's length, 'What about the headache?'

'As if I'd never had it.' She smiled, 'I lay with my eyes shut, listening to the birds and to the buzz of chainsaws in the distance then I must have dozed off. I woke up again and it was about ten, and I realised I'd never felt better.'

'Mmmm' he said doubtfully, and then, tightening his grip on her shoulders slightly, 'You'd better be telling me truth although, even if you are, I'm still going to hold you to your promise of going to see a doctor as soon as it's practicable.'

'Now are you going to tell me about your day?' she said after he'd changed into a fresh pair of shorts, 'If you don't, I'm warning you, I'm going to torture you,' she said pulling out a long hair that was growing on his shoulder.

'Ow! Alright, alright, I give up. I'll tell you everything,' he said, pretending to be afraid. 'These are the details of my exciting day.'

After eating, they headed down into Montecatini again, determined to have another go at speaking directly to the prostitutes. They decided it was better to split up: Layla would attempt to get into conversation with one or more of the girls on the main drag, while Luke would try Via Marruota where they had learnt that the girls were African. Layla wanted to be the one to approach the Africans but Luke refused point-blank. While Viale Leonardo da Vinci was well illuminated, with open bars and a regular police presence, Via Marruota was narrower, darker, and not frequented by anyone at night other than the prostitutes, their pimps and their clients.

He dropped Layla at a point from where it was easy to walk through to her destination and then drove ahead of her until he reached the junction with Via Marruota.

Turning right, he dropped his speed to little more than ten miles an hour and drove down the street taking a good look at each girl as he did so. He had been expecting to find similar girls to those on the main road with the only difference being their colour, but he was shocked by what he saw. On the main road, the girls stood still by the side of the road, often with mobile phones in their hands, which he assumed provided them with their pretext for standing by the side of the road without risking accusations of soliciting; usually, the only thing that clearly differentiated the prostitutes from the handful of genuine passers-by was the provocative way in which they were dressed. Other than the way they were dressed and the way they followed passers-by with their eyes, there was no overt attempt to obtain clients.

On Via Marruota, however, it was different. Although there were only four women working the street, he felt almost violated by the time he got to the far end of the road and prepared to turn round. The first woman he passed had leaned out and pushed her breasts upwards and outwards as he approached her while rotating her tongue suggestively; the second had held out her arm, waving her hand rapidly up and down from the wrist, leaving passers-by in no doubt as to her speciality; the third beckoned with one hand while sliding the other down the front of her skimpy shorts, while the fourth turned away from the car as he approached her, bent over and rotated her rear end suggestively.

He could feel he was sweating slightly as he pulled into a side street to turn round. He stopped and closed his eyes for a moment so he could think clearly. His heart was beating rapidly and he knew that what he was going to do scared him more than anything he'd done so far.

After waiting a minute, he started the engine again and pulled back out onto Via Marruota. He drove slowly past the first two women and pulled over by quick-wrist as he'd designated her. He wound the window down and she came over, leaned on the roof of the car and allowed the window-sill to push her breasts up.

'*Ciao, Bello.* You want fun.'

'How much?'

'Twenty euro, I give good hand job; thirty with mouth. You want more, you pay more.'

'How much more?'

'With condom in car, I do sixty. No condom one hundred; you want hotel – cost twenty-five extra.'

He took out his wallet, extracted thirty euros and placed them on the passenger seat. 'Get in.'

'OK. First I text your number to my friend – so no funny business.'

'That's fine. Just make sure she deletes it afterwards.'

She told him to turn right at the end of the road and then take the next right again. As he drove she slipped her hand onto his crotch and felt for his zip. He gently but firmly pushed her hand away.

'Not yet. Not while I'm driving.'

Less than five minutes after they'd started, she indicated that he should pull off the road onto a tree-lined track. He noticed that there were a couple of other cars parked under trees further on and he wondered whether other transactions were taking place, or whether one of the cars contained the girls' minders.

Her hand was across again while he was till turning the engine off and pulling the handbrake and his zip was open before he could pull her hand away. When he did, she looked at him with a mixture of puzzlement and fear in her eyes.

'It's OK. I'm not going to hurt you. The money's yours but you don't have to do anything; I just want to talk.'

She looked at him uncomprehendingly and he realised that her Italian might not extend far beyond the basic financial negotiations that she was used to conducting.

'*Preferisci che parlo inglese?*' he asked, and then repeated the question in English, 'Would you rather I spoke English?'

She shook her head.

'What language: *Italiano*, English, *Espanol, Francais?*'

There was suddenly a spark in her eyes. 'Francais, oui. Je parle un peu de francais.'

'*D'accord,*' he said, and assured her again that he meant her no harm and that he would pay her for her time so she wouldn't lose out or get into trouble.

'I can't,' she said, and shook her head, tears in her eyes.

'Please. It's important. I'm trying to find a girl, a relative of a friend of mine, and I think she may have been forced to come to Montecatini.'

'I can't. I don't know.' She looked frightened but he was sure it wasn't him that she was frightened of.

'Look,' he said, 'I don't know your circumstances but if there are people making you do what you do, I can help you. I know that sometimes girls are made to do what you do to help their families. If that's your situation then I can do my best to help your family as well.'

'You can't,' she said.

'I can try very hard, and I have lots of friends – some of them with more influence than I have.'

'It's impossible,' she said, desperation in her voice, 'You can't help them get across the Mediterranean.'

'No, I can't. But do you really trust these people to do what they say?'

'I have no choice.'

He sighed, 'OK. But you seem like a good girl. If there's anything you can tell me that will help me, I promise no-one will ever know where the information came from and, if there's any way I can help you, or your family in the future, I will.'

'And what did she say?' asked Layla.

'In the end, she agreed to tell me everything she knows, but it will have to be tomorrow. She was already pushing it a bit going back with only forty euros after spending twenty minutes with me.'

'Forty – I thought you settled on thirty.'

'I gave her an extra ten, so that if she were challenged, she could blame the client for keeping her but, at the same time, hopefully earn some credit by managing to get some extra money.'

'You're all heart,' she said with a smile. 'So what do we do now?'

'We need to come back in about an hour and a half. She wasn't sure where they were living but she said that she and the other African women can be picked up and taken back anytime between one-thirty and three. The people in charge use a van, and the women are in the back, so she doesn't really know where they go. The best she could do was to say that she's fairly sure they're living to the north of the town and that it usually takes about ten minutes to get there.'

'What about during the day? Surely she can see her surroundings then?'

Luke shook his head. 'She thinks that the building is a converted agricultural building. They're allowed outside but there's a thick hedge around two sides and a high stone wall around the other two.

She was fairly sure that there were no high buildings around, and there was no sound of traffic, but apart from that...' he shrugged his shoulders and grimaced.

'But, if we follow them, we'll be able to see where they go, won't we?'

'That's the plan, although it's not as easy as it seems in films or on tv. There'll be very little traffic about if we have to wait until half-past two or three and, if we follow them off the main roads and along little lanes, they'd have to be pretty stupid not to spot us.'

'So we won't learn very much,' said Layla disappointedly.

'That depends..... If the road they take when they turn off the main road doesn't have many turnoffs, then that limits the number of places they could go and, the woman I spoke to didn't think that the van does much climbing as it drives them home. Once we know which road they take, we can spend some time studying the area from the hills up above; all we need is a more powerful pair of binoculars. And then, after that, we can start following them much further along their route, as well as watching from the hills.'

'We could do with two cars,' said Layla wistfully.

Luke smiled, 'I thought of that. I'm going to Florence tomorrow morning to collect my aunt's sister's old Ducati from Alessio. He's had it checked over and says it's fine. Why don't you come along? I'm sure there'll be a spare helmet, and if there isn't we can buy one.'

'Mmmm. I'll think about it. By the way; when did you last ride a bike?'

'A few years ago. I used to have a Kawasaki 500 but I sold it when it failed its MOT and never got round to getting another one."

'And you expect me to just jump on the back when you haven't ridden one for years - and try not to fall off as you blast along the motorway!'

'Come on. You'll enjoy it – and we don't have to take the motorway, except for the first three or four miles. We can come off at Prato Est and then follow the line of the original motorway all the way to Pistoia. There are speed limits of fifty, sixty and seventy kilometres per hour all the way along – with plenty of speed cameras, so I'll be taking it very steadily.'

'Maybe... Let me sleep on it.'

He smiled, 'I knew you'd agree.'

'By half past one they had managed to approach Via Marruota from the far end and parked at a point from where the first of the prostitutes could just be glimpsed in the distance. They settled down for what could have ended up being a long wait. Layla offered him chewing-gum but he refused by pulling a disgusted face and they settled into an uneasy silence.

Just before two, a car drew up by the woman and Luke stretched his hand towards the ignition key. Layla reached out and stopped his hand with a light touch. 'Client... I think... She's not getting in... Look, he's going now – false alarm.' Luke sighed and leaned back in his seat again.

It was nearly twenty-five past two when they saw a dark panel-van turn out of a side street on the left and drive up to the first girl. Luke turned the key in the ignition and then looked at his watch. 'OK,' he said as the van moved off, 'we give it seventy-five seconds and then we go after them.'

'Why seventy-five seconds?' asked Layla, surprised.

'Because he was stopped for nineteen seconds when he picked the first girl up, and he's got four more to pick up. Seventy-five seconds gives him time to pick up four more women; if we go too soon, we'll have to pass them. When they see us behind them, I'm hoping they assume that we're just driving along the road, not that we've just set off.'

'Four more? I thought you said there were four altogether.'

'Four when I drove down the road, but another one was already with someone.'

They came in full view of the van again just as it was setting off after picking up the last of the women and, as it moved quickly away from the kerb, they were able to maintain a good distance without getting too close.

At the end of the road, the van turned left, as he'd hoped it would, and he was also pleased to see that there was still a little traffic about. With one car separating them they were able to follow the van along and round by the hippodrome and then onto the main road towards Lucca. At the first roundabout, the van turned right towards the hills and Luke followed, being careful to keep his distance. Shortly after, the road forked and the van headed left, while Luke took the right turn towards Montecatini Alto. Thirty seconds later he pulled off the road and turned the engine off.

'Let's give it a couple of minutes, then we'll turn round and go home. I need some sleep.'

'OK. I thought you weren't going to follow them off the main road.'

'I wasn't, but then they took the first roundabout and I knew it wasn't far to the fork. Whichever road they took, I was going to take the other. At least now we know for certain that they're kept in the same general area as Marelli's villa.'

Layla's eyes lit up with hope, 'Do you think they're being kept there?'

He shook his head, 'It would be nice if it were that simple but it would be far too dangerous to keep them at the villa. Marelli's all sorts of things, but one thing he's not is stupid. Although we think he's one of the one's behind the racket and that he's probably making a fair amount of money out of it, we've got no evidence at all to suggest he actually has any contact with the girls. What we need to do is establish links between Marelli and the people dealing with the girls.'

'Women,' corrected Layla.

'Sorry,' said Luke, 'I wasn't meaning to demean them, but the one I spoke to earlier was scarily young – it's hard to think of her as anything other than a girl.'

'Illegally young?'

'No. At least I don't think so. She could have passed for sixteen but I'm fairly sure she was just one of those women who look young for their age, although I doubt she was any older than twenty.'

Alessio initially ignored Luke when he opened the door and directed a broad smile at Layla.

'Wow! My sister did you an injustice when she described you as pretty. Why are you wasting your time with a has-been like this.'

'Nice to see you too, Alessio. As you've already worked out, this is Layla – who has been warned about you.'

'Hi,' said Alessio, stepping forward to kiss Layla on both cheeks and then giving Luke a friendly hug. 'Come in. I'll make coffee. Luke, show Layla round."

The flat was an unusual, but not unpleasant layout. The entrance, which came off the communal stairs gave directly into the living-room which was separated by a large arch from a dining area containing a round beech table for four people. Beyond the dining area the kitchen and bathrooms were parallel to each other and each had a window in the far wall overlooking an inner courtyard. At the other end of the entrance wall, a short corridor led, beyond the stairwell, to the street side of the apartment and two decent sized bedrooms. The first bedroom was obviously Alessio's but the second, even though the double bed it contained was made up, had a vague air of disuse.

'Theoretically, this is my room, as this is the address in Italy approved by the probation service when I was released on licence. A representative of the British Vice-Consul could do a spot check, but they never have so far, and I think it's highly unlikely that they ever will. I'm allowed to go away within Italy for a couple of days but if I do they have to be able to reach me by phone to make an appointment.'

Layla nodded, 'I know this is where you're supposed to be; it was the first place I tried to find you – but it didn't take long to work out that you weren't here. What happens if the authorities find out that you're not living here?'

He shrugged, 'As I say, it's very unlikely they'll ever check, but if they do, and I can't get back in time to persuade them that I do live here, then my parole will be revoked and I'll have to serve the rest of my sentence – but it's not going to happen.'

After they'd had coffee, Luke brought Alessio up to date with the progress they'd made and what he hoped to achieve when they had the use of the Ducati.'

'Then what?'

'What do you mean, "then what?"' asked Luke.

'I mean, let's say you trace the girls back to Marelli's villa or somewhere near there, what happens next? You can't just go barging in and say "you can all go home now" can you? Prostitution's not illegal, so unless some of them are prepared to give evidence that they're being forced or that someone else is making money from them, you won't have achieved anything except finding out where they're living. Why should the girls give you any more information when they're "at home", for want of a better term, than when they're out on the streets?'

'The hope is,' said Layla,' that where they're living, there'll be evidence linking whoever owns it to the traffickers in Sicily.'

'But you've still got to get in, and that won't be easy. You can't break in. Remember Luke's only out on licence, one sniff of a charge for breaking and entering and they'll lock him up and throw away the key. You've got to convince someone else to go in and do the job for you.'

'No!' said Luke. 'Absolutely not. You're not going anywhere near this.'

Alessio smiled. 'Your concern is touching, but don't worry, that wasn't what I was going to suggest. You know how Renzi and several members of his government are Florentines?' He waited for their nods of agreement. 'Well, as it happens, my old school, the Liceo Dante, is also the old school of Renzi and several members of his government – it's also the school where some of them send their children.' He smiled again, 'The son of one of them is a friend of mine and I'm sure that if he could be persuaded to drop a word in the right ear, we may be able to get an official raid.'

'Wow! Do you really think that that's possible?' asked Layla, surprised.

'The problem would be security,' said Luke, 'I find it very hard to believe that the local authorities aren't, at the very best, turning a blind eye to what's going on.'

'I agree, it's a risk,' said Alessio, 'but on the other hand, what other viable alternative do you have?'

'None,' responded Layla.

'Alright. So what do we need to do to get this friend of yours on board?' asked Luke.

'Get all the evidence you can, and then set it out clearly in a file – that should be easy for you with your police training. If the Italian needs tidying up a bit, I can do that, then I'll go to work on my friend. OK?'

'OK,' said Layla, and Luke nodded.

Alessio had managed to retrieve his aunt's old helmet as well as his father's so they didn't have to go and find a new one for Layla before setting off back. She clung tightly to Luke's back trying to relax and follow the movements of his torso, despite having her eyes closed for much of their way around the *Viali* before they turned towards the motorway. On the motorway itself, she managed to relax and enjoyed the sensation of speed before Luke slowed down as the exit for Prato Est approached. When she felt the bike begin to slow, she leaned forward and stretched a gloved hand beyond Luke jabbing it twice forward, indicating that he should follow the motorway instead of turning off. He inclined his head twice to show that he had understood and opened the throttle again.

When he came off at Montecatini and stopped in the short queue for the paybooth he tilted his head back and to the side and shouted, 'How was that?'

'Wonderful,' she shouted back.

He took it easy as they made their way around the southern edge of the centre, along the anonymous looking thoroughfare that by ten o'clock would have transformed into the hub of the red-light area. They stopped in the Co-op at Borgo a Buggiano and bought some red snapper to cook and eat before returning to the town to put their plan into action.

Just after midnight, Luke approached Via Marruota and drove slowly along until he saw the woman he had picked up the previous night. She was on the opposite side of the road tonight and he had to press the button for the window next to the passenger seat and then lean across to speak to her.

'Je suis retourné,' he said with a smile, 'Get in.' he pulled the handle on the inside of the door and then pushed it outwards a few centimetres.

She shook her head and then pushed the door closed with her knee, *'Va t'en!.'*

'I'll pay double.. Don't you need the money to help your family?'

He saw the girl's shoulders slump and he knew he'd won, although as he was fairly sure that none of the money the girl earned would ever find its way to her family, he took no pleasure in the victory. 'Come on. Get in.' She did as she was urged.

As he drove out towards the same spot as the previous evening she turned and said pleadingly, 'You have to pretend.'

'What?' he asked, confused, 'Pretend what?'

'You have to pretend I'm doing what I'm paid for. There are people around, keeping an eye on things - to protect us - they asked questions about last night, wanted to know why we just sat there.'

Luke thought for a moment, 'And what did you tell them?'

'I told them that you couldn't do it, that you started thinking about your wife and you wouldn't let me do anything.'

'Great', he thought, then out loud he said, 'OK. I'll pretend. Don't worry. You can tell them that what you said to me last night must have convinced me after I'd gone home and thought about it.'

When he had pulled off the road and killed the engine, she slid forward on the seat, twisted and pushing her very scantily clad buttocks against the door, dipped down so that she was well below the level of the windows, with her cheek resting on his right thigh and her right hand holding his knee. 'Make sure you keep changing your expression,' she said.

He eyed the expanse of exposed flesh at the bottom of her back and then placed his hands behind his head, lacing his fingers together, as much because he wasn't sure where else it was appropriate to put them, as because it was a part of the act he was forced to play out.

'Where are you from, originally?'

'I come from South Sudan.' She stopped and, at first, he hoped it was just a pause, but then, when she didn't continue, he realised that he would have to extract the information patiently, bit by bit.

'And how did you get to Italy? Did you come across from Libya?' He felt a slight movement of her head against his thigh, as though she'd started to shake it and then thought better of it.'

'No. I got across from Turkey to Greece, and then I managed to smuggle over to Italy.'

'So how did you get to Montecatini?'

'I was begging in the street in a town called Barletta, trying to get some money for food before moving on up the coast… and then a car stopped, with two men in the front and a girl from Ethiopia in the back.'

'And then?' he prompted, 'What happened then?'

'They said they knew people who could help me – who could get me some papers and find me work to do.'

'And they brought you here,' he commented. 'What about the other women?'

'I don't know. We don't talk much. It's better not to talk much.'

'OK. But you must see things and hear things. Do they all arrive in ones and twos like you did? Or do they arrive in groups?'

'I don't know. I'm not sure. Both, I think. I don't know.'

He unentwined his fingers and lowered one hand to stroke her hair, 'Try, please. It's important. Have any new girls arrived in the past few days?'

She sighed, 'A group of girls arrived in a van two days ago. I don't know how many. They sleep in a separate building.'

'The latest group from Sicily,' he thought. 'And what will happen to them? Will they be working on the street with you?'

'Only two of them. They moved over to our building yesterday.'

'And are they here on the road now?' he asked with a hint of excitement in his voice.

'No. They'll be taught what to do and what to say for a few days before they get brought out, and then they'll be paired up with another girl. They might work here or they might work in Florence, but usually it is just girls who look very young who work in Florence.'

'In Florence? Where? In the Cascine?'

She shook her head, 'I don't know; they say there is a very big park with lots of trees.'

'The Cascine,' he said, under his breath, and then, 'What happened to the other women from the group?'

'I don't know - it must be time to go back now – Please.' The desperation in her voice was evident.

'Just this one last thing, then we go back and I won't bother you again… unless you need help.' He felt terrible about abusing the power he had over her; he knew she was right that she had to get back, but it was too important an issue for him to pull back.

'Alright. I'm not sure, but sometimes, with other groups I've seen cars drive up with men in them. After a while they go away again, but they take one or two of the youngest girls with them. I think the others are taken away again in the van, I don't know where – now please, can we go back?' He could tell from her voice that she was on the edge of hysteria.

'Of course. Thankyou. Here's a hundred euros; hide it until you need it, and don't tell anyone else you've got it.'

He drove her back to her pitch and dropped her off and then drove over to the piano-bar where he'd left Layla.

'That was horrible,' he said when Layla asked him how it had gone. 'I more or less bullied her into telling me everything she knew and it felt as if I were violating her as badly as anyone else who just wants to use her body. At least she can be emotionally detached with them; I felt as if I were forcing her emotions out.'

Layla took hold of his hand and gave it a squeeze, 'You did well, and you shouldn't feel bad about it. If anything, having to put it into words might make her more aware of how she, like all the other women, is being exploited. And don't forget, that the things you found out could be very useful in bringing these people to justice. I thought you were a fan of Machiavelli, and didn't he say that "the end justifies the means"?'

Luke gave a little smile and knocked back the grappa he'd ordered as soon as he'd come in, 'He didn't actually. Most people think that that's what he said, but that's because most people, or at least most people in England, haven't actually read what he wrote. Rousseau even argued that the whole of "The Prince" should be read as a satire intended to show how cynical many rulers were... Having said that, I suppose you're right in a way: I need to look at the bigger picture; If we can put some of these bastards behind bars, we'll be doing her and others like her a big favour.'

An hour later, they drove to the almost deserted carpark at the top of the wooded park surrounding the main old thermal establishments, and he pulled up alongside the Ducati.

'Let's just run through it again,' he said as he slipped the helmet on. 'You park just outside the hippodrome, near where the refreshment stands are then, when you see the van, follow it but don't get within fifty metres. When they turn off at the roundabout, you carry on but send me a message so that I know they're on their way. I'll be waiting near the end of one of the side-streets and I'll pull out behind them and take it from there. If there aren't too many turnings, I'll be able to find out where they're going tonight - otherwise, I'll have to turn off and we'll pick them up further along the route tomorrow and try again. There's no point pushing our luck and getting spotted while we're following them.'

The plan worked as well as they'd hoped. At ten to two, the screen of Luke's phone lit up and he felt it vibrate in his hand. He ran his thumb across the screen and it showed that there was a thumbs-up message from Layla. He pocketed the phone without opening the message, slipped his plain black helmet on and turned the key on the bike. At the first sign of the glow of the van's headlights in the distance, he eased the bike forward, timing it so that he would arrive at the junction just after the van had passed but before it had gone so far ahead that its lights would have disappeared.

As it had the night before, the van took the left fork, but this time Luke flicked the indicator to follow. The road was about a kilometre long and fairly straight and, for a moment, Luke hoped that they were heading to Marelli's Villa which lay to their left; the van, however, drove straight past the high gates without giving any sign of stopping. The road ended in a T-junction and, although the van didn't indicate, it was obvious from its position on the road that the driver intended to turn right. Luke opened the throttle a little to close the distance, wanting to be seen, and flicked the switch for the left indicator.

When Luke reached the end, however, he didn't turn left, but instead turned the bike's lights off and turned to the right towards the glow of the van's rearlights which were about eighty metres ahead of him. There was no other traffic on the road, so keeping the van in sight wouldn't be a problem although, if the half-moon decided to hide behind one of the small clouds that were in the sky, then that would make things awkward.

For a couple of minutes he did his best to keep the van in sight, although he was aware that, as he had to go very slowly, it was gradually pulling away from him Then, as he looked up from a deep shadow that he'd assumed was a pothole, he realised that the van had stopped and was now just less than fifty metres ahead of him. He immediately killed the engine and allowed the bike to coast into the side of the road.

Luckily, the van driver showed no sign of having seen him, and he was able to watch as a pair of large, wrought iron gates swung over to allow the vehicle to pass, and then closed again once this had happened.

He took his phone out, swiped across the screen and entered his code, allowing him to access the message he'd received from Layla. *Menu – Messaggi – Apri - Rispondi –* "Bingo; going to have a careful look around". – *Invia.* He turned the phone completely off and then took the binoculars out of the back-box on the bike. The driver hadn't got out of the van so, either he'd telephoned to announce his arrival, or there was a security camera which had allowed whoever was beyond the gate to know he was there. It took him some time, but eventually he spotted a faint red dot in one of the trees facing the entrance. Once he'd identified the camera and worked out where its blind spot was, he carefully worked his way along the edge of the road, crouching down so his head remained below the level of the bushes which stretched along much of the roadside, until he was sure he was out of sight of the camera.

When he was able to stand upright immediately below the camera, he used the binoculars again to look for other security devices until he was pretty confident that there weren't any. Having worked out where it was safe to approach the wall, he squirmed along the edge of the road just outside the camera's field of vision and then crossed over quickly. A self-seeded tree growing close to the wall provided him with something to hold on to and he carefully pulled himself up until he was just able to see over.

Three buildings stood inside the enclosure: two were clearly restored agricultural buildings and the third was a modern looking metal barn without windows. The van was parked between the metal barn and one of the older buildings where a single light was showing. He could just dimly see one corner of another vehicle behind the van, possibly a Landrover Freelander although he couldn't see enough of it to be sure. He tried to train the binoculars on the window, but the ondulating branches of a shrub that partially blocked his view, not to mention his own somewhat unstable perch, made it impossible to get the focus right. He thought that there were two people in the room although there could have been more out of sight of the window.

As he watched, a rectangular patch of light suddenly appeared on the ground as a door in the front of the metal barn was opened from inside. A figure that he thought was female was silhouetted for a moment before she stepped outside and closed the door behind her. She turned towards the door for a moment and did something to it before stepping away and walking briskly over to the building with the light. When Luke's eyes had adjusted to the darkness again, he pointed the binoculars at the door and, although there was very little light, thought he could discern a padlock.

'But that's great,' said Layla, as Luke finished telling her what he'd seen, 'We don't just know where they're living, we know that they're

~ 296 ~

kept locked up while they're not working. That has to be classified as modern-slavery and it's only a short step from there to trafficking, especially as the majority of them, if not all of them, will be working with false papers.'

Luke frowned, 'No,' he said. 'We know what's going on, and what we know would make a good newspaper article, but legally...' he shook his head, 'legally, I don't think that what we've got would be enough to guarantee a conviction... especially as these people have obviously got very influential friends.'

'So, what do we need? What more can we do?' asked Layla looking somewhat put-out.

Three things. We need to be able to prove that the women who arrive are coming along the line illegally from Sicily; we need one of the women who's already here to agree to testify and we need to be able to tie what's happening into Marelli and people like him.'

'So we need help.'

'Certainly with the first one. We need Luana in Sicily and then Pusceddu in Rome to help us track one of these consignments of women all the way through. That'll be time consuming but relatively easy to achieve... It may be easier to get someone to testify once they know that the people controlling them here are behind bars, especially if they can be convinced that these scum never had any intention of helping their families. As for the third one, it's down to us; we have to be able to prove that there's regular contact between Marelli and the place where the women are being held.'

'Nice and straightforward then,' said Layla with more than a touch of disappointment, and then, pulling herself together, 'I'll get onto Luana first thing in the morning. It would probably be best if she were the one to talk to Pusceddu this time.'

Layla suffered from another headache during the night but, other than feeling tired, felt fine again by the time they had breakfasted.

'You're sure you want to come?' asked Luke, concerned. 'Wouldn't it be best if you stayed here and tried to catch up on some sleep?'

Layla smiled, a smile that, at least for a while, banished all traces of tiredness from her face. 'No. I need to be doing something and I'm sure the fresh air will do me good – and your company, of course. I just need a quarter of an hour to ring Luana first, then I'll be ready.'

Luke didn't insist. It was probably better for her to be where he could keep an eye on her, he thought – and he would enjoy the company.

The best phone reception was upstairs so Layla went up to her bedroom to make the call while Luke remained in the living-room and decided to catch up on news from England while he waited.

Whichever site he looked at seemed to be dominated by speculation about the forthcoming referendum; some, usually reliable journalists, seemed to be suggesting that the result wasn't a forgone conclusion, even that the unthinkable might happen and the Leave campaign might come out on top. He clicked onto the site of one of the red-tops and laughed out loud when he saw that they were promising the £350 million per week that they claimed they would gain from leaving the EU would be put into the National Health Service. They must be really desperate to resort to such obvious lies: surely even Farage, Gove and Johnson couldn't hold the British people in enough contempt to think that they were dumb enough to believe that. He saw that both the Leave and Remain campaigns were being led by Tories, none of whom could be trusted to tell the truth. Luckily, he thought, the social, cultural and environmental benefits of being part of the EU was so obvious that Remain were bound to win.

Shaking his head in disgust at the way the Tory government was wasting the country's money on a pointless referendum, he decided to ignore the news and turn to the sport.

He felt slightly uneasy about riding the Ducati dressed only in a t-shirt and shorts, something he'd never have dreamed of doing in the somewhat harsher climate of England, but it really wasn't practical to dress in full biker gear for what would be a fairly short ride under the sun on roads that wouldn't permit him to go fast enough for the wind to cool them down. He had a pair of training shoes to change into in the top-box along with a small rucksack containing the binoculars, two half litre bottles of water, some nuts and some cereal bars to keep them going.

They left the bike in a small lay-by not far from the works of the olive-oil consortium in Vangile and, once their helmets were safely stowed away in the top-box and Luke had replaced his boots with the trainers, they pulled on their baseball caps and struck out westwards, on what they hoped was a footpath, as if they were just out for an enjoyable stroll.

Eventually, they emerged on a small country road that, Luke was fairly sure was the one that ran past the buildings in which the women were being held. They headed down the road until Luke recognised the group of buildings in the distance. He indicated it to Layla and they stopped to decide how to proceed. Layla pointed out a low hill off the road to the right but further down the road and not far past the buildings.

'Why don't we walk past but then turn off and head to the top of that little hill. We can sit down and pretend to be having a little picnic and see if we can see anything with the binoculars at the same time.'

As they walked steadily down the road, chatting to each other as they did so demonstrating no interest in any of their surroundings, Layla began to limp slightly. When they were almost opposite the gate in the wall around the farm buildings, she put a hand on Luke's arm to stop him and bent down to undo her shoe-lace with the other. Slipping the shoe off she straightened up and, turning it upside down, shook it as if to remove a small stone, hopping as she did so to keep her balance. Luke steadied her and held on to her t-shirt as she bent down to replace the shoe.

'Three cars and a van,' she said, as they began to walk again.

'Well done. Any idea what models?' he asked.

'No. The gate was only open a crack and I was only able to get a quick glance. I think there was someone just inside the gate and I didn't want them to think I was interested.'

'Never mind. Hopefully we'll be able to see a bit more from up on the hill.'

They were lucky; before they had gone a hundred metres to the point where they had decided to leave the road, they heard the noise of a car behind them. Layla glanced back over her shoulder and tightened her grip on Luke's arm. 'One of the cars is coming out, and it's turning this way. You memorise the second half of the number and I'll get the first.'

'OK But remember not to look directly at them; we don't want them recognising our faces.'

'Got it?' he asked, as the white Lancia went past and they stepped back onto the road.

'I did,' she said, 'How about you?'

'Uh-huh,' he confirmed. 'As soon as we get up to the top of the hill. I'll make a note of it.'

From where they sat to eat their nuts and their cereal bars, part of the interior of the compound was clearly visible through the binoculars and Luke was able to add the number plate of a second vehicle to the one already recorded on his phone. There was no sign of any of the women, but they did notice that three flush-fitting metal window covers, that Luke had not seen the night before, had been pushed back on one side of the large metal barn to let some light in. There was also a fourth small building attached to the back of the barn which they guessed was some form of toilet block.

'What now?' asked Layla after they'd been there a while, 'If we stay here too long we'll be drawing attention to ourselves.

'Now, we go back round to the road and then, in a bit, take a left turn that will take us near Marelli's villa. It's good that the women are being kept so close to him but it doesn't prove anything; we still need to establish a link.'

Disappointingly, little could be seen of Marelli's Villa from the road; despite its elevated position; the perimeter wall and the olive trees in the park, which Luke noticed had been allowed to grow higher than was usual for well-maintained trees in the area, guaranteed almost complete privacy. They didn't linger, not wishing to draw attention to themselves, and any observer would have been convinced that they were far more interested in the view of the hills to the north.

'Two security cameras, I think,' said Luke, once they were about fifty metres beyond the end of the external wall, 'One covering the main entrance, and one covering the road. I'd be very surprised if there weren't more covering the other sides. Getting in without being seen would be almost impossible without specialist equipment, and probably inside help.'

'It's a shame we're not in a film; they always seem to manage.'

'If we were,' said Luke, 'I think it would probably be more Pink Panther than anything else.'

'Pink Panther? Wasn't that a cartoon series?'

He shook his head in mock despair. 'What a culturally deprived childhood you must have had. There were a series of Pink Panther films starring Peter Sellers as a bumbling French Detective called Inspector Clouseau. In the one I'm particularly thinking of – I can't remember whether it's the *'Return of the Pink Panther'* or *'The Pink Panther Strikes Again'* – Inspector Clouseau tries using several different disguises to get inside the villa of the man he suspects is a leading jewel thief. All the attempts finish badly and all the time, the jewel thief's wife is fully aware of what's going on.'

'Sounds riveting,' she replied drily, 'what's his wife got to do with it?'

'Never mind. Forget I ever mentioned it. What we need to do is decide what we do next. There's probably not a lot more we can do on our own apart from trying to establish a connection between Marelli's villa and the buildings where the women are kept.'

'What about the place where you went yesterday? Now that we know where both places are, can't you keep an eye on them both from up there?'

Unless I had much more powerful binoculars, which would attract attention, it's not really close enough. I need somewhere nearer.'

She thought for a moment, 'I'll tell you what; why don't we go back to the car, drive up to where you were yesterday and have a look from there. Even though it's too far away to use to watch them, we might be able to see somewhere else that allows us to keep an eye on the two properties without being seen.'

As neither of them had any better idea, that was what they did.

'There,' she said, pointing down into the valley. 'What about that?'

He looked in the direction she was pointing, but couldn't work out exactly what she was indicating.

'Where?' he asked.

'You see that little group of three pointy trees, just behind that white building down there?'

'Yes.'

'Well. If you look just above them and to the right, there seem to be the remains of an old stone building. Isn't there enough of it left to give cover to someone who wanted to see but not be seen?'

Luke raised the binoculars and swung them to the right until he located the three trees and then carefully raised them slightly and refocussed on the ruin that Layla had indicated. "Remains" had been almost a euphemism: there was little more than a heap of stones, although there was probably just under a metre of wall left at one end.

'It would be very uncomfortable,' he commented, as he surveyed the stones strewn over the ground on their side of the wall.

'Not as uncomfortable as being kept in a small compound all day and then being taken out at night to allow sick men to practise all sorts of perversions on you,' she said sharply. 'If you don't want to do it. I will.'

'Hey! Take it easy!' he said, lowering the binoculars and stretching a hand out towards her. 'I wasn't saying I won't do it. I was talking to myself really while I tried to work out how to do it. I won't be able to risk standing up, just on the off-chance someone might notice and start asking questions, but the biggest worry will be snakes. Those stones are the ideal hiding place for vipers now that the sun's out. They won't come out unless they feel threatened, but it's something I need to bear in mind, if I'm going to be lying there for a few hours.'

'Sorry,' she said, 'It's just that...' He put an arm round her shoulder and gave her a squeeze.

'It's alright. I understand.'

Before they left, he worked out what appeared to be the best way to get to the place they'd selected: a way that didn't involve passing either the villa or the agricultural buildings on the way. It was too late to set anything up for that day, but they agreed that Layla would run him down in the morning and pick him up again in the early evening before it was time for the women to be taken out into the town.

Taking a longer route back, they checked that at least part of the route they'd picked out from above was feasible and then went to buy a couple of picnic blankets for Luke to lie on as well as a large bottle of water.

When they got back to the house, Luke set to cooking while Layla went upstairs as she felt a slight headache and thought that going to lie down for half an hour might prevent it from developing into a full-blown, debilitating migraine. He had just gone out to collect a couple of large sprigs of rosemary for the *fagioli all'uccelletto* he was preparing when he heard Layla's phone upstairs. She answered almost immediately and all he could hear was the occasional muffled sound of her voice before all was silent again and he carried on cooking.

'How're you feeling?' he asked as she came down the stairs a little later, 'How's the head?'

She came and stood next to him, dipping the tip of a finger quickly into the bubbling beans and then sucking it clean, giving an approving nod.

'Better, but I've got a metaphorical headache now.'

He looked at her and raised an inquisitive eyebrow.

'You heard my phone?' He gave a sign of assent.

'Well, that was Diletta. Apparently, Damiano managed to get in to the villa and Marelli agreed to speak to him. He told him he was doing research project about someone called Clara Calamai, said that he remembered the interesting things that Marelli had said about her when he'd been with the Scout group to see a film there, and asked if Marelli had any books on her that he could borrow. Marelli obviously likes flattery and asked Damiano if he'd like to see one of Calamai's most famous films.

That got him taken down into the basement cinema where Marelli told one of his assistants what film to put on, and then left him to watch it for a couple of hours. For most of the time, the assistant was in the room but he did leave him completely alone a couple of times and Damiano had a quick look out of the door. Apparently, there are six identical doors leading off a central corridor; one of them is the cinema and he says that next time he goes, he's going to find out what's behind the others. His father's a builder, so he knows a bit about construction and he says that the walls of the cinema room are soundproofed and he thinks that some of the other rooms could be too.'

'I hope Diletta told him that there shouldn't be a next-time – especially if he's going to start wandering around places he isn't supposed to be.'

'That's the metaphorical headache, I'm afraid. Diletta now seems thrilled by what Damiano's doing, so she's not going to be holding him back. Apparently, when he saw Marelli afterwards and thanked him, he asked if this Clara Calamai was the best pre-war Italian actress and ended up with an invitation to see a film by someone else called, Doris something or other.'

'Doris! Not Doris Day, she didn't have any connection to Italy, and she wasn't pre-war either.'

'No, it wasn't Doris Day, but the name did began with a D: made me think of boxing for some reason.'

'Means nothing to me,' said Luke.

'Well, anyway, he's going back again and there's nothing we can do about it, so let's just hope he finds something useful and doesn't get into any trouble.'

It took Luke a few minutes to clear enough of the stones that were strewn across the ground all around the remains of the ruined building and to create a space that would be comfortable enough to spend the next few hours in. Before he finally settled down, he cast an anxious glance at the sky and particularly at the dark clouds that had gathered over Macchino. It was hard to tell which way the clouds were moving but he knew that, if he were unlucky, and it rained, it would be a torrential downpour that would render the observation point he had created unusable for two or three hours. Never mind; if he were lucky, the cloud would not burst until it had passed over him. At the moment, the effect of the strong sunlight contrasting with the dark cloud meant that the light was crystal clear and the colours of the vegetation were unnaturally bright.

He was lucky. At one point, when the cloud was directly overhead, a few heavy drops of rain fell, but it was a false alarm, and the danger slowly passed. For ten minutes, as the cloud cut him off from the sun, he felt cold, but he kept telling himself that it was only temporary and, so long as he didn't get wet, the sun would soon have the upper hand again.

Once the cloud had passed, It would have been very easy to doze off and he regularly shifted his position whenever he thought he was feeling too comfortable and at risk of sleeping. On a couple of occasions he found that an arm he'd been resting his weight on had gone to sleep and he had to shake it around for a while, grimacing as feeling painfully returned, before adopting a new position.

Very little happened for most of the morning: at various times, two cars and three vans arrived at Marelli's villa and another van, with one person in the front, left the compound where the women were housed, the gates being carefully closed behind it. The three vans that arrived at Marelli's villa left again almost immediately and, while he was careful to take a note of their registrations, he felt fairly sure that they were only independent tradesmen making standard deliveries. One of the cars stayed at the villa for about half an hour, while the other was still there at the end of the morning, however, as it was only an old Fiat Punto, he thought that it was unlikely to contain anyone of any real significance. The van that had left the compound returned after just over an hour and a half and again the gates were carefully closed behind it. 'Shopping trip?' he noted down on the notepad that lay by his side, and which he was gradually covering with doodles.

He fought against the urge to check his watch too regularly, knowing that he'd only be disappointed by how little time had passed since he last looked.

When it eventually got to one o'clock, he decided that he could allow himself to eat, feeling grateful that Layla had insisted on making him a thick sandwich with pecorino and Neapolitan salame, even though he'd insisted that he'd be fine with just a couple of cereal bars as he would be expending almost no energy during the day.

There was a lot to be said for occasional comfort eating, he thought as he washed the sandwich down with a swig from the litre bottle of water he'd brought.

Lunch, however, provided only a temporary diversion from the tedium of watching and, far sooner than he would have liked, he was again lying, leaning on his elbows, fighting off the temptation to close his eyes.

There was no activity of any sort around the compound and only a handful of vehicles entered or left the villa. He continued to scrupulously note down all the details he could; even though he wasn't sure if he'd be able to get the numbers discretely traced, there was always the chance that something might turn out to be useful as corroborating evidence – if, of course, they ever got to that stage.

A very new looking, dark-red Alfa Giulia Quadrifoglio with heavily tinted glass arrived just after three, followed closely by a four-by-four Lexus, again with tinted glass, but where he could pick out two jacketed men in the front, each with almost identical short hair and sunglasses. Luke allowed himself a wry smile; the two men might as well have worn sandwich-boards with "official bodyguard" written across them in block capitals. Either Marelli himself, or some important visitor, must have been in the Alfa. Something interesting, at last.

The Alfa and the Lexus were still there at half past four when a *motorino* arrived. While the gates had opened automatically for the other cars, the person on the *motorino* had to wait at the gate to speak to someone before being allowed in. The person who came to the gate, spoke to someone else using a walkie-talkie before waving the visitor in and closing the gates behind him. The number-plate on the rear of the *motorino* was bent and Luke was unable to see anything other than the PT indicating that it was from the Pistoia province, which was what he would have expected anyway.

The Punto that had arrived in the morning, left shortly after the arrival of the moped and, as it turned towards Luke, he was able to get a reasonable view of the driver and take a photograph. He doubted that they would be of any significance but at least it was something to do.

Finally, at half past six, as Luke was beginning to tick off the minutes before he could call it a day, a grey Golf emerged from the compound and turned left and then left again. He expected it to continue towards Montecatini as the van had in the morning, but instead it slowed down and turned into the entrance of the villa where the gates swung open. Suddenly, he felt fully awake again; at last, some sort of evidence connecting Marelli to the place where the women were being kept. Then he remembered his police training – no – it wasn't good enough – it was only circumstantial – if that. But at least it was a start.

The Golf left again and returned to the compound after about twenty minutes and about ten minutes later, the Alfa and its shadowing Lexus also left, although in the opposite direction. Luke made sure that he'd written their numbers down correctly when they'd arrived and then, after recording the details of a BMW X5 that left a few minutes later, he decided he'd had enough for the day and gathered his things together into his small rucksack.

'I've been to see Tardelli again – the policeman. I thought it would be a good idea to thank him again for setting up the meeting with the prostitute and also to ask him about other things, to try and give him the impression that I was interested in other aspects of Montecatini.'

'Good idea. Did he seem convinced?'

'Slightly relieved, I'd say. He spent far more time than I'd have expected telling me about the petty crimes that he says take up most of their time. According to him, major crimes are very rare here and most of the crimes that do happen are mainly due to tourists being careless. He said that there are so many who leave cars unlocked, or put handbags or cameras down while they're trying something on, or who walk around almost shouting out "hey, look at me, I'm a tourist; why don't you pick my pocket", that the criminals don't need to bother the locals. He did ask me about my cameraman, even though I was very careful when I spoke to him before to make it sound as if I only had a photographer with me temporarily.'

'And what did you say?'

'I told him that, as far as I was concerned, you'd finished the job with me and that I thought you were now doing an assignment for a nature and lifestyle magazine.'

He snorted, 'I suppose it's as good an excuse as any if I'm found loitering in the bushes with a camera. At least I shouldn't be accused of being a peeping Tom! Anyway, did you speak with Luana?'

'I tried but I only got her answer-phone. I left a message saying that I'd try again this evening if I didn't hear from her before.'

'Good, because I need to ask her another favour as well. There were several cars either arriving at or leaving the villa and the compound; I'm sure that either Luana or one of her old friends in the force will be able to trace the registrations.'

'Anything particularly interesting?'

He told her about the Golf, the Quadrifoglio and the Lexus.

'It's Tardelli…….. I spoke to the English journalist again…. Yes…. She avoided saying…… Claimed she was interested in knowing about other types of crime in Montecatini…… No; nothing like that. Mainly the types of crime that affects tourists: pick-pocketing, car theft – and things like that…. Yes, that's what I thought at first but there's one thing that worries me… her cameraman; she claims that he's finished the job with her and said that she thinks he's taking nature photographs somewhere….. It does sound plausible but there was something nagging at the back of my mind so I had someone do a bit more research on *Signorina* Simons. Anyway, it appears that she was the journalist who conducted the interview that led to the conviction of the English police computer analyst in the Guerrini case a few years ago. Now that could be just a coincidence but, looking at the picture of the policeman it struck me that there's a very strong resemblance to Simons' cameraman'……………… 'Yes. I've done that. Facial recognition software says that it's over 80% likely that it's the same person.' …………. 'Released on licence. Supposed to be living at a nominated address in Florence.' …… 'It's not part of our jurisdiction. We can only act if the British make a formal request.' …… 'You can. That's good. We'll try and keep an eye on him until then although I can only allocate limited resources.' ….. 'I will. Thank you. Arrivederla.'

Luke turned into Via Marruota and dropped his speed right down. There were women occupying the same spots as when he'd driven down the streets previously and he was subjected to similar explicit invitations to purchase what was on offer. The girl he'd spoken to before, however, was not there. Maybe -he thought – she's been picked up and will be back in place later. He turned into a side road towards the end of the built-up area and, after turning around, parked about eighty metres from the junction. He'd have to wait for twenty minutes – half an hour to be on the safe side – he thought.

Half an hour later, he drove back up the street, slightly more quickly than before, but not too fast to get a good look at the women as he passed; the girl still wasn't there.

At the end of the road, he turned right, made his way to the next roundabout and then came back. Turning into Via Marruota again, he pulled up next to 'long tongue' as he had named her, as he was certain she had been there previously when he'd picked up the other girl.

'Ciao' he said, with a smile, slipping a ten euro note between her ample breasts as she leaned into his window. 'I was here three nights ago and I had a good time with one of your friends. A girl with red skirt and with two rings in her left ear; she was the next one along on the street.'

The woman started to move away but he was too quick and had a firm grip on her wrist before she knew it. 'I think you're lovely too but I really wanted to see that girl again. There's another twenty euros for you if you can tell me where I can find her.'

He was rewarded for his offer by being spat at and, as he momentarily relaxed his grip in surprise, she pulled her arm away. Just then, a vehicle belonging to the municipal police came round the corner and pulled in behind Luke, switching its flashing light on as it did so. Two officers got out of the car and, hands on pistols, approached.

'What's happening here?' asked one of the officers unsmilingly.

Luke was about to speak but was pre-empted by the woman who began a torrent of abuse, directed mainly at him, although in a mixture of languages.

'Calm down. Calm down,' said one of the officers, 'or we'll have to lock you both up until you're able to explain in a civil manner. Now. Shall we start again? What's going on here?'

'I was just…' began Luke.

One of the policemen held up a cautionary hand. 'You'll get your turn. Let's hear what the lady's got to say. She seems to be the one who's upset here.'

'This man. He insult me. He offer money for sex – look!' and she extracted Luke's ten euro note and waved it in front of the police men. He give me this. He say I prostitute and want to give me more for do things with him. I am respectable tourist.' Her voice rose again and quickened as she spoke.

'I'm very sorry that you've been troubled this way in our city, madam. If you'd like to drop by the *Commissariato* in the morning to make a formal complaint, we'd be very grateful. I suggest that you go and rejoin your friends now.' the policeman pointed down the street to where the other prostitutes had been before they saw the police car. The two officers and Luke watched her swagger away down the street with her high heels, frayed blue hot-pants and crop-top.

'Get out of the car.'

Luke complied.

'Documenti, per favore,' said the second officer, stretching out a hand. Luke complied, pulling out his driving licence and his, slightly dog-eared passport.

'Turn round and put your hands on the roof of the car.' Again, Luke did as he was told.

'You got yourself arrested for kerb-crawling!" exclaimed Layla incredulously. 'How on earth did you manage that when half the men in Italy seem to be doing it every night without anyone bothering?'

He shrugged sheepishly, 'I was cautioned. I wasn't exactly arrested. Once I'd explained, numerous times to numerous different people, that I was a writer, trying to get information to help me write stories, they seemed to get bored and lose interest. Most of them seemed baffled as to why I'd been picked up, and just seemed to want to pass me on to someone else who could take a decision. They didn't really seem all that sure what to do about it and they obviously hear all sorts of excuses so I'm sure they didn't really believe what I said – or even care all that much. Eventually, a Captain gave me a piece of paper warning me about my future conduct and more or less told me to go away.'

She shook her head, 'I suppose that means you won't be able to get any more information from the women themselves. If the police see you there again, they'll take it more seriously, won't they?'

Luke's expression hardened. 'It means that I won't get the chance to find out why the girl who I spoke to before wasn't there tonight. There could be an innocent explanation – or, at least, as innocent as you can get in these circumstances – but there could also be a link between the girl who spoke to me disappearing and the police suddenly appearing as soon as I start to look for her. It's almost as if they were expecting me and were determined to stop me asking any questions.'

'Maybe,' she said, although he could tell from her tone that she wasn't convinced.

Then, changing the subject, she told him that she'd had a call from Luana while he'd been out. Luana had seemed hopeful of being able to provide evidence tracing one of the consignments all the way through from Sicily much quicker than they had dared hope. By using a little persuasion on her friend Gio, she'd been able to mobilise more resources and they had almost finished assembling a file that she thought would give them what they needed. She'd also given Layla the details of a *Carabinieri Maresciallo* in Buggiano who could be trusted absolutely and who was prepared to help. 'I'm meeting with him at ten, tomorrow morning.' She looked at her watch, 'So it's about time I was getting some sleep. I'll see you in the morning.'

'*Buonanotte.*' he said, 'See you in the morning.' He watched her ascend the stairs as he leaned back in his chair, flexing his shoulders that were aching after spending a good part of the day propped up on his shoulders. Watching the movement of her lithe legs and hips under the light material, he felt a sudden and unexpected wave of loneliness and tenderness wash over him. He sighed and rolled his head around his neck, trying to drive the thoughts away, 'Time for a glass of whisky,' he thought.

Twenty minutes later, he paused on the landing and looked at the face lying serenely on the pillow, picked out by the landing light that filtered through the door that had been left partially open to allow the cooler night air to circulate. He wasn't sure how long he remained there looking at her before he took a step forward and grasped the door handle in his hand. He looked for another minute, focussing on a wisp of hair that rose and fell as she breathed, then, he gently pulled the door towards him so that, while air could still circulate, Layla was no longer visible from the landing. Feeling disturbed, he slipped into the bathroom and got ready for bed.

Despite the warm sun on his back and the steep, tree covered hillsides, resplendent in late spring colours, by late morning, Luke was beginning to appreciate just how dull, lying in the same place for hour after hour could be. Just like the previous day, there was only very limited activity to be seen either around the barn complex or Marelli's villa. He studiously examined everyone and everything through his binoculars and noted down every little detail that could conceivably have the slightest relevance – but he was bored.

He regularly found his thoughts drifting to Layla: her head on the pillow as she slept; the determined look in her eyes as she'd insisted she was going to find out about Zahra; her vulnerability when she had one of her headaches; her lithe, lightly tanned body as she'd dived into the sea from the little beach on Lipari… He made a deliberate attempt to wrestle his thoughts away and focus on Judi; he tried to draw up images from their early days together, from their first holiday and from their honeymoon but, although he had no difficulty remembering the places with the colours, smells and sounds associated with them, he found that he couldn't conjour up an image of Judi's face. He thought back to when he'd first heard she was leaving him: the sorrow he'd felt and the anger he'd felt towards the person whom he'd held to blame – but the passion had gone and he couldn't rekindle it. He told himself again that it was all the fault of that article and that he shouldn't forget it, but he knew he didn't believe what he was telling himself and knew he needed to move on. He realised that whatever he'd had with Judi was over – if it had ever been more than an illusion anyway – and that, not only did he no longer care, but he was actually glad. Hopefully, it wasn't too late to make better choices.

Early in the afternoon, the BMW X5 that Luke's instinct told him was Marelli's arrived at the villa, the large gates swinging open automatically as the car approached and then closing again as soon as the top of the range SUV had passed through.

The same four by four Lexus that had accompanied the Quadrifoglio the previous day came along the road towards the villa about an hour later but, this time, didn't stop. Instead, it turned right at the junction and, slowing down to about fifteen miles per hour, drove slowly along to the entrance to the compound. There, the driver turned so that the car was placed diagonally across the road pointing at the gates, and sounded its horn – two short blasts and one long. The gate was opened by a muscular, fair-haired young man wearing jeans and a short-sleeved white shirt who Luke photographed while he had the opportunity.

The young man nodded to the passenger of the Lexus as it pulled inside, and then pushed the gates closed again. Luke watched the roof of the car as it moved away from the wall towards the buildings, hoping that he would get a good view of the occupants when they got out. Unfortunately, the car was driven round the far side of the main building before stopping so he was unable to see what was happening. He wondered whether to leave his observation point and try and get nearer to the compound. There was a point he could see that would allow him a better view inside but, to reach it, he would have to cross a stretch of open ground where he would be unable to avoid being seen. Reluctantly, he decided it was best to remain where he was.

Remaining where he was turned out to be the correct decision as less than five minutes passed before the Lexus reversed away from the building and turned to approach the gates again. Luke saw the same young man open the gates to let it out and then push them closed again.

This time, the driver accelerated to the maximum speed practical on the narrow country lane and, instead of turning left to pass in front of Marelli's villa, continued straight on, presumably to reach the main road slightly further to the west.

Luke picked up his phone to send a text asking if Luana had managed to trace the number-plate of the Lexus. As he lifted the phone, which had been switched to silent, he expected that, before he unlocked it, it would just show him the time but instead the screen informed him that he had three new voice-mails and two unread text messages. He went to the first of the voice mails and pressed 'play'

'*Ciao* Luke,' he immediately recognised the voice of Alessio, 'I was just wondering what time you'd be back. There's someone here to see you. Let me know.' Luke frowned. Alessio had obviously had someone with him when he rang and wanted to give the impression that Luke was staying there and had just popped out for something. The only thing he could think of was a spot check by the Consulate, to make sure he was complying with the conditions of his licence. Not very good timing but he was sure he'd be able to provide an acceptable explanation for his absence during the day.

'Luke. I've had a message from Alessio saying that someone is at his apartment looking for you. Give him a ring and give him some sort of excuse to pass on to them.' Alessio had obviously rung Layla hoping to reach him that way.

'It's me again. Alessio called me again using someone else's phone. It's more serious than it sounded earlier. The visitor was from the consulate, but he had a couple of what Alessio thought looked like plain-clothes police waiting outside for him. He said that they're going to call back again to see you this evening.'

The first text message had been sent a minute later than Alessio's voice-mail and said pretty much the same thing. The second was from Layla and just said, 'URGENT – LISTEN TO YOUR MESSAGES'.

He responded to the second message. 'Coming back now. Need to see you before I go to Florence.' then he sent one to Alessio,

'Enjoying walk in the hills – very poor reception – back in a couple of hours.'

He hurriedly gathered his things together, dropped a few of the loose stones to mask the place where he'd been lying, and walked quickly back to where he'd left the bike.

'It will just be an inconvenient random check; it had to happen sooner or later. Once they're convinced that I'm really staying with Alessio, they'll probably ignore me for the rest of the time I'm on licence. With a bit of luck, I'll be back by ten or eleven tonight.'

'If you say so,' she said doubtfully and began to turn away. He stopped her, putting a hand on her forearm, gripping slightly more firmly than he'd intended. She looked at him enquiringly.

'I know this isn't the right time, but I've had a lot of time to think and I've realised what an idiot I've been. No, let me finish,' he said hurriedly, as she parted her lips to speak. 'I blamed you for the breakup of my marriage, amongst other things and I was completely wrong. If anything I should have been thanking you and I apologise. No...' He raised his hand from her arm and half raised a finger as if pleading with her not to speak. 'That's not why I've been an idiot. I can rationalise those thoughts to myself and forgive myself for thinking that... where I've really been an idiot is in not being prepared to admit to myself how much I enjoy being with you... there's no comparison between being with you and being with Judi, in fact, it's difficult now to imagine not being with you... what I really want to know now is... is it too late? Can you forgive me for being so stupid?'

She was looking down at the floor and, with his heart in his mouth, he heard her sigh before she raised her head and took a step towards him. Her hands came up and went behind his head pulling his face down towards hers.

When their lips parted and she pulled back, he saw there signs of tears in her eyes, then she gave a radiant smile. 'I think ten would be better than eleven, don't you? Now, go and get changed; the sooner you're gone, the sooner you'll be back.'

While he changed, he filled her in briefly on what he'd seen during the day and asked her if she could chase up Luana about the number plates, while she told him briefly that her meeting with the Maresciallo had gone well and that she had a better feeling about him than about Tardelli.

Chapter Fifteen

Luke stood under the branches of a tree that overhung the railings surrounding one of the many private communal gardens that served the wealthier residents of Notting Hill. He had been there for almost two hours, walking on the spot occasionally to keep the circulation going in his legs as he watched the white Georgian house diagonally opposite with its burgundy door flanked by doric pillars.

Eventually, he saw a light go on in what he assumed was a bedroom on the second floor, while the light remained on behind the first-floor windows of what his limited knowledge of architectural layouts suggested must be the sitting room. He waited another five minutes to make sure that the person who had gone upstairs was staying there leaving the other resident of the house alone downstairs. Then he crossed over to the front door of the house.

He noticed that there was a spy-hole in the door and, after pushing the old-fashioned doorbell, he turned round so that his face was not visible when the man who he assumed had remained in the sitting-room came to the door.

His shadow suddenly appeared in front of him and he assumed that the light had been turned on in the hallway and was falling on him from the semi-circular window above the door. A few seconds later, he heard the sound of a chain being removed and a key being turned in the lock. He turned to face the house as the door opened.

The two men stood looking at each other for a while, Luke with the hint of a smile on his face and the other trying desperately to compose his features after the initial look of shock and panic that had assailed them.

'Hello, Cam. It's been a long time.'

'Luke,' was all the other could say. Luke smiled.

'You don't seem particularly pleased to see me.' He saw Cam McCreggan swallow, trying desperately to compose himself.

'When did… I thought… You know that…' and then with an effort, 'What do you want Luke?'

Luke raised a hand and McCreggan flinched, but it was only stretched out towards him offering a handshake. After a brief hesitation, McCreggan took it gingerly, as though fearing he was about to be the victim of some brutal judo move.

'Yes, I know. If I'd bumped into you a year or so ago I'd probably have punched you... but that's all in the past now. I've forgiven you, and I wish you well – both of you.' He saw McCreggan's shoulders relax a little although his face was still laden with suspicion. 'Aren't you going to invite me in? I waited until I saw someone had gone upstairs for the night before coming to the door.'

'And how did you know it wasn't me who'd gone up to bed first?' Asked Cam, who seemed to be slowly recovering some of his composure.

'You forget – although I obviously didn't know either of you as well as I thought I did, I do have a pretty good idea of both of your late night habits. I can't imagine you going to bed without relaxing with a glass of whisky first, and I can't imagine that Judi would wait patiently for you to finish it.'

'What do you want, Luke?' The earlier question was repeated as McCreggan showed no sign of either moving to the side or shutting the door in Luke's face.

Luke smiled again. 'I want to ask you a big favour, but I need to tell you a long story first.' He saw him hesitate. 'If the answer's "no", then the answer's "no", and you'll never see me again, but I need you to hear me out before I ask the favour... Hear me out; I think you owe me at least that much.'

McCreggan looked him in the eyes for a few seconds and then stepped to the side and, with a nervous smile, gestured Luke inside.

They went up a short flight of stairs to a wide landing with three doors leading off it. McCreggan opened the central door and led Luke into a comfortably furnished living room, the centre piece of which was a chocolate coloured soft-leather sofa with a recliner section on one end and a peninsula on the other. Two matching armchairs were set slightly back from the recliner end of the sofa facing a smallish round wooden coffee table, while a larger coffee table had been placed in front of the sofa. This table was made entirely of glass, with a bevel-edged top sitting on top of two substantial glass columns. The flooring consisted of large flecked white ceramic tiles and strategically placed brightly coloured rugs, that Luke saw at once had been placed to enhance the colours of the brightly coloured abstract paintings that lined the walls.

McCreggan had clearly been sitting with his feet up on the peninsula ending of the sofa before getting up to answer the door and Luke deliberately made his way over to the two armchairs to sit down. He wanted to make sure that his old friend was forced to change his position: he didn't want him to feel too comfortable, too soon.

McCreggan opened a fitted corner-cupboard, that Luke hadn't noticed as it blended in with the colour of the room, and took out an almost full bottle of Lagavulin and two glasses. He held the bottle up towards Luke and tilted his head slightly to one side. Luke nodded and McCreggan brought the bottle and glasses over to the small table.

Neither spoke as Luke watched him pour out two generous measures of the whisky then, as he was handed one of the glasses, McCreggan said, 'I take it you're not driving.'

Luke took a small sip of the whisky as the other sat down but didn't reply.

'Look, Luke. I really don't know what to say. I'm sorry that things had to happen the way they did. It just sort of... happened,' he tailed off lamely.

'I told you, it's OK. What's done is done and hopefully it will turn out to be what's best for everyone. But... like I said downstairs... I need you to listen to the story I've got to tell you.'

By the time he'd reached the point when he rushed to Florence and opened Alessio's door, more than two hours had passed and the amount of whisky in the bottle had dropped considerably.

McCreggan lifted the bottle to refill the glasses but Luke passed a hand briefly over the top of his glass to show that he didn't want any more at the moment.

'Have you got any decent tea, or are you still drinking that weird stuff from Waitrose?'

'Top quality Kenyan, if that's acceptable to you.'
'It'll have to be,' said Luke.

'So then what happened?' asked McCreggan, as he sat down again, having placed two pint mugs of tea onto the table.

There was no smile on Luke's face now. 'The official from the Embassy – apparently the cuts that you lot made when you were in coalition means that there isn't a Consulate in Florence any more – was quite apologetic, but he said that they'd had instructions from London that couldn't be over-ridden. Within twenty four hours I had to be on a plane for London accompanied by two security guards who'd been sent over specifically for the purpose and who would then accompany me to Winchester Prison.'
'But why?'
'Now that's a very good question. I've obviously had quite a lot of time to think about it and there's clearly something not right. Officially they'd been made aware that I wasn't complying with the residence conditions on my licence because, as a foreign national, my name had automatically been passed on when it had been officially recorded after the 'kerb crawling' incident. I don't believe that either the Italian or the British officials are that efficient... and as for the resources required on the British side, particularly after the cuts that your coalition friends have made to public services – it just doesn't add up. The people in Italy who had an interest in getting me out of the way have obviously got friends with the right connections in this country. The man from the Embassy seemed more surprised by what he'd been told to do than I was.'
'But that's incredible! You're implying that there are people in key positions here who're involved in international criminal activities.'
'Oh, come on, Cam. Don't sound so surprised. These links exist and they always have existed. Why do you think that dodgy Italian bankers occasionally end up suspended below London bridges? You can't be that naïve. Anyway, that's not something I want to go into now. I need to tell you the rest of the story, which is factual and not assumption.'

'OK, but I promise you, I'm going to look into it... Go on.'

'Well, as far as I was concerned, that was the end of my direct involvement in the story, but not of the story itself. The one positive thing to come out of my being removed was that the evidence we'd already put together got taken more seriously. Alessio let people know what had happened to me and, together with Layla, managed to put together the file of evidence that we needed to take to the minister who's the father of Alessio's friend.

'The morning after I was more or less arrested, the body of Damiano, the young man who was confident he could find out what was happening inside Marelli's villa, was found by a bend on one of the twisting mountain roads in the hills above Montecatini. According to the Police in Montecatini, he must have been knocked off, or lost control of his *motorino* after meeting a wild boar – perfectly believable except that there was no reason why he would have been on that road. Layla and Diletta went back to the *Carabinieri Maresciallo* and he agreed that it looked suspicious and wrote a report for Alessio and Layla to take to the minister.

'The Quadrifoglio I'd seen turned out to be registered to a Prato based textile factory, as did the Lexus. Discreet enquiries by our *Carabinieri* friend, showed that the Quadrifoglio was used by the CEO of the company, while the Lexus was used by his personal staff – which I presume is a euphemism for bodyguards.

'Obviously, I wasn't there, so I'm not exactly sure how it was managed, but the *Carabinieri* were authorised to carry out contemporaneous raids on: the compound, Marelli's villa, the home of the CEO in the hills near Vaiano and a number of other key locations back along the trail leading from Sicily.'

Cam McCreggan's mug had been held, forgotten in his left hand, a few centimetres from his lips as Luke had recounted the events that had followed quickly after his deportation. Now he glanced down and, realising he was in danger of spilling it, placed it down on the table.

'And were you right? Were the raids a success?'

There was a pause before Luke replied and McCreggan, without being aware of it, leaned forward in anticipation.

'Almost completely successful. The Sicilian end and a number of intermediate stages on the route were rolled up pretty easily, although I'm sure that alternative arrangements would have been put in place fairly quickly – the authorities know that while they might win some important battles, it's not a war with any end in sight.

'Four arrests were made at the compound and seventeen young women were transferred to official camps – although I'm told that six of them have since disappeared again.

'Where it wasn't quite as successful was the raid on Marelli's villa. They found evidence linking the site to the compound and traces that showed that Damiano's *motorino* had been moved in a van that was kept at the site but one of the men who works for Marelli insists that he gave Damiano and his bike a lift to the edge of Montecatini, as he was having a problem with his carburettor. He claims that Damiano was fine when he dropped him off and that he has no knowledge of what he did, or where he went after that.

'Marelli denied all knowledge of what was going on and his Estate Manager claims that he was the one who had links with those running the girls. I'm pretty sure that Marelli's really the one behind it, but I'm also sure that others will be very well paid for taking the blame and keeping his name out of it. One of the men who works for the businessman from Prato offered to testify against Marelli in exchange for his own freedom but, as Marelli's lawyers somehow got hold of a copy of the interview tapes, they were straight in there arguing that it was just a case of the man desperately trying to find some way of getting off himself and that it was a malicious allegation. The investigating magistrate had no choice but to rule the testimony inadmissible,' Luke leaned across to the whisky bottle and, without asking, refilled his glass.

'And?' said Cam, softly. 'Go on.'

Luke drained his glass in one swift movement but didn't put it back down on the table. He made sure he was looking McCreggan directly in the eyes before continuing, his face expressionless. 'Layla came to see me on the first visiting day, about a month later… The first thing she told me was that she was fairly sure that they'd managed to track down Zahra. Although Marelli was careful not to leave any traces, the businessman from Prato wasn't as careful. You probably wouldn't believe it but he'd kept records of all his dealings with girls as if he were keeping a set of accounts. They were able to see when he'd purchased girls, how much he'd paid for them and how much he'd made back at the end. Each record was accompanied by a photograph – or photographs. I'm sure you can imagine what sort of photographs they were. In the disposals column, sometimes there were prices shown along with the name of the buyer; sometimes, the girls seemed to have been passed on to his employees when he'd finished with them and some were just annotated as "soiled goods".

'A girl named Zahra, who seemed to be the right age, with characteristics that tied in with some of the details that Layla's sister had sent her had been sold on for three thousand euros to a farmer with a remote farm in the hills above Grosseto. The *Carabinieri* found the girl chained to the wall in a disused grain silo about a hundred metres away from his home. She'd appeared reasonably well fed but the doctors said that she'd clearly been repeatedly abused over a significant period. At that time, the girl was severely traumatised – as you'd expect – and hadn't said a word to the doctors who were looking after her. Because of her condition, Layla had only been allowed limited access to her at that time but, when she came to see me the following month, she was able to confirm that DNA tests had shown that the girl is almost certainly Zahra and, if it wasn't, then it was certainly someone else with a genetic link to Layla.'

'That's good news, isn't it?' said Cam softly, 'I mean, I know it's disturbing and traumatic, but it sounds a lot closer to the best case scenario than to the worst.'

Luke shook his head with a bitter, humourless little laugh. 'On Layla's second visit - after she'd brought me up to date about Zahra, she told me that she'd finally got round to seeing a doctor about those headaches she'd been suffering from.'

This time, as Luke paused, it was Cam who poured more whisky into his glass. 'I was always concerned that they were more than just stress related headaches but, as it's not really something I know anything about, I'd had to take her word for it. In reality, what she had was a tumour of the pineal gland.' Cam moved his hands slightly and gave a slight shake of his head indicating that, while he understood that this sounded serious, he too was entirely in the dark, never having consciously heard of the pineal gland.

'Tumours on the pineal gland are often benign, just causing headaches of varying degrees of severity as they swell and press against surrounding areas of the brain. Unfortunately, when they're malignant, if they're not diagnosed early on, they become more difficult to treat and if they're not treated...' he tailed off, and looked down into the glass that Cam had topped up.

'Metastatis,' said Cam, in little more than a whisper.

The nod of assent from Luke was so slight that if his old friend hadn't been watching him carefully he would have missed it. 'It took a lot of persuasion to convince her that she should marry me before she died, but we were married in the prison governor's office just before Christmas last year. For as long as she could, Layla travelled backwards and forwards between Italy and England, seeing me whenever she could and spending as much time as possible with Zahra and her therapists. Eventually, she couldn't travel anymore and moved into a hospice near the prison. Fortunately, I'd been transferred by then to the open prison at Sudbury, which made things a bit more manageable.' He stopped again.

'When?' asked Cam, gently.

'Eleven days ago... They've let me out on a four-day compassionate license – with a tag, of course,' he added bitterly, – 'so that I could attend the funeral. The funeral was yesterday and I need to be back by tomorrow evening.'

'I'm sorry,' said Cam, and then, suddenly wary, 'You said you wanted to ask a favour.'

There was a fleeting smile from Luke. 'I do, but don't worry, I'm not going to ask you to help me go on the run, or do anything else that would be inappropriate for someone in your position... As soon as the identification of Zahra was pretty certain, Layla started trying to get Zahra into the country using the Dubbs process but, as I'm sure you're aware, your old coalition friends have rowed back on the numbers of unaccompanied minors they said they were prepared to let in. Once we married, I became jointly responsible for the application. That was one of the reasons why we did it, so that I would become a relative, even if only by marriage. Of course, as a convicted felon, the adoption agencies find it difficult to see me as an appropriate parental figure.'

'So you want me to vouch for you, as a responsible person?' said Cam in a voice that betrayed a degree of relief.

Luke smiled and shook his head.

'So, what then?'

'Oh. If I thought that your vouching for me would be enough, then that would be ideal but the last petty official I spoke to more or less said "over my dead body", so I've been thinking of alternatives.'

'And you came up with...?'

'What I came up with, Cam, was you – or to be precise you and Judi. With your public profile and respectable veneer, the authorities would love you, especially if you agreed to waive your right to privacy.'

Cam frowned, 'I'm still not clear exactly what you want us to do.'

Luke looked him directly in the eye and said slowly and clearly, 'I want you and Judi to take over the application to formally adopt Zahra.'

*****

Discover other titles by Phil Whitney

Relative Values (2015)

Affairs of State (2016)

The Visitor's Guide to Florence and Tuscany (1986)
Guidebook

Off the Beaten Track in Italy (1990) Guidebook

Find out more about Phil Whitney at

https://www.smashwords.com/interview/PhilWhitney59

https://www.amazon.co.uk/Phil-Whitney

and

get regular updates at

https://facebook.com/Phil.Whitney.Author

Please leave a review for my book at your favourite
online retailer.

Please send any queries about my books to my
Facebook Author page.